MW01103860

SHERLOCK HOLMES
ON THE
WILD FRONTIER

by

MAGDA JOZSA

Australian-British spelling is used in this book.

This book and many more by this author available from amazon.com and other online bookstores. Check out the author's website at:

www.read4life.com

Copyright © 2005 Magda Jozsa

2nd Edition
Create Space Independent Publishing

ISBN:978–1–419602–603

This book is dedicated to my sister *Anna Richards*

April 1954 to September 2004

ONE

I was just turning down the lamps preparatory to retiring, when we heard—loud in the silence of the night—the clip clop of hooves on the cobblestones outside.

"Turn up the wick, Watson," requested Sherlock Holmes. "I believe the rider is coming here."

I did as requested.

Holmes went to the window and peered out. The hooves became silent as they reached our door and Holmes pushed up the window and leaned out. "Can I help you?" he called down to the horse's rider.

"I have an urgent message for Mr Sherlock Holmes," called a male voice in reply.

"That is I," said Holmes. He leaned out further.

I moved along to the second window and also looked out. The horseman, with a great deal of agility, hoisted himself up to stand upon his saddle. He reached up and handed the message to Holmes' outstretched fingers.

"Thank you," said Holmes, as his hand closed on the missive.

"I'm to await a reply," said the horseman.

Holmes nodded and drew back into the room. He opened the letter and read it quickly, then leaned out the window again. "I will be there," he said.

The horseman touched a finger to his cap in salute and dropped back down onto his saddle before continuing on his way.

Holmes closed the window and turned to me saying: "Fancy a trip to Sheffield, Watson?"

"What is in Sheffield?" I countered.

"Sir Eustace Plymouth."

My eyebrows went up a notch at that. Plymouth was a revered name amidst the peerage. "It is he who sum-moned you?" I asked.

"A matter of some urgency. He requests I come down on the first train tomorrow."

"What is it about then?"

"He does not say. States it is a matter of extreme urgency and importance and believes that I am the only man in England who can help him."

"Oh? Sounds a bit melodramatic."

"Just telling you what he has written," said Holmes, ignoring my jibe. "Needless to say, I'm going down in the morning. Train leaves at seven, Watson. Care to come?"

"Yes, I would like to, Holmes." I enjoyed sharing in Holmes' cases and this one was promising.

"Good, I will wake you at six." With that final comment, he disappeared into his room. I glanced at the clock on the mantle and hurriedly doused the light again. There wasn't going to be much time for sleeping.

I awoke to Holmes' hand on my shoulder. "Time to rise, Watson," he said in an unbearably cheerful voice.

"I have just closed my eyes Holmes," I growled in rejoinder.

"That was five hours ago. Come on Watson, sloth does not become you."

He left the room and I drew the blankets over my head, only to have Holmes open the door again and call out. "Into your clothes Watson or you will not have time for breakfast!"

If anything could make me move, it was that. There was nothing I hated more than starting the day on an empty stomach.

By seven, we were on the train to Sheffield and I was feeling a little less bleary eyed. "What do you think Sir Eustace wants of you, Holmes?" I asked.

"I have absolutely no idea, Watson. That he has asked for me makes me believe that the matter is one of some delicacy. Something very personal to him, no doubt – as to what that can be, I know not."

It was nearly ten of the clock by the time we reached Sheffield. Awaiting us at the station was a liveried footman and pony trap. Before long we were on our way to Plymouth castle, a thirteenth century structure of massive forbidding appearance.

"Impressive place," I remarked.

"Interesting too," replied Holmes. "Did you know that in the sixteenth century Sir Roger Plymouth was being compared to Count Vladimir Dracule of Transylvania. His reputation was just as bloodthirsty. See those spikes that adorn the towers? It is said that he used to decorate them with the heads of his enemies. His enemies being the fathers of the women he kidnapped tortured and murdered. Eventually, the peasants stormed these walls and dragged Sir Roger off to a much deserved fate. The castle is rumoured to be haunted by the ghosts of all those that he murdered."

"Really? I wonder ..."

Holmes laughed suddenly. "I doubt very much if we are here for that though. I am sure that our mission will be a much more down to earth one."

"Sir Eustace has quite a reputation for strictness, tyranny some would say," I said. "Perhaps he has some Sir Roger in him."

"Quite possibly. The trait is in the family. Anyway, here we are, so we can judge for ourselves."

The pony trap came to a halt in the cobblestone courtyard and a butler descended to meet us. "Mr Sherlock Holmes?" he asked, glancing at Holmes and myself with uncertainty.

"I am Holmes and this is Dr. Watson."

"Very good, Sir. His Lordship is expecting you. If you will come this way."

We followed the butler through a myriad of passageways and stairs until he stopped before a huge oak door, all of ten feet tall. He knocked and opened the door. It was an enormous room, and in the middle was a massive four–poster bed. In the centre of the bed, dwarfed by the heavy timber and drapes, was a wizened old man with white hair and beard.

"Ah, Mr Sherlock Holmes. Glad you could come," he wheezed, struggling to sit himself up. The butler was quick to assist. Sir Eustace waved him away. "Don't fuss!" he growled. "Leave us!"

The butler nodded and left the room, closing the massive door behind him.

"Well, don't just stand there, man, come over here where I can see you," ordered the old man crossly.

We moved closer. He looked Holmes over, taking in his lean build, his hawk like features, prominent nose and determined jaw. Holmes' unruly dark brown hair was slicked back off his forehead with pomade, which made his brow seem higher and more intellectual.

Finally, Sir Eustace's light green eyes locked with Holmes' steely grey ones. "Thought you would be older," he grunted.

"Age has nothing to do with ability, Sir Eustace," Holmes returned politely.

"Oh? Are you saying you are more capable than me?" he demanded.

"Yes, in this instance there is no doubt that I am, or you would not have sent for me." Holmes was not in the slightest bit put out by the old man's manner, nor his frosty glare.

"Impertinent young whippersnapper," he muttered, beard bristling.

Holmes smiled faintly.

Being unable to cower Holmes, he turned his attention to me. "And, who are you?" he demanded.

"Dr John Watson, Sir Eustace."

"I did not send for a doctor."

"Dr. Watson is my colleague. We often work as a team," explained Holmes. "Now, Sir Eustace, you are obviously an ill man and your doctor has warned you against smoking, yet you continue to do so. Egyptian cigarettes unless I am mistaken. I also see that you have recently updated your last will and testament and want me to find your son who is missing, and return him home before you die, is that correct?"

The old man's jaw dropped in surprise and I must confess I was also impressed. I had no idea how Holmes deduced all that but from the look on Sir

Eustace's face he was one hundred per cent correct.

"Well, they say you're a smart fellow. I wouldn't have sent for you if you weren't. But tell me, who was it that told you of this business? Was it Samuels?"

"The butler? No. No one has told me anything. The ash in the ashtray beside your bed is a distinctive light grey colour peculiar to Egyptian cigarettes—Alexandrian to be exact. I have written a small monograph on this particular subject and can identify one hundred and forty types of cigarette and their ashes at a glance. The fact that there are no stubs in the ashtray indicates that you are trying to conceal that you are still smoking. Beside you on the bed is a sheath of legal papers and I recognize the distinctive parchment used for last testaments. Also, on the bed is a photograph of your only son—Cathcart Pettigrew Plymouth. Had he been present, he would have been the one to greet us at the door and introduce us to you, not the butler. You sent your servant away which told me that the matter was a personal one. What could be more personal than an errant son?"

The old man nodded. "Not bad for a whippersnapper," he admitted smiling reluctantly. "I wish my son were more like you, young Holmes; a thinking man, rather than the fool he turned out to be. Still, I am an old man not long for this world. I am dying and he is my only heir. Perhaps his time in America has toughened him, made a man of him."

"America?"

"Yes. I want you to go there, find him and bring him back."

"Impossible. Do you realise how *big* the

Americas are?"

"Don't be impertinent. Of course I know how big it is. I have a letter from him giving his most recent location." He reached into the pile of papers beside him and pulled out a dirty yellow envelope. "Here."

Holmes took the letter and frowned. "This is six months old."

"So?" Green eyes met grey as he tried to stare Holmes down.

"So he could be anywhere by now."

"Read the letter, you impudent young pup," he ordered.

It is fortunate that I kept well back as neither man noticed my smile. Although Holmes was only in his early thirties, I have never ever heard him referred to as an impudent young pup before. Then again, by all accounts, Sir Eustace was over eighty, so perhaps to him two and thirty was little more than a beardless youth.

Holmes began to read the letter out loud. "Dear Father, I trust you are well. My recent stint as a professional gambler (which before you growl, is a respectable profession here on the frontier) netted me sufficient funds to outfit myself for a mining enterprise. I am now headed for Colorado to try my luck in the gold fields. Perhaps, when I have made my own fortune, you will revise your poor opinion of me."

"There," said Sir Eustace triumphantly. "He is in Colorado. You can go there and find him."

"Colorado, Sir Eustace, is the size of England, Scotland and Wales combined," pointed out Holmes.

"Bah! Are you saying you can't do it? That you're not up to it? Can't cope with anything a little challenging, is that it? Huh! Call yourself a detective? You probably couldn't find your way out of this castle!"

Holmes controlled his temper, though his eyes glittered angrily at the old man's gibes. He knew he was deliberately trying to goad him. "I did not say that I could not do it. I merely pointed out that Colorado is an enormous state and a search for your son in such a place would be time consuming," replied Holmes, enunciating each word distinctly. "I have a practice here in London. I cannot just abandon it and go traipsing around America for months on end."

"You will be well paid."

"Money does not come into it," countered Holmes stubbornly.

They glared at each other—a clash of wills. It was the old man who glanced away first. He suddenly looked weary. He was silent for a long moment before he began to speak. His voice was softer now, free of aggression and haughtiness. He was just a feeble old man missing his son. "Mr Holmes, I see that you are a courageous young man and an intelligent one. That is the sort of man I need to find my son. It is no easy task that I am asking of you—I *am* aware of the difficulties; but if anyone can succeed, it is you. I promise that your practice will not suffer from your absence for when you return I will sing your praises. You will be well compensated you and your companion, for any loss of income you might have earned had you stayed in London.

"I have money, but not strength. My time draws near and Cathcart is the last of my line. Can you not find it in your heart to help an old man? He is all I have, Holmes. Is it too much to ask to want to see him again before I die? I am not long for this world ..." he trailed off and looked up at us pathetically.

Now it was Holmes' turn to be silent. No one could ever accuse him of being an uncompassionate man. He sat down on the edge of the bed and helped himself to one of Sir Eustace's cigarettes without waiting for permission, lit up and said, "Why don't you tell me about your son, Sir Eustace."

The old man eyed the cigarette wistfully. Holmes took another from the box and lit it up also, handing it to him. They exchanged companionable grins as they puffed on the foul-smelling smokes.

"Cathcart has always been a rather clumsy, diffident boy. A quiet, timid mummy's boy. His mother spoilt him terribly as she was in her early forties when she had him. I was sixty-five. She considered him a miracle when he arrived and doted on him. I suppose it was pretty miraculous at that, considering our ages. She's been dead these past ten years God bless her soul. Unfortunately, I have never been able to see eye–to–eye with Cathcart.

"I tried to toughen him up, make a man of him. I even tried to enlist him in the army, thinking that that's what he needed. They turned him down. Can you believe it? Claimed he was too delicate or some such nonsense. Too stupid most likely. I will admit I gave the boy a hard time after that. Then, on his twentieth birthday, we had a fight ..." His eyes clouded with remembrance.

"I told him he wasn't worthy of the name Plymouth and did not deserve to inherit the title. I changed my will, writing him out of it. Told him that unless he proved himself worthy of the name he would remain disinherited and that I would leave it all to my only nephew who is a Lieutenant in the Third Northumberland Regiment."

"And the new will?" prodded Holmes gently.

"He's back in. Now, Wilbur only inherits if Cathcart dies without an heir." He sighed. "I was a foolish old man. I lost my temper. It was a bitter row. Two days later, Cathcart disappeared. He left a note behind telling me he was leaving to make his own fortune. Naturally, I searched for him, but he managed to elude my searchers. I never expected him to have the nerve to leave the country. I have to admit that surprised me. Two months later I received a letter telling me that he was in America and would not return home until he could make me proud of him. That was nearly two years ago. He will never make his fortune, Mr Holmes. He has a good heart, but he has never been able to do anything right. The longer he stays in that Godforsaken country, the greater the risk that he will not survive. In fact, I am surprised that he has lasted this long."

He looked at Holmes. "This trip to America has probably been an ordeal for Cathcart, but for you it would merely be an adventure. You hardly seem the type to shirk from danger. You would not be in such a profession if you did."

Holmes picked up the letter again. "He posted this from a town called Buzzard Gulch. I suppose six months is not so old a trail. One question, Sir. Why not hire an American detective agency—like the Pinkertons for instance? They are on familiar ground and would be more able to find him than me."

"I thought of it, but there is no one as dependable as an Englishman. Who knows with these Americans? Riffraff the lot. I would trust *you* to do your utmost. I would not trust *them*."

A faint smile touched Holmes' lips at the old man's blatant prejudice. "Let me confer with my colleague here. We usually work together and on a task of such magnitude I would value his assistance."

The old man nodded and Holmes drew me over to a far corner of the room. "What say you, Watson? Fancy a trip to the American frontier?"

My pulse raced a little at the excitement of such an excursion. "It would certainly be an adventure, Holmes," I said.

"Yes, it would. It may take months though. How do you feel about that?"

"There is nothing holding me here. I am game if you are."

Holmes clapped a hand to my back. "Stout fellow!" he said and I could see that he was as excited as I was at the prospect of an adventure in an unknown wilderness. We returned to the bed.

"Very well, Sir Eustace. I will need this photograph of your son and carte blanche with regard to expenses. If memory serves me correctly, the Southern Princess sails on Thursday. Watson and I will be on board."

Sir Eustace clasped Holmes' hand. "Thank you, my boys, thank you. I know I can rely on you both."

TWO

We spent the next two days paying bills and getting our affairs in order, as we had no idea how long we would be in America. Holmes obtained some additional information about Cathcart Pettigrew Plymouth and also all of the letters he had written to his father.

"Studying the correspondence of an individual often tells the trained observer more about that person than meeting them face to face," he said. "For instance, young Plymouth's writing is quite distinct. Notice the small script, it shows a lack of self–esteem. It is straight up and down with small straight strokes on the uppers. Here is a man with little confidence, one who is easily intimidated, yet curiously his Y's have an unusual flourish to the tail signifying an artistic streak—a repressed one, as indicated by the way the tail curls over onto itself, as if to tuck itself away."

"Holmes, as interesting as all that is, shouldn't you be packing? We leave tomorrow morning," I said. I was still in a bit of a dither wondering what I should or shouldn't take.

"What is there to pack?" he replied. "We have a long journey ahead of us. I suggest we take only the essentials, Watson. The rest we can buy on the way. We are more likely to blend in better wearing local clothing as opposed to our British ones."

"I suppose so," I said. It certainly simplified the problem of packing.

We were up by six the next morning. Our luggage consisting of two bags each was down by the front door awaiting the arrival of our cab. Mrs Hudson outdid herself with breakfast and wished us well.

"Mrs Hudson," said Holmes sternly. "I do not want any of my things touched during my absence."

"Touched they will be Mr Holmes. I am going to make the most of this opportunity. Those rooms upstairs have been crying out for a good clean and a new coat of paint. I will have it all done before you return and your precious things will be back in their places."

Holmes scowled, but surrendered without further argument, after all there was no quibbling with Mrs Hudson when she was in such a determined mood.

Before long we were on our way to the Southampton docks to board the Southern Princess, an American ship. We were to travel first class at the expense of Sir Eustace and Holmes carried a fat pocketbook for our incidental expenses. As we boarded the liner, we were greeted by the Captain and shown to our staterooms by the Head Purser. All in all it looked like we were going to have a pleasant journey.

I enjoyed the voyage over the next thirteen days and mingled with the other passengers, most of whom were Americans returning home. It was fair weather and made for a pleasant trip, which was just as well as I have never been much of a sailor and was prone to sea sickness on rough seas.

Holmes, on the other hand, rarely left his cabin. He surrounded himself with maps, guides and books about the American frontier and its people. I too had purchased a couple of books, but they were of a more lurid fictional nature. After all, one would have to be extremely gullible to believe that anyone could draw and fire a weapon in a quarter of a second. I was quite sure that the feats of the gunfighters were greatly exaggerated.

When I joined the army after finishing medical school, I had been looking for excitement and adventure. My subsequent injuries not long after I joined resulted in my returning to England a weak and broken man. It put an end to my dreams and, for a while, I thought that an adventurous life was beyond me. It wasn't until that fortuitous day in 1881 when I met and became Holmes' flatmate that my prospects changed. His generosity in allowing me to participate in his adventures had given me a new lease of life and, as my body healed from its injuries, so too, did my spirit.

Fully recovered now, my longing for travel and adventure was renewed and I looked forward to this opportunity, although I knew that Holmes himself was feeling somewhat ambivalent. On the one hand, he was reluctant to leave London for an extended period claiming that while he was away the 'mice would play.' Yet on the other, the spirit of adventure was strong within him also and he too looked forward to exploring a different side of life.

He had a tolerance and respect for Americans that was not commonly shared by most British. On the whole, Americans were usually considered brash, loud spoken, and vulgar by most well–bred Englishmen. I think Holmes admired their independent streak and hardiness in civilising a vast wilderness. As for myself, well, I knew few Americans. Those that I met on the boat were all well–spoken and pleasant company.

Certainly, I could not fault their manners.

On the last day of the voyage, Holmes deigned to come out and mingle. He took the Captain up on his offer of a tour of the ship and bombarded him with questions. I then introduced Holmes to the various people I had met and a lively conversation ensued. Holmes was in one of his charming, sociable moods, which was a vast contrast to the hermit–like existence of the preceding days.

Next morning, we stood on the deck, our eyes wide with interest as we steamed into the harbour of that magnificent city called New York.

"What is that, Holmes?" I asked pointing to an island that appeared to be under construction of some sort. "Are they building a lighthouse?"

"Hardly, Watson," returned Holmes dryly. "That, my friend, is the statue of Lady Liberty being constructed."

"Lady Liberty! I think I heard something about that. Wasn't it given to the Americans by the French?"

"Correct. They presented it in July 1884 in Paris and shipped it here a year later."

"It's pretty big."

"It is massive. What a shame we will not get to see the completed statue. I have no doubt it will become this city's most famous landmark in time."

I gazed at the island, squinting as I tried to pick out more details of what they were building. So far they had only constructed the huge feet of the statue and part of its legs.

When the ship docked, we returned to our staterooms and collected our bags before disembarking. We went through customs, declared our intention of staying for a short while only and were soon out on the street hailing a cab to take us to the nearest train station.

As we rode in the four–wheeler towards the city, I asked: "Where do we go next, Holmes?"

"Well, Plymouth did not stay in New York. The size of the city may have intimidated him a little. His next letter was sent from San Francisco, so that is where I would like to go."

"Shouldn't we just go straight to Colorado?"

"We could but we would be missing a vital link in the chain. If possible, I would like to retrace Plymouth's steps, city by city. We will learn more about him that way."

I frowned. It seemed to me we would save a lot of time if we went straight to Buzzard Gulch, Plymouth's last known address. What was the point of going to San Francisco?

Holmes read my thoughts, smiled and said: "How do we know that Plymouth did not double back and return to the city? Perhaps he found frontier living not to his taste. The only way we can be sure of being on his exact trail is by following his footsteps to the letter."

"Plus you want to see San Francisco," I replied.

Holmes grinned at me. "You are becoming very astute, Watson. I will have to watch myself. I won't be able to hide anything from you soon."

I grinned back at him. "A few days won't make a great deal of difference I suppose, and we should make the most of this trip. After all, Sir Eustace is paying. He should at least get his money's worth."

"Exactly!" agreed Holmes.

At the train station, Holmes enquired as to the next train for San Francisco. It was not quite as easy as we thought it would be, necessitating several changes to different lines and railroads. It seemed that here in America they had lots of privately own railway lines, unlike the four in England. As the clerk in the ticket office rattled of the various routes we could take to get to San Francisco, my mind began to wander, it was far too much to memorize.

Holmes listened to the man attentively, before deciding upon a route. "Very well," he said, after the clerk stopped talking. "We will take two tickets, one way to St. Louis on the Pennsylvania Railroad. When does the train leave?"

"Ten minutes."

"What?" I gasped. I had thought we would have at least one night in New York. Holmes thrust money at the clerk, who quickly made change.

"Platform six. You'll make it if you hurry, gents," he called after us as we hurried away from his window.

Holmes with the unerring accuracy of a compass found his way to Platform six in less than five minutes. True, we were moving at a rapid pace and I was panting by the time I tossed my bags onto the train and climbed wearily up after them.

A conductor met us near the door, as he was securing the exits prior to departure. He showed us to the only available compartment, which was occupied by a rather large lady with two grubby little children. I fervently hoped she was not travelling far. The trio stayed with us until we reached Philadelphia, by which time, both Holmes and I were ready to toss the juveniles from a window. They had annoyed us endlessly with questions and they poked and prodded at everything we owned while their mother just sat and smiled at us as if we enjoyed the irritating attention of her snot–nosed, uncontrollable offspring.

From Philadelphia we travelled on to Pittsburgh, sleeping on the seats. Our bags served as pillows, our coats as blankets. Not the most comfortable of positions I will admit, but at least we had no children hounding us. We took our meals in the dining car and returned to our compartment after. We did not dare leave it empty too long in case someone helped themselves to it. We were not sure how things worked in America, and as we had not had time to reserve it for our exclusive use, we worried that we would be saddled with other unsavoury passengers.

Our luck held however, for no one else entered our compartment. It could have been the thick cloud of smoke from our pipes that hung heavy in the air that kept them away. Whatever the reason, we were grateful. We saw little of the cities that we passed and did not get to leave the train until we reached St. Louis, where we overnighted. It was a pleasure to be able to bathe and sleep in a comfortable bed before returning to the rigors of train travel.

Next morning, we bought tickets on the Missouri Pacific line that took us to Kansas City, where we once again had to change trains. How Holmes remembered all these directions was beyond me for I noticed he had not even bothered to take notes when the New York ticket clerk listed the cities and the change overs

In Kansas City, there was a delay of some two hours before our next connection—the Denver and Rio Grande Western. Kansas City was swarming with all manner of people. The thing I noticed most was how openly the men went armed. Many had huge weapons at their hips. Near the railroad were stock yards full of bellowing cattle awaiting shipment to the east. It looked like a lively town and I was disappointed that we could not overnight here for it seemed to epitomize what I imagined a real frontier metropolis would look like with its wide main street and its plank sidewalks. Quite a novelty and nothing like the country villages of England.

We went to a small restaurant for a lunch of Shepherd's pie—a huge helping that made my eyes bulge in wonder. To my surprise, both Holmes and I were able to clean our plates. We loosened our belts a notch, paid for our meal and wandered out onto the plank sidewalk. We still had an hour before our train departed.

"Let's visit a saloon, Holmes," I suggested. In the lurid penny dreadful that I read on the boat, it described a saloon and I must admit to a certain curiosity.

"Yes, all right," he agreed.

We entered the Pink Lady and made our way to the bar. It was full of off–duty cow herders, still in their vile smelling garb. I wrinkled my nose with distaste. "I suppose these chaps haven't heard of bathing," I muttered.

"Shh," grunted Holmes in return. "Someone

will hear you and you're liable to have to defend yourself with a pistol."

The saloon's interior was interesting. Much different to the English bars I was used to. It was a huge room, with a long bar reaching the length of the room at one end. Above the bar was a dreadful painting of a nude whose flesh was a bright pink, hence the name of the place. There was tinny piano music being played and numerous tables. Some men sat at tables merely drinking, others were playing cards. A staircase at one end led upstairs to private rooms and scantily clad saloon women circulated amongst the men. They would have been arrested if they dared appear in an English pub thusly clad. Still, they had nice legs.

Holmes ordered two brandies and we turned to survey the occupants of the room. I glanced to where Holmes seemed to have his attention focussed. He was watching a corner table where six men were playing cards. It was obvious that something was happening for there was an unmistakable air of tension about the players. Suddenly one young man leapt to his feet—he couldn't have been more than ten and seven years old. His hand went to the revolver at his hip and he swore obscenely.

"Yer lyin' skunk!" he declared, glaring at the man dressed in a pristine white shirt, black string tie, and black velvet frock coat and trousers. "Yer cheatin'."

As if those words were a signal to the locals, those at nearby tables all scattered, leaving drinks and even chips discarded as they ducked for cover. The saloon girls too, made their way hastily to the stairs.

On either side of Holmes and me, the patrons also moved away. Foolishly we stood were we were.

The elegantly dressed man slid back his chair slowly and stood up. He pushed back his coat to reveal a pearl handled revolver. "You've had a lot to drink boy, apologize and I'll let you live," he drawled.

"Apologize nuthin'," declared the young cow herder. "Yer cheatin'. You pulled that damn Ace from yer sleeve, I saw yuh."

The other players at the table hastily made their withdrawal, leaving only the cow herder and the gambler, for that is what he had to be. My eyes were transfixed on the scene so that I never paid attention to what Holmes was doing.

The two men—well one man and a boy—glared at each other, their hands hovering over their pistol butts. I was wondering what they were waiting for. How would they know when to draw. Did they have to wait for someone to yell 'draw' before they pulled their weapons. It all seemed so senseless and it was an unfair match. The boy was drunk and hardly in a fit condition to engage in a gunfight, or any fight for that matter.

In the flash of an eye their hands moved, blurring in action and guns were whipped from their holsters in incredible, almost unbelievable speed. The gambler was the fastest. A mocking grin curled at his lips as he brought his gun up to shoot the boy, whose own pistol had become stuck in its holster. Suddenly from nowhere, a flying spittoon struck the gambler in the side of the head, causing
him to drop his gun.

The cow herder finally managed to pull his

gun free. He looked at the downed gambler, then turned his drunken, angry eyes onto Holmes, who had thrown the spittoon.

"Goddamned interferin' furriner!" he yelled and to my horror he turned the pistol in our direction and fired. The first bullet kicked splinters from the bar, the next smashed the mirror behind the bar and the third lodged itself in the ample midriff of the nude.

"Now would be a good time to leave, Holmes," I said, suiting action to words. We had pistols, but they were in our luggage at the train depot. Even if we were carrying them, we would never have returned fire. Holmes was quick to follow me, moving just as another bullet struck the bar in the place he had just vacated.

"Talk about gratitude," he muttered and I had to agree. Holmes had saved the boy's life and he showed his appreciation by shooting at us.

Fortunately the drunken cow herder didn't follow us once we were outside. We made our way to the depot. Our train was already in so we collected our luggage and climbed aboard. Frankly I was glad to be leaving this uncivilized outpost.

✠   ✠   ✠

Our next stop was Denver, where the train stopped only long enough to take on more passengers, water, and fuel before continuing on to Salt Lake City. Here we had time to stretch our legs as we awaited our next connection. As we sat on the platform, I was struck by a sudden thought. The very first case Holmes invited me to join him on was one he jokingly called *A Study in Scarlet.* Jefferson Hope was an

American who avenged himself upon two Mormons from this very place, Salt Lake City.

"What are you smiling at, Watson?" asked Holmes, interrupting my reverie.

"I was just thinking about Jefferson Hope murdering Enoch Drebber."

"Ah, yes. That was a few years ago now, wasn't it?"

"Yes. It was the first time I was privileged to witness you at work. They came from here, Holmes."

"Salt Lake City is crawling with Mormons." He nodded his head towards a group of people at the other end of the platform. I had not paid them any attention before, but now I looked at them more closely. It consisted of one man and four women with no less than nine children of various ages.

"They're all his wives?" I asked.

"Yes."

"Good heavens!"

Holmes chuckled. "Perhaps you should convert, Watson," he suggested.

"I don't think so. One wife would be enough for me." I glanced surreptitiously at the group again and wondered what those women saw in the man, for he was not exactly handsome. Fat and ugly was more like it. How did he manage to attract so many wives? After all, I was neither fat nor ugly, or so I have been told by women, and I had a head of thick brown hair, as opposed to the balding dome of the Mormon male. I wasn't quite Holmes' height, but five foot ten was still considered tall, and what is more, I was in the prime of life, yet he had four wives and I couldn't even get one!

"He is probably rich, Watson," said Holmes breaking into my thoughts again.

"Do you know how annoying that is, Holmes?"

"What?" he asked, standing up as our train steamed into the station.

"Reading my mind."

"Can I help it if your thoughts are transparent."

"And, can I help it if you should have been burned at the stake a century ago?"

"It is no remarkable feat, Watson. No witchcraft involved. I just watched your eyes. You looked at the patriarch of that family group and then carefully examined each of the women. He is not an overly appealing specimen and the woman are all reasonably attractive. It was not hard to divine that you were wondering how he managed to attract them. It was also not difficult to deduce that you despair your own partnerless state for you fingered your moustache as you looked at the man. I could see quite plainly that you considered yourself better looking than he and were puzzled that you could not attract a woman."

"It is rather unfair, is it not?" I said, smiling. Trust Holmes to turn a simple innocent thought into an exercise in deduction!

"I am sure, Watson that you will get all you desire. Stay patient do not be so keen to throw off the mantel of bachelorhood. Would a wife have let you come to America on a week's notice?"

"No, but then if I had a wife, I may not have wanted to come," I returned reasonably.

"Just as well you haven't then," muttered Holmes to his pipe.

"Pardon?" I asked, not sure that I heard him right.

"Nothing," he replied, settling himself into his seat.

This train, the Western Pacific had sleeping cars, so we travelled in relative comfort. We passed through Sacramento during the night and arrived in San Francisco the next day.

From the train station we located the Gainsborough Hotel, which is where Plymouth had stayed. The manager reported that Plymouth had expressed the opinion that he wished to travel west and a hotel clerk had purchased for him a first class one– way ticket to Denver.

We took rooms at the same hotel and returned to the train station to purchase tickets to Denver for the morrow.

Holmes pretended to be unmoved by the excitement of being in a strange city in a foreign country—alien to both us, despite being seasoned travellers throughout Europe, but I noticed his eyes were bright with interest as we took in the sights of this incredible place.

That evening we went to an area known as the Barbary Coast. It was teeming with assorted waterfront life, from gentlemen to sailors to cow herders. Tinny music mixed with quality instruments, emanating from the various buildings that lined the main thoroughfare. There were saloons, theatres and other establishments offering entertainment of all kinds. Anything a man desired could be had here for a price. We entered the Golden Palace Casino and took a table on the upstairs balcony. It gave us an excellent view of the stage.

On this stage was a line of dancing girls performing what the announcer called 'the latest sensation from Paris, France—the *Can Can*.' There was much energetic jumping and high kicks and displaying of shapely legs. I was fascinated. I noted, too, that Holmes watched the performance with interest also.

"They have nice legs, don't they, Holmes?" I said with a grin.

"Good calf muscles," was his offhand reply, but I noticed his eyes did not leave the dancers.

He was never the sort to be distracted by feminine beauty or wiles and scoffed at men who were. Still I learned something about my friend that day and that was that he could be held captivated by a shapely set of legs.

After the performance on stage ended, we decided to have a go at the games of chance. There were several games, some of which I was familiar with, others I had never heard of. We decided on roulette. We played this for perhaps an hour with little success. I was usually much luckier with the wheel, but not on this occasion. I observed that Holmes seemed to be more interested in studying the dealer than the game board. He bet sparingly, but his luck was no better than mine.

Finally, just as I was going to suggest we quit and return to the hotel, Holmes challenged the dealer. The man had just announced that no more bets were to be placed and that he was ready to spin the wheel. He tossed the ball in and started the wheel spinning. When his hand went down to the side of the table, Holmes said sharply: "Leave your hands where we can see them."

"What?" asked the dealer.

"I would prefer it if you kept your hands away from the concealed control switch. It would be nice to have at least one honest spin of the wheel."

"Hey, mister, what are you saying?" asked the tall, well dressed, thick moustached man beside him.

Holmes glanced at him. "This wheel is rigged. The dealer has been pressing a button to manipulate it. I have been watching him until I was sure. I am sure now."

"They're cheating!" exclaimed the man. Within seconds, his cry was taken up by the other players who glared ominously at the suddenly cowed dealer.

The proprietor of the establishment must have been nearby for we heard him calling for his hired henchmen to handle the trouble. Four large men, big on muscle, but perhaps not so on brains, came to the table and demanded to know what was going on.

"Your roulette wheel is fixed to ensure that no customer has a chance of winning," explained Holmes politely.

"We ain't got no crooked wheels in this place," said the largest of the four.

"Well, that is easily determined," said Holmes. "Just turn the wheel over and I will examine its mechanism. I believe you will find that there are a few additions."

"Tip the wheel, tip the wheel!" yelled big moustache suiting action to words. With the help of several other players the roulette wheel and table were upended.

Before Holmes could examine its mechanisms,

the henchmen began growling and advanced on us, meaning to beat us up and throw us out. I threw a punch at the fellow who grabbed me by the shoulder and Holmes lashed out at another; after that we had little more to do, for a wild free for all broke out. The enraged customers threw themselves at the toughs. More casino employees came running up only to also become embroiled in the fighting. I felt a hand on my arm and turned to defend myself, only to find it was Holmes.

"This way, Watson," he said, pulling me along.

We moved a short distance and took shelter behind an upturned table. Even as we ducked behind it, a bottle smashed against its surface.

"I see no reason for us to become involved in a common brawl," said he.

"Fancy the wheel being rigged. Things like that would never be tolerated in England," I said, quite enraged at being taken in so easily.

"Never give a sucker an even break," said Holmes, while I looked at him in surprise.

"I believe it was an American that came up with that," he explained.

"It is obviously the policy of _this_ place."

The battle raged around us. Occasionally we peeked out to see how it was progressing. From our viewpoint we saw gaming tables overturned, their heavy thuds accompanied by the clattering of chips that scattered over the floor. I winced to the sound of timber cracking as chairs and table legs were used as clubs and smashed over the heads and backs of un-lucky recipients. Bodies went flying, some to remain unmoving, others scrambling to their feet and continuing the fight.

A shower of glass rained down from the bar as the huge mirror behind the main bar was shattered by some missile or other. In a matter of moments, the establishment was turned from opulent elegance to a debris littered war zone.

"What a shambles," I said.

"It is the least they deserve for running a dishonest establishment," replied Holmes righteously. "In the meantime, I think we should make ourselves scarce, for it is only a matter of time before the local constabulary arrive."

I nodded in agreement and stood up, only to duck quickly as a bottle sailed past my head, narrowly missing it. "Hands and knees, Holmes," I suggested.

We crawled along, trying to keep behind furniture, occasionally having to thrust a fighting patron aside. It took a while, but we managed to make it outside and across the street just as several large carriages arrived packed with blue uniformed men carrying batons who hurried inside the building.

"The police have arrived," I said unnecessarily.

"Better late than never," returned Holmes. We had to walk several blocks before we could find a cab to take us to our hotel.

"I wonder if the rest of our trip is going to be as eventful as today, Holmes," I said as we entered our hotel room.

"I dare say it will. Despite the trappings of civilization, this is still a rough country."

✠ ✠ ✠

The next day we boarded the train that was to take us to the first stop on our journey west. Our fellow passengers for the most part, consisted of merchants, salesmen—or drummers as the Americans called them. Several families with intentions of settling in the west were also on board, as well as elegantly suited sporting men. Gambling was considered a respectable profession in the west and high-class gamblers were deemed the elite of the frontier, much as gentleman are considered in polite British society.

While I chatted to a farmer and his wife, Holmes struck up a conversation with two well-dressed gamblers. It was not long before they had the cards out and were demonstrating various card tricks to Holmes. He was so intrigued that he bought himself a pack of cards at the first whistle stop, barely making it back onto the train in time, for it had only stopped long enough to take on water and coal.

The further we west travelled the sparser the terrain became and the smaller the towns. The Denver & Rio Grande Western had sleeping births and travelled from San Francisco to Denver, which is the capital of the state of Colorado. It was an uneventful journey and extremely comfortable. I was pleasantly surprised by the trains themselves for I had been expecting primitive conditions, but the Denver & Rio Grande Western line offered comfortable carriages with a dining car, smoking car and even a bar. It was all very civilized.

It took a couple of days of travelling to reach Denver, in this our second visit, although I suppose I could hardly count the first for we had not left the train. It proved to be quite a modern city, by frontier standards. There were solid brick buildings and theatres and fashionably dressed men and women. The only discordant note was the presence of heavily armed men. In San Francisco and New York and indeed, in any of the larger Eastern cities, the citizens did not carry firearms so openly, but here in Denver, they seemed to flaunt their weapons.

We found rooms at the Imperial Hotel and learned that Plymouth had also stayed there some one–and–a–half years previously.

"You know, Holmes," I said as we strolled around town looking for a likely restaurant for our dinner. "I had expected conditions to be a great deal more primitive out here, but they are quite up to date and modern. Why they even have stone sidewalks!"

"True, but this is a major city, Watson. I think as of tomorrow, you will start seeing a change and not necessarily for the better. Make the most of tonight, for I doubt very much if we will continue to experience such comfort and luxury. The difficult part of our journey is yet to begin."

The next day, as our train did not leave until noon, Holmes and I undertook to find out Plymouth's movements. We learned that he had worked as a bartender, barber and finally as a bank clerk.

The saloon owner claimed he was the worst bartender he had ever seen even though when Plymouth had walked in for the job he claimed he was the best bartender in London.

The barber was just as uncomplimentary and even threatened to take a razor to him if he dared show his face in the shop again. Apparently, young Plymouth was a trifle clumsy with the blade and had been fired when he nicked the Sheriff's ear, who threatened to arrest him for assault.

Only the banker proved to have a few kind words for the runaway. Plymouth worked for him for over a year until his daughter Felicity, had returned from the ladies college in San Francisco. The banker claimed he had hoped to make Plymouth his son–in–law. He showed us a photograph of his lovely Felicity.

"What more could a man ask for?" asked the banker, proudly displaying the picture of a woman that only a father could love.

Holmes took a look at it and winced at the bucktoothed, buxom creature that smiled up at him. He handed the photograph back to the adoring father and asked: "So Plymouth was happy working for you until you tried to pair him up with your daughter—is that correct?"

"Yes. Then, when I was hinting he should name the day, he suddenly took it into his head to become a gambler. I don't know what got into him. Up until then he had always shown good sense and was the perfect gentleman. He quit his job and caught the first train west the very next day."

As we walked back to the railroad, I grinned and said: "I cannot blame Plymouth for running. After all he is quite a good-looking young man in that photograph you have of him."

"In his place I would have done the same," agreed Holmes.

THREE

The train to Buzzard Gulch was a rattly, primitive affair compared to the ones we had travelled on previously. There were no first-class carriages, but long communal ones with open seating. Our fellow passengers were less elegantly attired than those of the previous day and were a mixed group.

I noticed the garishly dressed drummers in their loud checked suits and the men from the gambling fraternity, but they all seemed to keep to themselves and were not quite as friendly as the ones we had met previously.

"They're dishonest gamblers, Watson," said Holmes in reply to my comment about their unsociability.

"Dishonest! How can you tell?"

"See the one with the green waistcoat?" I nodded. "Look at his hands and you will see his right forefinger has an ink stain on it."

"So?"

"He has a small ink pot in his coat top pocket which he uses to mark the cards when playing. The other fellow with him is his partner. He deals the marked cards to him and vice versa."

"Good heavens!" I said, a little startled by the thought. "I thought gambling was a respectable profession,"

"Keep in mind, Watson, that the further west we go, the lower becomes the standards. Men like that are little better than criminals, except that they rob the people over the card tables rather than at gun point. There are insufficient police to uphold the law and in many cases it is mob rule that retains order."

"In that case, I think I will stay away from card games," I replied.

"It would be wise," agreed Holmes. "Unless the players are honest gamblers, then it probably would be safe."

"As I cannot tell the difference between an honest and a dishonest one, I will not even attempt it." I said and Holmes smiled.

We reached our destination by late afternoon and as we alighted from the train I surveyed the town with dismay. It was as unimpressive as its name. Fancy calling a place Buzzard Gulch. Lining the main street, the only street, were clapboard structures with higher false fronts. The street was wide and dusty with wooden sidewalks in front of the buildings and dirt and mud everywhere else. At the edges of the sidewalks were hitching rails for the horses and water troughs. Hefting our bags we made our way to the only double storied structure in town, *The Herders Rest Hotel*, which was located across the road from the railway depot and beside the loading pens full of smelly cattle.

There was a horse–faced clerk asleep at the front desk, whom Holmes woke when he clanged the bell on the desk. The clerk blinked at us and growled: "Yeah, what?"

"We would like two of your finest rooms please," requested Holmes.

"Hmm," the clerk grunted and tossed two keys at us. "Sign the register. That'll be a dollar each in advance." His manner was insolent.

Holmes picked up the keys as I inscribed our names in the register. I noticed that many of the past occupants had merely signed themselves in with an X. "Is there a bell hop?" I asked.

"This ain't Denver," replied the clerk dismissively. "Doors are numbered."

"Come, Watson," said Holmes, picking up his bags. "We will leave this fellow to his ruminations. It is obvious he has wife troubles." That caused the clerk to look up at us in surprise. Holmes ignored him as we made our way upstairs.

I had room seventeen and he had nineteen. They were pitifully small rooms containing a bed, washstand and wardrobe and nothing else. Holmes' room was exactly the same, except he also had a chair. I dumped my bags and joined him in his room. He was perched on the windowsill, smoking. "Now what, Holmes?" I asked, helping myself to the chair.

"Now we start to trace Plymouth. We know he posted his last communiqué from here and none since. We know he planned on becoming a prospector. What we have to find out is which way he went. Perhaps he mentioned his next destination to someone? It was only six months ago, so the trail is not that cold."

"Perhaps we should try the general stores. If he bought supplies and prospecting equipment, he would have bought them here."

"Capital suggestion. In his letter he states that he won enough as a gambler to outfit himself for prospecting. The saloon keepers may also remember him." He fished out his pipe, filled it and lit it, before we left the hotel to check out the town, what little there was of it. Two saloons, the hotel, a dressmaker, and tailors shop combined, a bakery and a general emporium that sold everything from staple goods to explosives.

As we entered the store, the proprietor, a short bald fellow in shirtsleeves and waistcoat greeted us. "Afternoon gents, what can I do for you?"

"We are trying to locate a young friend of ours. He came this way six months ago, with the intention of becoming a prospector. Perhaps you may have served him?" said Holmes taking out the photograph and showing it to the storekeeper.

The man studied the picture and frowned for a moment before his expression cleared. "Oh sure, I remember him. Good looking young feller, real polite and he talked just like you."

"He's a countryman. What do you remember about him?" asked Holmes.

The storekeeper grinned. "The young feller fancied himself as a gambler. I don't think he knew much about gambling but he had the devil's own luck. I was in the Blue Bull when he hit his winning streak. Didn't matter how badly he played, he just kept on winning. Folks would've accused him of cheating, except he had no idea what he was doing or how he was doing it. I have heard of beginners luck, but I'd never seen it before. Anyway, he made himself a mite unpopular around here because of it. The marshal advised him to quit while he was ahead. So he decided he'd become a prospector. He will probably blow himself up as like as not." The storekeeper shook his head at the memory, before adding, "Mind you, I didn't sell him any explosives, didn't want any innocent folks getting hurt, if you know what I mean?"

"Did he happen to mention where he was going?" I asked.

"Nope. He caught the noon stage west if that's any help. First time I've ever seen a prospector travel by stage, they usually have a mule."

"Thank you Sir, you have been most helpful," said Holmes, shaking his hand.

"I could be even more helpful," offered the storekeeper. "Have you gents considered buying new hats?"

"There is nothing wrong with our hats, thank you," I replied, giving my Homburg a tap on its top, it was only two months old and in perfectly good condition. Holmes was wearing a similar hat.

"Well sure, there ain't nothing wrong with your hats for city living but out here, the sun'll fry your nose off'n your face quicker'n you could blink."

I decided he was just trying to sell us hats and was exaggerating the effects of the local weather. After all, our hats were perfectly suitable. "We will manage with what we have on, thank you," I said politely.

He shrugged. "It's your heads. How about guns then. There's all kinds of thieving skunks out west."

"We have weapons, thank you," replied Holmes, but on noting the storekeepers disappointed expression added, "Perhaps some of your finest cigars...?"

That made the fellow's day as he happily brought several boxes of cigars out for our perusal. Holmes bought a dozen. Next we went to the train depot and enquired as to the location of the stage depot.

"Right here, gents. We handle both. The mornin' stage runs east, the noon stages runs west. Which do you want?"

"West. How many stops does it make?" asked Holmes.

"Goes as far as Lucky Strike and makes one stop at the Wells Fargo way station for a team change."

"Lucky Strike is a mining town, I take it?" asked Holmes.

"A real boomer, so I'm told," agreed the station master.

"So if someone wanted to become a prospector, they would go there?" I asked.

"As likely a place to start from as any," he agreed.

"Thank you. We will take two tickets on the noon stagecoach to Lucky Strike," said Holmes taking out his well filled wallet.

"Er ... hope you don't mind my sayin' so, but that's a mighty fat wallet you're packing."

"So?" Holmes looked at him.

"Well, I'd advise you to hide if you want to keep it. There's been a lot of stage holdups of late and Lucky Strike'll be crawlin' with all kinds of tinhorns, claim jumpers, rattlesnakes, and every other kind of thievin' polecat you could name. They're likely to slit your throat for just your watch, let alone a fat wallet. Show that and you'll have more buzzards hoverin' round yuh than on a buffalo carcass."

"I see," said Holmes.

"You sure you want to go there? No offence but you gents don't seem the type to be goin' to a place like that. Hell you ain't even packin' iron."

I listened to this incomprehensible dialogue with puzzlement, and then looked at Holmes to see if he understood.

"Thank you for your concern," said Holmes, "we appreciate the advice and we do have weapons. Now, two tickets if you please."

The station master shrugged and issued the tickets. "It's your scalps."

We returned to the hotel. Back upstairs in Holmes's room I asked, "Did you understand what that man was saying, Holmes?"

"Perfectly, Watson."

"In that case what are tinhorns, claim jumpers, and ... polecats?"

Holmes smiled. "Colourful language is it not? Tinhorns are dishonest gamblers. Claim jumpers are thieves that steal other people's mining claims and polecats are a native species of wild cat that uh...climb poles." Holmes explained, sounding very knowledgeable, but I still looked at him dubiously.

"I will grant you the first two, Holmes, but I am not so sure about the third."

Holmes laughed. "Neither am I. Perhaps it is a term applied to dishonest people."

"I am a bit surprised about there being snakes in town though," I said.

"Snakes?"

"The station master said there were rattle-snakes in town."

"I think that is another derogatory term for untrustworthy people."

"Oh. What did he mean by packing iron. What do we need an iron for?"

"He did not mean the sort used for pressing clothing, Watson. Hog leg, Iron, Peacemaker etcetera are colourful metaphors for a revolver."

"These people have well and truly mangled the English language." I complained. "I can barely understand them."

"You will get used to them if we are here long enough."

We refreshed ourselves then had an indifferent meal at the hotel, retiring early, though it was difficult to sleep in the lumpy uncomfortable beds.

FOUR

The following day we had a mediocre lunch at the hotel before fronting at the train and coach depot. There was a Cobb and Co coach parked to the side and we made our way to it. The driver, a grizzled old veteran in dust covered buckskins, took our bags, and loaded them onto the roof of the coach. He said not a word but spat tobacco juice out at regular intervals, narrowly missing my boot. Frightfully disgusting habit!

Holmes examined the coach with interest, it being the first of its kind we had ever seen and tried to engage the driver in conversation. His replies were monosyllabic grunts, punctuated with a great deal of spitting, "No talker, he," said Holmes ruefully when he rejoined me. I glanced at my watch; it was almost noon.

"We might as well get in, I suppose," I said to Holmes, who nodded in agreement. He opened the door and we found that there was already one passenger on board. A whiskey drummer from the smell of him, and one who sampled his own wares.

We clambered past without waking him and took seats opposite one another at the window. The seat, though padded was quite hard.

"Not exactly built for comfort, is it?" I said.

"No, but it is built for speed," replied Holmes.

It was almost noon. The driver climbed up to his perch on the seat and the guard was in the process of climbing up when there came a commotion in the street.

A garishly clad woman with unnatural red hair and dressed in a bright red gown with a low décolleté, a feather boa and a large flowery hat was being escorted by the town marshal, several men and a group of screaming women who were brandishing parasols and brooms.

"Hold the stage!" called the marshal, hurrying forward.

"Flossie, you in trouble again?" asked the guard good-naturedly as he took the bags the marshal handed up to him.

"You know how it is, Jake," she grinned, not at all put out by the scene she was creating.

"Hussy! Hussy!" chanted the accompanying women.

"All right, that's enough," said the marshal, holding up his hand to silence the women. "I'm runnin' her out of town, so let this be the end of it."

He helped the woman up and she plonked herself down beside Holmes as I had the snoring drummer beside me. Her cheap perfume wafted over us and clogged our nostrils, almost making us gag. Lucky there wasn't any glass in the windows of the coach for we were going to need the ventilation.

"Howdy, honey," she said to him with extreme informality. Before Holmes could respond there was more of a commotion outside the coach with the marshal trying to clear passage for the vehicle to pass. Soon, with a crack of the whip and a cloud of dust, we were on our way.

"Hiyuh gents," greeted the woman. "I'm Flossie Dolittle."

"Miss Dolittle," greeted Holmes. "I am Sherlock Holmes and this is Dr. John Watson."

"A doctor huh?" She eyed me with interest. "Well ain't that handy. I got me an itch that won't quit; maybe you can take a look at it later."

"Er, yes perhaps," I replied, fearing just where that itch was.

"Who's sleepin' beauty there?"

"We have no idea," I said. "He was already asleep and on board before we arrived." I looked her over. She was not a beautiful woman; her face was plastered with too much rogue and powder, but she had an appealing smile and friendly demeanour.

"Does this sort of thing happen often, Miss Dolittle?" asked Holmes.

"Yup, all the time; gets irksome. Damn pious wo-men get jealous if their husbands come sniffin' round me."

"How unpleasant for you," returned Holmes politely, ignoring her appalling grammar.

She turned in her seat and eyed Holmes with interest. "Hey now, you're a real gent ain't you? Like one of them English Dooks or somethin'."

"We are from England, yes, but alas; do not have titles, bar the obligatory ones."

"Well you're both kinda cute in your funny little hats," she said.

I frowned, that was the second time someone had cast aspersions on our hats, which happened to be the latest fashion in London. I decided to change the subject. "Are you a performer then, Miss Dolittle?" I asked.

"Why I sure am," she laughed. "Strictly horizontal performances if yuh know what I mean," she added with a brazen wink at me.

"Ah, yes, of course," I mumbled as she grinned suggestively.

"It is unfortunate that you have lost your position here," said Holmes, still being polite.

"Well honey," she said, leaning closer and hooking her arm through his. "It's a position I could easy get into was you offerin'."

"I–I beg your pardon?" gasped Holmes.

"Weren't you offerin' to put some work my way?" she asked.

Holmes blinked at her in shock. "Good Lord, no! Not at all!"

"Too bad. Most my customers are trail trash. Never bin with a real gent before."

Holmes unhooked her arm, while I hid a smile behind my hand. "I understand that Lucky Strike is a gold mining town," I said changing the subject yet again.

"Yup," she agreed.

"I am sure you will have no difficulty getting work there, Miss Dolittle," I reassured.

"Sure enough. There's fifty men to every woman in these here parts, an' you don't have to keep callin' me Miss, makes me sound like a schoolmarm. I'm Flossie to my friends."

"It is customary to call a lady Miss on so short an acquaintance," I pointed out.

She laughed again. "I can tell you're furriners, no one around here'd call me a lady."

"Nevertheless ..." began Holmes.

She latched onto his arm again. "Now ain't you a cute one," she said. "What did you say your name was – Shylock?"

"Sherlock, Sherlock Holmes," said Holmes, trying to unhook her hand again, but gave up when she tightened her grip.

"What do you do for a crust, Sherlock?" she asked.

Holmes' eyebrow went up a notch at her over familiarity. Why, even I never called him by his Christian name and I had known him for several years. "I am a consulting detective."

"You don't say? Well, don't let 'em know you're a John Law in Lucky Strike, else you won't live to see the
day out," she warned.

"Good heavens, do you mean to say there is no law in the town?" I asked in amazement, such a thing being almost incomprehensible.

"There's a marshal, but I wouldn't trust him further'n I could throw this coach. He's on the take. You got a problem, don't go to him."

"Thank you for your insights, Miss Dolittle," said Holmes. "What else can you tell us about the town?"

"There's a shootin' every other day of the week. And the place is boomin' and burstin' at the seams with more thieven' polecats than you can poke a stick at. Whatever yuh do, don't drink the whiskey on accounta it's mostly snakehead rotgut. An' hang onto yuh wallets. They got bare-faced boys that'd eat dudes like you two for breakfast and that's a real shame." She patted Holmes' cheek. "Yessir, it'd be a real shame to have your purty face all mussed up."

"I assure you, Miss Dolittle I am more than capable of looking after myself," replied Holmes. If he was uncomfortable by her unwanted attention he hid it well.

After a while, she yawned, unhooked her hand, much to Holmes' relief, curled her feet up onto the seat and went to sleep, using Holmes' shoulder for a pillow. He was too much of a gentleman to remove her, but the flowers on her hat kept tickling the side of his face. I refrained from comment, knowing it would only irritate him.

✠   ✠   ✠

It was after the afternoon stop for a team change; we had travelled in silence for an hour or so when there was a sudden gunshot and a shouted oath. The coach came to an abrupt halt, causing me to fall forward into Holmes and the sleeping drummer into Flossie.

"Hold up!" he yelled waking up for the first time and looking around wildly. And that is exactly what it was. I looked out the window and saw the guard lying on the ground, a bullet wound in his shoulder.

"Everybody out," ordered the boss thief—a tall man with long brown hair and his face covered by a soiled blue handkerchief with red spots.

We disembarked from the coach and lined up.

"Search 'em," ordered the boss thief.

Another fellow came over to us and searched us. He took my service revolver from my pocket and tossed it into the bushes, then helped himself to my wallet and watch. Next he searched Holmes, tossing his gun into the bushes also. Holmes ignored this and continued to study the thieves. I had no doubt that he would be able to recognize them if he ever saw them again, such was his phenomenal memory and eye for detail.

They relieved him of his wallet, then turned their attention to the drummer, who had been shocked sober and helped themselves to his sample case. Flossie also handed over her reticule without argument.

It was all over and done with rather quickly and efficiently. There were four bandits in all. One wore two guns and kept us covered as the other three mounted, then he turned and leapt astride his horse. With a wild yell, they took off, galloping down the road. As soon as they left, I hurried to the wounded guard and called out: "Driver, throw down my bags please. I am a doctor."

The driver hunted amongst the bags and tossed down my Gladstone, which contained my medical kit. Although, I did not bring my actual medical bag, I had my equipment and supplies in a soft canvas sack for easier packing. I thought it prudent to bring it along as one never knew what one would encounter travelling in a rough, untamed country like this one.

As I worked on the guard, Holmes retrieved our pistols and studied the horse tracks of the thieves. To my surprise, I had an attentive audience as the drummer, the driver and Flossie squatted by me, watching every move I made as I probed for and removed the bullet.

"You can tell you're a real doc," observed Flossie, "yuh did that real neat. I've seen some fellers who claim they're doctors, real butchers they are."

The drummer nodded in agreement, while I marvelled at the stoicism of these frontier folk. The guard was conscious the whole time it took to probe for and remove the bullet and he barely uttered a groan. If this had happened in England, the woman would have been swooning, while the men would have clamoured for the police. These people were fatalistic about the robbery.

"He gunna be all right, Doc?" asked the driver. I glanced at him, it being the longest sentence he had uttered to date.

"Yes, he should recover with rest."

"Yeller bellied skonks," growled the driver. "Shot him from ambush they did."

"Is this a common occurrence?" asked Holmes coming up and returning my gun to me.

"Near Lucky Strike it is. Once a week." He spat his tobacco out onto the ground.

"What does the law do about it?"

"What law?" He spat again.

"The town marshal," I said.

"He's only in charge of the town, this is outside his territory."

"What about the county sheriff?" I persisted.

"Big county an' Ross Feenan's only one man," shrugged the driver.

The guard chose this moment to pass out. I finished binding his shoulder with material provided by Flossie from her petticoat. "He will have to ride inside," I said. Holmes helped me lift him and place him

[54]

on the seat. "Perhaps he could use your lap for a pillow, Miss Dolittle," I suggested. She nodded and climbed in also.

"I'll ride up top," offered the drummer. "Might help to clear my head."

Holmes and I boarded the coach and soon we were on our way again.

"It seems incredible that highwaymen can plunder at will, with no interference from the law," I said.

"We were lucky," said Flossie. "That kind of trigger happy scum don't care who they kill. Mighty fortunate neither of you gents tried to play hero on account you'd have been dead heroes."

"Did they get all our money, Holmes?" I asked, for Holmes was carrying our travelling expenses.

"No. Fortunately I took the station master's advice and hid the bulk of it."

"Didn't get mine neither," grinned Flossie.

"So they were willing to kill a man for a meagre sum?" I said.

"Scum like that'd shoot their own mothers for a dollar," shrugged Flossie, obviously well used to the rigors of travel.

"Well, Watson, you did say you wanted adventure," said Holmes, a faint smile at his lips. "This has certainly been an experience."

"One I could well have done without," I said. "The guard too."

FIVE

If I had been shocked by the callousness of the thieves, I was even more surprised by our reception in Lucky Strike. One would have thought that the late arrival of the stagecoach would generate interest and even alarm.

When the coach pulled up outside the stage depot, its manager wandered out chewing on a vile looking cigar. "Where's Jake?" he asked.

"Shot," grunted the driver.

"Dead?"

"Nope."

"Owlhoots?"

"Yup."

"That's it," I said, climbing out of the coach indignantly. "Sir, are you not in the least bit concerned that the passengers have been robbed...that the guard has been shot and could quite easily have been killed? What kind of service are you running?"

The depot manager looked me over. "Dude?" The question was aimed at the driver.

"Doc."

"Ah." He turned back to me. "Well, you see, Doc, it's thisaway. Coach gets held up regular like. Ain't nothin' I can do about it. Folks travel at their own risk. Stage line ain't responsible."

"Well, where is the law?" I demanded, forgetting for a moment what Flossie had told us about the town marshal.

At that moment a big, dirty unshaven man in a sweat stained undershirt, trousers and suspenders approached us. There was a tin star attached to his suspenders. "Someone holler?" he asked.

I am afraid I could not conceal my expression of distaste at the sight of him. I turned to Holmes. "Surely that is not the elected representative of the law, Holmes?" I asked incredulously.

"He wears the badge of authority," replied Holmes, taking a step forward. "Marshal, I can describe the highwaymen."

"The what?"

"The perpetrators."

"Huh?"

The man was a complete imbecile!

"The owl hoots, marshal," offered Flossie.

"Oh. Why'nt you say so? Anyways how could yuh describe 'em. They wore masks," replied the marshal looking Holmes over warily.

"How do you know they wore masks?" asked Holmes.

"Uh...they always do."

"Are you going to look for them?" I demanded, rather indignant at this state of affairs. This would never have happened in England!

"Nope." The marshal scratched his crotch and belched.

"Why not?"

They'll be long gone now."

"I think not, Marshal," contradicted Holmes. "Those horses over there at that saloon rail have been hard ridden in the last hour. The saddle on the black horse has a spur tear on the side flap. One of the thieves had a saddle exactly like that on a similar horse. If we go inside, I am sure I can identify the felons."

"The what?"

Holmes sighed resignedly. "The owl hoots."

"Uh...well...uh, I don't know about that. You cain't go accusin' law abidin' citizens. You ain't got no proof, mister."

"Proof can easily be established, Marshal. If I recognize the men inside, you can search them. If they are carrying our possessions, our wallets, watches etcetera, surely that would be proof enough even for you." Holmes reached into the coach and collected his walking stick. He began to stride towards the Golden Belle Saloon. "Coming, Watson?"

I hurried after him, with the marshal, drummer, Flossie and the depot manager trailing after us. It struck me that the marshal should have been leading, not Holmes. It also occurred to me that the marshal probably knew the thieves and was taking bribes from them to overlook their crimes. He certainly did not appear too enthused about their possible apprehension.

As Holmes strode towards the saloon, the crowd following us grew. Inquisitive citizens tagged along behind us, no doubt curious as to what was going on and not wanting to miss any of the possible action that Holmes' businesslike appearance heralded.

Holmes stopped at the hitching rail and examined the saddle that had caught his attention. Next he checked the back hooves of the four hard ridden horses, their coats still soaked with lather.

"Aha!" He exclaimed, holding the hoof of the last horse up. "At the scene of the crime I noticed that one of the horses was missing a nail from his offside shoe. This horse's shoe corresponds with that print. These animals definitely belong to the stagecoach robbers." Holmes let go of the hoof and straightened up. He approached the swing doors and stopped, peering over into the dark interior, allowing his eyes to become accustomed to the change in light levels. As he entered with his entourage in tow, the tinny piano music stopped and all eyes turned towards us. Holmes characteristically ignored the effect his entrance had on the crowd and scanned the room. Over at a side table were four men carousing with scantily clad saloon women. Holmes walked over and stopped in front of the table.

The man in the centre had long brown hair and a blue bandanna with red spots around his neck. Even I recognized him, for he had not bothered to change his clothing or alter his appearance in any way. I was astonished at the foolhardiness of these thieves that they would come to the very town where the stagecoach was bound for, it was unheard of.

He looked up at Holmes and a flicker of recognition showed in his eyes. "Well if it ain't fancy pants," he sneered, making no effort to hide the fact that he recognized us.

"You Sir, and your companions are under arrest for highway robbery," stated Holmes calmly.

The men laughed. Considering that all the men were heavily armed with guns readily accessible at their hips, I thought it prudent to draw my own gun and hold it concealed in my hand down by my side.

"Who's gunna arrest us then?" asked blue 'kerchief.

"The marshal," said Holmes, triggering an even louder outburst of laughter from the outlaws.

"Yeah, Marshal, come arrest us," grinned one

of the other men, a scrawny looking individual with a gun at either hip in a buscadero style gun belt.

"Uh...well...uh...," stammered the marshal, backing up so as to put Holmes and myself between him and the men.

"Very well," said Holmes coldly, "if the marshal is too cowardly, I will make a citizen's arrest. Unsheathe your weapons."

Sensing impending violence, the saloon women quickly untangled themselves from the robbers and moved away. As if that was a signal, the people at nearby tables started evacuating the vicinity and the crowd that had followed us in also ducked for cover.

"Make me!" snarled the boss thief as his hand darted up from under the table, his fist filled with a weapon.

Holmes flicked up his walking stick, the lower part separating to reveal a sword which he thrust at the thief, poking the tip of it into his throat hard enough to be felt, but not quite hard enough to pierce the skin. "Put your gun on the table," he ordered. As an added inducement he poked harder with the sword. The man paled as it broke skin and lowered his gun onto the table.

"All of you put your weapons on the table," said Holmes, glaring at the others, who stood dumbly, too surprised by Holmes' quick retaliation to react.

The scrawny man drew his left side gun and pretended to put it on the table, whilst at the same time he drew his right hand gun cocking back the hammer before the weapon cleared leather. It was a very fast, smooth move, but I was faster as my gun was already in my hand, having anticipated such treachery. I

brought my gun up and fired in one rapid action hitting him in the arm. He dropped both his weapons. At the same moment, Holmes quickly swung his sword stick at the third man who foolishly attempted to draw his weapon. The blade came down
onto his wrist, slicing into it deeply and his gun clattered to the floor. I pointed my revolver at the last man who raised his hands.

Moving over and taking care to stay out of Holmes' way, I quickly disarmed him and gathered up all the weapons, dropping them onto a nearby table.

"Now empty your pockets," ordered Holmes.

The thieves were quick to obey, being thoroughly intimidated. Flossie's purse plonked onto the table along with our wallets and watches which we retrieved. The drummer, who had kept well back during the confrontation, scuttled forward, and collected his wallet.

"Thanks Mister," he said, tipping his hat to Holmes before hurrying away.

"Marshal, take these men to gaol—I assume you *do* have a gaol?" said Holmes acerbically.

"Uh ... yeah," muttered the chastened marshal, his face shiny with sweat.

Holmes lined the outlaws up and, with the marshal leading; we herded them to the jail. It was left to me to search them and remove several small single shot weapons plus various types of knives from their persons before tending the wounded and installing them in cells.

"These men have been responsible for robbing numerous stagecoaches. It is your duty to hold them for the circuit judge. There is a judge is there not?"

"Uh...yeah," grunted the marshal. This seemed to be the sum of his vocabulary. He was thoroughly cowed and intimidated by Holmes' imperious manner.

Flossie was waiting for us when we returned to the depot to collect our baggage. "Sherlock, Doc, that was mighty impressive for a couple of dudes," she said hooking arms with us. "And your shootin' Doc, why you'll be the talk of the town."

"We did what we had to. One cannot allow criminals to escape or else the lawless will run rampant," I said, feeling rather flattered by her admiration.

She glanced at us just before she took her leave, her expression serious "Fellers, you've proven you can look after yourselves, but watch your backs, won't yuh. The marshal ain't gunna leave them locked up for long. When they get out they'll be gunnin' for yuh. You took 'em by surprise this time. To look at yuh no one would think you could act so smart and fast, but next time yuh tangle with 'em, it won't be so easy. That kind of scum would think nothin' of shootin' yuh in the back."

"Thank you for your concern, Miss Dolittle. Rest assured that we shall be extra vigilant. Fortunately our stay in this abysmal hamlet is only temporary." Holmes replied.

I held out my hand to her. "It was a pleasure meeting you, Miss Dolittle," I said. She smiled at me. "You too, Doc. If either of you fellers get to feelin' lonely, look me up, huh? It'll be on the house."

"Er...thank you for the offer." I said, while Holmes kept his face expressionless. After she moved off, we made our way to the nearest hotel.

SIX

We registered at the front desk and went up to our room. By city standards, by Buzzard Gulch standards for that matter, the place was a dump. Our room had two single beds. In one, the springs stuck up through the mattress, and in the other, the mattress sagged to the floor as the middle slats of the bed appeared to be missing. There was a chipped wash bowl and a cracked jug filled with dirty brown water. Flies buzzed around the room and as I dropped my bags on the floor, several bugs scurried to safety in the rising dust.

"Three dollars a night for this pigsty!" I exclaimed in disgust.

"It is a mining town, Watson. All the prices are likely to be inflated."

"Do you think we will find young Plymouth here?"

"Not in town, unless we are extraordinarily lucky, but perhaps somewhere in the diggings."

"I don't know how people can live like this."

"Hardy pioneer stock, Watson. They have courage and durability. They leave the safety of the east and come west; build towns with saloons, houses, and businesses. They farm the land and dig for gold but unfortunately in their struggle to make a living, the education of their children becomes neglected and this leads to several generations of poorly educated people—hence the atrocious grammar we have been encountering. Some can barely read or write their own names. It is not until a town actually becomes settled that consideration is given to the establishment of schools."

"But surely not all are illiterate or ignorant?" I argued.

"No, of course not. If the parents are educated, it follows that they will in turn teach their offspring. It is often the poorer classes who come west to make their fortune, hoping for a better life. Conditions in American cities for the poor are no better than in our own. Education is not a priority with them."

"Well you are right on one point their language is atrocious. I can barely understand them."

"And, they in turn can barely understand us. The Queen's English has become so distorted that it is no longer recognizable to them. We must remember to use simple words." Holmes walked over to the window which looked out onto the front street. "I can see an assay office from here. I am assuming that all miners have to register their claims to make them legal. If Plymouth has a claim here, he will have had to register it. It could save us some time."

"Good idea, Holmes. I'm not looking forward to an extended stay in this place. Do you hear that racket?" I was referring to the eternal clump, bang, thump coming from somewhere up the street and the loud raucous laughter and music from the saloons which flanked us on either side of the hotel.

"That thumping must be from the stamp mills and smelters. I can see the smoke from here. As for the bars, well one would assume that they will close at a reasonable hour," replied Holmes, not realizing just how wrong he was. After all, we were no longer amidst civilization.

We decided to leave our belongings in our bags, as they were far cleaner than the receptacles provided for storage. Holmes retrieved the bulk of our travelling expenses from where he had hidden it in his luggage. "I don't trust leaving it here," he said in answer to my look.

"Just as well you never had it on your person on the stagecoach."

"Yes, I decided to take the Buzzard Gulch station manager's advice. He seemed to know what he was talking about. Just as well, as those thieves managed to spend a good portion of what was in my wallet."

✠   ✠   ✠

The assay office was staffed by an elderly grey bearded man with thinning hair, thick glasses, and a limp. "Can I help you?" he asked politely, then adjusted his glasses and took a second look at us. "Er ... you don't look like miners?"

"You are quite correct, Sir, we are not," said Holmes leaning against the counter. "We are trying to locate a friend who had intentions of becoming one. I am hoping you can assist us with the location of his claim."

"Well, they all have to register here. If he has a claim, he will be on file," said the fellow, opening the ledger. "What did you say his name was?"

"I didn't. His name is Cathcart Pettigrew Plymouth."

The old fellow snickered at that. "That's some

moniker. Must be a foreign gentleman like your-selves."

It was strange being constantly referred to as foreigners, but at least this fellow didn't make it sound derogatory. He began to flick through the pages. "How long ago did he come here?"

"About five to six months ago," I said, also moving forward. We waited in silence as he studied the pages of his book leisurely.

"Ah...here it is. Called it The Pride of Plym-outh. Strange name, but I've seen stranger."

"Where is it located?" asked Holmes. The old fellow pulled out a large map and gave us directions. I removed a page from my notebook and made a rough trace of the route. "I don't suppose you would know when and if he comes to town?" I asked.

"No. I try to keep to myself. You have a ten-dency to live longer that way."

"Thank you," said Holmes, shaking his hand as I put my makeshift map away.

As we exited the clapboard building, I said. "It is getting fairly late; Holmes and we have not eaten since our early lunch. What say we get some dinner?"

"Might as well," he agreed. We walked along the plank sidewalks, dodging the occasional drunk be-ing thrown out of a saloon. Every third building seemed to be a saloon, brothel, or gambling den of some sort. There were no schools, no churches, and no public buildings except for the gaol. We passed a hardware store selling mining equipment at exorbitant prices. It was the same with the general store. Notice-ably, there were few women to be seen, except those plying their sordid trades. A decent woman would not have been safe on the streets in this town where every man seemed hell bent on pleasure.

During the time it took us to walk from the assayers to the eatery, we saw only one bonneted woman of elderly vintage and even she was accosted. We would have gone to her aid, but she clouted and poked the fellow with her parasol and discouraged him most effectively.

"This is an appalling state of affairs," I said. "Why that poor woman is at least seventy!"

"Men outnumber women one hundred to one here. Anything in skirts is fair game," was Holmes' reply.

During our stroll we also saw four fist fights and one drunken fool shooting his gun off randomly in the street. He managed to put a hole through a water trough, a signpost, and narrowly missed a pedestrian, who became irate and clobbered him with his own gun. The man collapsed and lay in the street as passers-by ignored him and continued on their way. We stopped long enough to drag him to the edge of the sidewalk, so he would not be trampled by horse traffic.

"Wonder where the marshal is," I muttered.

"Hiding no doubt."

The inside of the eatery was less foreboding than its name of *Greasy Harry's* suggested. It was actually rather clean, and despite the place swarming with customers, I espied a vacant table. I led the way. Once seated, a scrawny fellow in grease stained apron came over to take our orders.

"May we see a menu?" I asked politely.

"You can have steak 'n 'tators or steak 'n

eggs."

"Steak and potatoes, thank you," said Holmes, "and coffee."

He looked at me.

"The same." When he left, I smiled and said, "Nothing like a large choice."

"Actually, I am rather surprised that they have steak. Mining towns often have a meat shortage and have to rely on game animals."

"Someone must own cattle nearby," I said.

"Most likely."

That was the end of our conversation for our meal arrived and I tucked into it with gusto. The steak was huge and well-cooked and the pile of mashed potatoes rather high. I noticed that Holmes also had a hearty appetite and soon cleaned his plate.

It was perhaps eight o'clock by the time we finished our meal and coffees. Despite night falling, the sounds of revelry seemed to become louder rather than lessened. "Too early to go to bed," I said, after we paid the exorbitant sum of five dollars for our meals.

"I thought I might buy into a game of poker," said Holmes, a light of anticipation in his eyes. I looked at him in surprise, for I knew he was not normally interested in gambling. He usually considered it a waste of time and an occupation of fools. I glanced at him curiously. I had not realized that this violent, vibrant community had infected him with a suppressed excitement.

"You said all the gamblers here were dishonest?" I reminded him.

"Not all. I just have to be vigilant. I am sure I

can find an honest game in progress somewhere. Gambling, especially poker is an art form here, more a mental exercise than mere wagering."

"Well, as long as you promise not to lose all our travelling money ..."

Holmes smiled, clapped me on the back and moved towards the largest of the saloons we had seen so far. It was called Miners Paradise, but as we entered the noisy, smoky atmosphere, it struck me that it was anything but paradise inside. Two large muscle–bound thugs were tossing a protesting miner out who was loudly proclaiming that the games were rigged. He was unceremoniously thrown into the street.

Inside, Holmes walked around until he came to a vacant chair at a poker table. "Is this seat taken?" he asked.

"Help yourself," replied a well-dressed man shuffling the cards.

"Thank you."

I pulled up a seat from a nearby table and sat just behind Holmes. I had no desire to risk my money playing. I knew little about the game and was content to watch for a while.

"I'm Ace Bannon," introduced the well-dressed man, "to my left is Price King, Jack Fletcher and Rex Brown and this fellow..." he nodded to his right, "is Marty Kilgore."

"How do you do? My name is Sherlock Holmes. My friend is John Watson."

"It's a dollar to open. We're playing five card stud, no wild cards."

He nodded as Ace, obviously a professional gambler, listed the rules. Holmes took out his pocketbook and several greedy eyes fastened on to it. I shifted uncomfortably in my seat, all the better to keep the other bystanders in view. I did not trust them, especially now that they had seen the thickness of his note case. Holmes casually withdrew some notes and put the pocketbook away, oblivious to the interested stares. After he purchased his chips, Ace handed him the deck.

"New player deals," he said, and with that, the game was under way.

Holmes lost the first two games but won the following three. As the game progressed, the players soon lapsed into casual conversation. It turned out that I was right. Ace Bannon was a professional gambler from Boston and appeared well educated. King was a mine owner, as was Fletcher, whilst Brown and Kilgore operated stores. This was a private game, not run by the casino, so it was highly probable that it would be honest as the players all seemed to be respectable men.

"Would I be right in thinking that you'd be the two gents who caught them stage robbers today?" asked Fletcher.

"Yes, we assisted the marshal in arresting them," replied Holmes as he discarded two cards and picked up two kings in return.

"Assisted? Hear tell you did *all* the work." Fletcher grinned and the other gamblers joined in chuckling.

"Maybe we should pin the badge on you," suggested Brown. "We could use some real law in this town."

"Thank you for the compliments, gentlemen,

but our business here is brief and we do not anticipate staying long."

Holmes won that hand with a full house and play continued. I must confess that after the first hour or so, I became rather bored as a spectator. I decided to take a look around the saloon. As I wandered, I watched several games that were in progress. I had absolutely no idea of the rules of faro, but I had played roulette before in Monte Carlo, so at least that game was familiar. I decided to play for a while, betting cautiously. I had not forgotten the protesting miner's complaints as he was being tossed out and that incident in San Francisco had taught me that wheels could be rigged.

Several more hours passed. I did check up on Holmes' progress at intervals and was pleased to note that his pile of chips had grown rather than dwindled. He did not look like he was ready to quit yet, although some saloon women had attached themselves to the players. There was an attractive dark-haired woman in a skin-tight red dress hovering around Holmes. I smiled when I saw that. Knowing Holmes' attitude toward women, I found it rather amusing, especially when she draped her arms around his neck and leaned down over him nuzzling his neck. I could not hear what was being said, but I could imagine it was something along the lines of:

"Do you mind, Madam, I am trying to play cards here."

I noticed she straightened up but kept her hands on his shoulders. All these women were mercenary. She was no doubt more interested in his pile of chips than in him. I considered going over to join him again and engaging the woman in conversation but decided to get a drink first as my throat was rather parched from the smoky atmosphere.

At the bar, a big burly man in denim trousers, checked shirt and cowhide vest backed away and bumped into me as I approached.

"Hey, watch where yuh goin'," he snarled, his hand going to his gun.

"My apologies," said I, not particularly wanting to get into a brawl over such a trivial incident. It was easier to apologize than to point out that he bumped into me.

"Well, well, well, what have we here?" he asked, looking me over and grinning. It was evident that he had never seen anyone decently dressed before. I was wearing a dark grey fine pinstripe suit of the latest London fashion, along with matching waistcoat, white shirt, black cravat, and Homburg. Certainly, I was not dressed as outlandishly as he, so understandably I was rather nettled by his attitude.

"Ain't he purty," he said, nudging a fellow dressed similarly to himself in denim trousers, rough shirt, and spotted calfskin vest. From the smell that emanated from them, he and his friend were cattle workers—cow herders, or cowboys as I believe they are called, regardless of their age.

"It is obvious," said I, a little haughtily, "that sartorial elegance is lost on the inhabitants of this dreary outpost."

"Talks purty too," said the other cowboy. "I dunno what he said, but he sure talks purty."

"So where yuh from, Mavis?" asked the first.

"My name is not Mavis," I replied, my ire

rising. "And I suggest you keep a civil tongue in your head."

"I think he's sassin' you, Turk," said the other cowboy. The big one frowned.

"Are you sassin' me, dude?"

"Am I what?" I asked, not comprehending his question.

"I said are you sassin' me?" he repeated, glaring at me.

"Why don't you speak the Queen's English? I have no idea what you are talking about!" I retorted.

"He's a furriner, Turk!" said the other.

"Sure enough. Reckon we gotta make allowances for furriners 'coz they cain't talk Amurrican. Have a drink with us, Mavis and no hard feelins'."

I was about to refuse, but he draped a brawny arm around my shoulders. I am five foot ten myself, but he dwarfed me by a good six inches. His arm was like a thick tree branch. Not that I was afraid of him mind you, but I have never been foolhardy. I decided the quickest way to get away from these louts was to have a drink and then leave. "All right." I said.

"Three whuskeys!" bellowed Turk and the bartender complied, sliding the glasses down the bar. Turk handed the glasses round and said: "Bottoms up, Mavis. This'll put hairs on your furrin' chest."

I was tempted to inform him that that portion of my anatomy was already adequately covered, but again refrained, not wishing to prolong this association. I took a tentative sip from my glass and almost gagged on the fiery liquid which tasted more like lamp fuel than whiskey. I made to return my glass to the bar, but this caused the big cowboy to lose his amiability.

"Somethin' wrong, Mavis?" he enquired, his voice mild, yet somehow menacing at the same time.

I was too irritated to pay it much attention though. "My name is *not* Mavis and this is not whiskey!" I declared, throwing caution to the wind. After all, a man can only take so much.

"You too uppity to drink with us?" asked his friend, having drained half his glass in one gulp.

"Don't mind him, Sam," said Turk, grinning ferociously. "Mavis just ain't used to hard likker. Not like a real man. Wonder if he wears frilly drawers under his pants. Reckon I should get you some sasparilly instead, huh Mavis?" he offered.

"Or some of that coloured water that the bar gals drink," offered the other.

This insult to my manhood was just too much. I swung my right fist and struck Turk just above the belt buckle. I put as much force as I could muster behind the blow and smiled with satisfaction at the result. Turk turned purple and gasped, staggering backward until he tripped over an outstretched boot. He landed on the floor holding his abdomen and wheezing. I felt a hand on my shoulder and spun around, striking out with my left first in a precision timed move. I had no sooner come face to face with the second cowboy before my fist connected, sending him sprawling.

Considering that these Americans were all trigger happy, I decided to draw my gun as a deterrent against any further violence. Gun in hand, I turned to Turk, who had recovered enough to attempt to draw his own revolver from his lying position. A boot came down on his shoulder and the man sitting in the seat nearest him looked down and warned, "I wouldn't if I was you, Turk. That's the feller that took out Two–gun Tolliver today."

At first I had no idea what he was talking about, until I remembered the stagecoach robber I had shot. He had worn two guns. It seemed that the fellow had something of a reputation for toughness and gun fighting, for when Turk looked up at me, there was fear in his eyes.

"Uh...no offence Mistuh, I was just funnin' me 'n Sam. Didn't mean no harm. Sure sorry we called yuh Mavis, but we didn't know who yuh were. No hard feelins' huh?" He scrambled hurriedly to his feet and backed out, dragging his semiconscious comrade with him.

I straightened my hat and gave the seated man who'd given Turk the warning a friendly nod. I was feeling rather pleased with myself. Too bad Holmes hadn't seen me handling the thugs. I suddenly remembered I was still thirsty and drained the rest of my drink in a single gulp. I returned the glass to the bar and was about to move away when the liquid reached my stomach.

I felt as if I had just been kicked. I gasped and staggered, my stomach heaving, my head reeling. Through watery eyes, I saw the bartender looking at me curiously and croaked: "Water!"

He filled a glass with muddy looking water which I gulped down gratefully, not caring about its taste or colour. When I was able to think coherently again, I asked: "Just what sort of whiskey was that?"

"Snake head," replied the bartender. At my

blank look, he elaborated.

"Rot gut. The bar's got a still out back. When the stuff's cooked the boss tosses in a couple of snake heads for extra kick."

"Egads! They were barbarians! Shaking my head to clear it, I decided to rejoin Holmes. It was well past midnight. Perhaps he was ready to call it a night. I returned to the poker table. The other players were still there, but Holmes was not.

"Excuse me," I said, interrupting their play. "Do you happen to know where my friend has gone?"

The men grinned. "He cashed in his chips and took off after Lily."

"Lily? Was she that dark- haired lady?"

"Yep. She went upstairs and he took off after her quick smart. Can't say I blame the young feller," grinned Fletcher, giving me a wink. "She's some looker, that Lily."

"What is upstairs?" I asked.

"The gals' rooms," offered Brown, also grinning suggestively.

I was stunned. Surely this decadent atmosphere had not affected Holmes that much? I found it hard to believe. Perhaps she knew of Plymouth's whereabouts and Holmes had merely gone up to question her in private.

Suddenly there was a crashing of furniture and female squeals. I looked up. On the gallery, spilling out of a room where some six clad and partially clad females and rising up from amidst them was none other than Sherlock Holmes himself!

SEVEN

"Good Lord!" I gasped and hurried towards the staircase leading up to the gallery. As I raced up the stairs, I saw that Holmes had the brunette, Lily, by the ankles and had hoisted her upside down in a flurry of silk and petticoats and then he proceeded to shake her. Just as I reached the top of the stairs, he dropped the woman unceremoniously and dived into the midst of the others as yet another hectic scramble took place.

"Holmes!" I called, catching a glimpse of a trousered leg beneath the petticoats and heaving female forms. Holmes struggled to his feet again, despite two women hanging off him. He'd lost his hat and tie and his coat was torn, as was his untucked shirt. His hair was in disarray as well and his face was flushed as he panted from his exertions. However, he was triumphant.

"Holmes?" I repeated, a little uncertainly this time, wondering if perhaps I was interrupting something.

"I have got it, Watson!" he declared, holding his arm up high above his head. That is when I saw he was clutching his pocketbook. It all made sense now. The woman must have picked his pocket. Holmes went after her to recover it, only to meet with female opposition when he tried to retrieve it.

"I think now would be a good time to leave, Holmes," I suggested.

"Most assuredly, old fellow," agreed Holmes, shaking one woman off his arm, and unhooking the other who was gripping the back of his trousers.

"Oh honey, don't go just yet," called one of the women, making a grab for his coat tail, which he avoided by agilely leaping forward.

"We're just gettin' warmed up," added another grinning floozy.

The brunette in the red dress had regained her feet. She strutted over to Holmes, not in the slightest bit abashed at being caught stealing. She cuddled up to him and even embraced him, sliding her hand over his chest and on downwards. He in turn, gripped his pocketbook all the more tightly. "Yeah, don't go yet, honey. I've never met an English gent before," she said huskily. Then smiling roguishly, her hand wandering over his person, she added, "I'm sure I could stiffen' somethin' else besides your upper lip."

Holmes' mouth curled in distaste and he pushed her away roughly. "Come, Watson," he gasped, hurrying past her. I followed, trying desperately hard to keep the smile from my lips.

When we reached the bottom of the stairs, Holmes put his pocketbook away, only to discover his watch was missing. He turned around and looked up; the women leaned over the rail giving us a fine view of assorted cleavage. There was not an ounce of modesty amongst them. The brunette grinned cheekily at us and held up Holmes' watch.

"Lookin' for this, Honey?" she asked, swinging it to and fro.

Holmes took one step forward as if he were about to run the gauntlet again, but when one woman blew him a kiss and a couple others primped their hair, he proved that there were actually limits to his courage.

"Come, Watson," he repeated, grabbing my sleeve and pulling me along.

"But what about your watch?" I asked, glancing back at the grinning women.

"Forget about the watch," he snapped, moving forward at a sprightly pace. His cheeks were flaming as he forced his way through the crowd. However, by the time we reached the hotel, he had resumed his natural complexion.

I should not have, I know, but I could not resist asking, "Did you have a good time tonight, Holmes?"

He glared at me but answered. "If you are referring to the card game, then yes, I did. In fact I won a hundred dollars. If you are referring to the tussle with those thieving hussies, then my answer is most assuredly not."

"It has certainly been an eventful trip thus far," I said, sitting down on the corner of one of the beds, only to have the whole thing collapse in a cloud of dust.

Holmes came over and grinned at me. "Are you all right, Watson?" he asked, but the question lacked genuine concern.

"Quite." I disentangled myself and looked at the bed. "I think it will be safer sleeping on the floor than on the mattress." I poked at the sharp spring that was protruding with my toe. Holmes looked at the other sagging bed and nodded in agreement.

We stripped the blankets off the beds and spread them on the floor, removing only our boots, ties and coats before settling down. We lay there for a short while listening to the monotonous thump of the stamp mills and the laughter and music from the saloons.

It was impossible to get comfortable on the hard, wooden floor, so I reflected on our exciting day instead and a thought occurred to me. "Holmes, I don't mean to bring this up again, but I am curious. Why were you shaking that woman by the ankles?"

"I was retrieving my pocketbook, Watson."

"I realize that, but surely there was an easier way to go about it?"

"Not really considering where she had it hidden."

"Oh, where did she have it hidden?"

"Use your imagination."

"I can't. My mind boggles."

"It was hidden in the only place she could hide it—her cleavage."

"You saw her stash it?"

"No, I deduced it."

"Really? How?" I leaned up on one elbow and looked over at Holmes, although I could only make out his general shape in the darkness.

"Well, Watson, you saw how she was dressed. The garment was practically sewn onto her. Logically, there was only one place where she could hide it in a hurry and where there was ample room for concealment."

"I see."

"I could hardly have reached in for it," Holmes added.

I smiled, picturing the attractive dark-haired woman. "I would have," I replied, imagining the possibilities of the situation.

[82]

"Yes, but you are a doctor, Watson. You're used to handling portions of female anatomy."

I was thankful for the dark. Holmes did not see the huge smile that split my face at his naive reply. Obviously he had no concept of medical ethics or professional propriety.

"Ah," I said. "So that is why you dived back into the group of women. When the pocketbook dropped you went after it before one of the others could get hold of it."

"Exactly and believe me, Watson, they tried. I've got scratches on my back and hands to prove it. It was like being in a cage full of wild cats."

"I had a rather eventful night also," I said.

"Oh?"

"I had a run in with a couple of cowboys at the bar. They were rather rude and insulting." I then proceeded to tell him about the incident. At the end of my recitation, I added, "You know that fellow I shot, the one that was wearing the buscadero gun belt?"

"Yes?"

"Apparently he has quite a reputation as a gunman. When Turk the cowboy heard that I had shot that fellow, he cowed and became very apologetic, leaving without further fuss."

"Which means that you have now acquired a reputation as a gun fighter"

"Oh, I hadn't thought of that."

"Never mind. In this locale, such a reputation may actually prove useful. It is certainly nothing to be ashamed of."

"I suppose. You know, Holmes, I've been thinking that we should buy new clothes tomorrow

[83]

before we go to the diggings. I would rather blend in a bit more than have to defend myself every time some yokel insults my clothing. What is more, you are certainly in need of new garments."

"Yes, my apparel did rather take a beating," agreed Holmes. "I need a new shirt and coat ... oh, and a hat too."

I grinned in the darkness again. "And a watch," I said, unable to contain the chuckle that escaped at the end of my last word.

"Oh, do be quiet, Watson!" replied Holmes crossly.

I chuckled again as I lay back to try and get what little sleep I could.

EIGHT

I woke to the sunrise. I had managed to get three hours sleep, despite the noise. Holmes was already up, looking much the worse for wear. He was sitting by the window smoking and scratching.

"Must you scratch, Holmes?" I asked, a little irritably, for as I have mentioned before I was never at my best when I was tired. "You look like you have fleas."

"I think I have, Watson," he replied seriously. "I think they were in the blanket."

At that moment, I too began to itch. I leapt to my feet. "What a vile place!" I cried in disgust.

"It is not the best, but I've been in worse," Holmes agreed placidly.

"Well, I don't know about you, Holmes, but I think our agenda for the day should be to first purchase new clothing, then patronize a bath house and then follow that with a sound breakfast before hiring horses to take us up to the mines."

"You will get no arguments from me. In fact, believe it or not, most of the shops are already open for business. This place never closes so as to accommodate the shift workers from the mines and stamp mills."

"Good." I looked at the dirty water in the wash jug and decided against washing my face before venturing out.

We collected our clean underclothes and went to the general store come haberdashery, where we purchased new clothing for a hugely inflated price. I decided to keep my hat for there was nothing wrong with it, while Holmes picked out a grey Stetson which made him look rather dashing. My clothing was utilitarian, a plain grey suit of serge, light blue shirt and black string tie. I supposed I would look like a merchant, or even a frontier doctor. Holmes's choice was a little more flamboyant. Black frock coat, black trousers, dark green silk waistcoat, white shirt, and black string tie.

"You will look like a gambler in that," I said as he paid for our purchases.

"That's the whole idea, Watson."

Next, we made our way to the gent's bath house advertising hot baths, haircuts, and shaves. It sounded good. Anything to end this infernal itching. We were soon firmly ensconced in deep baths in a room containing some half dozen wooden tubs. Two others were already occupied by individuals dozing in the water. The enterprising proprietor had a huge boiler in the centre and attendants filled the baths from this. It also served to keep the room warm and all in all it was very comfortable.

An hour later we emerged, shorn, shaven and feeling cleansed. We decided to return to *Greasy Harry's* as the food had been quite good the night before.

Breakfast consisted of a mound of hash browns, four eggs, bacon, and sausages. It was ten times more than what we would normally eat at home; nevertheless, we cleared our plates, both of us. It was almost nine o'clock by the time we sat back with our coffees.

"I've been thinking, Watson." said Holmes,

leaning back in his chair. "We should buy horses rather than rent them. We could also buy provisions, saddles, blankets, and anything else we are likely to need, rather than return to this town. I do not fancy another night in that hotel, do you?"

"Not at all!"

"When we find young Plymouth, we will have to convince him to return with us. It may take a day or two. He is likely to have his own transport, then we can ride to the nearest railhead rather than travel by stagecoach again."

"Excellent suggestion, Holmes." I agreed heartily. "That way we would get to see some more of this country as well. Perhaps even get in a little hunting."

"Perhaps." Holmes was never keen on hunting animals. He preferred human prey.

"Before we leave town, do you think we should send a telegram to Sir Eustace, letting him know of our progress?"

"Yes, I suppose we should. Will you take care of that, Watson? I shall buy our supplies. Make sure you do not give him false hopes; after all, we haven't actually *found* his son yet. He may no longer be mining."

"Oh dear. You mean we won't find Plymouth today?" I was disappointed.

"We may. But, I have read his letters and we have found out a few additional things about him since. He doesn't stay long in any one job because he doesn't have the skills. The only one he was any good at he had to flee. As a bartender, barber, and gambler he was sorely inadequate. What's to say he is any better as a miner? He may have moved on to try something else."

"In that case, I will just say in my telegram that we are on our way to his last known location."

Holmes nodded. "That would be best. I will meet you at Lassiter's Barn. I noticed they have horses for sale and second-hand saddles." Holmes handed me some money. "You had better check us out of the hotel and bring our bags with you to the barn."

We finished our coffees, and then set about our respective tasks.

✠ ✠ ✠

An hour later, I joined Holmes at Lassiter's barn. He was haggling with the proprietor over the purchase of horses, saddles, and harness. Nearby were four sacks containing our provisions and cooking utensils and two blanket rolls. Holmes finally agreed to a price for two saddle horses and a packhorse. I was pleased about the latter for I was wondering how we were going to carry everything. It was nearing noon before we were ready to leave town. I was all for having lunch first, but Holmes insisted we push on.

"We cannot tarry any longer, Watson. Not if we want to find Plymouth's claim before nightfall."

The prospect of travelling unfamiliar mountain terrain in the dark did not appeal to me, so I gave up arguing. I saddled the horses, while Holmes loaded the pack animal. We mounted and headed for the trail leading to the diggings. Our exit from town took us past the marshal's office. He was dozing on the front porch, looking as unshaven, dirty, and repulsive as ever. Inside, glaring at us through the barred windows were the highwaymen. Two–gun Tolliver spat at me when I glanced at him. I shivered involuntarily, thankful that he was safely behind bars.

It was late afternoon before we reached the spot, which according to my makeshift map was the Pride of Plymouth. As we rode up, three filthy bearded fellows emerged. Two cradled shotguns which I noticed were pointed at us with unerring accuracy.

"Yuh want somethin' stranger?" asked one of the three coming to the front. He at least was not holding a weapon, but then again, he had no need to.

Holmes made to dismount but the clicking of hammers being drawn back on shotguns deterred him. He sank back into his saddle and said: "My apologies for disturbing you, but we are looking for The Pride of Plymouth mine. This location fits the directions we were given."

"Yup, you're here. What do yuh want?"

"We are looking for its owner, Mr Cathcart Plymouth."

"I'm the owner. Me and me pards here."

Holmes glanced around the camp, his eyes missing nothing. "I see. You purchased it from Mr Plymouth, then?"

His comment caused the men to laugh and the spokesman replied: "Yup, you could say that. We bought it." He was plainly lying and for a moment I wondered if these unsavoury rogues had murdered young Plymouth for his mine.

"Do you happen to know which way he went when he left?" asked Holmes.

"Nope."

"That is most unfortunate as there is a reward being offered for information that will help us locate him?"

"You lawmen?" he asked suspiciously.

"No, not at all. We have been hired by his father to bring him home to England."

"Ain't heard of England," said one of the shotgun–toting men. "Is that near Texas?"

Holmes smiled faintly. "No, it is in another country a long way from Texas."

"How much of a reward?" asked the spokesman, greed gleaming in his eyes.

"Fifty dollars for general information. Two hundred for his exact location the latter will of course, only be paid after he has been located."

"You got that money on yer?" he asked.

"Not the two hundred," replied Holmes.

I was glad he said that because I didn't like the look in the fellow's eyes. He would have been happy to slaughter us both for two hundred dollars. I just hoped he wouldn't do it for fifty.

"Well now he might've mentioned that he wanted to take up cow herdin'. He headed t'wards the flats when he left us."

"He was fit and well when he left here?"

"Fit enough."

"Thank you." Holmes reached into a pocket and pulled out a fifty dollar note which he handed to the man.

We turned our horses and left. As soon as we were out of ear shot, I said indignantly: "Why did you pay him, Holmes? For all we know they might have murdered Plymouth and stolen his mine."

"They stole the mine all right. Claim jumpers are what they are. Only I do not believe they killed him. More likely they just forced him out. He was outnumbered and I doubt if he would have put up much of an argument. It is unlikely that they would have bothered to kill him; he did not pose much of threat to them. From the look of the mine and their general threadbare appearance, I doubt if they have had much of a yield. Plymouth probably had even less, so I believe them when they say he rode away from here."

"Unharmed?"

"Perhaps a little battered and bruised, but alive."

We were halfway down the mountain when Holmes suddenly veered off the trail to the right. I stopped my horse and the pack horse I was leading and waited patiently for him to return. Holmes reappeared a moment later. "I have found the perfect campsite, Watson. It will be dark soon and we will need to set ourselves up for the night while we can still see."

I nodded in agreement. My stomach had been rumbling for the last four hours and I was hoping we would stop for food. I followed him into the clearing. It was well sheltered with an open space in the middle. I set about tending the animals whilst Holmes set up camp and gathered the firewood.

There was a crystal clear stream nearby from which he filled the coffee pot. When he had done so, I watered the animals and tethered them to a stout tree branch with the rope Holmes had thought to purchase. There was plenty of grass for them to graze on. By the time my chores were finished, Holmes had a pan on the fire.

"What is for dinner?" I asked, looking at the concoction with suspicion.

"Baked beans and bacon bits," replied Holmes. "I added the bacon," he announced proudly, as though he were a gourmet cook in an expensive restaurant. The beans were from cans, so they should at least be edible. Anyway, I was hungry enough to eat one of our horses and not inclined to be picky.

With dinner finished and our dishes washed, we stoked up the fire and rolled into our blankets. Holmes would never admit it, but the lack of sleep from the night before and all the unaccustomed horse riding had tired him, just as it had me. Living in London, we were not used to riding on a regular basis. I knew that by morning every joint and muscle would be aching. Fortunately it would only be a temporary discomfort and would soon settle in a day or two of continuous riding.

"Night, Holmes," I called out softly, only to receive a soft snore in return. I smiled and closed my eyes.

NINE

The sun was well up by the time I woke from a blissful sleep. To my surprise, Holmes was still in deep slumber. It was rare for him to sleep so much, but then again we had endured several hectic days with little rest, not to mention the additional exercise in Holmes' case. They do say tussling with women can tire a man. I grinned at the thought and got up. I set about relighting the fire which had gone cold and cooked breakfast. It was almost ready before Holmes deigned to rise and join me.

"Morning, Holmes," I greeted cheerfully.

He blinked at me for a moment, and then sat up, stretching and yawning. "There is something to be said for the sounds of nature and fresh air," he said. "What's for breakfast?"

"Bacon and eggs," I replied. "I thought I had better use up the eggs before they were broken." Holmes joined me by the fire and I dished up. We both ate hungrily, not caring that we had not yet attended our morning ablutions. Our civilized standards were becoming lax, I reflected. For a moment I considered letting my beard grow but decided against it. After all, one had to retain some modicum of civilisation when surrounded by wilderness. After breakfast, we washed and shaved by the stream and packed up our equipment. It was nearly ten o'clock by my watch before we broke camp and continued on our way down to the flats.

"Do you think we will find him on the cattle farm, Holmes?" I asked.

"Cattle *ranch*, Watson. It is a grave mistake to call it a farm. You see, in this country farmers and cattlemen do not get along and are always fighting with each other."

"Very well, cattle ranch," I corrected.

"We may locate young Plymouth, though I would not count on it. Our quarry is proving to be as elusive as I had feared. I knew this would be no simple task. Still, we may pick up some useful information."

"I wonder how many farm—ranches, there are."

"We will soon find out," said Holmes pointing to a makeshift sign with crude letters, reading:

CIRCLE A, KEEP OUT

"A warning to gold seekers, no doubt," he added.

We moved off the trail and proceeded across the range. In the distance we could see cattle being gathered by men on horseback. They left their chores upon sighting us and came galloping over, their manner belligerent. I recognized two of the riders as the cowboys from the saloon, Turk and Sam.

As the half dozen slid to a halt, I did not wait for them to speak, knowing that they would probably be hostile. That attitude seemed to be prevalent in this place. Instead, I said, "Hello, Turk, Sam, nice to see you again. My friend and I are here to see your employer. Could you direct us to the main house please."

"You know these fellers, Turk?" asked a burly man with greying hair at the temples and an air of authority.

"That's the feller that shot Two–gun Tolliver

and knocked out Sam's tooth."

The truculent air left the other riders as they surveyed me. The burly man looked me over dubiously. "Guess you must be a lot tougher than you look," he said. "I'm Hank Berman, the ramrod. What's your business with the boss?"

"Ramrod? Is that the same as a foreman?" asked Holmes.

"Yep."

"Then perhaps we need not trouble your employer. You are in charge of hiring the staff, are you not?"

"Yep. Hire 'n fire 'em. You ain't looking for work, are yuh?"

"No. We are trying to locate a fellow by the name of Cathcart Plymouth. Our last authority was that he had intentions of becoming a cow herder," said Holmes.

"Plymouth, you're lookin' for that useless dude!" Hank Berman snorted. "Come to think of it, he sounded like you two."

"So you know him then?" I asked.

"Uh huh, wish I didn't. Damn kid turned up here, lookin' a might battered and bruised. Said his claim had been jumped. Said he was through minin' and that he wanted to be a cowhand. I could see he'd had a rough time of it and took pity on him. I put him on the payroll. Biggest mistake of my life." His last comment brought snickers from the other men.

"That Limey was worse than useless," grinned Turk, then at my glare, hastily apologized. "Uh, no offence M...uh...what did you say yer name was?"

"I didn't say, but it is Dr. Watson."

Eyes widened. It occurred to me that there was a gunfighter of some repute who was also in the medical profession. Dr. Holiday, I think his name was, only he was a dentist, I believe. Perhaps they were likening me to him.

Holmes brought the conversation back on track. "What happened to cause you so much grief, Mr Berman?"

"Grief is right. That *#@! fool," he swore luridly. "Yuh should 'ave seen him trying to rope a steer. Tripped his own hoss up and broke its leg. Cost us a good cow pony. Then he set up the brandin' fire near the scrub and burnt out the north quarter 'fore we could get it under control, an' if that weren't bad enough, I gave him a last chance as a night hawk, guardin' the cattle we had ready for shipment. Do you know what that son-of-a-bitch did?" he challenged.

"Started a stampede," suggested Holmes.

"Damn right! He lit up a smoke right next to the herd an' set 'em runnin' straight fer the house. We managed to turn 'em but not afore they flattened the privy and the boss' wife's garden."

"That was most unfortunate," sympathized Holmes.

"Unfortunate my fat Aunt Lulu," growled the irate foreman. "The boss was livid. He was in the privy at the time. Near cost me *my* job. I sent the fool packin'."

"Do you happen to know in which direction he went after he left here?" I asked.

"He headed for the mountains. Said he was gunna try his durn fool hand at trappin'," offered Turk.

[96]

"Trappin?" I queried.

"You know, Doc. Huntin' an' trappin, wild critters and the like."

"Hunting and trapping, Watson," translated Holmes.

"Oh."

The foreman pointed us in the general direction and added, "The damn stupid greenhorn has probably killed hisself by now. Likely got his foot caught in one of his own traps."

"Thank you for your assistance, Mr Berman," said Holmes, touching his hat brim in a gesture of acknowledgement.

"Yer welcome. I only hope you gents have more savvy than he has."

"Any particular reason?" asked Holmes.

"Like Turk said, there's a lot of wild critters up in them mountains. Cougars, bears and the like." He looked over our equipment and us. "Ain't yuh got no guns?"

"We have handguns," I offered.

"Take my advice an' get yerself some long guns as soon as you can. Yer gunna need 'em."

"Thank you for the advice. However, we do not wish to return to Lucky Strike, are there any other townships on our route or in the mountains?" asked Holmes.

"Nearest town is Bigalow Peak, other side of the mountains. You'll be wantin' guns long before then. Reckon you should try the Tradin' Post. Mostly for trappers, but ol' Keehoe usually sell all sorts of stuff."

"Where will we find this Trading Post?" I

asked.

The foreman gave us directions which Holmes stored in his phenomenal memory. We thanked the cattlemen and returned to the trail to continue our journey.

"It would seem that young Plymouth is not exactly suited to life on the frontier," I observed.

"The more I hear about him, the more I wonder how he has managed to stay alive so long," replied Holmes.

We noon camped by a bubbling brook and admired the scenery that the elevated view gave us. From where we were we could see the mines that dotted the hillside, but as we travelled up higher, the less populated the region became. We were hoping to reach the Trading Post before dark. Holmes reasoned that if Plymouth wanted to become a fur trapper, he would need certain items of equipment. Therefore in all probability, he had visited the trading post as well.

TEN

The sun was just beginning to dip below the horizon when we spied a ramshackle building. There was a corral to one side with several horses in it and two lean–to type buildings at the back. On the porch sat a man with thick unruly black hair, a beard sprinkled with grey and a cigar stub sticking unlit from his mouth. He was whittling on a piece of wood, but his eyes never left us as we approached.

"Howdy," he greeted as we reigned up.

"How do you do," returned Holmes. "Is this the Trading Post?"

"Yup. Got everything you're likely to need."

We dismounted and, up close, I noticed that the fellow was much older than he at first appeared. He stood up and fitted a crutch under one arm. Noticing our glances at his missing leg, he said, "Grizzly took it."

"You were attacked by a grizzly bear?" I asked, rather shocked.

"Yup. Damn critter was a maulin' me somethin' fierce. But for Charlie he'd have finished me off."

"Charlie being a friend of yours," I guessed.

"Best friend any man could have," he agreed. He opened the door to the building and we followed him in after securing the horses. As we entered, a large wolf hound looked up from where it lay sleeping on a rug. It had a mangled ear and there were scars over its body where fur no longer grew. The dog yawned and stood up, revealing that he was minus tail and leg. "Charlie hassled the bear just long enough for me to get to me gun and blast its brains out. Legs went rotten on both of us. We was found by some other trappers and they doctored me 'n Charlie up some. Had to give up huntin' after that."

Holmes patted the dog in passing. It settled back into its bed after scrutinizing us carefully and deciding that we were harmless. The old fellow made his way behind the plank counter. Holmes moved over and leaned on it while I started to look around the store with interest. There certainly was an odd assortment of supplies and equipment to be had in here, up to and including a stuffed buffalo's head.

Holmes fished the picture of Plymouth out of his pocket and put it on the counter. "We are looking for this young man. His name is Cathcart Plymouth. Has he been here?"

The ex–trapper squinted at the photograph. "Sure. Called hisself Cart. Stayed here a week. Wanted to be a trapper but had nary a clue. Was mighty wet behind the ears. I wouldn't sell him the stuff he needed till he know'd how to use it. Had to teach him everythin'. Real green he was."

"Has he been back since?" asked Holmes. "I see you also buy the skins."

"Sometimes I buy skins and naw, he ain't been back. Probably got lost. It's easy to do in these mountains an' he warn't no woodsman. I reckon it was him that set fire to the ridge."

"Why would he do that?" I asked in surprise, coming over to join them at the counter.

"Cain't say. Don't reckon he did it on purpose, mind," replied the old fellow, "it's just he likely set up his campfire too close to the brush. Likely got his ass burned if 'n he warn't quick enough. Boy didn't have the sense of a seam squirrel."

I exchanged looks with Holmes. Plymouth had already caused one accidental fire by not looking where he was setting up camp. Obviously he had not learned from his first mistake. "Well, it shouldn't be hard to follow his trail then," I said with a smile, "we can just head for the burnt patches."

A smile also quirked at Holmes' lips at that, but he did not reply to my comment; instead he turned his attention back to the old man. "How long ago was this?"

"Three months, I reckon."

"What sort of horse was he riding?" asked Holmes.

"Sorrel gelding, white streak on its nose."

"Any points of interest in its shoes?"

The old trapper smiled widely, revealing several gaps in his teeth. "You look like a dude, but yuh talk like a hunter. Its left side front hoof had a bent nail in its shoe."

Holmes smiled warmly in appreciation of the compliment. "How has the weather been these past three months?"

"Midlin'. Ain't had much rain. Ain't been no strong winds neither."

I listened to this conversation but was not quite sure what relevance it had. No doubt Holmes had a reason for his questions and they evidently won the old trapper's approval. I had noticed that the Americans seemed to have little tolerance for inexperienced people or greenhorns as they called them. Yet once someone proved their ability, or aptitude in handling new tasks, they were accepted without question.

"You gents want to stay the night? For a dollar you can bunk in the lean–to and put your hosses up in the corral. Give 'em proper feed too."

"Yes, thank you, we would appreciate that. We also need to purchase some rifles," said Holmes.

The old fellow really beamed now at the prospect of a couple of customers.

"We could do with some extra food supplies too, Holmes," I added. "Our appetites have become quite ravenous with all this exercise."

We went outside and unsaddled the horses. I took our gear to the back while Holmes fed and watered them. The ex–trapper, Foster Keehoe by name, invited us in to dine with him in his small, but surprisingly clean kitchen. Holmes and Keehoe chatted like the best of friends.

I always marvelled at Holmes' ability to mix with all kinds of folk. Given that he could be so gregarious and sociable at times, it often astounded me that I should be his only close friend; but then again, intimacy was not something that came easily to him.

Holmes was curious about the mountains and the animals we were likely to encounter. Keehoe, in turn, was curious about England. "You tellin' me you don't have bears and cougars in England?" he asked, almost disbelievingly.

"Oh, we have bears, smaller ones. There is a wild cat in the highlands of Scotland, something similar to a bobcat. Then the usual squirrels and badgers and things."

"I once heard they don't wear guns over there, that true?"

"Quite true. It is not habitual for the citizens to go armed."

"It's not what?" He blinked at Holmes uncomprehendingly.

"My apologies. We don't usually carry guns," Holmes repeated in simpler terminology.

"What about yer law breakers?"

"They do not always carry guns either."

Keehoe's eyes widened. "Yuh don't say. What about yer lawmen?"

Holmes smiled. "No, they don't carry guns, not unless they are going up against someone who is known to be armed."

"Well doggone it, that's just plain crazy!" exclaimed Keehoe in disgust. "Yuh don't always know if 'n someone's carrying a gun 'til they up and shoot yuh."

I chuckled. "Can't argue with that logic."

After dinner, our genial host offered us some home brew. After my experience with the vile substance in the saloon, I was hesitant. Holmes however accepted the mug filled to the top, toasted the old fellow, and drank. I waited for the effects to hit him. When nothing happened, I asked, "How does it taste?"

"Smooth and mellow. Really, it is quite excellent," replied Holmes.

Apart from his eyes being brighter and his cheeks a little flushed, he seemed none the worse for it. I held out my mug and Keehoe filled it. To my surprise it was just as Holmes described it: smooth, mellow, and rather strong, but pleasing to the palate, nonetheless. "I say, this *is* rather good. And you claim it is homemade, Mr Keehoe?"

"Yup. The Jacksons have got a still in the high country. Make the best moonshine round these here parts."

"The Jacksons – they are mountain men?"

"Yup. Hill folk. Mean an' ornery 'round strangers, an' none too bright; but they sure know how to make whiskey."

"Would Plymouth have likely encountered them?" I asked, still sipping my whiskey, savouring the taste, and feeling a warm glow steal over me.

"Might have. For his sake, I hope not. It depends on which away he went. I'd advise you to steer clear of 'em as well."

"In that case we will endeavour to do so." I replied.

It was nine o'clock by my watch when we decided to call it a day. We said good night to Keehoe and settled down in the lean–to, feeling pleasantly warm internally and very relaxed.

"Say, Holmes, what is a seam squirrel?" I asked recalling that I had puzzled over that descriptive phrase.

"A flea."

"Oh. Colourful language these Americans have,"

"Very picturesque. Take our host for instance, Watson, he is quite a remarkable man despite being illiterate. His knowledge of nature and animal behaviour exceeds that of a Professor of zoology. He may not be able to write his name, but I would wager he

[104]

could describe either of us right down to your moustache without ever setting eyes on us, merely from reading our tracks at a campsite."

"Is that not what you do at crime scenes, Holmes?"

"Yes. The technique is the same. Just as a hunter can tell the size and age of an animal he is following I can trace my human prey. These trappers and mountain men and the Indians, of course, would all make brilliant detectives because they are trained from birth to observe minute details and extrapolate from there. My abilities are often considered remarkable in London, simply because they are unheard of. Here, they are commonplace. Noticing an imprint in the dirt or a broken twig can mean the difference between life and death in this harsh environment. My powers of observation which strike you as extraordinary are quite insignificant in comparison to the abilities of some of the people here."

"I can see you have taken to Keehoe," I said.

"The man is worthy of my admiration. I wish we could stay here for a few days. There is much he could teach me."

"We can if you like. A day or two is hardly likely to make much difference."

"You don't mind?"

"Not at all, Holmes. It will do the horses good to have a rest before we venture into the high country."

ELEVEN

The next morning, after we broke our fast, Holmes asked Keehoe if we could extend our stay. The old fellow was delighted and I could see he had taken to Holmes just as quickly as Holmes to him. Despite their age differences and educational opportunities, they were much alike.

We started the day by examining his rifle collection. He had several varieties, including a large, cumbersome Sharps buffalo rifle; an ex–Civil War issue single–shot Enfield; a model 1873 Winchester rifle and an 1873 Winchester carbine. I quite liked the smaller saddle gun, while Holmes admired the rifle, which he claimed was the best rifle ever made.

Keehoe approved our choices and sold us ammunition and also rifle scabbards to attach to our saddles. With weapons in hand, we went outside to practice and found they were rather close shooting guns with considerable accuracy. Holmes was delighted and Keehoe was pleasantly surprised. I think he assumed that because we did not openly display our weapons, we couldn't shoot. Both Holmes and I were reasonable shots and the guns were very well made.

Over the next five days, I loafed about currying the horses, patting the dog, and manning the shop, while Holmes spent all his time with Keehoe who instructed him in the finer points of tracking and sign reading. Sometimes I watched the two of them together, Holmes the student, Keehoe the teacher.

They would go for long walks in the forest,

and occasionally I would accompany them. On one such an occasion, we stopped in a clearing.

"Well, Mr Holmes," said Keehoe. "Look around and tell me what you see."

Holmes began to prowl around the clearing, occasionally dropping onto his face to study some minute trifle on the ground. I saw nothing. After almost half an hour, he stood up and brushed the dirt and twigs from his clothes. "There were two deer sleeping here but were frightened of by a mountain lion. I also detect tracks of some small animal, but I am not sure what."

Keehoe smiled. "Thems racoon tracks. What else do you see?"

Holmes frowned. "Nothing."

"Yuh sure? Look again." Keehoe sat down on a rock to wait patiently, as Holmes once again made a study of the ground.

When Holmes finished he came over to us, saying, "I don't know how I could have missed it. There was a fox here also, and a rabbit. The fox caught the rabbit."

Keehoe clapped his hands in delight. "Yep, yer durned right. Most folks would've missed it. Yuh did real good, boy."

Holmes smiled delightedly at the older man's approbation.

When not studying the wildlife in the woods, he would draw animal prints in the soft soil of the vegetable patch at the trading post and have Holmes identify each. He also, and more practical for Holmes' profession, made other signs, the kind likely to be made by man. I was roped into assisting with this as

Keehoe was not as agile as he had once been before his injury.

They had me take a walk, leaving a trail for them to follow. I was not to do anything obvious, just walk naturally, occasionally sit down, kneel or what have you. I had a half hour start before they followed. I was waiting for them by a stream when they arrived. To check that Holmes had been correct in his observations, he gave me a run down on what he found. He was spot on in every detail.

While Holmes was talking to me, Keehoe was looking around, now he turned to Holmes. "The Doc was busy here, why'nt yuh look around and tell us what yuh can find?"

Holmes nodded and pointed out what he discovered as he found it. "Watson wandered into this clearing, walking in a zig zag pattern. He went over to that rock and sat down, next, he went over to the creek and knelt down on the bank to have a drink, cupping his hands, so that some water spilled. Then he got up and went into the bushes ..." Holmes stopped talking and also went into the bushes while I flushed a little with embarrassment.

Holmes returned, flashed me a faint smile and continued. "He answered the call of nature and returned to the clearing to await our arrival, smoking two cigarettes in the meantime."

"If yuh felt the temperature of his stools, yuh'd be able ta figger on how long ago he'd passed."

"I will give that a miss, if you don't mind," replied Holmes, smiling faintly, before adding, "There is a slight depression here, and here that I can't quite make out."

Keehoe moved over to where Holmes indicated. He studied the marks, before saying, "Lie down on the ground, with your head in your hands."

Holmes did as instructed assuming a horizontal position, stomach down.

"Now stand up."

He did and studied the slight indentations that he had made. Understanding dawned. "Watson lay down here, those are the depressions from his elbows and the other are his toes."

"Yup. If he was a shooter, plannin' on ambushin' someone, he might leave a mark like that. Yuh might even see a mark from his rifle butt. An' see that little bit in the middle? It's from his belt buckle. If the ground had been softer, yuh could even see the pattern on it and of course yuh can tell how tall a man is from the length of his body."

I had to admit, I was impressed. To me, the marks were barely discernible. I had always thought Holmes' ability in sign reading to be remarkable, but now I realized what Holmes knew from the start, that Keehoe was his master.

Each evening, while we sampled his moonshine whiskey, he would spend hours teaching Holmes a strange sign language. I tried to learn it also, but by the end of the week, all I could remember were the signs for 'many horses' and 'food'. At least I would not go hungry or on foot, I thought with a smile.

Holmes, with his retentive memory and natural linguistic ability, had no difficulty picking it up, so that by the end of the week, he and Keehoe could converse solely in sign language.

The night after Keehoe gave him his first

lesson in this sign language, I said: "What do you need to know sign language for, Holmes. I doubt if we are going to run into that many deaf people."

Holmes chuckled. "It's not for deaf people, Watson. It is the universal sign language used by Indians of all tribes. I will be able to converse with them if we meet any."

"Is that likely?"

"Keehoe says it's their hunting season and that they usually come to the mountains for that and return to the plains during winter. So it is probable."

"Well, if Keehoe says so, then it must be so," I replied.

Holmes' hero worship of the older man was amusing to watch, touching too, for it showed me a side of Holmes that I had hitherto never seen. Traditionally, Holmes was always the teacher and I was the student. It was strange to see him asking questions and admitting to a lack of knowledge. Had we been back in London, he would never have admitted to ignorance, certainly not in front of someone else. He seemed to have developed a new humility that wasn't evident before. He looked up to Keehoe and treated him with the respect one would expect him to give to his father.

In return for Keehoe's lessons, Holmes taught him how to read and write. Each night they painstakingly went through the alphabet. Keehoe was not as quick a student as Holmes, but Holmes was untiringly patient. He did not mind how many times he had to repeat something.

As the days passed, Keehoe mastered the alphabet and was able to read some of the simple sentences that Holmes printed out for him. I will never forget that night, when Keehoe read his first sentence.

"Ch–ar–lee is my d–og and he say–ved my life!" he read. Both Holmes and I applauded, and he grinned from ear to ear.

"Congratulations, Mr Keehoe," said Holmes, smiling at him. "You can read."

"Who would've thought I'd ever be able ta do that?" replied the old man, still beaming.

"Shall we try some more?" asked Holmes. Keehoe nodded eagerly, as Holmes printed. FOSTER KEEHOE.

Keehoe studied it for a long moment, sounding the words out in his head; he looked up at Holmes in surprise.

"That's me. That's what me name looks like written."

Holmes nodded, still smiling tolerantly at him. "Why don't you try writing it?" he suggested gently.

Keehoe took up the pencil and laboriously scrawled out his name—another first. Keehoe was so excited that he filled mugs with whiskey and handed them around to toast the occasion.

"To the literate, Mr Keehoe," I said, raising my mug. We clinked metal mugs and downed our drinks, celebrating the event before they continued on with their lessons long into the night. Now that the alphabet was making sense to him, Keehoe was like a child with a new toy. He couldn't get enough of it and wanted to read everything that had a label on it.

Time passed rapidly and by the fifth day, I was hinting that we really should get a move on, as we had a job to do and that the longer we delayed, the further away Plymouth would get. Holmes reluctantly agreed. If he had his way, I am sure he would have stayed here until winter set in.

We saddled and loaded our provisions which Holmes paid rather generously for and turned to say our goodbyes to Keehoe who leant on the corral rail. I thanked him for his hospitality and shook his hand, while Holmes was almost effusive in his farewell.

"Mr Keehoe, Sir," he said, as he shook hands. "It has been an honour and a pleasure to know you."

"Likewise, Mr Holmes," he replied with a grin. "An' if you ever get sick of city livin', you're welcome here."

"Thank you, my friend. I will keep it in mind." He turned to his saddle bags and rummaged for a moment, before turning back. He held a book in his hand. I recognized it as the one he had been reading on the train. It was a collection of short stories about a famous frontiersman named Daniel Boone. "Mr Keehoe, I would like you to have this. You can practice your reading."

Keehoe's eyes lit on the book and shone with reverence, as if it was some holy object. "Really? Yuh don't want it?"

"I have finished it. It is yours." Holmes handed the book to him. The old man opened it and looked at the print in awe. I realized then that this was probably the first time in his life that he had ever held a book.

"Watson, may I borrow your pencil for a moment?" asked Holmes. I handed it over. Taking the book from Keehoe, he quickly wrote an inscription and signed it.

I read it over his shoulder: *To Foster Keehoe,*

the most remarkable man I have ever met. Sherlock Holmes. The old man accepted the book as Holmes handed it to him and when he looked up his eyes were misty with unfamiliar emotions. It was a rather touching moment; one could not help but be moved by the poignancy of the occasion.

The two men, one young, one old, looked at each for a long moment, sharing their thoughts before Holmes offered his hand. They shook firmly, sealing a pact of friendship and mutual respect.

"Goodbye, my friend," said Holmes softly, releasing his hand and turning away. That day he came as close to displaying the very human emotions that he always disdained, and frankly, I would not have been surprised had he shed a tear.

We mounted and were soon on our way further up into the mountains. Our destination was the burnt-out section on the ridge, Plymouth's last known location.

It was just after midday when we reached the ridge. The fire had spread for a good mile and it took over an hour to locate its origin, Plymouth's campfire. When Holmes saw it, he shook his head in disgust. "Really, you would think a grown man would have more sense. To set a campfire up beside a bush on a windy ridge is sheer stupidity."

I held the horses as Holmes examined the camp.

"Ah!" he cried a few minutes later.

"What have you found?"

"Left side front hoof, bent nail."

"Pardon?"

"The hoof print, Watson. This was definitely

Plymouth's camp and this is his horse. The weather has been fine, no rain, no strong winds. I should be able to track him easily enough."

"But the trail is three months old." I argued.

"True, but if the horse stands in a sheltered spot the prints may still be visible and naturally as we get closer and the trail fresher, it will be easier."

"Which way did he go then?" I asked.

Holmes scouted around for a bit longer before pointing to a narrow track. "That way. He went up hill to escape the fire."

As Holmes made to mount and move in the indicated direction, I asked, "Can't we stop for lunch, Holmes?"

"You and your stomach, Watson. At this rate it will take us months to track him down," complained Holmes, rather unfairly I thought, considering we had just wasted five days so he could learn more about tracking.

I did not bring that up, though, as he would only argue that it was ultimately to our benefit and well worth the delay. Instead, I said rather huffily, "Well, it is not my fault you are inhuman!"

Holmes gave a long-suffering sigh. "Chew on some jerky if you're hungry," he suggested.

I dug some of the hard, dried meat out of my saddle bag and looked at it dubiously.

We remounted and continued uphill, and as we rode, I chewed on the salty meat. It was tough, but not inedible. It helped to stave of the hunger pangs.

We found Plymouth's next campsite just before sundown and decided to settle there for the night. It was obviously a favourite camping place for travellers for there was a fireplace made of rocks. It made it easy for Plymouth.

"I wonder if he has had any luck as a hunter," I said, my earlier irritation with Holmes forgotten.

"I doubt it." Holmes held up a rusty old empty can of baked beans. "He is using his provisions. If he caught anything he would eat that and we would find traces of animal remains."

We quickly set about making camp for the night. By this time we had formed a routine and were rather adept at it. Holmes cooked, he was not a bad cook, although one or two of his concoctions were somewhat dubious and barely palatable, but for the most part they were edible. I tended the horses. Like our other campsites, there was a stream nearby. No doubt it was the same one we had passed several times as it came down on a meandering course from the top of the mountain.

TWELVE

We were now accustomed to sleeping on the ground and got a good night's rest. The following morning, we repeated our routine and were quickly back on Plymouth's trail. We followed his tracks continuously uphill for the next two days until we came to a clearing in the centre of which was a log cabin. Smoke came from its chimney and from a shack at the back of it. "Maybe they have seen Plymouth," I suggested and was about to move forward when Holmes reached out and stopped me.

"I think we should avoid this place. Unless I am mistaken, there is a still in that shack, which means that these could be the hillbillies that Keehoe spoke of."

"Put yuh hands where ah can see 'em," said a drawling voice with a heavy southern accent. "Git 'em up!" the voice ordered again when we were slow to react. We slowly raised our hands shoulder high. There was a faint sound and a huge, ugly, hairy man appeared from behind a tree. He was pointing a Sharp's rifle at us. "State yuh business in these here parts," he ordered.

"Now see here, my good man," said Holmes. "This is Dr. Watson and he is on his way to an emergency." I wondered if this uncouth mountain man would buy Holmes's bluff. To my surprise his eyes widened.

"A doctor, yuh mean a for-real sawbones?"
"Yes."

"Well I'll be damned an' what are yuh waitin' fer, Doc? The 'mergency is right here."

"What?"

"Me wife's 'bout ready ta pop one."

"I beg your pardon?" I really had no idea what he was talking about.

"She's havin' a young un. She don't reckon it's right. Asked me to fetch her a sawbones but ah got ta samplin' mah brew and done fergot."

I finally got the gist of his words. "A breech?" I asked. The burly man just shrugged uncomprehendingly. I looked at Holmes. "Holmes, I will have to help this woman if it is a breech birth. She could die if she tries to deliver, her and the infant."

"Whatever you say, Watson," shrugged Holmes. He always deferred to me on medical matters.

With the mountain man escorting us, we rode on to the cabin and dismounted. I fished out my medical kit and approached the house. The burly man led our horses away to water them, while Holmes fetched out his cigarettes.

Just as I was about to enter the building, two equally huge, but younger men came hurtling out of the house. "Whuskey skonks!" yelled one as he threw himself at me, knocking me to the ground. I fell heavily and landed on my left arm, trying to fight him off with my right. The other man attacked Holmes.

"Damn scavengers!" growled the one attacking Holmes. Holmes tried to reason with him but to no avail. I also tried to tell my assailant that I was there to help his mother, they had to be the mountain man's sons, so similar was the resemblance.

Holmes' attacker sent him flying into the woodpile and approached him menacingly. Holmes' hand closed over a stout piece of wood. He struggled to his feet and clobbered the big man as his punches had had no effect, but the log did the trick and the fellow collapsed. Holmes then staggered over to me and thumped my attacker across the back of the head, much to my relief.

Holmes rolled the dead weight off me and helped me to my feet. I was wheezing and trying to get my breath back after having had the life nearly squeezed out of me.

Just then, the older man rounded the corner, saw his sons down and jumped to an erroneous conclusion. "Mah boys!" he yelled in anger. "Yuh kilt mah boys!" He rushed at us, hands outstretched, fists clenched.

"I've had enough of this," said Holmes as he swung his log again striking the elder over the head. Father rapidly joined his sons in blissful slumber.

"Good God, Holmes, don't they care about the woman inside? What manner of men are these that attack innocent strangers for no reason?"

"Mountain men."

I went to open the door of the cabin with my left hand. The slight pressure I exerted caused me to yelp in pain. I drew my hand back and examined it worriedly.

"What's wrong, Watson?" asked Holmes, concern in his voice.

"I have sprained my wrist, Holmes."

"Badly?"

"Bad enough. I won't be able to help the woman inside."

Holmes glanced at the slumbering mountain men, then back at me. "But you have to!"

Was that panic in his voice? "Perhaps if you bandaged my wrist...?" I began.

"Yes, yes," he agreed eagerly. He picked up my kit and undid it, pulling out a roll of bandages. He bound my wrist tightly. I was concerned for it was already starting to swell, not to mention the pain which throbbed through it.

"Wait here, Holmes. I will check her out. It is possible that it is a normal birth which she could manage practically by herself."

"I hope so."

I entered the cabin, which proved to contain two rooms. I knocked on the door of the second room.

"Come in," called a world-weary female voice. I entered. The woman in the bed looked as toil worn as she sounded. Her brown hair was limp and her eyes sad. When she saw me, she looked surprised, "Who are you?" she asked; her accent southern also, but not quite so heavily accented as her male kin.

"I am Dr. Watson."

"A doctor? A real doctor! Lordy Lord and sakes a mercy!" She gasped. "I never figgered that no–good jackass would go get me a real doctor!"

"My friend and I were passing by when your husband told us of your condition. Are there problems with this birth?" I asked.

"Yup. This 'un don't feel like the others did. When it kicks, it gets me here. She indicated the lower left side of her abdomen. I put my hand to the spot and could feel the infant kicking. At this late stage of the pregnancy it should have been head down, with the feet at the top end. This was most definitely a breech. With my hand injured the way it was, I did not see how I would manage to turn the baby and help with what could prove to be an extremely difficult delivery.

"Are you having any contractions?" I asked.

"Yup."

"How far apart are they?"

"I've had three since yuh come in," she replied casually.

"Minor ones?"

"Nope. Hurt like all git out," she said. "Oops, there's another one now." It was truly amazing the stoicism of this woman. I was used to the more pampered ladies wailing and making a great scene with every contraction.

"Now Madam ..."

"Emily. You–all can call me Emily, Doc."

I smiled at her and said, "Well, Emily, your baby is the wrong way round and has to be turned before you can deliver. Unfortunately, your sons mistook us for intruders and attacked us before we could explain our presence. In the ensuing scuffle, I hurt my hand."

"Them fool boys. Ain't got a brain between 'em," she said. "You tellin' me you cain't turn it?"

"Not with my wrist like this," I replied holding up my injured arm.

"Damn fool menfolk! Always wrasslin' with strangers. I'm surprised they let you in."

"I am afraid we had to knock them out, your

husband as well."

"Won't hurt 'em none. Thick heads, the lot of the 'em." Despite my news she retained her calm and for that I was thankful. I had a feeling I would have enough drama contending with Holmes' hysterics when I told him what he would have to do.

"So what's gunna happen now, doc?" she asked, eyeing me with interest.

"As I said before, I am travelling with a friend. If you have no objection, he can assist with the delivery."

"He a doc too?"

"No...a chemist. I will instruct him as to what to do."

"He a gent like you?"

"Oh yes, most assuredly. My dear lady, I would never suggest this if it were not necessary. The baby has to be turned or it will die and your life is also at risk."

"Well, fetch him in then. Do what yuh have to do, Doc. I'll do whatever yuh say."

"Thank you." I nodded to her and hurried out.

Holmes was sitting on the porch rail. He looked at me as I came out of the cabin, stood up hastily and backed away, saying, "No, Watson! No, I couldn't!"

"Holmes, it is a breech; it has to be turned and I cannot do it with an injured hand."

"I can't either. I am not a doctor!"

"I will be there. I shall tell you what you have to do. There is nothing to it; it just requires two good hands."

"I can't, Watson." Holmes was looking rather

greenish at the very thought of it.

"Holmes, how often have I done things for you without question or argument? All you have ever had to do was ask. I have tackled every unpleasant task you have thrown at me and never complained. And now, for the first time in our acquaintance, I ask you to do one little thing..."

"It's not that little," mumbled Holmes.

"That woman could die and her baby most assuredly will. Do you want to be responsible for their deaths?"

"No, of course not! Couldn't you do it one handed?"

"No. That is impossible, Holmes. The baby is sideways in the womb, it needs to be turned and that requires two hands. I would do it if I could, Holmes, you know that and you know I would never ask you if the situation were not desperate."

Holmes was silent for a long moment.

"Doc, if'n yer comin' now'd be a good time," called the woman from the house.

"Holmes?"

He licked his lips.

"We don't have much time, Holmes."

"All right, damn it!" He strode into the house angrily and I smiled with relief.

"Wash your hands to the elbows, Holmes and come into the bedroom," I ordered. I entered the room and prepared the woman. Holmes removed his coat, rolled up his sleeves and washed his hands in the basin. He entered the bedroom and looked at his patient. She looked back at him with curiosity.

"Howdy," she greeted.

[123]

"Madam," said Holmes, his face expressionless. I quickly instructed him as to what he had to do and he did it. He detested every second of it, but he did it. As I watched him it occurred to me that his long, thin, artistic hands were better suited to the task than my short stubby ones.

"Can you feel its head?" I asked him, after several minutes of manipulating.

"Yes."

"Manoeuvre the baby so that it is head down towards the opening?"

"Done." Holmes' voice was as expressionless as his face.

"All right. Now make sure that the cord is not around its neck, then slowly guide it out. Emily, you can push now."

Holmes held the baby's head and guided it out. Soon the babe's shoulders were showing and then the legs. It started to wail and the woman, her face covered with a sheen of sweat gasped with relief. Her pain must have been intense, but she had not made a sound bar breathing. As Holmes held it, I washed the blood off the baby and cut the cord. Holmes wrapped it up and handed it to the woman. "It is a girl, Madam," said Holmes. He too was perspiring from the strain.

"Thank yuh," she said smiling weakly. "I always wanted a girl. What's your name?"

"Holmes, Madam."

"I can hardly call her Holmes. What's your first name?"

"Sherlock."

She smiled again. "And what's yours, Doc?"

"John."

"I'll call her Shirley Joanna Jackson, after the two of yuh."

"Uh...thank you," Holmes replied, a little startled.

"We are honoured," I said, smiling.

"There's a jug of Tennessee Dew on the kitchen shelf. Take it with yuh for payment. I reckon yuh deserve it."

Holmes nodded and exited, while I finished tending to the lady. It took another fifteen minutes to tidy up and finish off the birthing process. When I finished, I took her hand and said, "Emily, we should really be leaving before your husband and sons wake up. Will you be all right?"

"Sure, Doc. I'm fine now, was a mite worried before though."

"I cannot foresee any further problems. You are an extremely healthy woman." I hesitated a moment before continuing. "There's one thing; my friend and I are looking for another Englishman. Do you happen to know if any such man came by this way about three months ago?"

"Why sure. There was a fella. Don't know if'n he was English. Didn't stay long enough to say anythin'. Billybob just opened with his ol' Sharps and that feller hightailed it like a bat outa hell."

"Do you know which direction he headed?"
"South."

"Thank you. Thank you very much. All the best with your lovely daughter, Shirley."

I entered the main room of the cabin, only to find that Holmes had well and truly helped himself to the Tennessee Dew cooked up by the Jacksons. He was sitting at the table, a blissful smile upon his face and an almost vacant expression in his eyes. The stuff may taste smooth and mellow, but it was extremely potent.

"Holmes, it's time we left," I said. He did not appear to hear me. I had a couple mouthfuls of the liquor, grabbed Holmes' arm and pulled him to his feet. I helped him into his coat and then led him outside. "Get on the horse, Holmes," I ordered and thankfully he obeyed. It was just as well as there was no way I could have lifted him onto the animal. I then attached his horse's reins to my saddle and the pack horse to his, then led them both away from the shack. As we went past the heap of mountain men, I could hear them groaning their way to consciousness.

Emily claimed they had hard heads, it seemed that was true. Hopefully, they would be too engrossed with the arrival of their new sister to worry about coming after Holmes and me. He was certainly in no condition to fight them off should they come and neither was I. As we rode, Holmes suddenly broke out into song, "In a cavern, in a canyon, excavating for a mine, was a miner, forty-niner and his daughter Clementine..."

I looked back in surprise. I knew Holmes was musical for I had often heard him play his violin, but I did not know that he could also sing. His voice was a rather pleasant tenor. Fancy him singing a barroom ballad. That whiskey was lethal. Holmes would be mortified if he knew how he was behaving. I grinned in amusement and enjoyed the music as Holmes warbled on.

"Oh my darling, oh my darling, oh my darling

Clementine, you are gone and lost forever, oh my darling Clementine."

We rode for several miles with musical accompaniment before I decided to find a place to camp. It was already late afternoon. Fortunately it was not long before I found a nice little clearing on the banks of a stream. Holmes dismounted and plonked himself down on a soft patch of grass near the bank, then promptly keeled over and went to sleep. I looked at him in exasperation. Typical, now I was left to do all the work!

I unloaded the packhorse, then loosened all the saddles, but with my injured wrist I was unable to remove them. After that I set about gathering firewood and building a campfire. I prepared a stew and waited for Holmes to wake up.

It was a rather long and lonely vigil as the sky around me slowly darkened. In the distance I could hear the cries of a mountain lion and the snuffles and grunts of other nocturnal creatures nearer to hand. I hoped the cat was nice and far from here.

Holmes finally woke around seven o'clock that night. The first I knew of it was hearing his voice. "Where are we, Watson?"

I turned around as he approached the fire.

"Glad to see you are awake, Holmes."

As he came into the light I looked him over; he appeared a little disgruntled and seedy. "Can you take the saddles off the horses, Holmes? I couldn't quite manage that." I held up my injured hand as a reminder.

"Yes, of course." He disappeared into the darkness again and tended the horses. When he returned, I dished him up some stew, which he ate with little enthusiasm.

"You know Holmes, you did very well today," I said seriously.

He looked up and eyed me with disgust. "That was the most repulsive and horrible thing I have ever done," he said.

"Oh really, Holmes!" I chided. "Childbirth is a wondrous time. It is a privilege to be part of it."

"It was revolting," he insisted. "I don't know how you do it all the time."

"You would feel differently if it were your own," I said.

"I doubt it. I never want to speak of this again, Watson."

"All right. I never knew you could sing, Holmes," I said, changing the subject.

"Sing?"

"Sing. My darling Clementine never sounded so good."

Holmes looked down at his plate and could not meet my eyes as I chuckled.

✠   ✠   ✠

Holmes was still wide awake and alert when I rolled into my blankets by the fire. He sat silently smoking. I wondered what he was thinking about but did not disturb his thoughts. Before long, I soon dozed off.

I was roused from deep slumber by the whinnying of terrified horses and Holmes shaking my shoulder and whispering urgently, "Stay where you are, Watson!"

I rolled over and could just make out the shape of the yellow eyed predator as it stalked our horses. Holmes was levering a shell into his Winchester. He put the gun to his shoulder, took aim and fired. The big cat leaped and flopped as I quickly scrambled to my feet. Holmes approached the animal cautiously, loading another bullet into the breech just in case. His precaution was unnecessary; the animal was dead, head–shot.

"By Jove, Holmes, that was good shooting, and in the dark too."

"It was after our horses," he said, poking the dead beast with a toe. "It's a shame though. We are the interlopers in its environment. It was only exercising its right to exist.."

"And so were you, Holmes. We would not get far without horses, and what is to say it would have stopped at the animals," I said. My first thought on seeing the dead cougar was to skin it and take the skin home as a souvenir, however, after Holmes' comments; I thought it best not to mention my idea. It would not be well received. Holmes was not into hunting animals just for the sake of it and would most certainly frown upon my taking a trophy.

"You might as well go back to sleep, Watson," suggested Holmes.

He took the cat by the back legs and dragged it away from the campsite and jittery horses. I fished out my watch. It was only an hour or so until dawn. When he returned, I said, "It will be daylight soon, Holmes.

We might as well have breakfast and get an early start."

"Good idea," he agreed.

"Oh, by the way, I know which way Plymouth headed after he was scared off by the Jacksons," I added.

"How do you know that?" asked Holmes in surprise.

"While you were drowning your sorrows, I asked Mrs Jackson if she had seen him."

"Which way did he go?" asked Holmes, ignoring my reference to his inebriation.

"South."

Holmes smiled. "Good show, Watson."

THIRTEEN

The sun was just beginning to rise as we broke camp and headed south along the trail. It continued uphill for the rest of the day until we came to another ridge with deep ravines on one side. The scenery was breathtaking, the sky a deep blue azure and the view startling crisp and clear. The air was bitingly fresh and strongly scented from the pine trees. I inhaled deeply; you couldn't get air like this in London.

There were more mountains, blue and hazy in the distance and forests as far as the eye could see, stretching out in a sea of evergreen. It was such a vast expanse of wilderness that you had to see it to believe it. In fact I would be safe in saying it was unimaginable to city dwellers, or even for that matter, anyone from England. Our whole country could fit into this one state, and every precious inch of it was utilized, unlike this huge untouched land. The sheer size and magnitude of how far we had come in the past month and perhaps, how far we still had to travel was daunting.

"We don't get air like this in London!" I exclaimed, as I inhaled again, thumping my chest in enthusiasm when we stopped to rest our horses.

"No," agreed Holmes, promptly fishing out his cigarettes.

I shook my head in exasperation. "I swear to God, Holmes, fresh air is wasted on you. So is all this grandeur."

"Not so, Watson. I can appreciate nature's

beauty as well as the next man, but it has no practical use other than to please the eye. When I look at it, I see the eternal wilderness we still have to cover to complete our mission."

"Well, I don't care what you say. I am going to enjoy every minute of this trip and if I want to admire the scenery, I shall. I don't care how long it takes us to find our man. I like it here."

"Are you saying you do not miss the comforts of Baker Street or Mrs Hudson's cooking?" asked Holmes, his tone bantering.

"Perhaps Mrs Hudson's cooking a little. No offence Holmes, but your efforts sometimes leave a lot to be desired. Still, you haven't killed me with your cooking yet, so I must be getting used to it. I can understand why some men get the wanderlust and cannot settle. There is so much to see, so much to experience, it can get in your blood."

"Not mine. I would give anything to be lounging in my armchair before the fire smoking my pipe."

"Liar," I said without rancour, for he was enjoying the ruggedness of this trip as much as I. Holmes did not take offence at my words, but merely smiled and lit up his smoke.

☩ ☩ ☩

We spent the next three days making our way downhill towards a mesa. We had found intermittent signs of Plymouth, a half burnt out camp here and there and faint horse tracks. Obviously he had learnt a little with regard to fire making for now it seemed he kept a blanket ready, so that when the fire spread he was able to put it out quickly. We found fragments of burnt blanket every now and again.

"You would think" said Holmes, after finding yet another piece of burnt blanket, "that he would realize that it is the positioning of his campfire that is the problem, not the actual making of it."

"Apparently not."

"It still amazes me that he has managed to survive for so long."

I wondered that, too, although Holmes had voiced this thought before. His food supplies must have been running low by this time, just as ours were. Holmes had an aversion to hunting for sport; fortunately though, he had no qualms about hunting for food. We had begun supplementing our diet with jackrabbits and even wild turkey, which was absolutely delicious. It certainly made a tasty change from baked beans and jerky. We still had a few fresh vegetables in the food sack, and we supplemented these with wild roots and berries and such. I could not imagine young Plymouth being able to shoot very well and when we found his discarded traps, one had a piece of his boot heel still adhering to it.

"He stepped on his own trap, Watson!" laughed Holmes.

Initially, I thought that Sir Eustace had perhaps been a little harsh in describing his son, but now I had second thoughts. Cathcart Plymouth really was hopeless. He could not succeed at anything, no matter how hard he tried. He was willing, only inept. It was just as well that the old man had relented. It seemed he was only suited to being the son of a rich man, one who did not have to work for a living. Still, one had to give him credit for trying I suppose.

✠ ✠ ✠

We reached a long mesa by the fourth day and were travelling along it at a leisurely pace. I was almost dozing in my saddle, listening only to the plodding of our horses hooves, when Holmes' soft words broke into my reverie.

"Don't look now, Watson, but we are surrounded."

I looked up in surprise and glanced around. "What! Where?" The plains were deserted.

"We have been under surveillance for the past hour."

"By whom?"

"Indians."

"Indians!" I made to look around again but stopped on Holmes' sharp command.

"Eyes front, Watson!" Then in a more even tone, he continued, "Do not show fear. At any moment they will come hurtling towards us like a crazed mob. Take it in your stride. Above all else Indians admire courage. If you show fear, they will kill you without a moment's hesitation. If you show courage...well, we may have more of a chance to escape."

"Why don't we run now? Why wait to be captured?"

"We cannot outrun them; besides which they surround us."

"But I can't see them. Where are they?" I looked around discreetly and could see nothing.

"They are there, take my word for it."

Almost as if they heard him, a sudden cry went up and the mesa came alive with half naked horsemen whooping wildly and bearing down on us. It took all my nerve to sit calmly in the face of this onslaught. We continued to ride forward slowly. Holmes made no attempt to reach for a weapon and I followed his lead. It seemed like there were hundreds of red men, but as they came to a screeching halt a few yards from us, I could see there were not more than twenty. No matter, we were still outnumbered.

Finally we had to stop as we could go no further. Holmes held his hand up in a traditional greeting but said nothing. The leader of the Indians waved his lance about and spoke to us in a guttural dialect, which unfortunately neither of us understood.

Holmes began to gesticulate using the sign language that Foster Keehoe had taught him. I silently thanked the old trapper for those lessons; for I felt sure that our situation could only be improved by being able to converse with them. I also wished I had paid more attention. For all I knew, they could have been asking us the time of day, although, going by their body language, I doubted it.

"I am asking him what tribe he is from," said Holmes to me as his hands moved. The savage replied in kind.

"They are Pawnee."

"Is that good?" I asked, trying to keep the nervousness from my voice.

"It is better than if they were Sioux, or Apache, or any of the more hostile Indians. The Pawnee often work as guides for the army, so they have had more dealings with the white man than some other tribes.

"So, our situation is good, then?"

"I wouldn't go so far as to say that. They are friendly to the white man when they are outnumbered; however, we are the ones who are outnumbered, so I cannot say how they will react to us."

"Oh. So that means we're in trouble then?"

"Not necessarily," he replied.

I shook my head with exasperation. Who could follow Holmes' reasoning? "Why do you say that?"

"We are still alive, Watson."

FOURTEEN

Before long we saw campfire smoke, and then shortly after spotted herds of horses being guarded by Indian boys and then their tent-like dwellings came into view. Squaws going about their business stopped to stare at us as we rode by. The braves halted before the largest tepee and the leader of the band whooped, bringing the occupant out.

He was an elderly but ageless fellow, wearing the long, feathered headdress of a chieftain. In the centre of the headdress of white feathers was a single red feather. An elderly squaw also emerged followed by a younger one, who stood to one side passively.

The Indians motioned for us to dismount and the leader of our captors pushed us forward towards the chief. I stumbled and Holmes grabbed my arm to steady me. It would not do to fall flat on my face in front of the chief—such clumsiness would be considered bad form, and hardly likely to create a good impression. We stopped in front of him as he looked us over with shrewd brown eyes.

Holmes returned his scrutiny with interest, before raising his hand and saying both verbally and in sign language: "Greetings, Chief Red Feather. We are peaceful travellers that mean you no harm."

So much for the myth of the inscrutable red man. The Chief's eyebrows shot up surprised that Holmes knew his name. "You know of me?" he asked in passable English, much to my relief.

"Your name has travelled far," replied Holmes

solemnly, if not truthfully. "Many sing of your great deeds around their campfires. You are known as a great warrior who is famed for counting coup as many times as I have fingers on one hand."

The Chief nodded in agreement to Holmes' compliments. It was obvious his observations hit the mark and for this I was thankful. Who would have thought that his talents would serve him equally as well in the American wilderness as it did in combating crime in London?

"Who are you?" asked the chief, motioning for us to sit down.

"I am Holmes, a seer, and this is Watson, a healer. We work together."

The chief looked us over thoughtfully. "I have not heard of white men having seers," he said.

"We have them, for how else would we achieve what we have without them," pointed out Holmes.

The chief nodded again. "What do you see now?"

Holmes kept his face impassive and I kept my fingers crossed that he would not err now at this most crucial time. "I see that the hunting has been good this season and the tribe has food and skins to last them through the winter. But I also see that the tribe has suffered much in recent times. Your horse herds are small from much trading in past seasons. But fear not, for the future is brighter and you will regain back all that you have lost.

"I also know that the maiden yonder is your daughter and that she remains unwed bringing sadness to your tepee, for as you grow old you wish for many

[138]

papooses to carry on your name."

The flicker in the chief's eyes betrayed his surprise at Holmes' words.

"You are wise, seer Holmes," he replied. "And Healer, what can you do? he asked, addressing me.

"I can take away your squaw's pain," I said, having noticed the side of her face was swollen. An infected tooth being the most likely cause.

The chief nodded.

I stood up and the chief ordered his wife to approach.

"I will need my...uh...medicine bag," I said.

The chief nodded again and I went to my horse to retrieve my medical kit from the saddle pouch.

I examined the woman and saw it was indeed an infected molar. I sat her down and as gently as I was able, used my forceps to remove the tooth. I then had her rinse her mouth and pressed an alcohol-soaked swab into the recess to kill the infection and pain. After I finished, the chief spoke to her in his own tongue and she gave an affirmative answer. I hoped it was a favourable one.

Next the chief called out again and the shy, rather pudgy maiden scuttled into the tepee only to emerge moments later with a pipe and a skin pouch of tobacco. He filled his pipe, lit it, took a few puffs and then handed it to Holmes who also puffed on it with great relish. He then handed it to me.

I took a puff and only with great will power and effort did I prevent myself from choking. I surmised it would be considered bad form to cough and splutter on a Peace pipe. I am sure wars have been started over less. I only took the one puff and handed it back to the chief. The fact that he offered us the calumet was a good sign, I thought.

When the pipe was smoked down, Holmes took out his own pipe and tobacco pouch and offered the chief some tobacco. The old fellow's eyes lit up at the sight and he accepted eagerly. No doubt he preferred white man's tobacco to the foul Indian stuff.

Soon Holmes and the chief were puffing away happily. Nothing was said. The infernal silence was starting to grate on my nerves; after all, I wanted to know what was going to happen to us, if anything. Still, it was fortunate I suppose that I was used to Holmes sitting for hours on end in silence, it proved useful training for this occasion. These two were a matched pair. I believe however, that this was actually a test of patience or nerve or something of the sort on the Indian's part. It was hard to know what he was thinking or planning and lesser men would have been squirming long before now. I lit my own pipe so as to have something to do and tried to look as calm and relaxed as Holmes. Very little perturbed him.

The hunting party that brought us to the camp had long since dispersed and everyone was going about their business and ignoring us completely. We had not been searched, but I assumed they thought we were unarmed as we did not wear revolvers in open display as the Americans did. At least they did not appear to be hostile Indians.

"Are they going to kill us?" I asked casually, keeping my voice matter-of-fact and unconcerned. The chief spoke English reasonably well, which meant that he understood it as well. His face remained inscrutable at my words but you could almost see his ears prick up at the question. How we handled our captivity and possible death was also of interest to him. If we showed fear, we were doomed for sure.

"Too soon to say, Watson. I am hopeful that we will be able to convince them otherwise."

When our pipes were finished, the chief gave some orders in his own tongue and a pair of braves pulled us to our feet and pushed us along towards a vacant tepee. Our possessions less the rifles were returned to us. "At least they don't mean to rob us," I said with relief.

A short while later the chief's unwed daughter brought us food, smiling and appraising us. It was a little disconcerting when she squeezed my arm, feeling my muscles. Then she gave Holmes' arm a squeeze of comparison before leaving.

"What was all that about?" I said when she left.

Holmes shrugged. "Who knows. Perhaps she has never seen white men before."

The food she provided looked rather dubious but fortunately it tasted all right. With the inner man satisfied, I asked, "Holmes, you said the chief had counted coup five times. What is that and how did you know?"

"Did you not see the five scalps on his belt?"

"Those were human scalps?" I asked, disgusted at the thought.

"Yes."

"How revolting. So counting coup is merely another word for scalping?"

"No, not at all. Counting coup is when a brave goes into battle carrying only a lance or a small stick and nothing else. They usually only strike the enemy and leave them alive as this is considered highly honourable, more so than killing, since the enemy is likely to be fully armed. Most braves only do it once. To do it five times is the mark of a mighty warrior."

"I don't understand, Holmes. If they leave them alive how did you connect the scalps with counting coup?"

"I didn't really. Did you not see the five red hands painted on the chief's tepee? When a warrior goes to battle to count coup, he makes the symbol of a red hand on his chest. Normally, they leave their victims alive, and scalp them alive, as this is braver than killing them. But the Pawnee are not as warlike as some and the scalps on his belt were taken from the dead, not the living. It was a long shot, saying he took them counting coup, but with those red hand symbols on the tepee, I was fairly safe. He obviously likes to exaggerate his achievements. I doubt if there is an Indian alive that has counted coup in the traditional way five times. It is usually considered a suicide mission."

"And I suppose you guessed his name from the red feather in his headdress."

"I never guess, Watson, but you are quite correct. It was the single red feather that denoted its significance."

"This does not seem to be much of a prison," I said looking around the tepee. "We could easily escape."

"Not so easily. We are almost in the centre of the camp; we would be visible from all angles if we tried to crawl under the edges and there is a guard at the door."

I crawled over to the flap and lifted it to peer out. There was a large Indian on guard duty. He glared at me. I nodded casually to him, and then withdrew. Holmes had been right as usual.

"What do they mean to do with us?" I asked, settling back onto the pile of animal skins.

"I can't say. I'm hoping we impressed them with our powers. By the way, Watson, that was a good pickup on the squaw's tooth."

"I may not be able to observe the details of a man's life from his bootstrap, but I can deduce medical conditions readily enough."

"Quite so," he agreed.

\

✠　✠　✠

Several hours passed. We could hear drumming and chanting and when I took a peek outside the tepee's flap, I could see there was some sort of a council meeting going on with many of the older men puffing on pipes.

"I think they are deciding our fate, Holmes," I said.

Holmes joined me at the flap, ignoring the unfriendly glare of the Indian guard. Holmes studied the assembled group and the younger members of the band dancing around one of the fires. I glanced at him and for the first time since we were captured began to worry for Holmes' expression was anything but reassuring.

"What is it, Holmes?"

"It doesn't look good. I was afraid of this. It is one thing for them to be friendly to soldiers when they are outnumbered, but we are at their mercy here and I think they like the power this gives them. I cannot understand what is being said, but from the gestures some of them are making, I surmise that some of the members of the tribe have had bad experiences with white men and want to punish us for it."

"Oh." I licked my lips. This was probably the worst situation Holmes and I had ever been in. "Perhaps we should try and think of a way to escape," I suggested.

"I have been thinking of nothing else for the past three hours. At this point in time, there *is* no way. It's true we still have our handguns, but we are heavily outnumbered and wouldn't get very far if we tried to shoot our way out. Even if we did manage to escape, we wouldn't get far. The Indians, even an inferior tribe like this one, are superior trackers and it wouldn't take them long to find us. Furthermore, I don't want to abandon our horses, guns, and provisions, for we'd be unlikely to survive without them."

I nodded and sighed; once again Holmes was correct, only I wished he wasn't. I wracked my brain trying to come up with a solution but gave up after a while, it was a fruitless occupation. There was no way to escape. We were trapped here with our fate in the hands of the Indians and frankly, that was not a very comforting thought.

We passed a fitful night, trying to sleep to the sounds of drums beating incessantly. Evidently the Indians made a ritual of murdering white men. At first light, the chief's daughter once again brought us food. I thanked her politely and she giggled. She reached out and touched my moustache and giggled some more, for the native men did not have facial hair.

"She likes you, Watson," observed Holmes. "That could be a good thing; we may be able to turn it to our advantage."

I didn't see how, but I wasn't about to argue. Any chance was better than none.

After we had eaten, a large Indian opened the flap and gestured for us to come out. We were then taken to Red Feather's tepee. There were four other old men chiefs sitting on either side of him. As we stood before them, the rest of the tribe gathered around.

The chief began to motion with his hands and Holmes translated, "Many have suffered at the white man's hands. We have had bad seasons, we have lost horses, and we have been cheated by the white men in blue coats. You must be sacrificed to the gods to ease our suffering and your strength and endurance will bring good fortune to the tribe."

This was not good. I didn't like the sound of it.

"They mean to torture us," said Holmes softly to me. "The longer we last, the more luck we will bring them, or so they believe."

It would seem that we had failed to impress them suitably the previous day. Several braves hurried forward and we were grasped by the arms and hauled towards a couple of tall logs that had been embedded in the ground to form upright poles. We were lashed tightly to these poles.

Our situation had just gone from bad to worse for I did not see how we could escape from this. I wished now that I had pulled my revolver out when I had the chance and put it to the chief's head. Could have taken him hostage and bargained and threatened our way out of here: now it was too late. Perhaps if we survived their torture, they would let us go. It was not a pleasant prospect. My lips tightened and I thrust my jaw out as I decided determinedly that I would show no fear. I had read somewhere that Indians respected courage and that by showing no fear, they would respect me and perhaps they would finish me off quickly, rather than prolong the torture. At least I hoped so.

"It seems this is our last adventure together, Holmes," I said, ignoring the Indian who was busy tearing my shirt off and exposing my bare skin. Another was doing the same to Holmes.

"I'm sorry, Watson. I got you into this and I will never forgive myself for putting you in such danger."

"I came willingly. I do not blame you. Indeed, I have often thought that were I to die unnaturally, I would hope it was by your side during some great enterprise."

Holmes was silent for a moment before he said, "Thank you, Watson. A man couldn't ask for a better friend than you have been."

I was touched by his words, for it was rare for him to voice such sentiments. "What do you think they are going to do to us?" I asked, after noticing several braves sharpening knives.

"I believe they are going to skin us alive."

I could not contain the hiss of inhaled breath at the horror of his words.

"Try not to scream, Watson. It will only give them satisfaction."

"I'll try," I said, my voice hoarse.

By this time the drumming had restarted. "I wish they'd stop that infernal drumming!" I said irritation plain in my voice. "It's bad enough we are going to be skinned alive, but must I suffer a headache as well?"

Holmes chuckled, causing several Indians to look up in surprise. It was such an alien sound under these conditions. I was glad though, for it gave me the strength I needed to face the coming ordeal.

The drumming became faster and louder and the braves began chanting. Two, with gleaming knifes their edges as sharp as razors approached us and waved the knives in front of our faces in a sort of ritualistic dance. I just wished they would get it over and done with instead of dragging it out so insufferably. One put the point of his knife against my chest and cut. I bit my lip to keep from crying out, but the incision was just a tease, a slight nick. He was toying with me.

At that moment, there was a sudden commotion. The chief's daughter came running forward. She stopped in front of us and began to speak rapidly in her native tongue, I had no idea what was going on, but one look at Holmes' face gave me hope. Red Feather came forward and motioned angrily for her to move, but she shook her head. Instead, she turned and threw her arms around Holmes, hugging him, and then she released him and hugged me as well. After which, she turned and glared at her father. The other old chief's came forward and a pow wow was held. None of this was in sign language, so we had no inkling as to what was being said.

"Do you have any idea of what is going on, Holmes?" I whispered.

"I think the girl doesn't want them to torture us. Let us hope they heed her."

There was a great deal of argument. The girl continuing to stand protectively in front of us, while the braves with the knives objected to her interference and her father pleaded with her to get out of the way. She was insistent and it seemed, successful.

After a while, the crowd began to disperse and the maiden turned around and beamed at us both. Chief Red Feather came forward and started to speak in sign language. Holmes, as usual translated. "Plump Beaver wishes to take one of you for her mate. Do this and you will live and become honoured members of our tribe. Refuse and you die – slowly."

Holmes was untied so that he could answer. "Which one of us does she want?" he asked, speaking aloud and motioning in sign simultaneously, "and what will happen to the other?"

"She does not care; she likes you both. The other will also become a member of the tribe; you are not without talents. We will return you to your tepee. You have until the sun sets to choose." So saying, the chief turned his back on us and returned to his fire. I was untied and we were both bundled back to our prison.

"What a stroke of luck!" I enthused as soon as we were alone.

Holmes, on the other hand did not look overly keen.

"I don't know," he said. "Being skinned alive is comparable to being married."

I smiled. "Nonsense. All we have to do is have one of us marry her and win their confidence so that we can escape."

"I have a better idea," said Holmes, his eyes gleaming as the thought came to him. "You marry her Watson and drug the wedding feast. That will put everyone to sleep and we can sneak off in the night."

"Why do I have to marry her?" I argued. "After all, she doesn't care which of us does, and if they are all going to be drugged anyway, it doesn't make any difference who plays the groom."

"Alright, let's cut cards for it," offered Holmes, fishing out the pack from his saddlebag. Low card marries her."

"All right," I agreed. "That's fair."

Holmes shuffled the deck thoroughly and held it out to me. I cut the deck a quarter way down. My card was the seven of clubs. Holmes then turned up his card, the Ace of spades.

"I win!" he declared and now he did look enthusiastic.

"Well, I suppose it is only the ceremony I have to put up with. It's not like I have to go through with the honeymoon or anything. She will be sleeping deep by then."

"Exactly!' agreed Holmes. "I trust you have enough sleeping draught?"

"Yes, I think so." I hurried to my bag to check my supplies. Luckily the Indians had not touched it, medicine pouches being sacred to them.

FIFTEEN

Just as the sun set, we were once again brought before Red Feather. Plump Beaver, his daughter was also there smiling winsomely at us. Thank goodness she was going to be drugged I thought, otherwise I would have had second thoughts also, for she looked a bit like her namesake, a plump beaver, teeth and all. I stepped up the chief and said, "I will marry Plump Beaver."

The young lady in question threw her arms around me and hugged me and, much to my dismay, felt me all over. She wasn't exactly bashful. She was the Indian equivalent of a desperate man-hungry spinster. The chief was delighted; pleased to be rid of her no doubt, for she had sounded rather shrewish when she was nagging at him to set us free.

We were returned to our tepee and as I was about to go in, a bundle was thrust at me by a grinning Indian. I was bemused.

"What's this for?" I asked.

"It's time to get changed, Watson," explained Holmes.

"Changed?"

"Into your wedding clothes."

"The wedding is tonight?" I was stunned. I thought I would at least have a little time to get used to the idea and perhaps get to know my bride-to-be.

"The sooner the better. You don't want to stay here, do you?"

"No, of course not!" I unwrapped the bundle

and looked at the clothes which consisted of a breech clout, leather leggings, moccasins, and a buckskin shirt. Holmes could not keep the smile from his lips at the sight.

"If you dare laugh at me, Holmes...!" I warned.

"Never, Watson. I would never dare."

✠ ✠ ✠

I stripped and changed into the clothes provided leaving my underpants on. When I had dressed, Holmes looked me over critically.

"You look ridiculous."

"Now see here, Holmes..." I began icily.

"I am not laughing at you, Watson, but the Indians will. You cannot leave your long johns on under the breech clout, it looks ridiculous."

"Well I can't take it off, I would be...naked," I almost whispered the last word.

"The Indians do not wear underclothes," he pointed out. "They don't seem to mind."

"That may well be, but they're savages. I cannot run around half naked in front of women and children."

"Do you want to be the laughingstock of the camp? Worse still, do you want to embarrass your bride-to-be and her family? Remember, your prospective father-in-law is the chief, we must make a good impression, or otherwise they may change their minds and kill us anyway. In case you haven't noticed we are somewhat outnumbered..."

"All right. Don't nag!" I growled. I removed my underpants reluctantly and readjusted the breech clout. It was a long piece of cloth that one stepped over and pulled up between the legs to thread over a belt, so that half hung down the front to the knees and half down the back. I could not fault the coverage front and back, but the sides were exposed and frankly I was not used to such exposure. I felt naked.

"That's better, Watson," approved Holmes, keeping the smile from his face, with effort no doubt.

I just scowled at him still in bad humour. I was not comfortable wearing such meagre coverings.

"Don't forget the sleeping draught," Holmes reminded me. I took the packet and concealed it inside the buckskin shirt.

Ten minutes later the guard came and motioned for us to follow. We were led to the Chief's tepee. His wife was outside dressed in her finery. She smiled at me and patted the side of her face. I noticed that the swelling had gone down.

"At least you have won over your mother-in-law," whispered Holmes.

"Shut up, Holmes," I hissed back. He was enjoying my current predicament far too much. No doubt he considered it payback for my making him deliver the mountain woman's baby. I wish he had lost on the cut of the cards though; he'd be laughing out of the other side of his face then!

The chief welcomed me and clapped me on the back. The confounded drums began to beat again, but the tune was different and the party commenced. Indians danced around the fire for a while until suddenly the drums stopped and Plump Beaver came striding majestically towards us with several squaws in attendance.

[153]

She was dressed resplendently in a doeskin dress with a bear claw necklace around her neck. Her long black hair was loose and her head festooned with flowers. She actually looked quite pretty. She smiled coyly at me as she joined me, taking my hand in hers.

I wondered how she could so easily marry a complete stranger, but then again, who knew how Indians worked these things. I was surprised too, that her father would allow her to marry a white man, for mixed marriages were often frowned upon by both races. Still, I supposed that their interaction with the white man, made them more tolerant of me and the situation more acceptable. Or perhaps the chief was just desperate to get rid of his daughter. Considering that they had intended to kill us before, I figured that the latter was the most likely.

As a couple, we stood before the chief who conducted the service in his own tongue. When I was required to answer, he asked the question in sign language and Holmes translated. It all proceeded rather smoothly.

Initially, I was conscious of everyone's eyes upon me in my outlandish garb, but the nervousness soon passed and I ceased to notice how I was dressed. After the ceremony, there was a feast with much drumming and dancing.

There was a medium sized barrel off to the side, from which everyone was getting their drinks of water. I surreptitiously removed the packet of sedative powder and slipped it to Holmes, with a faint nod in the barrel's direction. He took it and quickly secreted it in his pocket. I could hardly leave as I was part of the main wedding party, but Holmes could approach the barrel as if to get a drink. He waited a few minutes before doing just that. When he returned he carried several tin cups, he handed one to me and the other to Plump Beaver. I guessed that my cup held un-drugged water.

She took a sip of her drink and then turned to talk to her mother, putting her cup down. Other Indians were drinking freely from the barrel as well. All was going according to plan. The celebrations went on until quite late. Some of the Indians were already sleeping. Plump Beaver also looked like she was dozing. I gave Holmes a nudge and he nodded. It was time we put our escape plan into action.

I tapped Plump Beaver on the shoulder and she opened her eyes. I smiled and held out my hand to her to help her up. She stood up and smiled eagerly, taking my hand, and leading me to the wedding tepee. She looked surprisingly awake, but I assumed this was just temporary. Hopefully she would fall asleep fairly quickly once we were inside the tepee and I could meet Holmes outside. It was his job to have our horses and gear packed, ready and waiting. However, this was not to be.

As the flaps of the tepee closed, Plump Beaver turned on me and threw her arms around me. She began to kiss me and I responded so as not to arouse her suspicions. She seemed remarkably awake though. I couldn't understand it. I thought she had drunk all her water. Oh, God, no! I just realized, she had put her cup down and her mother drank it instead. Plump Beaver was wide awake. What was I to do? She was a savage; how would she react if I did not appear enthusiastic? I had to appease her desires so that she would not voice her dissatisfaction and rouse the rest of the tribe. It would only give the Indians another reason to kill us, which had been their first intention anyway.

My thoughts were rudely interrupted when I felt Plump Beaver pulling loose my breech clout. The things I did for Holmes! I had no choice but to return her affections and hope that she would soon tire and go to sleep.

✠ ✠ ✠

It seemed like hours before I heard her quiet breathing. I was just thinking that my moment had come when Holmes peered in through the flap. He looked down at me where I lay beside Plump Beaver. "Get dressed, Watson. The horses are ready," he said softly.

I nodded and slipped my arms from around the girl. My own clothing had been brought to the tepee sometime earlier, so I quickly dressed, taking care not to disturb her. It would not do to wake her, for I did not think I had the energy to propitiate any renewed affections. I crept out and found Holmes waiting by our horses. The camp appeared to be in deep slumber, for most of the tribe had partaken of the water, everyone except Plump Beaver. I caught a glimpse of Holmes' disapproving face in the moonlight.

"Not a word, Holmes!" I warned, for I was not in the mood. What I had done, I had done for the two of us. It was not a matter of satiating carnal desires.

We walked the horses from the camp for a fair distance so the sound of hooves would not rouse anyone. Holmes led the way and soon we found a trail at the edge of the mesa which led down to the river below.

We rode for most of the night, trailing blankets behind us to cover our tracks, before calling a halt by the river and dropping wearily from our mounts. We figured we were safe enough here, as it was unlikely the Indians would follow us, knowing that this time we would be ready and likely to shoot first, rather than let ourselves be taken so easily. I must confess though, that I felt a little guilty about leaving Plump Beaver. Still, it's not like I had much choice in the matter and a forced wedding is no basis for a good marriage.

✠   ✠   ✠

Next morning, over breakfast, Holmes decided to voice his disapproval. "Really, Watson, I am totally appalled. How could you take advantage of that poor woman?"

"What? I didn't take advantage of her," I replied, becoming heated at his accusation. "So much for your lousy plan. She never drank the water! She was wide awake and expecting me to do my duty. I had *no* choice. It was either that or make her angry and suspicious. *She* made all the advances, not me!"

"Oh! In that case it is fortunate that it was you who married her. I doubt if I could have soothed her savage breast quite as expertly as you."

All of a sudden, I had a sneaking suspicion that something was amiss. "It was rather curious that I lost, especially when you were so dead set against marrying her in the first place."

"What are you saying, Watson. Surely you are

not accusing me of cheating?" Holmes sounded injured.

"Yes, that is exactly what I am doing. Admit it, Holmes, you cheated!"

Holmes looked down and couldn't meet my eyes.

Now I was certain. "You reptile, Holmes. You cheated!"

"I say, Watson, that's a bit harsh."

"No more than you deserve. You are a *reptile,* Holmes," I said, enunciating the word clearly.

"Well, I may have cheated a little," he finally admitted.

"You cheated a lot."

"Still, you have to admit you were far more adept at handling the situation than I would have been."

"That may well be, but really, how could you? I am supposed to be your friend. I was willing to die with you, and you set me up!" I was starting to feel really angry now at Holmes' duplicity. I trusted him and he deceived me.

Holmes stood up and approached the river to wash his coffee mug; his back was to me when he said, "What are friends for Watson, if you can't use them to your advantage?"

It was the wrong thing to say. I saw red. He had just implied that I was there to be used. I discarded my breakfast and advanced on him. He turned when he heard my footfall behind him and that is when I struck. My fist lashed out relentlessly, striking his jaw with enough impact to jar my arm.

He staggered back, off balance, tripped over a

rock and fell backwards into the water with a resounding splash, music to my ears. He was absolutely stunned. He sat up with water lapping about his waist.

"What was that for?" he demanded his surprise apparent.

"For cheating, Holmes. For deceiving me and for assuming I am here to be used whenever it suits you."

"Oh. Well, I confessed to it," he said, starting to get up, completely soaked and dripping water.

His lack of contrition just made me even angrier. I took advantage of the situation and struck the other side of his jaw, sending him plummeting back into the water again. Undeterred by my ire, he continued as though the second altercation hadn't even happened.

"I don't know what all the fuss is about; after all you seem to have survived the experience. Was it really that bad?" he added curiously, wisely choosing to remain seated in the water.

"No. It wasn't bad at all. Plump Beaver was very affectionate and accommodating."

"Well, I am truly sorry, Watson, but you have to admit you handled the situation well. Much better than I would have."

"Perhaps," I replied, only slightly mollified, not by his words, but by his bedraggled appearance. It did my heart good to know I had been responsible for it.

He regained his stance. "Look on the bright side," he continued, squelching his way to the bank. "You have often in the past boasted of having experience of woman on three continents. Now you can

[159]

make it four."

His comment brought an involuntary smile to my lips as I thought about what the fellows at my club would say to that. I said nothing. I didn't want to give Holmes any satisfaction from his treachery.

He collected his bedroll and took his towel and a change of clothing from it. I packed up the camp while he was changing and had the horses saddled by the time he was ready. We mounted and rode quietly for some minutes, before he asked, "So, you had a good time then, Watson?"

"Shut up, Holmes!"

He chuckled, only to break off with a gasp of pain as his injured jaw began to throb anew. That brought a smile to my own lips and I was maliciously glad he was suffering. Served him right!

SIXTEEN

It was nearly an hour later, before I thought to ask, "Are we going anywhere in particular, Holmes?"

"Yes. Didn't I tell you?"

"You have told me nothing."

"Your vicious attack must have distracted me," said he.

"Holmes," I growled warningly.

Sensibly, he chose not to pursue that particular subject. "I asked some of the Indians last night if they had seen Plymouth. Apparently when he saw them he ran until he reached the edge of the mesa. His horse stopped, but he didn't and fell down into the river."

"So he's dead then?"

"No. The braves who were chasing him saw him grab onto a log and float downstream. I am looking for sign of where he emerged."

We continued to make several stops along the bank to check for signs of Plymouth. After all, he had to come out of the river eventually. At our third such stop, Holmes stood on the bank surveying the river.

"You know, Watson. I don't think Plymouth did come ashore anywhere near here. The river is running too fast, wide and deep and unless he is an exceptionally fine swimmer, he would have had no chance."

"Then what do you think he did?"

"Well, he was hanging onto a log. If he had any sense he would have straddled it and rode it down river until the current lessened and the water became shallower."

"That being the case, we are not likely to find him today. I suggest we make camp here for the night. It's as good a place as any."

Holmes glanced up at the sun, nightfall was still quite a few hours away, however, he nodded in agreement.

I set up the campfire while Holmes tended to the animals. When I broke out the provisions, I saw that Holmes had supplemented our supplies with deer meat purloined from the Indians.

"Mmm," I murmured when I saw it. "How about a couple of steaks for dinner, Holmes?"

"Steaks?" He winced and I smiled. No doubt his jaw still hurt him.

"Stew?" I offered, still smiling.

"Yes, please."

When the stew was bubbling away on the fire, we availed ourselves of the river to bathe and wash our clothing. The rocks around our campsite radiated heat so it wouldn't take long for our clothes to dry.

By the time our meal was ready, we were clean, dry, and hungry. I was also feeling somewhat more civil towards Holmes. He was quick to note the change in my mood and chatted happily about Colorado, its trees, mountains, and animals. I retired not long after sundown, having slept little the previous night. Fortunately, Holmes refrained from comment, knowing when to leave a subject well enough alone.

Next morning, we were up bright and early and after breakfast continued our journey downstream. Half a day passed before the force of the river lessened and we found a place suitable for crossing. Holmes reasoned that if Plymouth wanted to get out, he would do so on the other side of the river as being opposite to the mountains. Plymouth's goal would be to find a town as he had no food, water, or transportation.

A short while after we forded, we found a log on the bank with some chequered cloth attached to a sharp branch sticking up.

"He tore his shirt," I said.

"Yes. He came out here and flopped on the bank, probably from exhaustion. Lay here," he pointed, "for some time, then started to walk that way."

We followed the faint marks, scuffed rocks, new brush growth indicating where twigs had been broken by someone passing through in the past and continued on until we found what appeared to be a road. It was overgrown but had definitely been a major thoroughfare at some point in time.

It was as we travelled along this path that the mishap occurred. It was no fault of Holmes', just one of those things. We were plodding along at a steady pace when Holmes' mount stumbled and he almost fell, managing to retain his seat only in the last instance. He quickly dismounted and examined the animal's leg.

"Broken?" I asked.

"No. Just twisted. I can't ride him though."

"You can ride the packhorse," I suggested.

"No. The beast is already heavily laden. I will walk."

"In that case, we shall take turns to walk," I offered.

Holmes nodded his thanks and took the horse by its reins. "If we're lucky," he said as he began to walk, "we will come upon a town."

It was almost dusk when we called a halt and made camp. We were both footsore and weary, having taken turns to lead the injured animal. There was no handy stream and the terrain was dry. I took extra care in building the fire and gave thanks that Plymouth had lost his matches and possessions when fleeing the Indians. The brush and undergrowth would have burned wildly here had he tried to make camp in his usual fashion and it's extremely doubtful that he could have outrun the fire this time.

We turned in early and were up again at first light. As I cooked breakfast, Holmes, with great agility, climbed the tallest tree he could find. He was up there for quite a while before coming down.

"I saw cattle in the distance, Watson. There could be a ranch and where there is a ranch there are horses. I think we will have to detour. I may be able to trade my horse for another, or at least purchase a new one."

So, after breakfast we changed our course and headed across country. Fortunately it was open range, there were no fences to circumvent. It was late afternoon before we saw smoke, so vast was the holding. It was practically the size of an English county if not two. I finished my stint of walking and gratefully remounted as Holmes once again took the reins of his horse.

Another hour and a half passed before we reached the corrals and outbuildings. Several people wandered out from various dwellings, including the rancher and his wife and children. The woman glanced at us briefly before dismissing us as itinerants and returning inside the house, shooing her children in before her. The rancher came forward.

"Howdy," he greeted. "See you run into a mite of trouble."

"How do you do, Sir," greeted Holmes. "My horse stepped in a gopher hole and twisted his foot. I was wondering if I could trade him for another or purchase one if possible."

"You're outa luck, Mister. All my horses have been rounded up ready for the trail drive at the end of the week. Can't spare nary a one."

"What about that one?" I asked, pointing to the grey horse in a corral by itself. My question triggered an outburst of laughter from the watching men and caused the owner to grin.

"Well, yeah, you're welcome to him, 'ceptin' he's a wild one. Ain't been tamed yet on account of nobody can stay astride long enough."

"I see," said Holmes. "So if I can ride him, you would trade him for my horse?"

"Why sure," replied the grinning rancher. "No offence feller, but you sound like a furrin' dude."

"No offence taken. We are foreign."

"From England," I offered.

"You ever ride a wild hoss before?"

"No, I cannot say that I have," Holmes replied honestly.

"Well you've got nerve I'll give you that. Ride him and welcome, Slim," said the rancher. I smiled faintly at the sobriquet he had just tagged onto Holmes.

By this time, quite a crowd of off–duty ranch hands had formed around the corral, all curious to watch the proceedings. The rancher looked around at them. "I need a volunteer to show the dude how it's done. Any takers?"

"I'll do it, boss," offered a lanky man with a southern accent.

"You watch him careful, Slim. Tex'll show you how to do it if'n you don't want to bust your neck," offered the rancher to Holmes.

"Thank you, Sir."

Tex and two other cowboys entered the corral. They saddled the horse and attached a bridle and bit. The horse endured all this without protest. The two handlers then held the horse's head as Tex approached. As soon as he put a foot into the stirrups, the horse became jittery, and was it not for the two men holding its head, it would have started jumping straight away. Tex settled himself into the saddle and hooked one hand under the pommel. He nodded to the other two to indicate he was ready. The instant they let go, they ran for the fence and clambered over it as the animal began to pounce and buck wildly.

It swerved and bucked and ran straight for the fence. Tex was admirable, but even he could not stay astride for very long. He hit the dust with a thump and rolled under the fence quickly to avoid being trampled.

"Er...Holmes, perhaps we should just ask if we could store our baggage here instead. I do not like your chances of riding that beast. It really is quite savage."

I have never yet seen Holmes show fear and he did not do so now, however there was a trace of concern in his eyes. "We are unlikely to return this way,

Watson, unless you want to revisit the mesa ...?"

"No!" My reply was vehement.

Holmes' lips quirked. "That being the case, we need another horse. I have always ridden fairly well. There is no harm in trying."

I did not voice the thought which came to me at his comment. There was a great deal of harm in trying. He could end up with broken bones, or worse, a broken neck!

"Your turn, Slim," grinned Tex through the dust which covered his face. "Just make sure yer feet are firm in the stirrup and yuh've got a grip on the pommel. An' when yuh fall, let yerself go limp, don't tense up. Hurts less thataway...oh yeah...and uh, make sure yuh git out of its way when yuh come off on accounta it'll try and stomp yuh fer sure."

"Thank you, Tex," returned Holmes politely as he removed his hat and coat. These he handed to me as he approached the corral. The two horse handlers also came forward and entered with him. They caught and held the horse while Holmes mounted. Holmes' backside barely touched the saddle before he was lying in the dust at our feet.

"Howdy, Slim," grinned the rancher looking down at him. "Back so soon?"

Holmes flushed a little at the chuckles from the watching men. He was a perfectionist in all things and excelled in everything he ever attempted. To have been thrown so easily and quickly chaffed him somewhat. Holmes stood up, dusted off his clothes and returned to the corral. The handlers held the horse and up he climbed. This time at least he managed to stay on board for several hops before hitting the ground. I winced at the thud he made. He quickly rolled out of the animal's way and just as quickly remounted, only to be thrown again.

The cowboys, who had been chaffing him good naturedly at the start, had fallen silent as they witnessed Holmes' grim determination to master the beast. Time after time he was thrown, only to struggle to his feet and climb back on. With each fall, I noticed that his movements were less brisk and I started to worry at the possible damage he was doing to himself.

He mounted for what was perhaps the seventh time, when the horse leapt high in the air. Holmes flew off and landed heavily, winded. The horse snorted, nostrils flaring, ears back. Holmes lay helpless on the ground, unable to get breath enough to move. I leapt over the corral rail and ran at the horse, flaying Holmes' coat about to distract it, while Tex jumped in and dragged Holmes out. As soon as Holmes was safe, I dashed after him with the horse hot on my heels.

Holmes sat up grimacing in pain; he struggled up and regained his feet.

"Holmes...give it up," I advised, but he shook his head, still breathing heavily.

The rancher looked at him with admiration and sympathy. "Your friend's right. Give it up, Slim. This hoss is just plain unbreakable. I reckon that's why Red Feather wanted to get rid of him."

Through a haze of pain, Holmes blinked at him. "What? Red Feather? This is an Indian's horse?"

"Yup. Traded him for beef. Told us it was saddle broke, reckon he lied."

Holmes straightened up, holding onto his left

side as he did so. Despite the pain he was experiencing, he proved his mind was clear. "Indians do not lie." He frowned. "This horse belonged to Red Feather and he claimed it was broken in. Did you see anyone riding it?"

"No, he led it in."

Holmes sighed mightily, wiped the sweat soaked dust from his face and brushed the hair from his eyes. "I wish I had known this seven falls ago."

He re–entered the corral, waving away the horse handlers and approached the grey from the right side. When he reached it, he held it by the bridle and blew into its nostrils muttering soothing noises. Then he patted its neck and moved to its side. I held my breath. What was Holmes up to? Did he realize he was on the wrong side? He slipped his foot into the stirrup, the horse did not flinch, next he mounted and sat upon its back. The horse continued to stand statue still.

"I see it, but I don't believe it," muttered the rancher in awe.

Holmes clipped the horse to movement and it began to trot gently around the corral. After several circuits, Holmes guided it over to us, the stunned spectators.

"This horse will do nicely, Mr...I'm sorry, I don't know your name?"

"John Jenkins," replied the rancher. "I don't know how you did that, Slim," he added, his voice reflecting his wonderment.

Holmes smiled. Once again he had triumphed and in the process succeeded in amazing his awestruck audience.

"What in blue blazes did yuh do to that hoss?" asked Tex, coming closer. "In all mah years of hoss handlin' I've never seen nothin' like it."

Holmes smiled again and dismounted, giving the horse one final pat. He climbed out of the corral his movements surer. "It is fortunate I studied several subjects during our voyage here. Indian lore particularly fascinated me. You told me the horse belonged to Red Feather and he claimed it had been broken. White men mount from the left, Indians mount from the right. It went wild every time someone tried to mount it from the wrong side. By mounting it from the right, the Indian side, it thought I was one of its native handlers and so let me ride him."

"Well I'll be damned. Reckon you earned that hoss, boy," said the rancher. "An' I reckon they must breed 'em tough in that England place."

"Tough enough," I agreed before asking Holmes, "Why did you blow in its nose?"

"Indians do that to calm and reassure their horses. I saw them do it when we were in Red Feather's camp."

"Yuh was in Red Feather's camp and yuh got out alive?" asked Tex, his eyes wide with disbelief.

"We parted amicably," smiled Holmes.

Fortunately, he did not go into details, much to my relief. I glanced around at the cowboys; they were all looking at Holmes with renewed interest. Now when they addressed him as Slim, it was not faintly derogatory, but respectful.

"I wonder, Mr Jenkins, if we could purchase a night's accommodation here and continue our journey tomorrow morning," said Holmes.

[170]

"Stay as long as you like, no charge. Could use extra hands for the drive if you're interested." I was aware that we had just been bestowed a high honour. It was not often that 'dudes' were made such an offer.

"Unfortunately we have business to attend, otherwise we would have been delighted to learn cattle driving," replied Holmes, also pleased by the offer. I knew that his adventurous soul would have relished such an opportunity.

We unsaddled our horses and put them up in stalls for the night, giving them oats and hay for a change of diet. As we tended to them, I looked at Holmes. "You appear to be in pain, Holmes. Are you injured?"

"I'm not sure. I am bruised and shaken and every joint aches, but I do not think anything is broken."

"Not for want of trying."

"My own fault really. I should have asked from where they had obtained the horse. I assumed they captured it from them wild. I could have avoided these aches had I done so."

Having tended the animals, we took our belongings into the bunk house. There were several spare cots and we helped ourselves to two. I then made the mistake of breaking out my medical kit and ordering Holmes to remove his shirt.

"Are you a sawbones?" asked Tex.

"A what?" I asked as Holmes obeyed my orders.

"A doctor?"

"Yes."

"Really?" asked a short bald-headed man named Curly. He was the cook, or chuck boss as they called him. "You know, Doc, I got me a boil on the back of me neck that's been troublin' me somethin' awful."

"Oh," I said. "I can take a look at it if you like," I offered—big mistake, for all the other cowboys began to list their ailments and clamoured for my attention also.

"I take it there is no doctor nearby," said Holmes.

"Ain't one for near a hundred miles," offered Curly.

"Well gentlemen, I suggest you line up in order of seniority and I will attend to you after I have seen to my friend here," I said.

'In order of what?" asked a tow haired young man with buck teeth aged around ten and seven.

"In order of age, yuh dope," said Tex, whacking him on the back of the head with his hat. "Means you're last."

Holmes was smiling by this time, wincing only when I poked at him. He said softly, "Looks like you have your work cut out for you, Watson."

I just rolled my eyes before saying, "You have one cracked rib on the left side," I then supplied him with some ointment with which to rub into his bruises and strapped the rib tightly. His bruising was quite extensive and likely to get worse over the next few days.

When I turned around, I was greeted by a long queue of eager faces, with a beaming Curly in front proudly displaying his boil. There was humour in the situation which I could appreciate with my first couple of patients, but by the time I reached the last, I was a little irritated. Half their problems were imaginary, the other half minor or preventable. When I reached the tow haired boy, whose name was Pete, his complaint was that his feet hurt. As soon as he took off his boots I could see why—they were a size too small!

There was much good-natured joshing of him after my discovery, but it was not unkind in any way. The fellows seemed to treat him like a younger sibling. In fact, they all seemed and acted like a bunch of unruly school- boys. Quite a likeable group really, though I must say I was relieved, when I was finally free to wash up and sit down to a meal dished up by Curly.

SEVENTEEN

The next morning as we partook of breakfast with the cowhands, there came an interruption. The door opened and a lady entered. This brought on a sudden scramble as the men hastily rose to their feet. Holmes and I followed suit.

"Please boys, stay seated," she said and I recognized her as Jenkins' wife. She approached us.

"I understand that one of you gentlemen is a doctor?"

"That is I," I replied.

'I wonder if you would take look at my son, doctor. He has been complaining of stomach pains and he has a fever."

"Of course!" I stood up immediately and collected my medical kit, following her from the bunkhouse. As we walked, she apologized.

"I really am sorry, Doctor. I had no idea who you were yesterday or I would have had you stay in the house. I didn't learn of your profession until this morning. My husband only told me that the two of you had stopped by because you were in need of a horse, he did not mention you were professional men. I understand your companion managed to tame that wild stallion in the corral?"

"Yes, and it is quite all right, Mrs Jenkins. I enjoyed the company of your staff. They are a most amiable group of men." As we walked towards the house it occurred to me that doctors in this country were highly regarded, especially those in isolated

[175]

frontier communities. T'would that it was the same in England, where many a doctor could barely eke out a living.

She led me into the house and to her son's bedroom. I could see at a glance the child was rather ill. "How long has he been like this?" I asked, hurrying forward.

"He woke me around two o'clock this morning complaining of a sore stomach, but he was not feverish then. I thought it was just a tummy ache. I gave him some Croton oil and reassured him before returning him to bed."

I checked the boy's temperature which was dangerously high. He was also suffering from acute upper right quadrant pain. Recently, in fact it was in the last issue of *The Lancet*, I had read an article describing a similar condition. It was called appendicitis, meaning an acute inflammation of the appendix, which is a small organ attached to the end of the caecum.

Up until recently most people died of this condition and it is only in recent times with the advent of new anaesthetic techniques that it has become possible to operate and remove it. The operation itself was unremarkable; the difficult part was to keep the patient unconscious during it. From the child's feverish state I feared that the appendix was not only inflamed but could quite possibly have ruptured. If that were the case it was an extremely serious condition. I told the mother this; after all, she had a right to know.

"Oh my God," she gasped. "He's going to die?"

"He could die without medical attention. However, I am here, so his chances have improved somewhat. I will have to operate to remove the appendix. It is still quite a risky business though; there are no guarantees. If it has ruptured, then the resultant infection could be fatal."

I thought I should warn the woman, for my equipment was extremely basic. I did have some chloroform in my bag and as long as I maintained a clean environment and sterilized my tools I had a good chance of succeeding. Certainly, I had to do something. Inaction on my part could be as fatal as action. I looked at the woman. She had seemed fairly level-headed, now I was not so sure I could rely on her to assist me. She was quite pale with shock as I explained the dangers of operating versus not operating to her. She called her husband in and I repeated my comments.

"If an operation is the only chance he's got, then do it, Doc. I know you'll do your best," said Jenkins, looking as worried as his wife.

I nodded in assent. "I wonder if you would be so kind as to call my friend in. I will require his assistance. I am also going to need boiling water to sterilize my instruments and clean sheets for his bed." They nodded and hurried out to do my bidding. Holmes joined me five minutes later.

"The boy has an inflamed appendix, Holmes. I need someone to act as anaesthetist while I remove it. I am not sure if the mother or father are up to the task, whereas I know I can rely on you."

"Of course, Watson. How long will it take?"

"About an hour, but I am afraid we cannot leave today. I will need to stay close to observe the child for the next four and twenty hours, to ensure that he is out of danger."

Holmes nodded. "Just as well you were here, Watson," he said.

"If I had known I was going to have so many patients in this country, I would have brought more medical supplies with me."

We set about organizing a makeshift operating theatre. Holmes was to man the chloroform and apply the pad at intervals to ensure the child stayed unconscious. I also showed him how to monitor the boy's blood pressure and pulse.

"Look at it this way, Holmes. By the time we go back to London, you will be experienced at delivering babies and anaesthesiology."

"Two skills I hope I will never have to use again," he replied gravely.

When my instruments were sterilized, I proceeded with the operation which, I am pleased to say, went smoothly. Though I had never performed it before, it proved to be quite a simple procedure, especially as the appendix was still intact and had not ruptured as I feared. The risk of course was in opening the boy up and exposing him to contamination. An hour later, the boy was resting comfortably, appearing none the worse for the experience. As a matter of fact his temperature had come down significantly and I was hopeful that he would make a full recovery. We washed up and I packed away my instruments. Mrs Jenkins then led us into the parlour where she and her husband expressed their gratitude.

"Think nothing of it," I said. "We were glad to help."

That was when I noticed Holmes' distraction. He was studying a large oil painting above the fireplace.

"What a magnificent painting," he said, and it truly was. "It looks rather new."

"Yes, it is. I bought it for my wife last time I was in Harkin's Hollow."

"Harkin's Hollow?"

"It's a farm town about twelve miles from here. It is closer than the county seat, so I buy my supplies from there. Sell them beef occasionally too."

"Who is the artist?" I asked.

"Some fellow who married the marshal's daughter,' replied Jenkins.

Holmes leaned closer. "I think I can make out the name, Plymouth."

I looked at him. "It would seem that our search is at an end."

"You know the feller?" asked Jenkins.

"He is the man we are looking for," I replied. "You say he married the marshal's daughter?"

"Yes, so I heard."

"It seems we have delayed you," said Mrs Jenkins.

"Not at all, my dear Mrs Jenkins," replied Holmes urbanely. "It was my horse which delayed us."

"And it doesn't matter," I added. "After all, if he is happily married in Harkin's Hollow, a day or two is not likely to make much difference. He will still be there tomorrow. I would like to keep an eye on your son for the next four and twenty hours, just to make sure there are no complications."

"We would be most grateful. You must move into the house, Doctor, both of you," she insisted.

"Watson can," replied Holmes. "I am quite happy to stay where I am, thank you. There is no need to trouble yourself on my account."

✠ ✠ ✠

The day passed uneventfully. I was given a room next door to the boy's. Holmes was invited in for dinner but returned to the bunkhouse after. I retired just after ten, the child's condition was stable and he had even managed to tolerate a small amount of fluid.

All was silent until the early hours of the morning, when an urgent drumming of hooves raised the household. Jenkins ordered his wife to stay inside as we hurried out. Semi–clad men tumbled from the bunkhouse. The rider was none other than Tex.

"Rustlers!" he cried as he came to a sliding halt. "They shot young Pete!"

"Guns and horses!" called Jenkins, rushing back into the house to fetch his weapons. I followed suit. Even as I joined the others hastily saddling horses, I saw Holmes was amongst them. He had his rifle with him and a lantern.

In a surprisingly short time we were all thundering to where the night herders had been attacked. Half the herd gathered for the cattle drive had been scattered, the other half run off by the cow thieves. I expected Holmes to move forward and take command of the situation, but instead, he handed the lamp to

Jenkins to check the ground for sign.

I hurried over to the body of the young tow haired boy. His chest was bloodstained, his eyes open, his face pale in death. I draped the blanket that one of the hands gave me over him. There was nothing I could do for the boy. Jenkins checked the tracks, then returned to the waiting men. He detailed Curly to take the body home and ordered the rest of us to push on.

We followed the tracks easily in the moonlight for there were a great many of them. Half an hour later we could see the peaks of rocky ridges that lined a natural gateway through the mountain trail.

"Mr Jenkins," called Holmes, riding forward to join the rancher in the front. "Rein up. I believe we are riding into a trap. Can you stop here for a moment while I scout ahead?"

Jenkins hesitated for a moment, then said, "Well you've proven you're a smart young feller, Slim. We'll wait here."

I rode forward to join Holmes, but he shook his head. "Wait here, Watson. It is easier if I go alone."

Holmes rode slowly around the bend in the trail and disappeared from our view. He returned ten minutes later. His face looked serious in the moonlight.

"They're up ahead all right," he reported. "The cattle were driven through the canyon, but only by four men. There are tracks veering to the left and a large mound of rocks providing ample cover to shield them and their horses."

"But why stay there? It slows their escape," said Jenkins, looking puzzled.

"Hastens it you mean," countered Holmes. "They knew Tex escaped to raise the alarm. Herding cattle, they cannot travel as fast as unhampered horsemen. Their only chance is to ambush us as we ride past."

"What can we do? We can't let them get away with my herd."

"I have a suggestion," offered Holmes, his eyes glinting with suppressed excitement.

"Go for it young feller," nodded Jenkins.

"If we attach blankets, brush or whatever we can find from ropes being dragged by the horses, they will kick up quite a dust cloud that we can use to our advantage."

"And we go through under the cloud of dust," said Jenkins.

"Not quite. That would only result in us being trapped between two groups of criminals. No, the horses could be quite easily managed by two men at most while the rest of us circle behind the raiders. The dust will provide a distraction while we get into position."

Jenkins grinned as Holmes continued. "It is possible that the two men with the horses will be shot at, but if they stay in the middle of the herd and stay low, their risk will be minimal."

"Let's do it," said Jenkins decisively.

The men quickly and quietly gathered mesquite, blankets and dead logs, anything they could find that would kick up dust. These they bundled and tied via several ropes to the backs of the horses. Holmes decided that the horse handlers should wait five minutes before moving them through. It would give us

[182]

time to move up on the rustlers. Holmes had drawn us a rough sketch in the dirt as to where we were going.

The thieves were behind some large boulders. Holmes wanted to get behind them, which meant climbing up the rocks, so that we would be behind and above them. We could not scale the rocks in complete silence. That's when the horse herd would come in and create a diversion.

We all walked silently to the base of the rocks at the very back of the cow thieves. Suddenly the silence of the night was broken by loud whoops and the drumming of hooves. We started to climb, with Holmes in the lead. When the horses came into view the rustlers began shooting into the dust cloud. We used the racket caused by their gun fire to scuttle up to the top of the rocks, where all eight of us lined up along the top and readied our weapons.

"Let them waste their bullets," Holmes whispered to us. As the dust cloud cleared, one of the outlaws began swearing obscenely:

"What the hell...!" He stood up for a better look. "There ain't no riders down there!"

"That is because we are up here," announced Holmes. "Drop your weapons. You are outnumbered."

The five outlaws turned in shock. Their rifles were empty, but they quickly drew their handguns and fired upon us. When a bullet whizzed past my ear close enough to singe my hair, I did not hesitate to retaliate. We gave them a chance to surrender, but they refused. A savage gun battle ensued.

The thieves were desperate. They knew that only the rope awaited them for the murder of the young cowhand.

[183]

I heard one of our group gasp and drop his gun to clasp at his arm. Finally, the shooting died down; the cordite hung heavy in the air and as the smoke cleared we looked at the scene of carnage. All the bandits were dead or dying. By comparison only one of our group was wounded and not seriously so. Even as we emerged from our cover and clambered down the rocks, the last rustler's eyes glazed over and he breathed his last. Looking at their sprawled and bloody bodies, I suddenly felt sick.   What   a blood bath! Each bandit must have been shot several times. I glanced at Holmes. His lips were compressed and firm and he too looked a little pale. We were un-used to such bloody violence. True, I saw something of it in Afghanistan, but that was war, and Holmes saw death in many forms in his work, but usually only one at a time.

It all happened so swiftly, a kill or be killed situation. Justice was quick, deadly, and rough in this country and not something I think I could ever get used to. I quickly patched up the wounded cowboy and we used the outlaw's horses to ride through the canyon to where the other two cowboys awaited us with the rest of our horses.

Jenkins led the way after the remaining four rustlers and the cattle. Half an hour later we found the cattle milling around, but there was no sign of the thieves. They must have guessed that their comrades had lost the gun battle and fled. For this I was grateful as I did not think that I could have handled any more bloodshed.

We collected the dead outlaws on our way back. It was almost dawn before we sighted the homestead again so there was hardly any point in going to bed again. I checked on my young patient, before washing up and joining the crew in the bunkhouse for breakfast. It was a solemn meal, all boisterousness gone as they grieved for the loss of their friend.

Holmes and I stayed for his funeral, then saddled up, said our goodbyes, and left, making our way back to the old trail which led to the farm town of Harkin's Hollow.

Holmes was silent and frankly I was in no mood for idle chatter either. Having known young Pete, even briefly, made his death more personal to us. The suddenness of it and the violence which followed had left a pall on our moods so we rode in silence.

EIGHTEEN

It was early afternoon before we shook off our depression and felt up to conversing again.

"It is a rough country with rough justice," said Holmes. "The lawless outnumber the enforcers one hundred to one. Isolated regions are a law unto themselves as they rarely see a duly elected official. If the rustlers had not died in the shoot-out, they would probably have been hung from the nearest tree."

I sighed. "I know all that, Holmes; it was just the brutality of it that appalled and sickened me. As a doctor it goes against all my instincts."

"Well, our journey is almost at an end. Plymouth is happily married in Harkin's Hollow. According to the cowhands, it is a farm town full of 'god–fearing folk, more intent on prayin' than hell raisin'." He affected Tex's accent for the last sentence.

I smiled.

"There is only one saloon which closes on Sundays. It is considerably more civilized than Lucky Strike. Apparently they even have a church and a school. Our task now will be to convince Plymouth and his new wife to return to England with us."

"I will not be sorry to leave, even though for the most part it has been an adventure and I have enjoyed some aspects of this trip more than others. Still, it is always nice to go home."

We only stopped long enough to rest the horses and chew on some jerky before continuing on our way.

The sun was starting to dip in the sky when Holmes reigned up abruptly. He stared ahead. I followed his gaze. Over the tree line were rising spirals of smoke: thick, dark columns that boded ill.

"That is not chimney smoke, Watson," said Holmes, before spurring his horse to a run. I dug in my heels and followed, with the packhorse picking up the pace as well.

Fifteen minutes of hard riding brought us to the lip of the hollow and we were able to witness the carnage for ourselves. Even from where we were, we could hear the cries of anger and the sobbing of grief. Numerous buildings were on fire, including the church. There were dead lying in the streets and bloody people walking around dazedly.

"My God! What has happened here?" I whispered awe struck with horror.

Holmes just shook his head, as shocked as I and nudged his horse forward. I followed.

As we rode closer, I saw it was mostly the town's businesses which were on fire, the bank, the store, the marshal's office. On the steps of the latter lay a grey bearded man with a bullet hole in his forehead and a silver star on his chest. A young woman held him in her arms, sobbing pitifully. I did not need Holmes' deductive skills to guess that this was the marshal's daughter, Plymouth's wife. Holmes' face was grim and I doubt if mine looked any lighter. A short way ahead of us, a woman cradled a motionless child in her arms; his clothing was bloody.

"Holmes, I have to help the injured," I said. Holmes nodded.

"Of course. I will also see what I can do to

help."

We dismounted. I hurriedly unpacked my overused medical kit and approached the woman. I knelt down beside her.

She clutched the child tightly.

"I am a doctor," I said gently, loosening her grip. To my relief, I saw that the boy, no more than six years old, was unconscious, but not dead. He had been bullet grazed on the right temple. I did what I could to stem the bleeding and clean the wound.

"Is your house still standing?" I asked the woman. She nodded. "Then I suggest you take your son home and put him to bed. He will be all right, he just needs to rest."

"My husband...?" she asked.

"Where is he?" She raised her eyes towards a building which was almost burnt to the ground.

To my horror, I saw a pair of protruding legs and nothing more. I bit my lip and shook my head. "Take your son home. He needs you," I repeated as gently as I could.

I noticed that there were several people trying to help some of the wounded and went over to them. "I am a doctor." I said as I approached them. They appeared rather dazed so I decided to take command. "We need to set up a temporary hospital and bring all the wounded there. It will be easier than trying to treat them one at a time in the street." I explained to them.

An elderly man looked up at me from where he knelt by an unconscious victim and nodded. "Use my house," he said and pointed to a building a few doors down. "They didn't touch it," he added grimly.

Together we picked up the wounded man

whom he had been trying to treat and carried him to his house. As we walked, I asked: "What happened here?"

"Renegades. They robbed the bank and stores and looted the saloon. They were crazy, just shootin' at anything that moved, didn't make no mind to them. I just thank the good lord that my wife died last year and didn't have to witness this."

We put the wounded man on the kitchen table and I uncovered his wound to begin my examination.

"I'll send the others this way," the old fellow offered.

"Thank you," I replied, "and if there is anyone with any medical knowledge, midwives, veterinarians, anyone at all, send them as well. I think I am going to need some help."

"Mighty fortunate you coming to our town right in our hour of need, Doc," said the fellow.

I nodded. The bullet was lodged in the victim's hip, but I foresaw no difficulty in extracting it. I set to work at once, before the influx of patients started arriving. It would not take long for word to spread that I was here.

I had just removed the bullet when a stout elderly woman arrived supporting a younger woman, who held a blood-soaked cloth to her shoulder.

"I'm Ma Bolton," she said. "I'm the midwife, vet and doctor of this town."

"I am Dr. Watson."

"A real doctor?"

"Yes."

"Praise the lord!"

"If you could act as my nurse and treat the

[190]

lesser injuries, I will attend to the more serious ones requiring surgery. Also if you could send them in one at a time in order of urgency, I would be most grateful."

She looked me over with curiosity. "You talk funny, but you seem to know what you're doin'." She sat the wounded woman down on a chair and left the room. I glanced at the woman. "Bullet in the shoulder," she said. "Finish what you're doing Doc, I can wait."

"Thank you."

Throughout the afternoon and well into the night, the injured kept coming. I saw Holmes several times helping to bring the wounded in and cart the treated out. His clothing was soiled from helping rescue people from burning buildings and carrying blood-soaked wounded. He too worked tirelessly.

Ma Bolton proved to be an invaluable assistant and I was grateful for her help. I doubt if I would have managed without it. It was two a.m. by the wall clock when Holmes and the house's owner returned. They dropped wearily into chairs and watched as I tied off the last stitch in an adolescent's leg. I was using regular sewing cotton by this stage as my own supplies had run out long ago.

My patient thanked me politely and rolled his pants leg down, before limping from the room. I dropped wearily into a chair. Ma Bolton, with energy to spare, wiped the table down turning it back to its original innocent purpose. I noticed that she had been cooking earlier but could not take the time out to either eat or drink. She placed plates on the table and began to dish up.

Holmes and Sam McKee (the house owner), pulled their chairs closer to the table. "It was like an answer to our prayers when you showed up Doc, you and your friend. You both saved a lot of lives today," said old Sam.

"The doctor was the livin' wonder," enthused Ma. "Get that into yuh before you plumb collapse."

There was silence as we tucked into our food. I had not realized I was so hungry. I felt much as I had as a young surgeon in Afghanistan on days of battle as casualty after casualty was brought in; torn, bleeding and shocked. Today was much the same and coming so soon after the incident at the cattle ranch, I too was at risk of battle fatigue, shock, and depression. This was life on the frontier at its most raw, its most primitive.

Once our meal was finished, Ma set about washing up. I was amazed at her energy; she had worked as hard as the rest of us yet remained tireless. Holmes leaned back in his chair and lit up a cigarette, breathing in the smoke gratefully. I borrowed a smoke off him and lit up also.

"Mr McKee," I said, once I had my cigarette drawing satisfactorily, "you said the town was attacked by renegades. What exactly are renegades?"

The old man's eyes clouded. "Scum! The lowest kind of sidewinder! White trash, border jumpers and outcast Injuns."

"How many were there?" asked Holmes.

"Fifty, sixty maybe. Can't say I stopped to count 'em."

"Good Lord!" I was stunned. "So many?"

"That's why they didn't just rob the bank; they

stole everything that wasn't nailed down."

"What about getting up a...posse, I think you call it?" I asked.

"Couldn't, even if we wanted to. There ain't enough able-bodied men left. The rest are wounded, dead, or too old to be of much use, like me." His voice was bitter.

"If what I saw today was anything to go by," said Holmes gently, "you were extremely useful."

The old man gave him a watery-eyed nod. He was silent for a moment before continuing. "We're farmers here, not killers, and they are, every last one of 'em. We wouldn't stand a chance. That kind of scum prey on towns like this and avoid big ranches and towns which are more able to defend themselves. We were sittin' ducks."

"How long can they continue to run roughshod over the territory before the law apprehends them?" I asked.

"Years!" snorted Ma Bolton. "It'd take years. By the time the federal law gets organized in this state, the scum move on to the next and raise hell there."

"I wonder..." I began as a thought occurred to me.

The others looked at me politely. "I'm sorry. I was just wondering aloud if the rustlers we clashed with yesterday belonged to this group of renegades."

"Highly likely, Watson. They were probably stealing the cattle for food."

"Then we were very lucky that there were so few of them, or we wouldn't have stood a chance."

Holmes said nothing, just sat puffing his cigarette in silent contemplation. I glanced at him feeling

[193]

somewhat concerned. If the last two days had been overwhelming for me what was it doing to Holmes' sensitive nature? He professed to be unemotional, but he could and often was touched by the plight of others in need.

He could never turn down a client who was desperate and many a time had taken pity on some poor wretch who had turned to crime out of desperation. He could not have spent all day in this massive carnage and not been affected by it. It worried me, for I knew he was prone to fits of the deepest depression and lassitude. And it was at such times that he turned to the dreaded cocaine to relieve his anxieties.

NINETEEN

Ma Bolton returned to her own cottage at three a.m., while McKee offered us blankets and floor space, which we accepted gratefully. We washed at the kitchen trough and changed out of our soiled clothing. I was well and truly exhausted by this time, as was Holmes. Yet once I turned out the lights and climbed into my makeshift bed, Holmes made no move to follow suit.

"Aren't you going to bed, Holmes?" I asked.

'Later perhaps," he replied, filling his pipe.

"Really, I must protest. You are physically exhausted, Holmes. You have worked harder today than in any previous day of your life. You need to rest before you collapse. Your will cannot sustain your constitution for ever you know."

"My body is resting," he said, lighting the pipe. "But my mind is racing along. Can you in all good conscience ride away from this hamlet, knowing that a band of renegades are on the loose and that it is only a matter of time before they pillage and massacre another village full of innocents?"

"But what can we do? We are only two men."

"Yes, only two men. Still, it only takes one man to start a war." He glanced in my direction. "I am all right, Watson. You go to sleep. I promise I will too when my mind tires itself."

"That'll be never," I muttered as I lay down.

Holmes' lips twitched in response.

✠ ✠ ✠

When I woke several hours later, I found Holmes still perched cross legged on the settee, a blue cloud rising from his pipe. His eyes were closed and he appeared to be in a deep meditative state. Yet I had no sooner opened my eyes than he proved he was fully alert.

"Good morning, Watson," he greeted.

I sat up. "Did you sleep at all, Holmes?"

"In a fashion." He uncurled his long legs and stretched.

"So have you figured out how we are going to defeat sixty renegades?" I asked sceptically.

Holmes smiled. "Not quite. I have some vague ideas. I need to know the geography before I can come up with anything definite."

"Well, if we are going to go up against that many, I want a Gatling gun instead of a rifle." I was being sarcastic, my temper a little irritable from lack of sleep.

By the time we had washed and shaved at the well in the back yard, McKee was awake and calling us in to breakfast. He was at the stove cooking.

"Good morning, Mr McKee," greeted Holmes.

"Mornin' Mr Holmes," he returned. We sat down at the table and he dished up. It was over breakfast that Holmes brought up the purpose of our visit to Harkin's Hollow.

"Mr McKee, it was not chance that brought us here yesterday, but purpose. We are looking for a countryman of ours, Cathcart Plymouth. We believe he is married to the marshal's daughter."

"Why sure, I know Cart Plymouth. Boy's got

real talent. You should have seen the old town, before those thievin' skunks hit us, we had the fanciest signs in the state."

"I did not see him yesterday, not among the dead," Holmes stated flatly.

"I never saw him yesterday either," said McKee. "After breakfast, I'll take you over to his missus. It's the least I can do. She lost her pappy yesterday, so I sure hope Cart's still in one piece."

✠ ✠ ✠

After breakfast as promised, he took us along to a small cottage standing at the edge of town. It was a tidy little house, surrounded by a neat garden. McKee knocked on the door. It was opened by the pretty young woman we had seen weeping the previous day over the body of her dead father. She had black circles under her reddened eyes, indicative of a sleepless night.

"Mr McKee," she greeted, looking at us curiously. Then with a woman's instinct, her eyes fastened on me.

"You're the doctor, aren't you?" she asked. "Did... did you treat my husband yesterday?"

"Ah...no," I replied, a little uncertain how to go on.

"Sarah, these gents are from England too. They're friends of your husband."

"Oh? Come in please," she said, stepping to the side.

"I'll be on my way then," offered McKee with a brief nod at us. "Your stuff is safe at my place and you're welcome to stay there as long as you like."

"Thank you, Mr McKee," I said. "You have been most kind."

He touched a hand to his hat brim in salute to the woman as he left.

Inside, she led us to a neat parlour. "So you are friends of Cathcart?" she asked.

"Actually, we have never met him. We are here on business for his father," Holmes replied. "My name is Sherlock Holmes and this of course as you guessed, is Dr. Watson. Now, am I to understand that your husband is missing??"

"Yes." Her eyes clouded. "My father was killed yesterday when those raiders came and I was so grateful that Cathcart was not here. Only I expected him home by sundown and he never came. I thought maybe you had treated him, Doctor and that he was laid up somewhere."

"No, he was not brought to me. I would have recognized him," I replied.

"And I checked the deceased," reported Holmes. "He was definitely not amongst them."

"Then where can he be?" she cried her voice desperate.

"Calm yourself, dear lady," said Holmes, taking her arm and guiding her to a seat. "We are here to help. Where did he go yesterday?"

"He went up river. He was going to do some painting and took his stuff with him. He promised to be home before dark. He...he's not very good with directions. Sometimes he gets lost."

"Could he have got lost yesterday?" I asked.

"The smoke would have led him home," she

countered, while Holmes nodded in agreement.

"I couldn't go look for him, the renegades stole most of our saddle animals...and... what with Dad..."

"We quite understand. Watson and I will go look for him."

"I want to come with you," she said. "Just give me a minute to change."

"I don't think..." began Holmes, only his words were wasted as she hurried from the room, not waiting for a reply.

"Let her come, Holmes. She has had grief enough. This at least will give her something to do."

When she returned, our eyebrows shot up. She was wearing denim trousers and a checked shirt, with a man's coat over the top. Her thick honey coloured hair was piled up under her hat, a battered old Stetson. She also carried a rifle and looked grimly determined. I had no doubt whatsoever that she knew how to use it.

The three of us then returned to McKee's house and saddled our horses. Sarah Plymouth borrowed McKee's saddle to use on the packhorse, and then led the way upstream. We rode for little over an hour before Holmes called a halt.

"He was here," he said, dismounting. On looking around we found Plymouth's paint and easel hidden under a bush and a half–finished canvas. There was no sign of Plymouth and more importantly, there was no sign of blood in the idyllic spot he had picked to paint. Holmes circled around looking for sign. He even rode his horse across the stream and checked the far bank before returning to us.

"Plymouth was here, painting. He must have heard the gunfire coming from the village, because I can see where he began to pace in his agitation. He thrust his art things beneath the bush and resaddled his horse. By this time, I would say that the smoke was visible. He crossed the stream and began to head back, only to encounter the renegades. Fortunately, he saw them before they saw him and had the good sense to hide behind a large rock. It looks like he has chosen to follow them."

"Oh, but why? Why didn't he come home?" she asked, looking worried. Knowing Plymouth's lack of woodsman's skills, I could understand her concern.

"I don't know," replied Holmes. "Perhaps, considering that your father was town marshal, he thought to follow them and then return with information as to their whereabouts. He would assume that the townsmen would form a posse to go after them. He of course had no idea of the carnage they left behind."

"But it's so unnecessary," she said, frowning.

"To a westerner," agreed Holmes. "The renegades left enough tracks for a blind man to follow, but I doubt very much if Plymouth thought of that. He's not...uh..." Holmes paused trying to think up a tactful way of saying Plymouth was hopeless.

"I know he's no frontiersman, but he has other talents. He's a wonderful artist. I think you're right, that is just what my darling husband would do. He has the heart of a lion...uh...just not the skill."

Holmes appeared amused. At least this young woman had no illusions about her husband's shortcomings. I smiled to myself. Plymouth was probably

[200]

congratulating himself on the wonderful tracking job he was doing.

"We shall return to town, collect our belongings and follow him," stated Holmes decisively. "And, I assure you, Mrs Plymouth that we will continue on until we find him."

She looked at Holmes curiously. "Might I ask what your business with him is?"

"His father is dying and wants him to return to England to claim his inheritance. It is his wish to see his son before he dies. Of course we had not counted on him being married; still, I think you would like England, and now that your father is gone there is nothing to hold you here," said Holmes with satisfaction in his voice, while I winced at his tactlessness.

"What he means is that, had your father been alive, you would have been torn between the two," I modified, trying to tone down Holmes' comment.

Her eyes looked at me sadly. "You're right, Doctor. I wouldn't have wanted to leave Father. Now there is nothing but bad memories in Harkin's Hollow."

"You would like England. Certainly it is not as big as America, but it is just as beautiful, in a different way to the ruggedness of this country." I continued, hoping to distract her. "Plymouth castle is a magnificent structure and they own most of the land for two counties."

"Castle? Cathcart lives in a for-real castle?"

"Yes, built in 1252," I added. "Has he never spoken of his birthplace to you?"

"He said he had a fight with his father and wasn't welcome there. But that's all he said. He didn't want to talk about it much."

"Well, his father has had a change of heart. Sir Eustace regrets the argument that drove his son away." I explained.

"So does Cathcart, I think," she said.

TWENTY

We returned to Harkin's Hollow and collected our belongings. It was as Holmes was loading the packhorse that Sarah Plymouth approached him. "You'll have to give me time to find another horse," she said.

"You do not need a horse," he replied.

"The pack horse is heavy loaded," she pointed out. "It would slow us down my riding double with you."

Holmes stopped what he was doing and looked down at her. "You do not need a horse and you will not be riding double, simply because you are not coming."

"I am," she returned evenly.

"It is inappropriate for you to come with us. We will be travelling and living roughly. There are no luxuries or accommodation other than the open sky for a roof and the ground for a bed."

"You are forgetting, Mr Sherlock Holmes, that I was born and raised in this country. Many is the time that Dad took me hunting in the foothills. I'm probably more comfortable camping out than you are with all your city ways!" Her cheeks flushed as her temper rose.

I remained silent, wondering how Holmes would handle this wilful young woman.

Holmes frowned. "Madam, a woman of good character does not ride off into the wilderness with two men she has only just met."

"Are you saying that you are likely to molest me?" she challenged.

"No, of course not!" I gasped, shocked at the very idea.

"Then I am perfectly safe," she said triumphantly.

"You are safe from us perhaps, but not the renegades. We will be following them but they outnumber us. What if we were to be captured? Watson and I would no doubt be killed, but you Madam, would suffer a much worse a fate. If we are to assist your husband, we cannot do that *and* protect you as well," argued Holmes.

"I can protect myself."

"Huh!" Holmes grunted, his own temper rising. "I have heard that before, usually just prior to when the woman starts screaming for help from the nearest man!" Holmes was not always the most diplomatic of men as he just proved.

Her eyes fairly glowered. "That may be how it is with those milksops in England, but it's not the way out here!"

"Madam, you will *not* be coming with us. That is my final word on the subject. We will return here with your husband. I suggest you find other things with which to occupy your time whilst we are gone." Then to me he snapped. "Mount up, Watson, we're leaving!"

He quickly checked that the packhorse's load was secure and mounted his own horse taking the lead rope in one hand and urging his mount into movement. As we passed the lady, I stopped long enough to reassure her.

[204]

"Trust us, Mrs Plymouth, we will not return until we have your husband safe and sound."

"Thank you, Doctor, but I'd rather come with you."

"I am sorry. You really will be much more comfortable waiting back here than on the trail. It is no place for a woman." As we rode away, I made to glance back at the forlorn figure.

"Don't, Watson!" barked Holmes. "You will only weaken."

"I think you were a bit harsh with her, Holmes. After all she has just lost her father and now her husband has disappeared. You could have shown her a little compassion."

"She is like a stray dog. If I had shown compassion, she would have followed us. We do not need a woman cluttering up our campsite. It is far too much of an inconvenience."

"For you no doubt," I muttered. Holmes ignored me.

✠　✠　✠

We set up our night camp in a small clearing, some five miles from the spot where Plymouth had been painting. It was easy to follow the renegades trail as there was a plethora of horse prints. The outlaws made no attempt at concealment. It was obvious that they did not fear reprisal from the town folk or from the law. Holmes had procured a map from McKee which he spread out by the fire and studied intently. After a while, he gave a grunt of satisfaction and folded the map up carefully.

[205]

"If the renegades continue on this route, it will take them into Arizona," he said.

"Is that good?"

"Possibly. Once we have located Plymouth we will need to get ahead of them. The geography is particularly suited to what I have in mind."

"You have a plan then?"

"The merest glimmer of one, Watson. It depends on several factors, none of which I have at present."

"Like a cavalry platoon," I suggested.

Holmes' teeth flashed white in the firelight as he grinned at me. "Typical Watsonian response. You never change, old fellow. No matter the circumstances, you are the one constant."

I was not sure if he was complimenting me or insulting me, so I said nothing. Instead, I dished up our meal. We decided to have an early night so that we could start at first light the next day.

It felt like I had only just closed my eyes before I was woken by Holmes' hand upon my shoulder. It was still dark and I blinked in surprise.

"Quiet, Watson," whispered Holmes. "I heard a horse. Collect your gun and conceal yourself. I am going to go up the trail and scout."

I nodded and stood up, pulling my revolver out of my pocket. I moved past the clearing to a large boulder nearest the trail as Holmes swiftly disappeared in the darkness, moving on silent feet.

It was a few moments before I heard the clip clop of hooves on the trail. I marvelled anew at the acute sense of hearing that my friend possessed. He had been asleep yet woke to a sound so faint that it was only now becoming detectable to me.

A moment later, there came a gasp and a thud and Holmes' jubilant yell, "Bring a light, Watson. I have him! ...Her!"

I fetched a blazing faggot from the fire and hurried forward, pondering Holmes' amendment. How did Holmes know his captive was female? It was pitch dark under the heavy overhang of foliage. I raised my torch and held it up illuminating Holmes sitting on his captive. Her hat had fallen off, revealing long, light honey coloured hair; none of which would have been visible in the dark. He must have made his discovery by feel. Oh well, he always did say a good detective used *all* his senses.

"Mrs Plymouth," said Holmes, still sitting on her.

"Get off, you great ox!" she gasped, winded from her fall.

Holmes scrambled off and offered her his hand to help her up. She slapped his hand aside and stood up unaided.

"What the hell did you think you were doing?" she demanded.

"I was capturing an unwelcome intruder," returned Holmes.

"Are you all right, Mrs Plymouth?" I asked.

"At least one of you is a gentleman," she said, glaring at Holmes.

He glared back. "I told you to stay at home."

"And I told you I was coming," she shot back. I had to admire her spunk.

Holmes sighed theatrically, turned his back on her and began to march back towards our campsite. As he passed me, I heard him mutter: "Women!"

I smiled and took the reins of her horse. "I must say you took rather a risk following us like this. Something untoward could have befallen you in the dark."

She smiled at me. "I know this trail like the back of my hand. I don't know why your sidekick is so obstinate. I'm likely to be real useful. I can be your guide."

"We have managed quite well without a guide to date," I pointed out. "Please do not judge us by your husband's standards. Not all Englishmen are so inept. I used to be in the army and am used to roughing it, and Holmes has considerable woodsman skills, despite our living in the city." I was a trifle defensive, as it was a constant irritation to me the way the Americans assumed us to be hopeless in the wilderness just because we were city dwellers.

"No offence, Doc, it's just your friend's not real polite," she replied, sounding a little peeved.

"He's just shy around woman," I said, wondering what Holmes would think of my description of him. Not
much I'd wager.

We returned to the clearing. Holmes had built up the fire and as she moved over to join him I unsaddled her horse.

"At first light you can return to the village," he said.

"At first light I will travel along with you or follow you, the choice is yours."

"Let her come, Holmes," I said, coming over to join them. "It will be much safer for her if she travels with us and time saving too. We will not have to keep watching our back trail."

"I assume then Watson, that you are willing to take responsibility for her?"

"If you like." I agreed without hesitation.

"Hey! I can take care of myself!" She was indignant.

"So you say. That, of course, remains to be seen," replied Holmes dismissively. He kicked off his boots and returned to his blankets. Deliberately he lay back and closed his eyes, completely ignoring us.

"Shy? Mean, more like it," she hissed at me.

I smiled. It was going to be an interesting expedition if   Holmes and Sarah Plymouth continued to clash wills. She was the victor of this round.

She spread her blankets by the fire, head facing my direction, feet in Holmes'. She undid her coat and that was when I noticed the weapon belt around her slim waist.

"Egad, is that a revolver at your hip?"

"It was my Father's. He taught me how to shoot when I was knee high."

"I hope it's not loaded," muttered Holmes, opening one eye.

"It's no use unloaded," she replied, her voice dripping with sarcasm.

Noting the position of her blankets, Holmes rolled over onto his side, back towards us and grumbled, "Don't shoot me in the backside."

"I'll...!" She made as if to kick him in the rear, but I caught her arm and pulled her back.

"That would not be a good idea," I advised.

"Maybe not," she sighed, 'but it would give me a heap of satisfaction."

Yes Sir, this was going to be an interesting trip indeed.

TWENTY–ONE

The sun had just risen when I woke to the pleasing aroma of frying bacon. I sat up. Mrs Plymouth was cooking. Holmes was shaving by the stream, using a small mirror balanced on a tree branch for checking his progress.

"Good morning," I greeted.

"Morning, Doctor. You'll have time to wash and shave before I dish up." She was bright and chirpy.

Holmes looked at me sourly as I joined him and broke out my shaving gear. He was not fond of bright and chirpy females first thing in the morning. Actually, he was just not used to females full stop. "Remember, you're the one who wanted her to stay," he reminded me softly.

"It is better than her following us," I replied just as softly. "And she would you know; besides you would only worry about her. At least this way we can keep an eye on her."

"That's the problem with these American women; they do not know their place," he growled. His masculine ego had no doubt been somewhat bruised by her defiance.

"Still, you have to admire her courage."

"The only thing I admire about her is her rear," he stated flatly.

"Holmes!"

"Nothing would give me greater pleasure than to see the back of her."

I chuckled at that. Typical Holmes. "You know, the two of you would get along much better if you did not argue so much."

"There is no need for argument if she does what I tell her to do," he countered stubbornly.

I sighed. "Holmes, compromise is the key word when dealing with women."

"You may compromise, Watson. I do not. I never have and I never will."

He wiped his face and stepped away from the mirror, giving me room to complete my own ablutions. I did not say it aloud, but felt it was only a matter of time before Holmes learned the meaning of compromise. I was quite sure that Mrs Plymouth was more than capable of teaching him.

✠   ✠   ✠

We continued to follow the renegades' tracks, working on the assumption that Plymouth was following them. It was a safe assumption as at intervals Holmes found signs of a lone rider hiding behind bushes, rocks, and the like.

"At least we know he's alive," I said comfortingly to Mrs Plymouth.

"Not for long. He didn't have any food with him except for a packet of sandwiches and a canteen of water," his wife replied, a worried look creasing her brow.

"He has existed on less," Holmes replied tartly. It was plain that Mrs Plymouth still rankled under his skin like a burr beneath a saddle.

"Poor Cathcart," she sighed.

Holmes rolled his eyes at me as if to say that at any minute now she was going to start blubbering. However, she was made of sterner stuff than that.

✠   ✠   ✠

That evening, Holmes declared that he would cook dinner, even though Mrs Plymouth offered. He was making a stand to prove that we did not need a woman accompanying us. Mrs Plymouth just shrugged and helped me tend to the horses.

"What's up with his highness tonight?" she asked and I could not help chuckling. Holmes could be a bit aristocratic at times.

I chose my words carefully before responding, "Be patient Mrs Plymouth, it will take a while for Holmes to get used to your presence."

"Call me Sarah," she offered, then added, "well, he'll just have to get used to me because I'm not going anywhere."

When Holmes served up dinner an hour later, I looked down at the slop on my platter. It really looked quite disgusting. I thought it prudent, considering his mood, to refrain from comment and picked up my spoon and manfully began to eat it. It wasn't one of Holmes' better concoctions and tasted rather foul.

Mrs Plymouth was less tactful. "What the hell is this?" She asked, screwing up her nose at the 'food' on her plate.

"Stew," replied Holmes curtly, picking up his own spoon.

"Hogwash!" she declared.

"I beg your pardon?"

"This isn't stew. It's hog food. I thought you said you could cook?" she said, eyeing him challengingly.

"This is perfectly good edible food," Holmes replied coldly.

Mrs Plymouth stood up, her actions exaggerated and deliberate. She took her plate to some bushes and emptied it onto the ground. She then rinsed it and helped herself to the provisions and fry pan and within fifteen minutes, there came an appetising aroma to tantalize my taste buds. Catching my hopeful look, she added extra contents to the pan. I smiled at her in appreciation, only to turn and catch Holmes glaring at me. He obviously considered me a traitor. I tried to look contrite, but could not resist saying, "Well it is awfully revolting, Holmes."

Stubbornly, he continued to eat his slop, or I should say, made a pretence of eating his slop, for after the first spoonful he barely touched it.

I quickly emptied and washed my plate. Forty minutes later we sat down to a decent meal.

Holmes would not concede defeat, but from that time on, it became an undiscussed rule that Mrs Plymouth did the cooking and we tended the horses and gathered the firewood. Certainly the quality of our meals improved greatly.

Up until now I thought that Holmes and I were managing quite well with the cooking, yet, somehow, using exactly the same ingredients she could whip up an appetising repast the equal of anything prepared in a kitchen with proper facilities. I noticed too, that Holmes always cleaned his plate even though he offered very little by way of compliments. I doubt this caused Mrs Plymouth much pain for she graced him with a smug grin each time he handed back his empty platter. The country air gave us both excellent appetites.

As the days passed, we developed a routine of sorts. She was usually up before us each morning, which surprised me, for I knew how light a sleeper Holmes was. However, I assumed that he only pretended to be asleep to allow her some privacy when rising. We were existing under primitive conditions and some propriety had to be maintained, although I must admit that she did not slow us down in any way, nor did she complain and she certainly knew her way around a camp site. Holmes had become a little more accepting of her presence, even though he still did not wholly approve of it.

Their clashes became less frequent as the days passed. I believe Holmes had developed a grudging admiration for her capabilities, for she was indeed a very able young woman. For her part, I often caught her watching Holmes and listening intently to him when he explained something to me, be it to do with sign reading or a deduction of great detail on some minute source.

She admitted to me that she had a reluctant respect of Holmes' abilities and acknowledged that despite being a city dweller he, to use her words, had a lot of trail savvy. Still, her attitude towards him remained truculent, and his towards her was icily civil.

On the third day as we continued to follow the river upstream we came upon a magnificent waterfall. It was an amazing sight. The water cascaded from above, the noise deafening as it crashed upon the rocks at its base. It would have made a perfect scene for Plymouth to paint. I was inclined to dally, but Holmes insisted we push on as soon as the horses were rested.

We travelled several miles upstream until the thunderous roar from the waterfall was a faint and distant sound.

"We are unlikely to find a better place to camp," said Holmes reigning up. There was still at least two hours of daylight left, but the clearing was idyllic for a campsite.

"Great!" enthused Mrs Plymouth. "I'm going to have me an all over bath."

"That would not be wise, Mrs Plymouth. The river's current is exceedingly strong here. It could be dangerous."

"I'm a strong swimmer."

"I advise against it," he insisted, his ire rising.

"You can advise all you like. I'm having a bath. I itch with trail dust 'til I can't stand it no more." She glared at Holmes, then looked him up and down. "You look like you could do with a bath yourself," she said, somewhat rudely.

Holmes scowled. "A lady does not comment on a gentleman's hygiene."

"A gentleman should not require a comment!" was her tart retort.

He glared back at her. She met his eyes unflinchingly, until Holmes frowned. Then, finally, with a sigh of resignation he said, "Then at least let me pick a suitable place for you."

"All right," she agreed sweetly, in stark contrast to her previous manner. (I knew it would not take him long to learn how to compromise!)

Holmes moved further upstream and found a shallow pool where the water had collected in a circle of rocks. She looked at it dubiously.

"It is well screened by bushes and trees. You will have all the privacy you require and more importantly, it is safe."

"Thank you, Mr Holmes," she said sweetly, dropping her saddle bags down. "I'll start dinner after I've bathed," she called after his departing back.

We quickly set about the routine of making camp for the night. I fed and watered the horses while Holmes gathered the firewood and made a rock fireplace. Suddenly, the peace and tranquillity of our picturesque camp was broken by female screams. Next moment, we saw Mrs Plymouth in the river, being swept along by the current. She waved one bare arm at us and clutched a floating branch with another.

"Blasted woman!" snarled Holmes. "Get the rope, Watson!" He ordered as he pulled off his boots and socks, throwing his hat and coat after them. I collected the rope and handed him one end which he knotted tightly around his waist. He dove into the river as soon as he had done so and swam strongly towards the terrified girl.

I hurriedly tied a loop in my end of the rope and slipped it around my waist to safeguard the lifeline from being accidentally pulled from my grasp.

By the time Holmes reached the log, he was panting with exertion, for he had been swimming sideways against the current to reach her. He grabbed onto the log gratefully.

"You can't come here," she cried. "I'm naked!"

"I'm not here to gawk at you, blast it!" growled Holmes, his irritation plain. "I'm here to rescue you."

"Well, you don't have to be so nasty about it," she replied, her own voice laced with annoyance.

"Now stop this nonsense, move around and latch onto me," he ordered brusquely.

"I–I'm naked," she repeated.

"Fine, I'll leave you to drown then, so as to preserve your modesty," he replied sarcastically.

She glared at him, clutching the tree and trying to remain respectably submerged. They glowered at each other for a moment until Holmes, with one hand clung onto the log and with the other; he awkwardly unbuttoned and removed his shirt. This he thrust at her, growling, "Put it on." Just as awkwardly, she complied while Holmes averted his gaze.

I was running along the bank by this time, trying to keep level with the log. The rope was taut. I chanced to glance up ahead and had a thrill of horror. "Holmes!" I shrieked. "The waterfall!"

Holmes looked up. Not all that far ahead were scattered rocks, indicating the place where the water cascaded over the edge in a thunderous torrent to crash upon the jagged rocks at its base. Holmes quickly manoeuvred himself around the log, not caring if she was adequately covered or not.

"Climb onto my back and hold on," he instructed the frightened girl.

She did as ordered without argument, realizing their danger.

Holmes let go of the log and shouted, "Start pulling, Watson!"

I did. It was no easy task as I was fighting against the current, which was determined to drag them over the waterfall. If the rope had not been secured to my person I would have lost it several times over. As it was, I was nearly dragged into the water and only the sturdy heels of my boots saved me as I dug them into the riverbank.

Holmes assisted as best he could by swimming. Little by little, they came closer to the shore. Finally, it was shallow enough for an exhausted Holmes to stand up. The woman still clung to his back, hanging on like grim death.

He cursed under his breath when he stubbed his toe on a submerged rock as he waded onto the bank. Once on shore, he dumped Mrs Plymouth unceremoniously to the ground, flopping down beside her and panting hard from the effort.

After a few moments, the heaving of his chest settled and he ran a hand through his wet hair, pushing it out of his eyes.

Sarah Plymouth clad only in Holmes' sodden shirt looked at him, a curious expression in her eyes.

Holmes, conscious of her gaze and his bare chest, stood up. "Why didn't you stay in the pool I selected for you?" he demanded.

"It wasn't deep enough for a proper bath," she replied, her voice a little unsteady from her close call.

Holmes looked heavenwards and closed his eyes. "Give me strength!" he said, as if in prayer, before turning to Sarah and saying, "Just *once* I wish you would do what I tell you."

"Well, you're so damn *bossy!*" she returned as a reflex rejoinder, despite being unnerved by the incident. She looked down and bit her lip as tears sprung to her eyes.

Holmes ignored her and began to stride back towards the camp. I held out my hand to her and helped her up.

"Will you be all right, Sarah?" I asked gently.

She blinked her tears back and nodded.

I coiled up the rope and we walked back to the camp together. By the time we reached it, Holmes had already changed out of his wet things and was spreading them over a rock to dry. She hurried past to where she had left her own belongings.

"You could have been a little more sympathetic, Holmes. She could have drowned," I chided.

"And whose fault would that have been?" he said, raising his voice so she could hear. "Confounded woman! Had she listened to me her life would never have been in jeopardy in the first place. She takes after her husband, bumbling jackass that he is!"

"Holmes, that is hardly fair. She is nothing like Plymouth. Look I know this was her fault, but she feels bad enough already. She *knows* she could have got you both killed. Must you rub it in?"

Ten minutes later, Mrs Plymouth rejoined us. She hung Holmes' sodden shirt up on a bush and dropped her saddlebags down by her blanket roll. Silently she set about preparing dinner.

Holmes smoked his pipe just as silently.

Dinner was a rather subdued affair and it was not until after dinner, when Holmes was collecting his now dry clothing that she humbly approached him. "Mr Holmes."

He finished folding his shirt before turning to face her.

"I'm sorry," her eyes were downcast. "I know you hate me. But truly, I didn't mean to cause any trouble. Y…you saved my life today."

"I don't hate you," he denied. "But you are a troublesome female." At her sorrowful look, his features softened and his anger dissipated. "Forget it. Think nothing of it," he said finally. She continued to look up at him and he returned her gaze, studying her face. He tapped her under the chin with one finger and said gently:

"I just wish you would do what I tell you. I do know what I am talking about you know, and it's with your best interests in mind."

She looked contrite. "I know—*now*. I'm sorry. I promise I will do whatever you want me to from now on."

An involuntary smile came unbidden to Holmes' lips. "Hmm. I will believe *that* when I see it."

She smiled tentatively in return; then unexpectedly, stood up on tiptoe and kissed Holmes on the cheek before returning to the fire. He blinked after her in surprise and although I was not sure, I thought I detected a faint flush upon his cheeks.

TWENTY–TWO

The next day proceeded much as had the previous days. Except that Sarah Plymouth was much more subdued and I could not help noticing that she spent a great deal of time studying Holmes, as if seeing him for the first time. If he was aware of her scrutiny, he gave no evidence of it.

On the third day, Holmes discovered sign that Plymouth was subsisting on berries and plant roots.

"At least they're not poisonous," Holmes reassured her.

"And he's not starving," I added.

"I guess, but berries and roots aren't very filling; the poor dear must be wasting away," she sighed.

It was only natural that she was concerned for her husband, but, I noted, she was not as concerned as she had been initially. Whereas her infatuation for Holmes was growing by the day. She jumped to his every command and admired everything he did. At first I considered it rather amusing, but now I was not so sure. After all, she *was* a married woman. I knew Holmes would never take advantage of her, only his attitude towards her had also changed. *He* was much more tolerant of her than he had been, and he even took time out to explain things to her when she asked.

That night, after I rolled into my blankets on one side of the fire and Sarah Plymouth on the other, Holmes sauntered over to a rock to have his last cigarette of the night. I had observed over the last two nights that he was retiring later than the rest of us. The renegades' tracks were much fresher and I believe he was becoming more cautious.

He took responsibility for lighting the fire when we camped and he also selected the wood, the type that would not smoke, so as not to attract attention of the killers. On this particular night, I detected several pinpricks of light in the distance; they were no doubt from our enemy's campfires.

I was half asleep when Mrs Plymouth stirred and rose silently from her blanket. I pretended I was asleep as she padded over on bare feet towards where Holmes sat.

"Mr Holmes," she said, keeping her voice soft, but in the dead silence of the night, even those soft tones carried.

"Mrs Plymouth," he returned.

"Sarah, won't you call me Sarah, please?"

"You should return to your bed Mrs...er...Sarah."

"Sherlock..." At his frown, she amended her words. "Mr Holmes, do you believe that it is possible for a woman to love two men equally as much at the same time?"

That question caused me to prick up my ears and watch them surreptitiously.

Holmes did not look at her, preferring to continue to stare out into the darkness. "No. I do not believe that is possible, unless you are taking it in the context of a mother loving both her husband and son."

"No, I am not and you know it. I believe it *is* possible. If I wasn't married to Cathcar ..."

"You are married," interrupted Holmes, as he turned to face her.

"But if I wasn't?" she hinted.

"You would still be in Harkin's Hollow," he replied, not taking her bait.

She sighed.

"Don't you care for me at all?" she asked, reaching out and taking his hand. I could see Holmes' face in the moonlight. I had always thought of him as a rather stern man. Cold, unemotional, and even ruthless at times; but now, although his expression was serious, there was no harshness or coldness about his features.

"Sarah, I am flattered that you care for me, but you are mistaking gratitude for love. You are grateful that I saved your life and that in turn has become an infatuation in your mind. You are young, only one and twenty and you have been through a traumatic time, what with losing both your father and husband on the same day. It is only natural that you would turn to an older man for comfort."

"You're not so old," she argued.

"Old enough when compared to you, young lady," he replied sternly, causing me to smile. "Anyway, as I was saying; this is just a passing phase. The minute we find your husband you will forget you ever felt anything for me other than irritation."

She smiled up at him. "Okay, I admit I was irritated at first, but you have an awful lot of nice qualities too; although you can be a little overbearing and condescending at times."

Holmes' teeth flashed white in a grin. "And I am set in my ways, work incessantly, have no time for women and smoke too much."

[225]

"No time for women? You should make time. You're missing out on an awful lot, you know."

"Perhaps. Then again, perhaps the best women are already married."

That comment raised my eyebrows a notch, was Holmes actually flirting with her?

"You hope," she returned with a throaty chuckle. "But you never answered my question. Don't you care for me at all, even a little?"

"You are a persistent creature, I will grant you that," he answered, hedging.

She eyed him challengingly, awaiting his reply.

He sighed, pinched out the flame and flicked his cigarette stub away saying, "I admire your courage and determination in the face of adversity and I also admire your independence. I will admit that your company has not been as disagreeable as I initially thought it would be, especially since you have been doing what you are told..." his eyes twinkled as he said the latter, "and you have certainly been no hindrance, but I do not care for you in a...uh...romantic sort of way, if that is what you are after."

She sighed. "Well, I asked for it." Suddenly she smiled impishly and added. "You said it was only natural that I would turn to an older man for comfort, so will you?"

"Er...will I what?"

"Comfort me?"

That had Holmes stumped. "How?"

She moved closer and slipped her arms around him. He quickly straightened up.

"Hold me," she whispered.

Holmes stood helplessly for a moment as she snuggled closer to him, her arms around him tightly. His arms came away from his sides and he held them out, at a momentary loss. With some hesitation, he put his arms around her and held her to him, lowering his head to rest his chin on the top of her head, his eyes closed. They stood like that for a long moment before she eased her grip and pulled back slightly. His arms came away and rested on her shoulders.

"I guess Dr. Watson was right," she said.

"Pardon?"

"You're not really mean, you're just shy."

If Holmes was embarrassed, I could not discern it, equally, I could not tell if he was furious with me or not.

"Er...yes...well...uh...it is time you retired Mrs Ply–uh...Sarah."

"If you will too."

"I will directly," he replied.

"Do you think we will find Cathcart tomorrow?"

"I *hope* so," he replied fervently, causing her to chuckle again. She returned to her blanket roll and snuggled down. Some ten minutes later, Holmes also turned in. Just before rolling onto his side, he said softly. "Goodnight, Watson."

I smiled under my blankets but did not reply.

TWENTY–THREE

The next day I noted the change in Sarah Plymouth's attitude   to Holmes. She no longer stared at him moony-eyed but related to him more as though he were an older brother. I was relieved that the situation had been resolved without developing any possible complications.

It was just after ten o'clock in the morning when we came upon something which gave us new cause for concern.

Holmes, riding ahead of us, held up his hand to halt us. "Stay back," he ordered, dismounting hurriedly. We watched as he studied the ground, following invisible marks. He dropped to one knee and poked at the dirt. He was so engrossed he did not hear the soft footfall behind him; did not notice Sarah's arrival until she gasped.

"That's blood!"

Holmes stood up and quickly draped an arm around her, turning her away from the sight of the blood spots on the ground.

"Watson!"

I hurried forward and took her into my arms to hold her back, so as to leave the sign undisturbed. Holmes continued to follow the trail of blood, while I held the struggling woman.

"Mrs Plymouth, stay steady. Holmes will tell us what he has found when he has finished studying the sign. Just stay patient."

"It's Cathcart's blood, I know it!"

"Maybe, but there is not a lot of it and there is nobody here," I added.

"They could have buried him!" Her voice trembled.

"Carrion like these renegades would not bother with such niceties. If they had murdered him they would
have left his body for nature's predators to devour."

"Oh!" She slumped in my arms and I cursed my tactlessness.

Holmes returned a few moments later and his face was grim. "They have Plymouth," he stated. Seeing her distress, he continued. "From what I can gather, he is still alive. That blood is insignificant, not enough to be from a serious wound, more likely a blood nose, nothing more. There was a small group of renegades here. They came upon him, fought with him, and bloodied his nose. Plymouth tried to run, but they gave chase. He is their captive. They had him tied and he was walking behind their horses."

"Where's his horse?" I asked.

Holmes looked grimmer. "The animal was injured. They secured it tightly to a tree so it could not move. It has been mauled by a bear; there is very little left of it." Holmes passed me his brandy flask and I put it to Sarah's lips. The fiery liquid brought colour to her cheeks.

"He *is* alive," Holmes repeated. "We must push on. We're not all that far behind them, and..." he hesitated a moment before continuing, "from now on, we will eat cold food. It is too dangerous to risk lighting a fire at night."

Our mission had become urgent. For some reason the renegades did not kill Plymouth, but I knew that Holmes, like me, considered it only a matter of time before they tired of their captive. Who would have thought when we started this search that Plymouth would prove to be so singularly elusive?

✠   ✠   ✠

That night we camped in the entrance of a small cave and ate unheated can food. Holmes had us up and moving before first light. This day of travel brought a change in the scenery. What previously had been green and mountainous was now arid and rocky, the landscape barren. We conserved our water, giving some to the animals first and rationing it for ourselves. We did not camp that night until nearly two o'clock in the morning. Holmes was pushing us onward at a relentless pace. We had to cross the desert terrain before our water ran out. By midday the following day, Holmes announced that we had crossed the border into Arizona. I noticed that he was studying his map more frequently than he had been hitherto now.

"There is a town not far ahead," he announced. "If we do not stop for lunch, we will make it before sundown."

We pushed on and just as he predicted we saw ramshackle buildings rising up from the desert sand. There was no smoke coming from the chimneys and it looked particularly desolate.

"That's odd," commented Holmes, frowning.

"It's a ghost town," explained Mrs Plymouth.

"Still, there will be wells," said Holmes and I nodded. Our canteens were empty and neither Holmes nor I had washed or shaved in two days.

Near the edge of the town was a broken signpost. Holmes dismounted and picked up the board. It read, in crude faded letters, *FORTUNA*.

"A mining town," he said, dropping the sign. We stared at the single street. Tumbleweeds rolled down the wide deserted thoroughfare. Hitch rails sagged and most of the rooves had fallen in. The biggest building was an old saloon and it also seemed to be in the best condition. A few doors down was a derelict barn. Half of its front was gone, but the section still standing was in reasonable nick and some of the stalls still had hay in them. There was also a working pump nearby. Sarah found a rusty bucket with a hole in the bottom and plugged it with a rock, making it useable. With the three of us working together, we tended the animals and made them comfortable, before considering our own needs. After all, they were our lifeline. Without our horses we would never make it out of the desert alive. Once they were settled, we made our way towards the saloon.

We were halfway across the street, when a bullet whined over our heads causing us to throw ourselves to the ground in haste.

"Take that, yuh thievin' varmits! Yuh done took it all an' there ain't no more. Come any closer an' I'll put a bullet 'tween yer yeller bellied eyes!" yelled an aggressive, slightly quavery voice.

"Elderly man," said Holmes softly. "Perhaps I can distract him while the two of you run for cover."

Holmes raised himself and called out. "Now

see here my good man, we have nothing to do with the..." He threw himself back into the dust hastily as a bullet sent his hat spinning. That was when Sarah Plymouth took control of the situation.

She stood up and dodged Holmes' hand as he made a grab for her.

"Listen up, you mangy packrat. The sun has scrambled your brains if you think we're renegades. We're not here to steal anything, we just want shelter. Shoot at me and I'll bend the barrel of your rifle over your fat head!" she declared truculently.

The response to her insults was a wheezy chuckle. "Durned if'n you don't sound like my Ellie-May, whose done been gone all these years."

Holmes and I raised ourselves cautiously as a bewhiskered old timer emerged from a ramshackle building that looked as if it was about to collapse at any moment. He wore a grey confederate kepi and an old grey rebel coat. His face was time ravaged by the elements, but his eyes were surprisingly bright.

"How was ah to know if yuh was one of 'em or not?" he said in a heavy southern accent. A relic of a bygone era. He looked us over.

"So the renegades came through here and stole your gold?" asked Holmes, attempting to dust himself off. A crafty look came to the old man's face and I realized then that he was not wholly sane.

I had heard about such men. They spent their entire lives searching for the elusive yellow; wandering the deserts, living in ghost towns; hermits for the most part, senile for the rest. Generally they were considered harmless unless they felt that they or their gold was threatened.

[233]

"Mebbe they did and mebbe they didn't," he replied.

"But you just told us they did," pointed out Holmes reasonably.

"What's it to yuh?" the old prospector challenged, fingering his battered rifle.

"We are hunting them."

"Just you two dudes an' the gal? Huh, an' folks reckon ah'm crazy!"

"They attacked my hometown, killed my father and kidnapped my husband," explained Sarah.

"Thought he was your husband," said the old man nodding towards Holmes. I smiled faintly. Holmes would consider such a comment as an aspersion on his character.

We made our way to the saloon. Contrary to my earlier thought that the prospector was a hermit, our host, once he no longer considered us a threat, proved to be rather gregarious and garrulous. He informed us that there was a bathtub in the kitchen and a working pump in the back yard. Sarah claimed it first, taking the opportunity to cleanse herself of accumulated desert sand and dust. I eagerly anticipated my time, for I itched something dreadful.

The old fossicker's name was Ezekiel Buckett, but we were urged to call him Zeke. He had come to Fortuna in 1866, after the end of the War Between the States. It had been a wide-open town back then, a boom town, much like Lucky Strike. He met his wife here and buried her here ten years later. When the mines petered out he stayed, not wanting to leave his wife's grave. He had some success mining but was cagey about how much he had found. He was originally from Texas and proved it. Whenever he said the word "Texas" he doffed his battered old hat and held it to his chest reverently.

"Tell me, Zeke, you wouldn't happen to have any dynamite on hand, would you?" asked Holmes casually.

"What would you be wantin' with dynamite?"

"I have an idea as to how we can defeat the renegades, recover everything stolen from the citizens of Harkin's Hollow and also recover your gold."

"You want to blow them up, Holmes?" I asked, rather shocked at the thought.

"Not quite, Watson." Holmes fetched out his map. "This is where we are," he said pointing to a dot on the map. The renegades are somewhere between here and Screaming Woman Canyon. And here...," he pointed again, "is Fort Lonsdale."

"Yup, yuh got all that right," agreed Zeke. "I buy mah supplies from the Fort an' try to avoid that blowhard Colonel Sawbitt."

"Why?" Holmes looked at him in surprise.

"He hates Southerners. Hate 'em worse'n pizen. Threatened to toss me inta the pokey 'coz I was wearin' mah grey. Plum unreasonable he was. Claimed I was tree–son–us." He pronounced the last word carefully.

"Treasonous? What nonsense!" I said. "The war ended twenty years ago!"

"Try tellin' the Colonel that."

"Hmm, that could pose a problem, I was going to ask you to bring the army to us, Zeke," frowned Holmes. "On my calculations the renegades will reach the canyon in three days. They are travelling much slower than us. If we can trap them inside the canyon, the army will be able to take them easily. They need to be stopped once and for all so that no other small towns fall victim."

"Cain't argue with that," grunted the old man, "but there ain't no way Sawbitt will come with me."

"That's all right, we will have to go with my alternate plan," replied Holmes.

"What is your plan, Holmes? Surely you don't mean to dynamite the entrance and exit to the canyon?" I asked curiously.

"Only one side, Watson. After they have entered the canyon we blow up that end, then keep them at bay on the other."

"Why not blow up both ends?" I wondered.

"If I blocked both ends it could take days to clear a path through and we won't be able to retrieve the stolen goods until that happens."

"What about Cathcart?" asked Sarah, appearing in the kitchen doorway, drying her hair with a towel. Obviously she had been listening to our conversation as she bathed.

"Ah, yes. I have not yet decided quite what to do about him. It depends on where he is being held and how heavily guarded he is. If possible, I will try to effect a rescue prior to trapping them in the canyon."

"How will we get the army to come?" I queried.

"That will be your problem, Watson, because you are going to fetch them. Sarah, Zeke—that is if you want to come with us, Zeke, and I will keep them bottled up, you will fetch the army back to the canyon where they can engage the criminals. What can you tell me about Fort Lonsdale, Zeke?" asked Holmes turning to the prospector, who looked rather eager at the thought of engaging in a battle once more.

"Like ah said, it's run by Colonel Mortimer Sawbitt, a real horse's neck and a rebel hater to boot. I buy mah supplies from the Sutler's near the fort and steer clear of the ol' coot."

"Well, Watson is not of southern extraction, so perhaps he will have more luck with the Colonel. Now, Zeke, is there any way we can get ahead of the renegades without being seen?"

"Yup. Know me a shortcut. Most folk think the canyon *is* the shortcut, but it ain't. It's hard ridin' though. Yuh reckon you're up to it?"

"If you can do it, then I am sure we can," said Holmes.

"Well ah don't know, what with you two fellers bein' furriners an' all," frowned Zeke doubtfully. "Yuh reckon you're tough enough?"

"Yep, I reckon we are," agreed Holmes easily. It occurred to me that if we stayed in this country too long, Holmes would wind up talking like a frontiersman.

"We'll have ta travel at night," added the prospector. "Too hot crossin' the desert in the day."

"In that case, perhaps we should eat now, have our baths and get some sleep until nightfall."

"Well, yuh can count me in, ah got a score to settle with them bastards, beggin' your pardon, Ma'am," Zeke apologized, doffing his hat to Sarah.

"That is exactly what they are, so no apologies are needed, Zeke." She smiled at him. "Give me half an hour and I'll have dinner on the table," she promised, disappearing back into the kitchen, which also had a working stove. It seemed Zeke used the saloon quite a bit.

"Will you have enough dynamite for Holmes' purpose, Zeke?" I asked.

"Yup, got heaps. Was plannin' on blastin' new tunnels, but when the first one caved in and took a coupla buildings with it, ah figured, ah'd better stick to the hard way of doin' things and never used it."

"Excellent!" Holmes was looking pleased. "Your company will be invaluable, Zeke."

"Well anythin' to get me gold back." He gave Holmes a gapped toothed grin which Holmes returned.

"What if the army Colonel will not come, Holmes?" I asked when we had finished eating and Zeke had disappeared into his hidey-hole or wherever he lived in this town.

"He will have to, Watson. I will be counting on you. The army is crucial to my plan, after all there is no way the three of us can stop sixty renegades on our own."

I sighed. Sometimes Holmes' faith in me was more than my faith in myself. He read my mind again and clapped me on the back.

"Buck up, old chap. I wouldn't ask you to do this if I didn't know it was well within your capabilities."

"Thank you, Holmes," I said, pleased at his compliment, though unfortunately like always, he ruined it.

"Besides, there is no one else I can send. The Colonel hates southerners, so he would never listen to Mr Buckett. And I could never send a woman on such a mission, alone, across the desert at night. You are the only one left."

"Thanks very much, Holmes," I replied, my tone a little bitter at his comment. He looked at me, faintly amused before adding:

"That is why I like it when you accompany me on difficult cases, Watson; it is always good to have someone you know you can implicitly rely on to be at your back."

I glanced at him. Holmes was an expert at the backhanded compliment, but his last statement seemed sincere. "Really?" I asked, wondering if he would re-nege again.

"Yes, really. Why, Watson, if you had not been here with me, I would have had to marry Fat Beaver!" The amusement fairly twinkled in his eyes as he teased me.

"Her name was Plump Beaver," I corrected, but his humour was infectious and I could not stay an-noyed with him for long. "All joking aside, Holmes, I promise I will not fail you." I swore.

"You never have yet, that is why you are such an erstwhile companion." I felt a flush of pleasure at his praise, which I considered was genuine this time and swore solemnly to myself that I would not falter.

We settled down and slept for the next few hours, only to be woken by Zeke's whistling as he loaded his donkey. Actually he called it a burro, which was sort of a cross between a donkey and a mule. He seemed to have packed up all his worldly possessions. On noticing our questioning glances he said:

"Ah figured it was time ah left this place and went home to Texas." (more obligatory hat doffing).

[239]

"When ah get mah gold back ah can git home in style."

Holmes smiled. "Seems like a jolly good idea," he agreed.

We rode throughout the night, Zeke riding double with Sarah as his burrow was so heavily laden and only stopped to rest the horses at intervals. By the time the sun rose, we were well out of the desert and into rocky terrain.

"See that," said Zeke pointing. We looked and could see smoke spirals. "That's them thievin' polecats."

"We are well ahead of them," said Holmes rubbing his hands together in satisfaction. "Excellent!"

We dismounted and watered the horses, before helping ourselves to cans of food. Holmes moved away from the horses and sat down upon a rock. There was a faint rattling sound which I was unfamiliar with. Then I had the shock of my life, for young Sarah had drawn her gun and pointed it straight at Holmes.

"Don't move, Mr Holmes," she said, her voice low with grim warning. Holmes looked startled as he stared down the barrel of her revolver. Without warning she pulled the trigger. It wasn't until she actually fired that Holmes moved and when he did so I realized that she was not shooting at him, but slightly beyond him. A long snake with a diamond patterned skin and a strange tail had loomed up behind Holmes, disturbed by his presence. Sarah's shot had taken its head clean off.

"Rattlesnake?" asked Holmes, looking at it.

"Sure enough. You woke it when you sat there."

Holmes smiled at Sarah. "Thank you, Sarah. I take back any aspersions I may have cast upon your shooting ability. You saved my life."

She smiled warmly at him. "Guess we're even then, huh?"

"I guess we are," he replied, a new respect in his eyes for the young woman.

We were not used to meeting women of such skill and courage. The frontier women were a different breed from their pampered city cousins. Truth to tell, I found this strong independent streak to be rather becoming and Sarah was no less feminine for it, despite how unconventionally she was dressed.

After we finished our cold breakfast, Holmes turned to me. "Do you feel up to starting out for the Fort now, Watson?"

"Of course, Holmes." I replied, trying to look eager, although I would have preferred having a nap. The sun was already beating down unbearably upon us and I wished I wore a Stetson like Holmes. The wider brim on his hat gave his face more protection from the merciless sun than did my Homburg. My nose was already red and blistering. On Zeke's advice, I knotted his spare bandanna around my face to protect my sore nose from further damage.

"We shall make the canyon later today. The outlaws should be there late tomorrow and from what Zeke says, they will probably camp inside the canyon, giving us a little time up our sleeves, but you will have to arrive with the reinforcements by the very next day at the latest. I will dynamite the far end, so the renegades cannot reverse, but it will only be the two of us,

[241]

three if we count Sarah, holding them at bay at other end and that is where you must bring the army."

"I understand, Holmes," I replied. "Can you give me some directions as to the quickest way to the Fort, Zeke?"

He did as asked and also gave me directions back to the far end of the canyon. I wrote it all down in my notebook so I would not forget. Unlike Holmes I did not have an infallible memory.

"That is perfect, Zeke. Anything else I should know?"

"Yup." The old man dug out a battered confederate flag. "Take this with yuh for good luck, and if'n that mean ol' colonel won't come, wave this in his face an' he'll soon come arunnin' after yuh."

I did not particularly want the flag but could not refuse it for to do so would offend the old fellow.

"Thank you, Zeke; I will treat it like the crown jewels." I shook hands with him and Holmes.

"Good luck, Doc," said Sarah, giving me a kiss on the cheek. "And don't worry. I'll look after Mr Holmes."

"After your recent demonstration, I'm sure you will," I said returning her smile.

TWENTY–FOUR

After I rode away from the others, it did not take long to be overwhelmed by the awesome desolation surrounding me. I was very much alone in this strange country. While I was not afraid of getting lost; Zeke's directions had been crystal clear, I still felt overshadowed, minuscule even, amongst the towering red buttes. They were certainly magnificent to look at and I could imagine Plymouth's artistic heart yearning to paint the scene which stretched before me, but like Holmes, instead of seeing its grandeur I saw only the obstacles in my path.

Mindful of the time limit, I only stopped to rest the horse and chew on jerky. It was reassuring when I came upon Zeke's first listed landmark, Needle Rock, which needless to say fitted its name. I was feeling very tired by this time as we had been on the move since midnight, nevertheless, I forced myself to keep going. If Holmes could go for several days without sleep when puzzling some deep criminal enigma, then surely I could go without for something even more perilous. I knew how little chance Holmes and the others had once they trapped the renegades in the canyon. Three rifles and a few dozen sticks of dynamite would not contain them for long. They were well and truly outnumbered, and I was also worried to as to how Holmes was going to rescue Plymouth without endangering his own life unnecessarily.

The sun had just set as I rode into the dusty civilian settlement that had sprung up around the fort.

[243]

I was tired, sunburned, thirsty and hungry, but decided to approach the fort commander first so as to give him time to organize his forces.

I rode up to the gate and was halted by a smartly dressed young soldier in blue. He held up his rifle and gave the traditional order, "Halt who goes there?"

"Dr John Watson to see Colonel Sawbitt," I announced, adding, "It is a matter of considerable urgency."

He looked me over dubiously. I realized I probably looked none too impressive, being rather toil worn and covered in trail dust with nearly two days growth of beard. However, my voice and manner must have convinced him for he called for his superior, a fresh faced lieutenant to take me to the Colonel's office.

I was led into an outer room and asked to wait as the Lieutenant announced me. A moment later, he held the door open for me to enter.

The Colonel, a white bearded man with cold blue eyes glared at me frostily and eyed me up and down as if I were a sewer dweller that had crawled to the surface.

"Doctor...Watson, was it?" he asked.

"Yes." I replied. I did not offer my hand, for his manner discouraged such courtesy.

"Hmm," he muttered, still eyeing me in disgust.

"Excuse my appearance but I have ridden long and hard on a matter of some urgency," I said, helping myself to a seat. I wasn't going to stand in front of him like some errant schoolboy.

"What's the emergency, Doctor? The Apache

[244]

kid?"

"Who?"

He scowled at my ignorance. "You aren't here to report an Indian attack?

"Oh—no, not at all. I am here to report that there is a large group of renegades headed this way. They attacked the township of Harkin's Hollow in Colorado and are now in Arizona. There are at least fifty to sixty of them. They have also kidnapped the son of Sir Eustace Plymouth, one of the richest and most important men in England."

"England! You're English!" He made the words sound as if they were something vile and foul tasting.

"Why...uh, yes." I was a little confused by his attitude.

"I was wondering what that damned foreign accent was!"

"Well, really Sir, there is no need to be so insulting!" My hackles rose. "I came here in good faith, asking for your help to apprehend these renegades and..."

"Damn Britishers," he swore luridly, "you're as bad as they are!"

Now I was really confused. "What? Who?"

"In the war, you damn Britishers were on the side of those rebel scum. You sold them guns in exchange for cotton. Don't think I don't know. You're as bad as they are, worse even! The whole lot of 'em should have been wiped out!" His face was red and almost apoplectic with anger. "Simpson!" he roared. The young Lieutenant ran in. "Throw this bum out!"

"Now see here Sorebutt..." I began in protest,

my face also becoming red.

"What?" He raged at my accidental mispro-
nunciation of his name.

"If the name fits...!" I returned hotly.

"Out!" roared the other.

Two hefty soldiers came running in on the
Lieutenant's command and I was grabbed by the arms
and unceremoniously dragged out and tossed outside
the compound gates. As I sat in the dirt, spluttering
with indignation and rage, a second feeling came over
me. *Failure.* I had failed Holmes. I could not bring the
soldiers to the rescue. I felt so utterly miserable that I
could easily have sobbed like a girl-child.

Seeing the curious look of the young soldier
on guard duty at the gate, I picked myself up with as
much dignity as I could muster and said to him, "Your
Colonel is a pompous ass!"

"Yes Sir," he said, grinning and giving me a
salute.

His agreement did little to improve my mood. I
led my horse to the nearest livery stable for care and
made my way to the Sutler's. Here I bought a meal
and a large whiskey. What was I to do? I had to bring
help. That stupid, prejudiced Colonel would never listen to reason. He hated southerners and he hated the
British and he was not prepared to listen to anyone of
those persuasions. He did not care that a gang of mur-
derous felons were advancing this way. The man was
a complete imbecile! I drowned my sorrows, ignoring
the curious stares of the other patrons, many of them
off-duty soldiers.

I had been there for a little over two hours
when an old prospector, much like Zeke in appearance

arrived.

"Hey Buck," greeted one of the soldiers, "Seen anymore pink Injuns?"

"Git off with yuh," growled the old man to their teasing. I returned to the bar for a refill.

"Why are they picking on that poor old man?" I asked the bartender.

"Fool got high on rotgut. Came stormin' into the fort claimin' there was hundreds of Injuns on the warpath and headed this way. The colonel got his troops ready and charged out."

"So?"

"You know what they found?"

"No, what?"

"Three squaws and a papoose squatting round a campfire."

"Oh."

"The old fool was lucky he cleared off 'fore they got back. Sawbitt would have tossed him in the guardhouse for life. Ain't nothin' he hates more'n civilians wastin' his time."

"Except perhaps ex–rebels and the British," I returned.

"Tangled with him have yuh?" asked the bartender.

"Yes." I put some money on the bar and said, "Give the old fellow a drink on me." I then returned to my seat, an idea slowly beginning to take shape in my mind.

The old prospector accepted the complimentary drink and downed it quickly before coming over to my table to thank me.

"Join me, won't you," I offered, the idea

strengthening.

"Me name's Buck Trimble," he offered.

"Dr. John Watson," I returned. "I wonder Mr Trimble; you are a prospector are you not?"

"Yup, been prospectin' for nigh on thirty years."

"I don't suppose you would happen to have any dynamite?"

"Nope. Got me a half tin of blastin' powder," he offered. My eyes lit up.

"That would do. Would you be willing to sell it?"

The old fellow gave me a toothless grin. "Depends what yuh want it fer," he said slyly.

"Let's just say I have a score to settle with a certain bullnecked Colonel who shall remain nameless," I replied, smiling faintly.

"In that case, yup, I'll sell you me powder. I'll even thrown in all me fuse as well."

With our business concluded to our mutual satisfaction, I returned to the stable and for a small fee, the owner let me sleep in the loft for the next few hours. There was nothing I could do until after the fort had settled down for the night. It was risky what I was planning, but it was the only way I could think of to get old Sorebutt to follow me. I smiled at the mangling of his name, it certainly fit.

I dozed quite contentedly until eleven p.m., after which time I quietly saddled my horse, checked, and fused the tin of gun powder and dug Zeke's flag out, stowing it in my pocket for quick access. I rode around to the back of the Fort and secured my horse. It would not do for it to wander off.

Using the rope I had procured earlier, I made a loop and tossed it up over one of the wooden spikes of the Fort's back fence. It only took minutes to scale the stockade and climb over, and as I cleared the top I ducked quickly so as not to be seen by the night sentries. Fortunately it was dark and the moon was obscured by drifting clouds. Next, I went to the centre of the compound, dodging behind water troughs and parked wagons as I made my way closer to the flagpole. There was no flag flying on it at this time of night, it having been removed as per military custom. With a bit of fumbling, I managed to run Zeke's battered relic of the extinct confederacy up the pole.

With the first part of my task completed, I entered the colonel's office which providentially for me was not locked. I lit a candle stub and placed it under the desk so as to shield its light, along with sheets of paper, pen, and ink that I found on the desk. I ducked down under and printed out in big letters: *RULE BRITANNIA!*

Using medical adhesive to join the pages together, I strung them up behind his desk like a proud banner. I could not help grinning as I did this. If that did not get him pot boiling mad, my final act of vandalism should be enough to set them chasing me.

I snuck outside and made my way to the officer's latrine. Picking the central one, I dug in the dirt behind it and buried my can of blasting powder beneath its back wall. I made a little furrow and ran my fuse along it, covering it up as I went. I had been fortunate that old Buck Trimble had so much fuse and that he had been willing to part with it. Of course it helped when he knew I was going to use it on Colonel

Sawbitt. The fuse reached the side of the stable, so I just covered the end of it with a rock to keep the morning dew off it. As there was nothing more I could do until daylight, I made use of the stable, finding an empty stall to sleep in.

The trumpeting of reveille woke me. A glance at my watch told me it was five in the morning. I splashed water onto my face from a nearby bucket and went cautiously outside. There was still very little activity in the yard and as yet no one had noticed the red and blue flag flying proudly in the morning breeze.

I grinned with malicious pleasure in anticipation of my next act. I had always been an honest, law abiding citizen, but there was a certain thrill of excitement that came with breaking the law.

Bleary eyed soldiers were moving to the ablutions hut and patronizing the latrines. It seemed like now would be the ideal time to give them a wake-up blast. I fished my matches out and lit the fuse. It spluttered to life immediately and the thin covering of dirt over it did nothing to quench its flame. I leaned against the side of the stable wall and waited.

I was not disappointed. There came a roar as the can exploded. The central latrine flew up into the air from the force of the explosion, only to come crashing down several feet away, splintering into pieces. Seated on the latrine, his face as red as the end I was unfortunate enough to view was none other than Colonel Sawbitt.

He leapt up but tripped over his pants which were still down around his ankles. I showed myself briefly, saluted him and called, "God save the Queen!" Then I took to my heels and raced towards the ladder leading up to the back wall where my horse waited.

"Get him!" screamed the Colonel, but it was no use, for the soldiers were confused and disorientated at the unexpected attack. Pandemonium reigned. I quickly untied my horse and mounted, leaving a trail of dust in my wake. It wouldn't take them too long to get organized and there was no doubt that the irate Colonel would come after me personally, more importantly, he would not come alone.

When I finally stopped to rest the horse, I picked a high vantage point and viewed my back trail. Sure enough, there was a large dust cloud following my route. I grinned with pleasure.

✠ ✠ ✠

It was mid–afternoon when I heard gunfire interspersed with explosions. "Holmes!" The battle to keep the renegades boxed in had begun and only three people (four if they had managed to rescue Plymouth) stood between sixty killers and freedom. I spurred my horse to additional speed and prayed that the soldiers would not tarry.

Even as I rode, I drew my carbine from the saddle boot with one hand. As I came level with the canyon's natural gateway, I dismounted, quickly grabbed my saddled bag (it contained my spare ammunition and medical supplies), gave the horse a slap to send it on its way before dashing behind the nearest boulder for cover.

Glancing up, I saw Holmes as he stood up momentarily to throw a stick of dynamite. The moment he tossed his lethal missile, he spun and dropped suddenly as if struck by a bullet.

"Holmes!" I yelled. "I'm coming!" I was about to leave the cover of the rocks and attempt to climb up to where the others were, but Holmes' face appeared around the side of one of the rocks they were sheltering behind.

"Stay where you are, Watson. It's just a scratch. Where's the army?"

"Coming, they are not far behind me." I replied and hoped fervently that I was right.

At that moment a swarthy bearded face appeared before me, levelling a revolver. I brought my rifle up and fired. He collapsed his head bloody. I stayed on my guard after that and fired at anyone trying to exit the canyon on foot.

Ten minutes later, the gunfire was interrupted by the sound of bugles tooting out the command for charge. Despite my antipathy for the arrogant Colonel, I had to admit they made an awe-inspiring sight as they came charging forward, sabres drawn. I thought it prudent that I remain concealed as they swept past me into the canyon and within minutes were engaged in mortal combat with the surviving renegades. Feeling it was now safe to do so; I slung my saddle bag over my shoulder and made my way up to where the others were.

A short climb brought me to their position. Holmes grinned wearily at me, and Zeke clapped me on the back. Sarah Plymouth, brandishing an empty rifle blew me a kiss and sitting off to one side was none other than the elusive Cathcart Plymouth. He had a split lip and a black eye and was looking a little undernourished, but otherwise he was well enough. It also appeared that he had not taken part in the fighting.

I moved over to Holmes. His left sleeve was torn and bloody, but he had Sarah's neckerchief bound around his arm.

"I might as well tend your wound, Holmes," I said, fishing out my medical kit.

"Good to see you, Watson," he replied, rolling up his sleeve. "Did you have any trouble getting the soldiers to come?"

"Some. They will probably want to arrest me. I blew up the Colonel's latrine and ran Zeke's flag up the flagpole. He hates the British as much as he hates southerners."

"You blew up his latrine? My dear fellow!" Holmes was astounded.

"While he was on it," I added, unable to stop the wicked grin which sprung to my lips.

"You are shameless, Watson," chuckled Holmes.

"Well doggone it Doc, if yuh ain't the livin' wonder!" exclaimed Zeke. "Yuh say mah flag's a flyin' in the Fort?"

"Yes, Zeke, on the main flagpole."

"Hee hee," wheezed the old timer gleefully. "Ah wish ah could have seen ol' Sawbitt's face when he saw that."

"And I called him Sorebutt when I lost my temper," I confessed, still grinning.

Holmes smiled again. "Watson, I let you out of my sight for two days and you turn into a positive villain."

"Perhaps we should escape now, while the soldiers are busy," I suggested.

"We can't. We have to retrieve what was stolen from Harkin's Hollow," replied Holmes. "Don't worry, Watson. I won't let the bigoted blowhard arrest you."

"He'll probably arrest you too," I muttered mournfully, fearing that the Colonel was one character Holmes would not be able to sway. I cleaned and bandaged his arm which was, as he had said, little more than a scratch. Considering the odds, they had fared remarkably well. Of course, the dynamite helped. It not only threw the bandits into confusion, but also accounted for a great many of their number.

By this time the sound of shooting had diminished to the occasional sporadic burst as the remaining outlaws paid dearly for their lives. The soldiers proved to be the ultimate victors.

We waited for the rounding up process to begin before entering the canyon. When Sawbitt saw me, he roared and came galloping over, with several blue uniformed men following.

"Arrest that man!" He demanded.

Holmes moved forward and stopped in front of me, but it was to no avail. One burly bellicose soldier knocked him from his horse before he could even voice a protest and a wild melee broke out. More soldiers came over as Holmes and I defended ourselves vigorously.

Old Zeke joined in with a wild rebel yell and young Plymouth tried, but was knocked out almost immediately. His wife took exception to that and leapt upon the back of the soldier who did it, scratching at him and screaming abuse in the most unladylike language I have ever been privileged to hear. Chaos reigned until we were brought down by sheer weight of numbers.

"What is the meaning of this atrocious attack?" demanded Holmes, sounding imperious, even if he did not look it, with one eye blackened and a cut lip.

"You are all under arrest!" exclaimed Sawbitt triumphantly.

Holmes straightened up to his full imposing height; his grey eyes glittering, boding ill for the bumptious Colonel.

"'Ten–shun!" He roared, causing Colonel Sawbitt to stiffen to attention involuntarily. "You call yourself a soldier!" Holmes continued while I glanced at him in surprise. His voice had taken on the unmistakable twang that is so characteristic of the American accent.

"You attack citizens for no reason! You need to be coerced to engage the enemy in battle, and more importantly, you set your dogs upon *me*!"

"Uh...!" The Colonel was looking stunned, clearly quite overawed by Holmes' manner.

"And if that wasn't enough, you create an international incident by harassing a British subject who appealed to you for assistance!" Holmes glared at the Colonel who seemed to have shrunk into himself.

"Well, what have you to say for yourself? Hmm, huh? It had better be good because when Washington hears of this outrage...!"

"Uh...well...uh..." stammered the Colonel.

"Well man, don't stand there stammering like an imbecile. You do know who I am, do you not?"

[255]

demanded Holmes.

"Uh...no."

"What! Your stupidity knows no bounds! I am General Baines Smithfield–Jackson, first Adjutant to the President of these United States!" As Holmes announced his imaginary title with flourish, I noticed Sarah staring at him wide-eyed. She had never seen him in action before. I had and was having a difficult time controlling my mounting laughter. My face underwent a series of contortions as I tried to keep an expression of righteous indignation on it.

"Oh, yes, yes, of course I have heard of *you,* Sir!" gasped Colonel Sawbitt, lying through his teeth. "I didn't recognize you, Sir. You're not in uniform."

"Of course not, you bilious buffoon. I am in mufti!"

"Mufti?"

"If I escorted these people in full dress uniform, it would bring attention to our group. This is a mission of considerable importance, the less people who know of it the better."

"Er...yes, Sir," muttered Sawbitt, thoroughly cowed by Holmes' manner and assumed rank. "I am sorry, Sir. I didn't know. Er...what is your mission?"

"Do you think I am at liberty to inform every two–bit petty officer of my assignment?" Holmes was playing a big-shot army General to the hilt.

"Er...uh..." stuttered the other.

Holmes continued to glower; then, as if relenting, he said, "This gentleman whom you have treated so cavalierly, is none other than the eminent British entomologist, Dr. John Watson. He is here at the request of our government to find a solution to the cock-

[256]

roach plague in Colorado."

The Colonel blinked in surprise. "But there are no cockroaches in Colorado," he said.

"That is because he has been successful!" returned Holmes triumphantly, not missing a beat, despite his blunder. "However, that is neither here nor there. We detoured when we encountered these renegades. Naturally I took control of the situation and sent Dr. Watson to fetch you, and what did you do, you threw him out!"

Sawbitt scowled and whined to Holmes, "But, Sir, he tried to murder me."

"Nonsense!"

"No, true. He blew up my personal latrine. I was sitting on it at the time. He should be hung for that."

"It is you who should be hung," I returned hotly, "for exposing your oversized rear to innocent bystanders!"

The Colonel turned red and spluttered incoherently for a moment.

"The Doctor has told me all about that incident and your unsightly exposure. As you refused to listen to him, let alone help him, he had to take extreme measures to ensure that you pursued him and arrived in time to help. I am sure it is going to take all my diplomatic skills to mollify the good doctor *and* the British government when they hear of how you treated one of their citizens. When President Cleveland is informed of this you will be lucky if you are not busted back to private and on stable duty for the rest of your natural life!" Holmes threatened.

"Please, Sir, it was all a misunderstanding. I

had no idea you had anything to do with him. H–he never mentioned your name...I will do whatever I can to make amends. Dr. Watson, please accept my sincerest apologies ..." The Colonel was almost grovelling. It was a pleasant change.

I sniffed. "I may accept your apology Colonel Sorebutt, but only on one condition. I would like you to add two more flagpoles to your Fort and fly the confederate and British flags every Sunday for the rest of the year. It would symbolize your new attitude. I have never encountered a career officer with such an all-consuming bigotry of a vanquished enemy such as our good friend Ezekiel Buckett represents. As for how you treated me, *well!*"

Holmes nodded approvingly. "Yes, Doctor, that sounds like a reasonable request. Sawbitt, you will do as he says. I will be sending officers periodically to check that you are adhering to this new ruling. *They* will be in mufti too and if they report any ill-treatment or bigotry on your part, then you will be hearing from me."

"Yes, Sir. Anything you say, Sir," agreed Sawbitt eagerly.

"Very well. Now, Mrs Plymouth can identify the property of the people of Harkin's Hollow. I trust that you will organize for a detachment to deliver the horses and supplies back to the town. We will personally take charge of the stolen money."

"And I want mah gold," piped up Zeke.

The Colonel glared at him but dared not say a thing.

"Naturally, Mr Buckett," said Holmes deferentially. "You, Colonel, will take care of the dead and wounded renegades and I expect you to send a detail to unblock the entrance to this canyon. My group will ride on ahead as we have business to attend elsewhere."

"Yes, Sir," replied the Colonel, throwing Holmes a smart salute. Holmes returned it, appearing every inch the professional soldier.

"You won't mention this incident to the President; will you, General Jackson, Sir?"

"That's Smithfield-Jackson." Holmes corrected, glaring frostily at the Colonel.

"Sorry, my apologies, Sir."

"If you accede to the doctor's request, I am willing to overlook your ineptitude in this matter, and if he in turn is willing to drop any charges he may have laid against you for your assault, I do not see any need for the matter to go further."

"Yes, Sir! Thank you, Sir!"

Sarah Plymouth quickly set about identifying the property of the citizens of Harkin's Hollow, while I took a look at Cathcart Plymouth, who was only now beginning to rise.

By the time we had the bank money secured to Holmes' saddle and Zeke had loaded his gold onto his mule, Sarah came riding up leading a pair of horses. "I collected a horse for you, Zeke; I thought you could ride it home. It belonged to one of the outlaws. He won't be needing it anymore and it will save you riding double with one of us. The other horse is for Cathcart."

"Thank yuh, Missy," replied the old Prospector, grinning from ear to ear.

We parted from the soldiers soon after, travelling for quite a while so as to put as much distance between us as we could. We had no desire to encounter Sawbitt again. Our destination was Harkin's Hollow as Sarah and Plymouth wanted to pack up their possessions before returning to England with us.

TWENTY–FIVE

It was not until we made camp the following night that I had the opportunity to ask Holmes how he had rescued Plymouth from the renegades.

"I would rather listen to your story, Watson," he countered.

"I have already told you pretty much what happened at the Fort, Holmes," I replied dismissing my escapades. "I am more interested to know how you managed to get young Plymouth away.

"Oh, very well. After you left us, we made our way to the canyon and located the ideal position to camp. I left Zeke in charge and returned up the trail until I could see the outlaws. I remained hidden until they made camp. It was actually rather easy as they had been imbibing copiously of the stolen whiskey, including the Indian members of the band. I had been worried about them, for had the Indians been on sentry duty, my task would have been an extremely perilous one. The guards were the soberest of the lot and frankly that's not saying much.

"Plymouth had been tied to a tree well away from the fire. In fact, there was no one near him at all. I simply crept up from behind and cut his bonds free. He crawled behind the tree and we returned to my horse. I doubt if they even noticed he was missing until daylight. They certainly did not fear him and they never bothered to even look for him.

I nodded. "Then what happened?"

"I reunited him with his lovely wife. While

they were thus occupied, Zeke and I rigged one end of the canyon with some of his dynamite sticks. When the outlaws rode into the canyon, I lit the fuse and blocked the entrance. While they twisted about in confusion I ran along the rim of the canyon and rejoined the rest of the group at the opposite end where you found us. You should have heard the roar the explosion made, Watson, it near deafened me. It will take the army quite a while to clear the blockage.

"It took some time for the renegades to realize that they were trapped, when they did, they made their way to the exit, but a few sticks of dynamite strategically thrown held them at bay. It was most fortunate you turned up when you did, old fellow, for I used up the last stick just as you arrived and our ammunition was running low."

Holmes explained all this matter-of-factly, but in my imagination I could visualize him creeping silently upon the outlaw's camp at great personal risk. The outlaws would not have treated him quite as leniently as they apparently had treated Plymouth. This train of thought raised a question.

"Mr Plymouth," I said, turning to the young man sitting with his arm around his smiling wife. "Why did the renegades take you prisoner? I would have thought that they would have been more inclined to kill you."

"They were going to, Doctor, but I told them I had a very rich father and was worth more to them alive than dead. They planned on ransoming me. I had hoped to be able to escape long before then, but they kept me securely bound and only fed me enough to keep me alive. I cannot tell you how delightful it was to hear a fellow countryman's voice whispering to me in the darkness. It was like a miracle. I thought I was the only Englishman in the state."

I smiled. "Well you certainly led us on a merry chase, young Plymouth.'

"It is over now, Doctor. Sarah and I have been talking. There is nothing to hold her here anymore and she is more than willing to come to England with me. I would like to see father again, although in the past we haven't always seen eye-to-eye. I think this time he will have to admit I have done something right. The smartest thing I have done since coming to this country was to marry Sarah. I... well, I wasn't too successful prior to that." He gave his wife a hesitant smile and squeezed her around the waist.

She smiled tolerantly back.

I managed to conceal my own amusement at his words. "I am sure he will approve your choice of partner, but you have other talents as well. All you have to do is show him one of your paintings, they are most impressive. You have a rare talent young man."

"Do you really think so?"

"Indeed I do," I replied warmly.

"I agree with Watson," added Holmes. "You have a great future ahead of you as an artist."

✠   ✠   ✠

It took us four days to reach Harkin's Hollow; the return journey being much quicker than the outward one, as we no longer had to proceed with caution or follow tracks. A crowd turned out to greet us and Sarah was quick to tell them of our involvement in capturing the renegades. Their thanks and praise were effusive and overwhelming. Holmes and I received many a handshake, and slaps on the back. Knowing how much Holmes hated such ostentatious displays of gratitude, as opposed to warm appreciation of his art, it was sheer torture for him. To his credit, he endured it with seeming good humour.

I made a round of my patients to ensure that they were all recovering and also came in for my fair share of additional gratitude from them. We once again stayed at McKee's house, preferring to let the young couple have the
night to themselves.

✠   ✠   ✠

The next day we helped load a covered wagon with Sarah's belongings and Plymouth's paintings. We had decided to travel cross country to Phoenix and board a train there for New York. Plymouth did not want to return to Denver for fear of encountering the banker's daughter. She had frightened him terribly. I also did not want to retrace our steps in case we encountered Red Feather's band. Holmes was the only one who was disappointed as he wouldn't have minded seeing the old trapper, Foster Keehoe again.

Our parting was delayed by a tearful Sarah as she bid farewell to the friends and neighbours she had known all her life, consequently it was late morning before we were finally on the move. Ezekiel Buckett decided to stay in Harkin's Hollow for a few days. He, too, had been given a hero's welcome and was lapping up the attention. He said he was going to return to

Texas, but I had a feeling he would end up staying in this sociable little town for his remaining years. Certainly he could do a lot worse.

Over the next two days our journey progressed uneventfully as we made our way to the Arizona border again. I was thankful that our route to Phoenix would take us nowhere near Fort Lonsdale. I had no desire to see the bumptious Colonel Sawbitt again. Once in a lifetime was enough for me.

It was on the third night, as we made camp that Holmes pulled me aside just after dinner. "Watson, we are being followed."

"What?" I was astonished. Holmes glanced at the Plymouths, noting that they seemed to be engrossed with each other. Pulling me by the sleeve he led me away from the fire.

'Shield your eyes against the light from the fire and look up there," he instructed. I did. Faintly in the distance was a small star of light that winked and flickered. "It's a campfire," Holmes explained, not that it needed explaining.

"What makes you think they're following us?" I asked. "After all, there is no law against other travellers camping out."

"I spotted them yesterday but was not one hundred per cent sure that they were not just innocent travellers and I saw no evidence of their campfire during the night. They would have been approximately where we were last night. Our fire glow would have been visible for miles when we camped there, so should theirs have been, but I did not see it. They took care not to let their fire be seen."

"Perhaps they just found a better camp site

than us," I argued, not wholly convinced. I felt that the adventures of the past few months had made Holmes overly suspicious of everyone and everything.

"I concede Watson that it is possible that those travellers yonder may have nothing to do with us, but there is no harm in taking precautions, after all, this is a dangerous country for the unwary."

"Agreed, Holmes. So what do you want me to do?"

"Do not mention it to the Plymouths. There is no point in worrying them needlessly."

It was all right for me to worry though, I thought wryly.

"However," continued Holmes, "we should keep an eye on our back trail. Tomorrow I propose to make a little detour. If those travellers also make the detour, you will have to admit that I am right."

"Very well, Holmes," I agreed. Tomorrow Holmes would realize that he was wrong and that the other campers were on their way to Phoenix, just as we were. Whether he admitted it or not was another matter.

We returned to the campsite.

"Everything all right, Mr Holmes?" asked Plymouth.

"Yes. Watson and I were merely admiring the nocturnal fauna."

"Cathcart has been telling me all about England," enthused Sarah.

"I am sure you will enjoy it," I said, smiling at her. "You will be the Queen of Plymouth castle."

"Cathcart says he's met the Queen. She was a guest of his father once."

"Holmes has met Her Majesty also," I bragged.

"Are you an aristocrat, Mr Holmes?" Sarah asked, big eyed.

At times he certainly behaved like one I thought, so it was an understandable mistake.

"No. I am of the common lot. On occasion Queen Victoria has availed herself of my professional services," Holmes replied.

"You must be pretty good at what you do," said Sarah. "Uh...what do you do, exactly? I don't think I ever asked."

"I am a consulting detective. When the official police come unstuck or other private enquiry agents need help they come to me, tell me their problems and I am usually able to put them on the right track."

"That's why Cathcart's father hired you?"

"Yes."

"He wanted the best," I added, "and Holmes is certainly the best in England and Europe."

Sarah smiled and added, "And in America too."

"You must be exceptional for father to select you. He's very fussy, to put it mildly. Tell me, Mr Holmes, did you and Dr. Watson have much trouble in tracing me?" asked Plymouth.

"No, not really. Your trail was rather easy to follow."

I smiled at Holmes' reply, believing it unwise to mention that path of burnt out destruction he had left in his wake wherever he roamed.

TWENTY–SIX

The next day Holmes took me aside and gave me directions as to which way I should go. I took the lead and Holmes brought up the rear of our little wagon train if you could call one wagon that.

Towards mid-afternoon, he suggested he try hunting for some fresh meat. Ordinarily that task would have been mine, but this, I knew was merely an excuse on his part to check our back trail.

Some two hours later we heard a rifle bark twice in quick succession. When we came to a fork in the road, I motioned for Plymouth to take the left turning, deliberately positioning myself and my horse in front of a large rock, which had the words PHOENIX and an arrow carved into it. Holmes wanted us to detour, so detouring we were.

About an hour later as I was leading the buckboard into a clearing suitable for camping, Holmes rejoined us. He had two rabbits slung from his saddle.

"Not much luck I am afraid," he said in greeting. "Still rabbit stew is better than nothing." He left the rabbits with Sarah and joined me as we tended the horses. Plymouth was not overly adept at animal handling I had noted, so I sent him to gather firewood instead, although it would be Sarah who lit it.

"Any luck, Holmes?" I asked softly.

"They detoured, Watson," he replied just as softly.

"Did you get a good look at them?"

"Not their faces. There are four of them, but

they were too far away. What I did see was the lead rider dismounting and studying the trail at intervals. They were checking our sign. Harmless travellers on their way to Phoenix would not do that."

I sighed. I hated it when he was always right. "Why on earth would anyone want to follow us?"

"Well I can think of at least seven reasons," said Holmes airily.

"Such as?"

"They could be thieves who prey on other travellers: they could have been employed by Colonel Sawbitt to attack us: they could be renegades who managed to escape and are after us out of revenge: they could even be those highwaymen we apprehended in Lucky Strike."

"But they are in jail, Holmes," I objected.

"You will recall that Miss Dolittle expressed doubt that they would remain in jail long enough to be tried. Frankly, that marshal did not impress me greatly. I have no doubt that once we left town he released them."

"If it is the highwaymen, how come it took them so long. One would think they would have caught up with us long before now."

"Well, they would have had to detour to avoid the mountain men and the Indians. I am also sure that Foster Keehoe would have misdirected them if they asked our location. It takes time to pick up a trail."

"I suppose," I murmured a trifle doubtfully. "Anyway, you have only listed four reasons, Holmes, what are the other three?"

Holmes made a face at me and said blithely, "Your interruption caused me to lose my train of thought."

I snorted. Trust him to blame me! He chuckled at my reaction, for we both knew he had exaggerated, as usual. He always said he had seven reasons, or five theories, or six what have you, when half the time he barely had one! I was not unduly annoyed though, after all, he was just being Holmes.

By the time we rejoined the others, dinner was cooking. We said nothing of our fears to the Plymouths, but come bedtime, after they retired to their wagon for the night,   Holmes nudged me.

"Do you want first watch or second, Watson?"

"First watch?"

"Yes. It would be prudent to keep guard just in case they come sneaking up on us."

"Oh, in that case I will go first. What time do you want me to wake you?"

"Do you think you can stay awake until midnight?"

"Easily." I collected my rifle and blanket and moved away from the fire. I found a rock to lean against and, to keep my mind alert, thought about all the people we had met on our travels so far.

Time passed slowly. It was my intention to let Holmes sleep until two, but by twelve thirty my eyelids were beginning to droop and my head kept nodding.

Suddenly I heard a soft footfall. My head jerked up and my rifle clattered to the ground.

"Really, Watson," chided Holmes in the precise clipped tones he used when he was displeased. "If I were a murderer I could have slit your throat ten times over."

"I wasn't asleep, Holmes!" I denied. "I heard you approach. I was just momentarily startled."

Holmes gave a grunt which could mean anything, then said, "Well you might as well go to bed. I will take over now."

I tossed him my blanket, picked up my rifle and returned to the fire, rolling gratefully into Holmes' vacated bedroll. I am sure that I was asleep as soon as I closed my eyes.

✠ ✠ ✠

I awoke to the smell of cooking and soft voiced conversation.

"Good morning, Doctor," greeted Sarah cheerfully. "You're a sleepy head this morning."

I sat up, "Just feeling my age, my dear," I replied, only to be greeted by her laughter.

"You're not *old*, Doctor. Is it impolite for me to ask what your age is?" she asked.

"Possibly. I am four and thirty but sleeping on the hard ground has added a few years to my bones," I said. I was rewarded by her chuckle, which was a very pleasant sound first thing in the morning. Still, I could hardly tell her I was sleepy because I had been awake half the night. Of course, Holmes looked none the worse for his lack of sleep, but then again, he was used to it.

✠ ✠ ✠

We made good time this day with Holmes forcing the pace. We were in barren country, devoid of human life, except for ourselves and our pursuers. It

[272]

concerned him that we were so exposed and isolated. We could not count on Cathcart Plymouth to use a gun, he was as likely to shoot one of us as one of the enemy. Sarah was a good shot, but Holmes had qualms about asking a woman to participate in a gun fight despite her involvement in the one with the renegades, so the defence of the camp rested solely with us.

It was late afternoon as we approached a river. I noticed Holmes was looking about him incessantly. I slowed my pace so that he would catch up.

"What's wrong, Holmes?"

"I am not sure but I know something *is* wrong, Watson. I cannot see anything, but I can feel it in my bones. I sense we are being watched. There could be danger here. Our pursuers could easily have overtaken us in the night as they do not have to drag a wagon along with them."

"You think they are waiting in ambush ahead of us?"

"Yes, that is highly probable. Imagine if we were attacked whilst fording that river up ahead. It would be like shooting fish in a barrel."

"But we have no choice, we have to ford."

"I know." Holmes looked worried. He clipped his horse into a trot and moved up alongside the wagon. "Sarah, have you forded rivers with a wagon before?"

"Sure, heaps of times."

"Then I would be obliged if you would take the reins. Mr Plymouth, can you please get into the wagon bed and stay there until the wagon is across the river."

"Really, Mr Holmes!"

"I insist. You will only distract your wife if you stay up front. She will need to concentrate."

Sarah looked at Holmes shrewdly. She had not spent all this time in our company without getting to know us and knowing instinctively when something was wrong. Holmes gave a small nod to her mute question.

"Yes Cathcart, Mr Holmes has a point. You can hit all sorts of potholes and things in the water and it's real easy to fall off the seat. I'd be happier if you were in the wagon."

"Oh, all right," he grumbled.

She looked Holmes directly in the eyes, "Any other instructions?"

"Yes. If I yell, get the wagon moving as fast as you can across the river. Do not stop and do not look back. Once on the other side, take cover."

Instead of wasting time with questions, she merely nodded. This was yet another difference between a frontier girl well used to the dangers of life in her harsh environment and a pampered city Miss.

"Draw your rifle, Watson," instructed Holmes.

We took up our positions on either side of the wagon as we approached the river. There were high rocks on both sides of the trail. It was then that Holmes detected the sudden flash of sunlight on a rifle barrel.

"Move 'em!" he yelled slapping the rump of the nearest horse. The wagon increased in speed as Sarah whipped the horses into movement. Holmes aimed his rifle in the direction he'd seen the flash and fired. His bullet ricocheted behind the rock causing two men to rear up in shock. I pulled the same trick on the other side of the path and elicited a similar response.

Soon, Sarah was past the danger zone and entering the water. The outlaws didn't have a chance to fire upon us for we kept up a barrage of fire at the rocks, creating a dangerous ricochet effect. All they could do was run for their horses and get away from the rocks as quickly as possible. I heard one yell and knew I had made at least one hit. I was all for going after them, the heat of battle burning in me.

"No, Watson. We took them by surprise this time. If we go after them they have the advantage of numbers. Let's get across the river while we can."

We urged our horses into the water and soon joined the wagon on the opposite bank. Sarah had drawn it to the side and was now crouched at its rear with rifle in hand; ready to give us covering fire if needed. Fortunately it was unnecessary.

"I say," called Plymouth, as we joined them. "Bandits! What a rum lot! How did you know they were there, Mr Holmes?"

"I saw the sunlight glint off a rifle barrel."

"Jolly glad you have such eagle eyes."

"We can't stop here," stated Holmes, "so let's get moving again. I would like to keep on going for as long as the horses can take it."

It was eight before we called a halt for the night. Holmes chose our campsite with care. Once again, we followed the same procedure as the previous night. I stood guard until midnight, and then Holmes took over. I made sure I was fully alert when he came to take over for me. It wasn't hard to be so, as the attack by the river had convinced me once and for all that we were being followed by malcontents.

Holmes had the uncanny ability to wake at any given time he desired without the aid of an alarm clock, so when he joined me on the dot of midnight, I said, "If you move up that way a bit, Holmes," I pointed, "you can see their fire." Holmes nodded and walked to where I had indicated. I had noticed the fire glow earlier. It did nothing to reassure me for it meant that our pursuers had not given up on us. We had merely bought ourselves some more time.

Next morning we broke camp just after sunrise and kept up a good pace until early afternoon when Cathcart Plymouth called a halt. "Mr Holmes, I insist we stop and make camp earlier today. Sarah wants to bathe and our clothing needs washing. I know you are trying to put distance between us and the outlaws, but I am quite sure that you and the good doctor discouraged them thoroughly yesterday. They are unlikely to come after us."

"I beg to differ Mr Plymouth," countered Holmes.

"That is your prerogative. Nevertheless, I must insist. You are, after all, working for my father and by proxy, for me; therefore I should have some say in matters."

Holmes' eyes narrowed as he glared at the young man, who had chosen this most inopportune time to try to exert his authority. That was the problem with so called noblemen, sooner or later they always pulled rank, believing their titles gave them that right. It occurred to me then that there were not many titled men who actually did deserve their titles. Birthright had nothing on genuine achievement. It seemed to me that there were more worthy untitled men about than titled. Naturally I said none of this; I was more interested to witness the inevitable clash, for Holmes was not a great admirer of the elite.

"Mister Plymouth, you are hardly in a position to dictate to me," replied Holmes, glaring at the younger man. "It is true your father employed me, but I am a free agent, meaning that I am free to reject his employment at any time. Should I do so, I doubt very much if you or your wife would ever make it to Phoenix alive."

Plymouth then demonstrated a stubborn streak. "I think we could manage. After all, I travelled extensively through this wilderness on my own before meeting Sarah."

"And burnt down half the country in your wake," scoffed Holmes rudely. "Not to mention causing a stampede that almost trampled a ranch house, being chased by mountain men and Indians and losing your horse and possessions. Oh yes, you were very adept."

Plymouth flushed angrily but could hardly deny Holmes' accusations. He opened his mouth to reply, but Sarah cut in quickly:

"Please Cathcart, Mr Holmes, don't fight. Cathcart, Mr Holmes saved my life and he saved yours too. He and Dr. Watson only have our best interests at heart. I don't want them to leave. Frankly, I feel safe with them here. Mr Holmes, we *are* getting awfully dirty and have run out of clean clothes. I don't want to show up in Phoenix looking like trail trash. It's a real city after all. If we travel all night tonight, could we please stop long enough tomorrow to bath and do the laundry?" She looked pleadingly at Holmes.

I remembered my conversation with Holmes about compromise. It seemed like that had been years ago. Sarah was offering an olive branch, now the question that remained was whether or not Holmes would accept it. He was silent for a long moment as he considered her proposition. Finally he said, "Very well, Mrs Plymouth, we will do as you request. Please note that it is only because I have a great deal of respect for *you* that I am agreeing to this although it is against my better judgement."

"Thank you, Mr Holmes."

Plymouth looked churlish as if he wanted to keep up the argument, but Sarah took his arm and lead him to the wagon. "Come on, dearest," she said. "The horses needed the rest, so this stop was not wasted."

They climbed aboard the wagon and we were soon underway again. As we moved over to our horses, I noted Holmes' fists were tightly clenched. "That girl is worth ten, no, twenty of Plymouth!"

"You like her don't you, Holmes?" I asked, looking at him curiously.

"I respect her, Watson."

"No, it's more than that."

He shrugged. "Under different circumstances..." he never finished his sentence; he did not need to.

TWENTY–SEVEN

We travelled all night, stopping only long enough to rest and feed the horses. While they rested, we ate cold tinned food. It was during one of these stops that Plymouth approached Holmes. Holmes ignored his presence until the other spoke.

"I am sorry, Mr Holmes. Sarah has told me how you saved her from drowning in the river at considerable risk to your own life. I admit I have not exactly been the world's greatest woodsman, but it was rather jarring the way you said it. I honestly do not believe that there is any more danger, however; Sarah says I should trust your instincts as you have been proven right thus far. I apologize for pulling rank on you. I too feel much safer with you and Dr. Watson present."

Holmes finally deigned to look at him.

"Apology accepted," he said curtly, before replacing his pipe back in his mouth and looking away. Plymouth took the hint and returned to the wagon walking with eyes downcast and shoulders hunched.

"You could give in a little, Holmes," I said softly. "That young fellow has a serious self–confidence problem."

"It is not up to me to cure it."

"At least he apologized. That shows he has some potential."

"Hmm."

I shook my head. It was no use trying to talk reasonably to Holmes when he was in such a mood.

He resented Plymouth's words. He was hired by Plymouth's father, yet acting in a deferential role to his employer or employer's son was just not in his nature. Holmes rarely went out of his way to kowtow to the whims and fancies of those that paid him for his services. He considered himself a specialist: the fact that they came to him put him, in his opinion, in the superior position. I smiled to myself. I could never imagine Holmes in the army. He would be brought up on insubordination charges on his first day if he were a private. But then again, he would settle for nothing less than commander. Perhaps that is why he manufactured his own profession. It gave him power. He was a law unto himself. These thoughts and fancies I was having was interrupted by Holmes calling for us to mount up and move on.

We travelled all night and for the better part of the morning before Holmes called a halt. Sarah and Plymouth had taken turns to sleep in the wagon, so both were reasonably bright eyed, whereas Holmes and myself had remained in the saddle. Holmes was none the worse for it, but I can tell you, I was ready to drop off the horse at any moment.

We had arrived at a tributary of the larger river we had crossed several days previously. There was plenty of waterside shrubbery about to afford privacy whilst bathing and copious places to hang our clothing once washed.

"We will stop here for six hours before moving on," announced Holmes. Sarah flashed him a grateful smile and was quick to unhitch the horses. She hurriedly grabbed up several stuffed sacks of clothing, a towel and her toiletries and moved on downstream.

"The area past these bushes is off limits," she called cheerfully, leaving her husband to attend to the team animals. I did not offer to help him either, as I was eager to have a wash and a nap. A fifteen minute bath followed by a five and a half hour sleep would do me the world of good.

I bathed and washed the clothes I was wearing, changing into my last pair of clean undergarments, then I found myself a spot in the sun and promptly went to sleep. Holmes also did his laundry and bathed before returning to the camp to keep guard. It was inhuman the way he did not need to sleep as regularly as I and could often go for days on end without it.

✠   ✠   ✠

I was woken from blissful slumber by Sarah's screams. I came instantly awake and grabbed my pistol, dashing towards where we had left the wagon. I noticed Plymouth was no longer bathing, which meant that he was also in the camp. As I rushed to their aid, someone fired at me, kicking up dirt in front of my bare feet. I stopped abruptly and took in the scene.

There were four men in the clearing; this time they did not wear masks so I had no difficulty recognizing them. They were indeed the highwaymen who robbed the stagecoach. One filthy beast was holding a struggling Sarah, clad only in her petticoats and camisole. Seeing her made me suddenly self-conscious of the fact that I too was similarly undressed The boss thief of polka dot bandanna fame grinned mirthlessly.

"Drop 'em," he ordered. Holmes and I dropped our weapons, not because of any threat to us, but because the thug who was holding Sarah put his cocked gun to her head as an inducement. "Which one of you is Plymouth?" Polka dot bandanna demanded.

"That is I, unhand my wife!" Plymouth stepped forward.

The boss thief raised his gun. "Say adios, Dude."

"Now, Watson!" yelled Holmes, throwing himself at Plymouth and sending him flying, after which he then threw himself to the ground to retrieve his own gun and I followed suit. Never had the cold metal of my revolver felt so good as my hand closed upon it firmly. I had no sooner taken hold of it before bullets began to spatter around me. I rolled to make a moving target, stopping only long enough to return fire. The fellow known as Two–gun Tolliver was dead set on perforating me and came damnably close to succeeding. One bullet actually burned across my back. I could feel the heat of it as it passed. I aimed for his heart and saw him drop.

Holmes, at considerable risk to himself had aimed at and head shot the man holding Sarah, ignoring the guns of the other killers that were firing at him. Fortune smiled on him, for apart from a bullet searing his hair, he was unharmed.

The minute she was free, Sarah dropped to the ground and crawled to safety, away from the line of fire. She was unarmed and knew it was pointless to attempt to join the battle.

Plymouth had drawn his own weapon and was firing it wildly at the outlaws. While he only narrowly missed hitting his wife, he did manage to shoot our packhorse, tearing its rump. The poor animal would surely have fled had it not been tethered so securely.

I continued firing and moving until my gun was empty, as did Holmes. The silence that followed the deafening roar of guns was almost as spectacular as the attack itself had been. When the smoke dissipated, only Holmes and I were standing. Plymouth was on the ground, but uninjured, and Sarah peeped out from behind a rock.

The outlaws were down. Three dead, one dying and begging. "Yuh gotta help me, Doc," he begged of me.

I grimaced and moved over to him. When we had joined in the hunt for the rustlers and participated in the fight, I had been sickened by the carnage. This was a similar affair, but I had no such feelings. Perhaps I had become hardened, immune to bloodshed after having seen so much of it. I am sure that I have shot more people on this trip than I ever did in Afghanistan. I knelt down beside the man: one look at his wound told me there was nothing I could do for him.

Holmes also came over and demanded: "Who sent you after us?"

The outlaw looked up at him, his eyes already starting to glaze.

"Like...you..." he gasped before breathing his last.

Sarah ran to her husband. Both young people were wide eyed.

"Who...who were they?" gasped Plymouth.

"Watson and I helped arrest them in Lucky Strike after they robbed the stagecoach we had been travelling on. They obviously wanted revenge."

I threw a surprised glance at Holmes, knowing perfectly well that this was not entirely true—his question to the dying outlaw bellied that.

"Take your wife upstream, Plymouth, while Watson and I clean up this mess."

Plymouth's sensitive face was pale and shocked and it was more Sarah leading him away than vice versa.

"Search them, Watson," said Holmes dropping to his knees beside the dead outlaw and going through his pockets. I did likewise on another. They had around two hundred dollars on their persons and little else. We removed their weapon belts and dragged them away from the clearing to an area where there was some soft, sandy like earth. We improvised digging implements and began to scoop out graves.

As we worked I said: "Holmes, if they were after us for revenge, why did they want to know who Plymouth was?"

"Excellent point, Watson. The truth is they were after Plymouth, not us. It was he that they came to kill. You saw the boss thief, he aimed at Plymouth first. One would have thought they would shoot us first as being the more dangerous. The fact that they hated us was just an incidental bonus to them. Someone hired them to kill Plymouth of that there is no doubt."

"But why?"

"Why indeed," returned Holmes, a faraway look in his eyes, as he became lost in thought.

"What did that dying man mean 'like you' he said. What was like you? Was he trying to tell us something or ...?"

[284]

"Oh, he told me plenty. I believe that what he was trying to say was that the man who hired them was British like me. That of course is entirely logical, for no American has any reason to kill Plymouth."

"It may be logical to you, but it doesn't make much sense to me. If someone wanted to kill Plymouth, why wait until now. They had two years to do it."

"Perhaps this person did not think Plymouth would ever return to England and therefore posed no threat. Now that we are bringing him home the situation changes."

"Perhaps he knows why?"

"I doubt it, Watson. Plymouth is ignorant of this threat, of that I am fairly certain and I would rather not tell him, either. He does not have his father's character. It is fortunate that his wife is made of sterner stuff." Holmes fell silent for a moment before adding, "You and I will have to be extra vigilant from now until he is home again. Tonight, if on some pretext you can distract him for a while, I will have a word to Sarah. After all, she is with him at times when we are not. She also knows how to shoot. We can trust her not to panic."

I agreed with his assessment. Over the past month we had come to know young Sarah and I admired her spirit. Plymouth on the other hand, had not impressed me greatly. He had a sensitive artistic temperament but was essentially a rather weak man. I could understand why his father was so disappointed in him. For a man so strong to have a son so weak must have been extremely disheartening. Certainly, he meant well, but could not follow through on his intentions. It was fortunate that he had found himself a strong and capable wife. Although, I hoped she wouldn't tire of taking care of him as opposed to his taking care of her, the way it should be.

✠   ✠   ✠

It took us two hours to bury the bodies. As it turned out I did not have to find an excuse to separate Sarah from Plymouth, for he was feeling ill and was having a lie down in the wagon. Holmes quickly explained the situation to her and she nodded grimly.

"Don't worry, Mr Holmes, I'll keep my gun close to hand at all times. Have you any idea who it can be?"

"Actually I do, but—" he held up his hand to silence her questions. "But that can wait. I need proof first. If we have no further delays we should make Phoenix in two days. When we are there, try to keep him in the hotel until we board the train to the coast. Anytime we are out in the open, Watson and I will stick close. It would be better not to tell him; he's had shocks enough already."

"I am so glad you are here—both of you," she said warmly, her eyes on Holmes.

A faint flush suffused his cheeks and he replied rather curtly, "That's what we are being paid for."

"Don't pull that line on me. I'm one of the commoners, remember?" she said smiling. "Anyway, you can't fool me. You would risk your life to save others whether you were being paid or not."

A faint smile touched Holmes' lips as they exchanged intimate glances.

It was a shame that Sarah was married; if she hadn't been then perhaps Holmes would have ...? I let the thought trail. It seemed that Holmes had about as much luck with women as I did. All the truly admirable ones were already taken! I sighed, bringing their eyes to me in question.

"The sooner we are safe and sound in England, the happier I will be," I adlibbed. Holmes would not have been amused at my thoughts. Romantic claptrap he would have called it.

As all the outlaws were dead, Holmes now deemed it safe to stay where we were for the night, which was fortunate as I had only been asleep for an hour before they showed up. We did not have to stand guard either, which meant we could get a decent night's rest.

TWENTY–EIGHT

As Holmes predicted, we reached Phoenix after two days of constant travel. On arrival we sold our horses and the wagon to a stable owner and checked into the Grand Hotel, which had bathrooms on every floor. It was the most luxurious hotel in the city. Sarah hinted to Plymouth that they make the most of the facilities and room service and rest in their comfortable room. He agreed readily enough, for the hard travel had worn him out and he was still suffering the effects of shock from the shootout. Despite his experiences in America, he had been fortunate to avoid the sights of violence, even though he himself was a victim several times. The sight of the dead bodies and blood had quite unnerved him.

It occurred to me that it was providential that he had not been in Harkin's Hollow when the renegades attacked, such trauma would have destroyed him completely.

With the Plymouths safely installed in the hotel, we purchased new clothing and bathed before venturing out to find the sheriff's office. This being a frontier city and not a two–horse town as the quaint saying goes; the building we were looking for was quite an imposing structure with a brick courthouse adjacent to it.

We entered the office to see several desks occupied by deputies busy with paperwork. It looked more like a metropolitan police station except that they did not wear uniforms. All had the customary silver star pinned to their vests.

"May I help you?" asked one young man coming forward.

"We would like to see the Sheriff," returned Holmes just as politely.

"In regard to what?"

"To being attacked by four assassins on our journey here," stated Holmes. I held up the sack I was carrying.

"We have their belongings here to assist you with identification," I offered.

The young man nodded and went to an inner office; a moment later he motioned for us to enter, following us in.

"How do you do Sheriff Pearce," greeted Holmes, offering his hand. I too had noticed the name on his door so it was no great feat of deduction. "My name is Sherlock Holmes and this is Dr. Wat..."

He was interrupted as the Sheriff leapt up out of his chair. "Sherlock Holmes! *The Sherlock Holmes*?"

"Er...yes." Holmes was nonplussed, after all it was still early days in his career and though his fame was spreading throughout England and Europe, he was still an unknown on this continent.

"This is indeed an honour, Sir. An honour!"

"You have me at a disadvantage, Sheriff. I fail to see how you could possibly know of me."

"I was born in England. My parents came here when I was a babe. My cousin is Tobias Gregson of Scotland Yard. We correspond regularly. He speaks very highly of you and sends me newspaper clippings and the like. I am very interested in your methods, Sir, very interested. They are not unlike some of the ones we use here," explained the Sheriff, beaming with delight.

When it came to his work, Holmes was as susceptible as a female to flattery.

"Ah...yes, Inspector Gregson; one of the Yard's brighter sparks," replied Holmes politely, although that was not how he described Gregson recently when he was called in to fix a case mismanaged by the detective. I believe the term he used then was 'turnip brain.'

"I welcome this opportunity to discuss crime detection techniques with you," beamed the Sheriff.

"Certainly, but first we would like to report an incident," said Holmes, helping himself to a seat.

The sheriff offered his cigars around and we helped ourselves. I lit up gratefully. I had been somewhat apprehensive as to how the law would take the news of our shootout and the death and burial of the four outlaws. Considering the sheriff's attitude to Holmes, I now felt we had nothing to worry about, and so it ultimately proved.

Holmes took the Sheriff into his confidence and explained about the attack on Plymouth's life. The Sheriff immediately offered to place a guard on their room and Holmes gratefully accepted.

Sheriff Pearce then entreated us to join him for dinner at the best restaurant in town and spent most of the time questioning Holmes. Holmes was in his element giving examples of his peculiar ability to observe and deduce and the local diners were the targets of his eagle eye. The Sheriff was beside himself with delight. He wanted us to stay longer and was highly disappointed when we informed him we were leaving the next day.

"Must you go? There is so much you could teach me," he said.

"We can always correspond, Sheriff," offered Holmes generously. The fellow's eyes lit up at that and he nodded eagerly. I smiled to myself; Holmes did not realize what he was letting himself in for if the sheriff's eagerness was anything to go by.

He then offered to buy us drinks at the best saloon in town, which we naturally accepted. Sam Pearce really was very jovial company and highly entertaining, nothing like his cousin Gregson, who always took himself so seriously and was willing enough to use Holmes to solve his cases but reluctant to give credit. Still, he must have had a higher opinion of Holmes than we thought for him to write about him to his cousin. Gregson was a dark horse indeed.

It was as we left the restaurant that we encountered a disturbance on the main thoroughfare. There was a brawl in progress spilling out from a general store. The man in the centre was around six foot three inches tall, dressed in fringed buckskin shirt and trousers. He had the high cheekbones that signified Indian blood and he was barefoot. He was fighting with a bellicose apron-wearing man, whom was in all probability the store's owner.

Before the Sheriff could intervene, two of his deputies were on the scene. The Sheriff strode forward. "What's going on here?" He demanded.

"The damn half breed attacked me for no reason!" accused the shopkeeper hotly and I took an instant dislike to him.

"Not true, Sheriff," said the Indian. "Me come to sell skins. Ratcliffe only offer to pay half what worth. I say no. I go to other shop. Ratcliffe say they his skins. I try to take skins back, he try stop me. Me not do business with crook."

"He's lyin'," claimed Ratcliffe.

"This is easily fixed. Take your skins, Little Bear, and go," ordered the Sheriff. "As for you, Ratcliffe, this is not the first complaint of unfair trading made against you. I suggest you change your ways or you will be up before the magistrate."

The Indian nodded his thanks to the sheriff and reloaded his packhorse, while the shop owner stood by glaring at him the whole time.

"Sorry about that, Mr Holmes, Dr. Watson. Little Bear is a half-breed. His mama was a full-blood Shoshone and his father was a trapper. He hunts and traps in the high country then sells his stuff in town. We've never had no trouble with him before."

"It seems to me that he was not the instigator of this set-to, either," I said.

We continued on to the saloon and spent a pleasant evening in the Sheriff's company. Various notable locals like the Mayor, the bank manager and others joined us. Pearce introduced Holmes in glowing terms as the 'most eminent criminal specialist in London.'

By the time we left the saloon and walked the short distance to our hotel, Holmes was flushed and beaming with all the compliments and praise he had received.

"Careful, Holmes," I said with a grin as we approached the hotel's doorway. "Your head may not

[293]

fit through."

"Pardon?" Holmes looked at me in surprise.

"Your head has become notably swollen," I replied.

"Huh! You are just jealous! It is actually a rare treat to meet a regular law enforcer that can appreciate exceptional skills and talent when he sees it. Unlike those Scotland Yarders who are happy enough to take the credit for my work but reluctant to acknowledge it."

I conceded him his point but could not wipe the smile from my face. Our room was next door to the Plymouths.

Outside the Plymouth's door was an elderly deputy chewing on a cigar stub; his chair leaning back at an impossible angle. He gave us a salute as we passed.

Holmes stopped only long enough to ask, "Any problems, Officer?"

"Nary a one," replied the other, cigar stub stuck fast in his mouth.

✠   ✠   ✠

The next morning while we were having breakfast with the Plymouths in the hotel dining room we were distracted by a disturbance in the street. Holmes stood up and hurried to the nearest window and I followed his example wondering what was going on. Phoenix had struck me as being a civilized town, certainly not one prone to riots. We heard yelling, screaming, and chanting. I couldn't quite make out what was being said.

[294]

"What's going on, Holmes?" I asked.

"Lynch mob. I'm going to go to the jail to see if the sheriff needs any help."

"I'll come too," I decided.

"Plymouth, you and your wife stay here, we will return shortly," ordered Holmes. Even as we walked out onto the hotel porch, we spotted the young deputy from the day before hurrying in our direction.

"He's looking for us," said Holmes, waving to attract his attention.

The Deputy hurried over. "Mr Holmes, the Sheriff'd be mighty obliged if you would help him on a case of some urgency."

"What has happened?" I asked curiously, as we hurried along to keep pace with the young man.

"Ratcliffe's been murdered and it looks like Little Bear did it. The crowd are clamouring for his neck."

"If it is so clear cut, why do you need me?" asked Holmes.

"Sheriff ain't satisfied and wants your opinion. He's hoping having you investigate will quiet down the mob. We've never had anything like this here before."

We reached the sheriff's office and forced our way through the crowd to climb onto the front porch, which was barricaded by deputies armed with shotguns.

"Thank God you came, Mr Holmes," greeted the sheriff, looking frazzled.

"Hang the injun!" came a voice from the crowd.

"We don't want no murderin' half-breeds!"

yelled another. "Hang him 'fore he kills other honest citizens!"

"I would not have thought Ratcliffe was so popular," I stated.

"He's not," replied the sheriff sourly.

Holmes studied the crowd and picked out the two men who seemed to be doing most of the yelling and egging the crowd on to further violence. Someone threw a brick which shattered the front window of the office and the cry of 'Hang him!' went up.

The sheriff fired his shotgun into the air and won a temporary silence. "Everybody shut up!" he ordered. "This feller here is one of the best detectives in the world. I want him to investigate Ratcliffe's death. He will prove one way or another if Little Bear is guilty. If Little Bear is guilty he will be tried under the due process of the law and not by a lynch mob."

The sheriff glared at the crowd and began to single out individuals. "Tom Meeker, I see you. How do you think your wife would feel knowing you helped lynch a man that might be innocent? Could you look your kids in the eye? Sam Crehan what about you? Lynching is no better than murder. You're the one that campaigned for the city council to appoint more deputies. This is what we're here for. We can't call ourselves civilized men if we resort to mob rule as soon as a crime is committed. Give us time to investigate. Go home to your families and leave the law to us."

His words were having an effect, for some of the men began to look sheepish and backed away. Quite a few remained though, loitering, watching us silently.

"What evidence do you have against Little Bear, Sheriff?" asked Holmes.

"His footprints. They're as clear as day. You see, he knocked over a sack of flour when he was fighting with Ratcliffe and stepped in it. He's the only man in town that goes around bare foot and the footprints at the store are unmistakably those of bare feet. What's more, he didn't return to his cabin last night but stayed in town in Claymore's barn. He had that fight with Ratcliffe earlier in the day and could still have born a grudge. When the crowd went for him, he ran here."

"What does he have to say about it?"

"Says he didn't do it. Said he slept all night in the barn and never budged. But we can't prove it."

"I see." Holmes looked at the remaining group of men and singled two out, his keen eyes noting everything about their appearance. "Is the body still at the store?"

"Yes. This riot started soon after the body was discovered and we haven't had time to do anything but fort up here and protect Little Bear."

Holmes turned to the two men he had picked out. "I wonder if you two gentleman would come with us?"

"Why?" asked a thin rat-faced fellow suspiciously.

"I would like to have two impartial witnesses to watch that the evidence in the store is not tampered with during my investigation." The two men exchanged grins.

"Yeah, sure, why not," rat face agreed and the other nodded.

[297]

Pearce frowned at Holmes' choice of witnesses but said nothing.

"If you will kindly wait here a moment, I just want a quick word with Little Bear before proceeding to the shop," said Holmes, politely. "Sheriff?"

The sheriff nodded and led Holmes into his office. Little Bear sat inside on one of the desks looking worried.

"Mr Little Bear," began Holmes. "Who knew you were in the barn last night?"

"Claymore did."

"Anyone else?" The Indian shrugged.

"It no secret. Claymore could've told someone. I not know."

"May I look at your feet?"

The Indian's eyes met Holmes' and a faint smile twitched at his lips as he held his feet up for Holmes to examine.

"Thank you," said Holmes. "That will do. We will go to the store now, Sheriff."

The sheriff looked puzzled at Holmes' lack of questioning. "Why did you pick those two layabouts to come as witnesses?" he asked. "They're nothing but troublemakers. Never did an honest day's work in their life but always seem to have money. I wouldn't be surprised if they weren't the pair responsible for stirring up the lynch mob."

"I wouldn't be surprised, either," agreed Holmes, succeeding in confounding the sheriff even more. Well, he did want to see Holmes in action, now he had his opportunity.

We made our way to the store with the two loafers who did nothing but insult Little Bear and declare how kind and wonderful Ratcliffe was.

The sheriff snorted. "Ratcliffe was a mean, penny pinching bastard, no one in town will even miss him!"

At the store, we stopped by the door at Holmes' request. "If you could all stay by the door, gentlemen I will go study the scene." He entered and stopped just inside the doorway. The floor was coated with flour and a clear set of footprints showed up in it. Bare footprints walking towards the dead man and also to the safe and back again.

Holmes' eyes scanned the room, missing nothing. "Where are the sacks of flour usually stored?"

"On that far shelf?"

"I see. And what is your theory, Sheriff? asked Holmes, but before the sheriff could answer, rat face chimed in.

"Theory! Hell, any fool can see that Little Bear was here. He came in, fought with Ratcliffe and killed him. Then he rifled his safe and left. His prints are as clear as day. He's the only man that goes barefoot in this town."

"So you wear your boots to bed, do you?" asked Holmes.

"Huh?"

"If Little Bear is the only man who goes barefoot, one would then presume that every other man in town never removes his boots."

Rat face scowled. "You sayin' it ain't the Injun?"

"Well, it was very obliging of him to spill the flour and then walk through it several times to ensure everyone would see his footprints."

[299]

"It was accidental."

"Strange sort of an accident it is when the flour is not spilled during a struggle as you suggested but spilled from the doorway here."

"What?" The sheriff looked surprised.

"Please observe, Sheriff, the arc of trajectory made by the flour. It is narrow at the door here and spreads out into the room. It is consistent with someone standing by the door and throwing the flour out, therefore the sack was not broken open during the struggle. What is more, even a blind man could see that there is flour *on top* of Ratcliffe. If the flour was already on the floor it would be beneath him."

"He could've rolled over," suggested rat face's companion helpfully.

"Dead men do not usually roll, or make any kind of movement," I pointed out.

"The injun could've rolled him lookin' for the keys to the safe," said rat face triumphantly.

"It's possible," agreed Holmes, "and also easily checked. If he had been rolled over, then there will be flour on both sides of the victim. It is these footprints however that interests me. They are clearly significant, do you not agree, Sheriff?"

The sheriff looked at the footprints. "I don't understand," he said. "They're the prints of a bare foot."

"Notice the toes?"

"Not clearly. You can tell they're toes, but they're all squashed together and hard to define."

"Correct. Would it be possible to bring Little Bear over here?"

"I guess." The sheriff sent the young deputy

who had accompanied us back to the jail and he returned a short while later with three heavily armed deputies and Little Bear.

"Mr Little Bear, would you be so kind as to take a step on to the flour, beside that footprint?"

The Indian nodded and did as directed. As soon as he stepped back the sheriff gasped. "As you can see," said Holmes, smiling faintly, "the toes are clearly defined. You can see each one distinctly. That is because Little Bear never wears shoes allowing his toes to spread. When I examined his feet at the jail, I could see there was no trace of flour on them, nor was there any on his clothes or on the hem of his trousers. At a glance I knew that these were not his footprints but were the footprints of man who regularly wears shoes. Now if you will just give me a moment, I will make a closer examination and perhaps I will be able to tell you just who did commit this crime."

Holmes entered the shop and moved along the edge of the flour, studying the floor carefully. He made an examination of the safe with his usual detail and then moved over to the body. For the witness' sake, he rolled the body over and we could all plainly see that his right side was clean and free of flour, which proved conclusively that the flour had been spilled after Ratcliffe was dead. Holmes returned to the doorway.

"Anything?" asked the sheriff hopefully.

"One or two things. The murder was committed by two men. One clubbed Ratcliffe to death and relieved him of his keys. He opened the safe and helped himself to the money. The second man took a bag of flour down and tossed it out, some of the flour dribbled down onto his waistcoat. The murderer then walked carefully back towards the door, keeping to the edge of the flour, but not too successfully, I am afraid. There are traces of his passage indicating a booted man had been in the shop *after* the flour had been thrown. Then either the first or second man removed his boots and walked across the floor leaving a clear trail of prints. They obviously witnessed Little Bear's altercation with Ratcliffe earlier in the day and decided he would make the perfect scapegoat."

"It could be anyone," said the sheriff.

"No. Actually it is these two men here." On Holmes' words two of the deputies moved closer to our two witnesses.

No wonder Holmes wanted them to accompany us. He must have detected something that made him suspicious of them from the start.

"Observe this man's waistcoat," said Holmes directing our attention to the second man, who paled under our scrutiny. "This man is our flour thrower, which means his companion is the murderer. There should be traces of flour adhering to the soles of his boots."

"Lift up your foot, Gavel," ordered the sheriff.

"Damned if I will," said rat face, trying to back away, only to crash into one of the deputies. The big deputy grabbed his leg and twisted. Rat face fell to the ground giving us a clear view of his boot soles. In the ridges of the leather were traces of flour.

"I'll be damned," gasped the sheriff. "Get their boots off," he ordered his deputies. They complied and within minutes both men's feet were revealed. Rat face was evidently not hygienically minded for he hadn't bothered to wash his feet and traces of flour remained between his toes.

"There is your murderer and his accomplice, Sheriff. Little Bear is innocent."

"Take them away," ordered Pearce and the deputies hauled the two loafers to their feet and dragged them away."

"The sheriff turned to Little Bear. "Thank you for your co-operation, Little Bear. I would appreciate it if you stayed with us until we have had time to spread the word of your innocence. We don't want some fool lynching you out a misguided sense of civic duty."

The Indian nodded to the sheriff and threw a rare smile at Holmes before returning to the jail with the young deputy...

Sheriff Pearce then offered his hand to Holmes. "It's a real pleasure seein' you in action, Mr Holmes. A real treat."

"You are welcome; however, if Watson and I do not run we will miss our train."

"Don't worry about that, I'll make sure they wait for you."

Holmes and I returned to the hotel and collected both our luggage and the Plymouths. We were some ten minutes late in reaching the train, but the sheriff was true to his word. As we arrived, he was in the midst of a heated argument with the irate station-master and engineer. We were bundled in like celebrities and I could not help but be amused on seeing all the curious faces look out at us as we boarded. We found our way to an empty first-class carriage.

"I hope they loaded my things," said Sarah worriedly.

"Yes, the wagon was unloaded and stored here yesterday," I reassured her, "they would already have loaded it."

We settled back in our seats and fished out our smokes.

"Mr Holmes," asked Plymouth, "why was there a deputy outside our room last night?"

"Oh, the sheriff wanted to ensure we would have an undisturbed night."

Plymouth accepted this reply happily enough. It occurred to me that he was not overly bright.

TWENTY–NINE

The journey back to New York was uneventful. Holmes and I stayed close to the Plymouths and overnight, Holmes and I took, turns standing guard outside their room. We made sure that Plymouth was never alone. If he suspected anything, he made no mention of it. By the end of the week-long journey, I was starting to wonder if perhaps Holmes had been mistaken. The killers could easily have learnt about Plymouth. After all, if they had been following us, they knew we were searching for him. The question could have been one of harmless curiosity. Their real objective could always have been revenge upon Holmes and me.

In New York, we avoided the poorer sections and stuck to the more genteel regions of the impressive city. It was certainly a rival for London in size and sophistication. Sarah wanted to go shopping, as her clothing was quite outdated when compared to city fashions, and certainly extremely poor when compared to London ladies fashion.

Holmes still had quite a bit of the advance travelling expenses from Sir Eustace, so, after buying our passage on the Northern Star—an American steamship—he indulgently handed her over a considerable sum. To our dismay, Plymouth wanted to accompany her, which in turn meant that we had to go as well. It was not long before we began to resemble native bearers as her purchases mounted.

I have never gone clothes shopping with a

woman before and I am emphatically sure that Holmes never had either, but I can tell you this, it is exhausting! I swear, if I ever get married, I will *never* go shopping with my wife. Sarah eventually took pity on us when Holmes' complaints became vociferous to the extreme. We finally hired a cab and dumped her purchases onto its floor before we three collapsed inside with extreme fatigue. Meantime, as we slumbered, the cabby kept pace with Sarah as she strode along with no sign of tiring. She had amazing stamina; truly she put us mere males to shame.

We had dinner in Plymouth's suite, and admired Sarah as she modelled one purchase after another for us. Plymouth, of course, was delighted. While I thought she looked rather enchanting. She would set the London social scene on fire with her vivaciousness and her wholesome good looks. As for Holmes, I am ashamed to admit it, but he slept through most of it, making no effort to conceal his boredom.

The next day we boarded the Northern Star without incident. As we checked into our rooms, Holmes said, "Stay doubly vigilant during the voyage, Watson. This is the murderer's last chance."

"Will we keep up the night guard duty as well?"

"No. I do not think that will be necessary, after all Sarah is with him and unlike the towns, no one can break in through the window."

✠   ✠   ✠

The first three days of the trip were rather

pleasant. All of the other passengers were Americans on their way to England and I was often stopped with questions about my country and the best places to see. Holmes' unsociable demeanour discouraged such questions from strangers. As I got to know my fellow travellers I found that there were no other Englishmen aboard bar us and Plymouth. It became our practice to take turns to keep the Plymouths under surveillance whenever they were on deck or mingling with other passengers.

On the fourth day, mid-afternoon of a pleasant sunny day, I found Holmes loitering near a doorway, his eyes towards the stern of the ship where the Plymouths were looking out over the rails. Plymouth had assumed a precarious perch on the railing and Sarah stood by. The water streamed out behind the ship leaving a white trail as the ships steam powered it along at tremendous speed.

"Hello, Holmes." I greeted. "Why don't you take a break? I will take over now for a while if you like."

"Thank you, Watson. I would like to check out our fellow passengers and see if I can spot anyone suspicious."

"Actually, by taking a break, I meant a stroll around the deck or doing something to relax."

Holmes smiled wryly. "Looking for suspicious people is relaxing."

I shook my head. "You never change, Holmes."

As he made to leave me he said, "Stay wary, I have a presentiment that something will happen, and soon."

"What? Have you seen something?"

"No. It is just a feeling. Stay sharp."

"Trust me, Holmes."

He gave me a nod and left, whilst I leant back against the wall and fantasized that it was me and the woman of my dreams standing so romantically at the stern. It was not Holmes' fancy, but marriage had always been one of my aspirations.

At that moment a rather attractive redhead came through the door, she saw me and smiled. "Well hello," she said. "It is Dr. Watson, isn't it?"

"Yes."

"You're the Englishman," she stated.

"Right again," I said, smiling at her in return.

"What are you doing hiding here all on your own?" she asked.

"Oh, just passing the time of day," I replied. She really was rather friendly, as were all the Americans. As she engaged me in conversation, I kept one eye on the Plymouths. I noticed a nondescript uniformed crew member drawing level with them and was distracted momentarily by the redhead as she touched my arm.

"I say, Doctor, are you going to the fancy dress ball tomorrow night?" As she asked her question, my eyes turned to meet hers only to swing back on Sarah's scream.

I rushed over. Plymouth had fallen over the rail and was dangling on the rope which was strung around the side. Below him, the huge propellers churned, promising instant death to anyone caught in its lethal blades. I leant over the rail but could not reach him.

"Hang on!" I cried to him, and then gasped to Sarah, "What happened?"

"That crewman came past and pushed him over!"

The redhead started screaming for help. Holmes was among the first to arrive. He took one glance at the situation and peeled off his coat before climbing over the rail and hanging onto the outside of it. He hooked his feet into the lower rung of the rail and commanded, "Watson, hang onto my feet," and then even before I had taken hold he began to lower himself down backwards, until he was stretched full length upside down, hanging only by his feet, which I hung onto with all my might. His outstretched hands grabbed Plymouth's wrist and with sheer strength alone began to pull him up.

"Climb up over me," he ordered the pale faced Plymouth, who gripped Holmes' belt and pulled himself up. By this time, other crew members had arrived and leaned over to grab Plymouth when he came within reach. Holmes then flipped himself up in an excellent demonstration of acrobatics and I helped pull him in over the rail. His face was grim and sweat beaded his brow.

"What happened?" he demanded.

"A crewman pushed him over!" exclaimed Sarah indignantly.

"Watson?" Holmes looked at me.

"I only took my eyes of them for a fraction of second, Holmes. I did see a man dressed in uniform walking past. I glanced away for a moment and then Sarah screamed."

"What distracted you?"

I glanced at the redhead. Holmes followed my eyes and sighed with exasperation. "Figures," he muttered, a trifle rudely I thought. He went over to the redhead.

"Excuse me, Miss. May I ask why you chose this particular time to engage my friend in conversation?"

She looked surprised. "He was standing by the door when I came out."

"No one put you up to it then?"

"Why no, of course not!"

"Did you happen to see the crewman who pushed Mr Plymouth over?"

"No. I'm afraid my full attention was on Dr. Watson."

Holmes turned his back on her abruptly losing all interest in her as a witness and returned to us.

"Watson?"

"Medium height, brown hair. Pretty ordinary looking actually. There was nothing remarkable about him at all." I said, describing the crewman as best as I could. Sarah nodded in agreement of my description.

"I cannot believe that it was a member of my crew," stated the Captain, who had only just arrived and been informed of the incident.

"Frankly Sir, I do not believe it *was* a member of your crew, but a passenger disguised as one. The uniform was probably stolen."

"Who might you be, Sir?" asked the captain.

"I am Sherlock Holmes and the fellow who was pushed overboard is the son of one of the wealthiest and most prominent men in England," replied

Holmes.

I knew Holmes only revealed Plymouth's status to enlist the Captain's aid. He would be more likely to help us if the passenger concerned was one of some importance.

"Sarah, take your husband back to your room. We will join your both presently."

She nodded and took Plymouth's arm, leading him away. He was still trembling from his ordeal, although it seemed to me that Holmes' rescue was far more dangerous than Plymouth's fall, for he had to take the full weight of the other man as he climbed over him, using only his feet for support. If I had let go, he would have fallen to his death.

A futile search was then made for the attacker, but as the description was rather vague there was not a lot to go on. Those who had seen him had paid little attention to his appearance. We did, however, find a purser tied and stripped with a bump on his head hidden in a cleaner's cupboard.

Although he did not say so, I knew Holmes was immensely annoyed with me for not being alert enough to catch the man. If it had been Holmes, he would not have been so easily distracted. To make matters worse, he did not actually say anything about it to me. If he had ranted at me, like he sometimes did, I would not have minded, but his silence was worse because it made me feel all the more guilty for having failed him so.

As we dressed for dinner, I could stand his silence no more. "All right, Holmes, say it."

"Say what?"

"Tell me how useless I am. How easily I let

myself be distracted by a female. What a miserable failure I was ...!"

Holmes stopped tying his tie and looked at me, the merest twitch of a smile on his lips. "Why would I say all that?" he asked.

"Why, because it's true. If I hadn't been distracted, I might have caught the fellow, or better still, I could have prevented him from pushing Plymouth over."

"I doubt it."

"What?" I stared at him in astonishment.

He smiled at my expression. "I doubt if you could have caught him. He planned his move perfectly. The redhead certainly aided him, but her arrival was a coincidence, which he took full advantage of. Plymouth, fool that he is, was sitting on the rail. A two-year-old child could have pushed him over. It was just a stroke of luck that he managed to grab the rope, otherwise he would have ended up under the propellers. As for you, if you had rushed the fellow, there is the possibility that he would have tossed you over also, and although I have no love for Plymouth, I certainly would have missed your company."

"S-so you don't blame me?"

"Of course not. If I had been there, I wouldn't have been able to prevent Plymouth being pushed over either. The devil was rather cunning. By dressing as a crew member, he made himself invisible. Had he approached as himself, I have no doubt that you would have paid more attention."

I was relieved by Holmes' words, only I still could not help feeling a little guilty. Maybe he was just saying all this to alleviate my feelings.

"If you're not angry with me, Holmes, why were you sulking?"

"Sulking?"

"Well, you haven't said a word to me since we found the unfortunate purser."

"Ah, Watson, you take things too much to heart. I thought you knew me better than that. I have been thinking, not sulking. Forgive me, I did not mean to snub you. I have been lost in a world of my own."

Now I smiled with relief. His explanation was entirely in keeping with his character. I suppose I was too sensitive. I should be used to Holmes' ways by now.

[314]

THIRTY

We received an invitation to dine at the Captain's table and Holmes accepted, believing it would be safe enough for the Plymouths. While the people at the table conversed sociably, I noticed that Holmes appeared distracted. He seemed to be paying a great deal of attention to the table nearest the captain's. There were half a dozen people seated at it. Two of the couples seemed to be acquainted with each other. The other two men were obviously strangers to the others but chatted amiably enough with them. I failed to see what it was about them that interested Holmes.

After a while, Holmes reached across the front of me to tug Plymouth's sleeve.

Plymouth looked around.

"Would you recognize your Cousin Wilbur if you saw him?" Holmes asked.

"Wilbur Carstairs? Good heavens, no. The last time I saw him was when I was about six years old. Just before his parents went to India. I haven't seen him since."

"That is what I thought," nodded Holmes.

"Holmes," I said softly when Plymouth turned his attention back to the other diners. "Is that whom you suspect is behind the attacks?"

"He stands to inherit a great deal if Plymouth dies – Senior and Junior."

"But how does he know about the will?"

"Ah, well, that is still to be determined. Perhaps a confidant in the house keeps him informed of the latest developments. It's too early to say for sure. Anyway, I believe I have located him."

"One of the men at that table?"

"Very good, Watson. I am pleased to see that our years of cohabitation have not been entirely wasted."

"Which one?"

"The brown-haired man."

"He looks very ordinary. Dressed like an American too."

"So are we. It means nothing. You can always tell an American by the way they hold their forks, Watson. Observe our dinner companions if you will. They're holding their forks tines up, plus the fact that they transfer the fork over to their right hands after cutting their meat."

"Why yes of course, I hadn't noticed!" I looked down at the fork in my own left hand. It was facing tines down and naturally we never changed hands after cutting.

"The man at the table is using the European method, like us. If he is British why would he wish to conceal it unless he doesn't want to be recognized as such."

I threw several surreptitious glances towards the man in question, until Holmes nudged me to desist. "You will make him suspicious, Watson," he chided.

Holmes timed his meal to end the same time as his prime suspect. When that fellow made to rise, Holmes did also, saying, "I've left my cigarettes in the cabin. I'll just run down and fetch them. I won't be long."

As he backed away from our table, he accidentally bumped into the brown-haired man who had just risen. "Oh, I do beg your pardon," apologized Holmes.

"That's quite all right," said the other in an American accent.

I felt a pang of disappointment. It seemed Holmes was wrong. The fellow was an American. Perhaps he had European parents and learned his table manners from them. It certainly seemed that he was not Plymouth's British cousin.

Holmes gave the man a nod and a smile and left the room. The man also left. Holmes took his time about returning. Dinner was long over and I was just thinking that we should return to our cabins when he put in an appearance. From his expression, I knew that he didn't want me to mention the brown-haired man in front of the Plymouths.

"You took a long time, Mr Holmes," said Sarah with a smile.

"Do you imagine that I would collect my cigarettes and not take time out to have one," he replied placidly.

This was an outright lie for I could smell no smoke on his breath as is usually the case when someone has just had a cigarette. I had no idea what he could have been doing for the past forty minutes.

"We thought we might have an early night tonight," said Sarah and Holmes nodded approvingly. Then, to my surprise, Cathcart Plymouth asked a question which proved he was not quite as dense as I supposed.

"Mr Holmes, why is someone trying to kill me?"

"Oh, you mean that incident today?"

"No, I mean all the incidents, including you or the doctor sitting guard at our door and Sarah is sleeping with a loaded gun under her pillow. I know you all think that I am a weakling, just as my father does but I have a right to know."

Holmes and I exchanged glances as his wife exclaimed. "Oh, Cathcart! I don't think you're a weakling at all. I think you're wonderful and brave. It's just that you're so sensitive and Mr Holmes did not want to worry you needlessly. After all, until today, it was only a suspicion." She looked at Holmes in silent appeal.

He nodded and said, "Your wife is absolutely correct. We were hired by your father to find you and to ensure your safe passage home. As his heir your importance has increased, making you a potential target."

"Only it is no longer potential, but actual," Plymouth replied bitterly.

"Yes." Holmes looked him over closely. "My apologies for keeping you in the dark. The others were simply obeying my orders."

"Whom do you suspect?"

"I am afraid it is merely conjecture at this point. Your father has revised his will making you the primary beneficiary. Should you die, your Cousin Wilbur Carstairs inherits."

"But I've been in America for two years, why wait until now to attack, if it was him?" cried Plymouth in disbelief.

"Prior to your father changing his will, your cousin stood to inherit the lot regardless of you being alive or dead, therefore, you were no threat to him. Since your father's change of heart however, his chance at receiving a rich inheritance has dwindled, especially now that you're married, for it will eventually go to your offspring. His only hope is to kill you and Sarah and he must do it before you are reunited with your father."

"The attack was only on me today, not Sarah."

"You are the one he has to get rid of first. He would no doubt have taken care of her later."

Plymouth had paled visibly but retained his nerve. "Of course you cannot prove it's Wilbur."

"No, and unfortunately you cannot identify him."

"Yes, that's true. There is one thing that might help though. Wilbur has a big red birthmark on his right shoulder. About three inches wide. I remember seeing it when we were children."

Holmes smiled in appreciation. "Excellent!"

"Well, I don't know how that helps us all that much," I argued. "We can hardly go around baring the shoulders of all the male passengers."

"Of course not. However, once we have our man we can readily identify him," replied Holmes.

"I hate to think that my own relative may be responsible. Could it not be someone else? Someone with a grudge against me?"

"I doubt it. You didn't make enemies in America, except for perhaps that Barber you worked for." There was amusement in Holmes' eyes as he mentioned the latter.

Plymouth flushed with embarrassment.

"No," continued Holmes. "It's not revenge. The only reason anyone has to kill you is greed. If they merely wanted to kidnap you, I would suspect ransom. Still, as I said before, at this early stage it is merely conjecture."

"What would you like us to do?" asked Plymouth, slipping his arm around Sarah. "We are in your hands."

"Thank you. Do much as you have been. Do not order room service. If you want something, Watson or I will fetch it for you. Do not admit any strangers, including the ship's staff and above all, keep your door and windows locked."

We escorted them to their cabin before returning to our own room. I could hardly wait to ask him about the brown-haired man. As soon as Holmes closed the door I swung round.   "What   really took you so long when you left the dining room, Holmes?"

"I followed my suspect."

"But he was an American!" I protested. "I heard him speak."

"He's as American as I am," replied Holmes in an American accent. "Anyone with a modicum of acting ability can impersonate an accent, especially if it is only for a short duration. He kept his comments and answers to a minimum during dinner. He knew he could not maintain it in a heated discussion with the other Americans because they would be sure to notice the accent."

"Oh." Such a simple solution had not occurred to me. "Are you sure?"

"Fairly sure. I've asked around about him also; it seems he mostly keeps to himself, except during meal times. He's deliberately avoiding contact with the other passengers to limit the conversational opportunities. Still, I wouldn't mind having a look at his right shoulder."

"We can hardly assault him and strip him," I replied with a smile.

Holmes grinned briefly before taking out a cigarette. "Shame, it would simplify matters. Still, instead of keeping watch on the Plymouths, it may be prudent to keep an eye on him."

"I must say young Plymouth surprised me. I thought he was completely oblivious to everything that was going on."

"As did I. I confess I underestimated him somewhat. I have long since dismissed him as a buffoon. Be that as it may, there is no harm done."

We decided to stay in our room for the night, as Holmes foresaw no danger overnight with the Plymouths safely in their room. There was no need for either of us to spy on the brown-haired man until the morrow, or so we thought.

✠ ✠ ✠

It was still a little early for sleeping, so I immersed myself in my scribbled notes and was rewriting a more detailed account of our travels and adventures in America. It was around half past ten. Holmes had sprawled out on his bed and I would have thought he was sleeping but for the spirals of smoke puffing up occasionally from his pipe.

I looked up from my writing at a faint thumping sound. "Do you hear that, Holmes?" I asked.

"Hmm?" Holmes glanced lazily over at me.

"That banging sound."

Holmes sat up and swung his feet off the bed, also listening intently. He tossed his pipe onto the bed and hurriedly slipped into his shoes. "That's coming from next door!"

As he raced from the room, I followed him, picking up his pipe as I passed. After all, I didn't want us to set fire to the ship.

He ran to the Plymouth's door and banged on it. The thumping coming from inside was renewed. The door was locked. We put our shoulders to it and forced it open.

Sarah was bound and gagged, lying on the floor with her feet up against the wall of our room.

Holmes hurried over to her and removed her gag before undoing her hands and helping her up.

"Who did this to you?" I asked.

"Cathcart."

"What?" gasped Holmes in astonishment. It was the last answer he expected to hear.

"He's gone looking for the murderer. Oh, Mr Holmes!" Tears rolled down her face. "He tricked me. Took me by surprise and tied me up to stop me coming to you. He said he would catch the murderer himself and prove to everyone he was not a hopeless nincompoop, whatever that is. He has no chance!"

"Don't worry, we'll find him. How long ago did he leave?"

"About ten minutes ago. I worked my way off the bed and started kicking your wall, but I was afraid you wouldn't hear me banging with my bare feet."

"All right, Sarah, stay here. Watson and I will go look for him. You might want to ring for the purser to have the door repaired while we're gone." Holmes gave her hand a squeeze of reassurance and we left.

"Where do we start, Holmes?" I asked as he led the way to another deck. "We'll check out our suspect's room. It's possible that he's still there and Plymouth has not yet encountered him."

At the door numbered 23C on the lower deck, Holmes knocked loudly. There was no answer. I glanced around warily as Holmes pulled his picklock set from his coat pocket. With me shielding him should anyone come along, he went to work upon the lock. The door was open in seconds. We entered quickly. The room was empty.

"Search through the drawers, Watson!" snapped Holmes.

I hastened to obey. "What am I looking for, Holmes?"

"Anything that may confirm his identity."

Holmes up-ended the man's suitcase and sorted through it messily.

I searched the cabinet drawers. "Here!" I exclaimed, holding up the man's passport.

Holmes hurried over and almost snatched it from my hand. I read the name in the passport over his shoulder.

"Vincent Craggill." read Holmes aloud, frowning.

"It's not Wilbur Carstairs," I pointed out, rather unnecessarily. "This man has no connection with Plymouth."

"Hmm." Holmes tossed the passport back into the drawer as I hurriedly repacked the suitcase. It seemed we had the wrong man.

"There must be some other explanation for his holding the fork the wrong way," I added.

"Hmm," grunted Holmes again. He did not like to be proven wrong. "Never mind, we still have to find that idiot Plymouth," he said, finally. We left the room, not bothering to lock the door. The unfortunate man would probably think he left it undone himself.

"We will have to split up, Watson. You take the places of entertainment and I will check the exterior. If we don't find him within the hour, we'll meet at the Mahogany Bar on the top deck. If you see Plymouth, bring the fool with you."

I nodded and took off in the direction of the ball room. I searched it and saw no sign of Plymouth. As I came out I ran into Sarah who was now fully dressed. "Oh, Doctor. I couldn't just stay in the cabin and wait. I want to help with the search."

"All right," I said, knowing it would be pointless to try to send her back. "I'm about to check the gaming room. Holmes is checking the decks. Perhaps you could go along and see if Plymouth is near the bow," I suggested.

"Which is?" she asked, not being nautically minded.

"That way, to the front of the ship."

"All right," she agreed and went off in the appropriate direction. I searched the gaming rooms to no avail and the bars (of which there were several), but I did not see Holmes, Plymouth, or even brown hair. I decided to make my way to the Mahogany Bar at the top. I had no sooner walked out of the warm confines of one of the lounges onto the wind-chilled deck before I heard a scream coming from the front of the boat.

"Sarah!" I cried aloud and began to run in that direction.

Ahead of me, leaping over the rail from the upper dock in a single bound, was Holmes. He raced along with formidable speed. In front, near the rails, I saw Sarah Plymouth struggling with the brown-haired man. Cathcart Plymouth was lying at their feet, unconscious.

Sarah screamed again as the man pushed her up against the rail and began to force her over.

Holmes was almost upon him but was not quite quick enough to prevent the villain from shoving her over.

Sarah disappeared over the rail with a final scream.

Holmes hurled himself bodily at the man. In the lights that had come on suddenly, I saw the man stab at Holmes with a knife. I was still running to reach them but had slowed down considerably as I was gasping for breath. I drew my revolver, but my chest was heaving so much I dared not fire. I had to get closer.

Other people were beginning to emerge—the ship's crew and passengers. It was one of the crewmen that had the presence of mind to turn a light onto the struggling figures. As another drew level with me, I gasped at him to stop the ship; that there was a woman overboard.

[325]

He turned and ran, no doubt looking for the captain.

I was almost to the railing when Holmes thrust the man half over the rail. He pushed, forcing the man's knife hand away from him. The man appeared to teeter on the brink, gravity pulling him inexorably further out. Suddenly, he dropped his knife and grabbed at Holmes' lapels as he lost his equilibrium completely and fell, pulling Holmes with him into the dark waters of the ocean.

There were life buoys tied along the edge of the rail. I quickly pocketed my gun and pulled out my penknife, slashing through the ropes and dropping several buoys into the water, yelling, "Holmes!"

More crewmen came forward, one bringing a powerful lantern. He directed the light downward. The ship was still moving forward, although I noticed its speed had decreased.

"There!" I yelled, pointing to two small dark dots. The crewman directed his light in that direction. I could see Holmes and the man named Vincent Craggill still fighting. He had lost his knife but was doing his best to drown Holmes. As for Sarah, she was nowhere to be seen.

Soon, the darkness swallowed them up and we were past them. Shortly after, the captain arrived demanding to know what was going on. Plymouth still lay on the deck, blissfully unaware of all that was going on around him and to tell you the truth, I had not stopped to examine him. Frankly, I did not care whether he was alive or dead. I was more concerned that his foolishness may have caused the death of two far superior and worthy people. Holmes and Sarah.

Rapidly, I explained to the captain what happened. He was quick to react. Engines were turned off and the ship eventually came to a halt, but we had travelled miles from where the two had fallen overboard. The ship began to retrace its route but was far too slow as it had to turn around first, so a long boat was lowered. While this was happening, I did take a quick look at Plymouth. He had a nasty crack on his head but nothing more. I detailed a couple of crewmen to take him back to his room and have the ship's medical officer attend him. It was my intention to go with the lifeboat.

Half an hour passed before we were ready to set off. It was pitch dark and the sea stretched out before us— vast and desolate. I only hoped Holmes had managed to win the deadly fight with Craggill and had found one of the life buoys I had tossed over. As for Sarah, I knew she could swim, but how would she manage weighted down by her female garments? They were not conducive to swimming. They would be more an impediment, an anchor around her neck. I feared we were already too late to help her. I went cold at the thought.

As the six sailors rowed silently, I sat at the bow and trained the light out into the darkness, making occasional sweeps in a wide arc, so as not to miss anything. I waited some ten minutes before shouting, "Holmes!"

My words echoed back at me. As we moved closer to where we assumed they had gone over, I called out again and again, my heart heavy with dread. "Holmes!" I yelled at the top of my voice, but the wind carried no welcome reply.

"There!" yelled one of the sailors, pointing with an oar. I shone the light in the required direction. There was a man floating in a life buoy. At this distance I could not tell if it was Holmes or Craggill. We drew closer. The man was lifeless. We used the oars to bring him closer and pull him on board. It was Craggill and he was well and truly dead.

I saw another life buoy floating in the water but it was empty.

"Where's the other feller?" asked one of the sailors.

Where indeed? I refused to consider the possibility that Holmes had drowned and was even now sinking slowly to the bottom of the ocean. If he were alive, what would he do? I thought quickly, trying to put myself in Holmes' place. Three buoys had fallen into the water when I released them, there were only two here.

"He must have taken the third buoy and swum back after Sarah. If we continue in the direction that the ship had come from we should find them," I suggested.

The sailors put their formidable muscle behind their efforts and soon the long boat was cutting through the water powerfully. It seemed we rowed for an eternity on this endless stretch of water. I continued to yell out their names at intervals, but as the distance lengthened, my fear that they were lost grew. Imagine then my joy when suddenly I heard a reply coming faintly from the darkness.

"Watson!"

I stood up, holding the lantern. "Holmes! Sarah!"

"Watson, over here!" came the reply, stronger now; louder.

The boat moved closer to the sound of his voice and finally I could make out two heads bobbing in the water clutching onto the buoy.

Holmes raised a hand in a wave to us. As we drew level, I saw that Holmes was holding onto Sarah and she in turn hung onto the buoy. She was alive and conscious.

I put the lantern down and hurriedly leaned over the side to pull Sarah on board. She was minus her dress, clad only in her under garments and shivering violently. Once in the boat, one of the sailors wrapped a blanket around her.

Next, I turned to help Holmes aboard, he was also shivering uncontrollably. I quickly handed him a blanket which he draped gratefully around his shoulders. Before flopping, he gripped my hand tightly.

"I have never in my life been so pleased to see you, Watson," he said, his voice betraying his emotion.

"Nor I you, Holmes," I returned, helping him to sit beside Sarah. The sailors turned the boat and began to row back towards the ship, which was only now coming into view.

"Sarah, are you all right?" I asked, looking her over with concern.

"Freezing, but alive," she said, teeth still chattering. "It was a close one, Doc. When I fell in the water, my dress kept dragging me down. I had a hell of a time trying to get out of it. I'm a pretty good swimmer, but the water was ice cold and I could see the ship getting further and further away. I thought I was done for." She looked at me and from her expression I had an inkling of the utter terror and dread she must have felt, being alone in the ocean in the pitch dark in the middle of nowhere.

"I was starting to tire when, like an angel from heaven, Sherlock arrived." She glanced at Holmes and reached out her hand to him, taking his in her own. "I owe you my life, again," she said.

"Your life would not have been at risk if that turnip-brained husband of yours had done as he was told," replied Holmes.

I noticed that he had not objected to her calling him Sherlock this time, nor did he remove her hand. For that matter, she did not object to his insulting her husband; although in this instance, I thoroughly agreed with him.

I looked at the dead body lying near us. It was also covered by a blanket. "I guess you were right, Holmes. He was the assassin after all."

"Check his right shoulder, Watson. See if it is Cousin Wilbur. The passport could be false."

I undid the man's shirt and exposed his shoulder. It was blemish free. "No, it is not he," I said as I covered the body up again and looked at Holmes. "How did you manage to overcome him?"

"It was not easy," Holmes admitted soberly. "He did his damnedest to drown me. Fortunately I was the better swimmer. I could hold my breath longer."

Although Holmes said nothing more on the matter I could picture it in my imagination. The two men struggling desperately to push each other under the water, then, Holmes diving under and pulling the other down by the legs and holding onto him like grim

death until the other ran out of air, his own lungs nearly bursting with the effort. Finally emerging victori-
ous, he rises to the surface and gulps in the air gratefully. I could see him dragging the body over and
hooking it onto the buoy and then, with his unerring
sense of direction head back for Sarah, pulling the
third buoy along with him. I could imagine his relief
at finding her tired, but alive and wondered what took
place at that meeting.

If his greeting to me was anything to go on, I
am sure his relief at finding her was equally emotive.
Something must have transpired between them for as
they sat here, hands clasped tightly in each other's,
they shared an intimacy that had not been noticeable
before. Perhaps Holmes had let his guard down and
was no longer able to conceal his personal feelings.
He liked her a great deal and I knew it must have been
an effort on his part to remain detached from her.

We drew up alongside the ship, hearing the
claxons sounding, warning of our approach. All the
deck lights were on and the passengers gathered at the
rails curious to see what was going on. Before long we
were being assisted on board. Sarah was escorted to
her cabin by a maid while the captain accompanied
Holmes and me to ours.

As Holmes stripped out of his wet clothes and
dried himself, he repeated his story to the captain. The
captain agreed to hand the body over to the authorities
once we arrived at Southampton. After he left us, I
handed Holmes a brandy, which he accepted eagerly,
before throwing himself down onto his bunk. With his
glass empty, he looked up at me. "How is Plymouth?"

"Had a crack on the head. He will live."

"Damn fool!" Holmes almost snarled the words and I was in complete agreement. "He doesn't deserve to live!" Holmes was still fuming. "The sooner we return that useless imbecile to his father, the happier I will be."

"At least there will be no more attempts on his life," I said, trying to cheer him up.

"Thanks for reminding me!" Holmes scowled darkly. "The threat is not yet over. This Craggill fellow was merely a hireling. It stands to reason that Wilbur Carstairs could not leave his commission and travel to America."

"Then if we can prove that the two were associated, we will also have proof of his guilt."

"I doubt if we will find any connection. Carstairs is an intelligent adversary. He has taken great pains not to appear in the matter, so it is reasonable to assume that there will be nothing to connect him with Craggill. He would have made sure of that. To tell you the truth, Watson, if it were not for the fact that as Plymouth's wife, Sarah is next in line to inherit, and therefore in grave danger, I would willingly abandon the idiot to his fate."

"Holmes, you don't mean that," I reproached.

"I do. What the devil is it to me who inherits old Plymouth's fortune? I do not even care about his promised fee. If it were only young Plymouth's life at risk, I would say to hell with him and return to Baker Street with my conscience clear."

I stared at Holmes, rather stunned by his vehement statement. These were indeed strong words for him. It also gave me insight into just how deep his feelings for Sarah Plymouth were. Nearly losing her tonight had brought them to the surface. He would never acknowledge those feelings, nor act upon them, but he could not prevent himself from having them. What a shame Cathcart had not been murdered, thus making Sarah a widow. Holmes would not be bound by any constraints then. It was interesting to speculate as to the possibilities of a union between her and Holmes. She was really the ideal woman for him, strong, independent and a free spirit. All the things Holmes admired in a woman.

I shook off my thoughts and instead said, "You have been through a rather harrowing ordeal, Holmes. I suggest you retire now and get some rest."

He nodded. "Perhaps another brandy, Watson?"

I refilled his glass and poured one for myself, raising my glass in a toast. "To friendship," I said, smiling. I was gratified to see the glimmer of a smile spring to Holmes' lips in return.

"And there never was a truer, stouter, and more reliable friend than you, my dear fellow," he replied, raising his glass to me.

"Nor a more courageous and remarkable one than yourself, Holmes," I responded, my heart warmed by his show of comradeship.

He smiled. "I never doubted that you would come to our rescue tonight, Watson. I rather took that for granted."

"Just as I take it for granted that you will always come to mine."

THIRTY–ONE

It was nearly lunch time before we woke. Holmes was looking much better than the night before. We shaved and dressed and went next door. It was Sarah, looking bright and refreshed and none the worse for her ordeal who answered our knock. Cathcart Plymouth was sitting up in bed, his head bandaged. He grinned at us, which was the worst possible thing he could have done, for it served to raise Holmes' ire.

"I know what you are going to say, Mr Holmes," he began, "but I was just so sick of being mollycoddled. I wanted to do something myself. Sarah tells me you caught the man who attacked me and that it wasn't my cousin."

"You have no idea what I am going to say," growled Holmes, glaring at the young man, his grey eyes cold.

"Huh?" Plymouth blinked in surprise.

"Did she also tell you how close she came to drowning because of your stupidity?"

"Sherlock!" Sarah grabbed Holmes' arm to stop him, but it was too late.

"What?" Plymouth gasped at Holmes' words.

"Yes, Plymouth. While you lay dozing upon the deck, the assassin threw your wife overboard...!"

"What!" Plymouth was aghast.

"Sherlock, please?" pleaded Sarah.

Holmes turned towards her and said harshly, "He's a grown man. He has to learn that there are consequences for every action. He cannot go through life with his head buried in the sand, blissfully ignorant of the havoc he causes. His ignorance could have *killed you!*"

I have seen Holmes irritated before, but I had never seen him in the grip of such an ungovernable rage. I knew that if he did not get control of himself, and quickly, he would say something that he would regret. I feared that he would inadvertently reveal his feelings for the other man's wife.

"Holmes is right, Sarah," I said hurriedly, cutting in to give Holmes the time he needed to regain command of his temper. "Young Plymouth himself just said he did not want to be mollycoddled. It is only fair that he knows what happened last night."

She looked at me, her eyes sad; then glanced back at Holmes, who, apart from his clenched fists, appeared noticeably calmer.

His eyes softened slightly as he looked at her reproachful expression. "I am sorry, Sarah, but he should know. You cannot continually go on protecting him. What kind of man hides behind a woman's skirts?"

"Not you, that's for sure," she said softly.

I hoped that Plymouth could not hear her words for her tone of voice was anything but impersonal.

She took a deep breath and turned to her husband. "You see, Cathcart, when I saw that man hit you over the head, I attacked him, only he got the better of me and threw me overboard. Mr Holmes came rushing up, but was too slow to catch me, especially as the killer turned on him and attacked him with a knife.

They fought and both went overboard. It was Dr. Watson who stopped the ship and came back for us with a rowboat. Mr Holmes killed your attacker while they were fighting in the water and then he swam back for me." She stopped for a moment studying her husband's face, which had paled significantly.

"I would have drowned for sure if he had not come back for me. I–I had gotten rid of my dress because it was weighing me down, but the water was freezing. I had been trying to stay afloat for over an hour and was beginning to tire. I ... well, I don't think I would have been able to last much longer if Sherlock had not reached me when he did. I was almost gone when I heard him calling me; it was like a miracle."

Plymouth sat silent for a long moment. "I see," he said finally.

I wondered if he noticed her lapse and the repeated use of Holmes' Christian name. He turned and looked at Holmes who had calmed down considerably as Sarah spoke and appeared more his normal detached self.

"I can see why you think I am such a fool, Mr Holmes. I had no idea that my actions caused all that chaos. Perhaps it would have been better if he had killed me, then Sarah would not have to be tied to such a miserable excuse for a husband," he said bitterly.

"Oh, Cathcart! Don't be silly. You know I love you..."

"Do you? Or is it Sherlock Holmes that you love?"

I felt a pang of guilt at his words and wondered if Holmes did as well. I glanced at him, but his face

[337]

was impassive.

Sarah sat on the sickbed and held her husband's hand. She looked him squarely in the eyes and said with open honesty: "I do love Sherlock. How could I not? He has saved my life three times already and yours too, four times in fact. I admire him and look up to him and yes, he *is* courageous, but such courage comes naturally to some men. He is like...well; he's like the older brother I never had. It is you I married."

I glanced surreptitiously at Holmes. His face was wooden, expressionless: but his eyes, what was that unfathomable light in them? Desire? Jealousy? Pain? I could not read him at all.

Plymouth still looked doubtful.

"You have wonderful qualities, Cathcart. I know you're no gallant adventurer. It's not in your nature to be that. I knew what you were like when I married you. I figured I had enough savvy for both of us. You have a wonderful talent for painting, what does it matter that you can't make a campfire or fight very well. Dr. Watson has told me that you are filthy rich. You can hire people to do that for you. You can have a personal guard even; it's really not that important."

"But I can't protect you," he said, staring down at his hands, not meeting her eyes.

She bit her lip, then a faint sparkle of amusement appeared in her eyes. She threw a glance at Holmes and we saw her smile before she said those familiar words: "I can protect myself."

Her comment brought about the desired effect. Both Holmes and I started to laugh while Plymouth looked at us bewilderedly.

"Wh–what's so funny?" he asked plaintively.

She was smiling more broadly now. "That's what I said when I first met Mr Holmes and Dr. Watson, before they had to rescue me the first time. It's kind of a standing joke now, I guess."

Plymouth offered her a weak, tentative smile, still suffering from his acute lack of confidence that had only worsened with Holmes' display of anger.

She patted his hand, still smiling. "Truly, I *can* protect myself. I made the mistake last night of throwing myself at that man. If I'd had my gun with me, I would have shot him instead. It's just that I was so distraught when I thought he'd killed you."

"Really?"

"Yes, really."

His smile became a little less tentative.

"I would never intentionally risk your life. You mean everything to me, Sarah."

"I know that dearest," she replied, kissing his cheek.

"Holmes and I were about to go get some breakfast," I said cheerfully. "Shall we send some down for you?"

"Yes, please. Thank you, Doctor." She smiled at us as we withdrew and left the young couple alone.

Once out in the corridor, Holmes lit up a cigarette. He inhaled deeply, then said, "Thank you, Watson."

"Pardon?" I was confused for a moment.

"For taking over. I nearly lost it when I saw him sitting there with that stupid grin on his face. He has absolutely no idea of the devastation he causes

[339]

wherever he goes. To think a woman like that..." he broke off suddenly, realizing that he almost said more than his normally reticent nature would allow.

"Are you all right, Holmes?" I asked.

"There is no justice in this world, Watson," he replied with a sigh.

I looked at him searchingly, before reminding him, "She's taken, Holmes."

"Hmm." His response was a half laugh, half grunt that said nothing, but conveyed everything. At my continuing look of concern, he added, "I will be all right, Watson. I have my work."

I nodded.

THIRTY–TWO

With the assassin dead, the rest of the cruise progressed rather pleasantly. I thought of looking up that charming redhead, but unfortunately for me she had turned her attentions to someone else.

It was the last day of our journey. The sea was rather rough as there was a storm brewing. We were all on deck, except for Plymouth, who was in one of the lounges drawing charcoal sketches of the passengers. As the ship began to heave, so did my stomach.

"You're starting to look a little green, Watson," observed Holmes.

"Uh, yes. I'm feeling rather queasy."

"Why don't you go lie down in your cabin, Doc," suggested Sarah.

"Yes, I think I will," I agreed and staggered away, finding it difficult to keep my balance. I had not realized it at the time, but our position on deck had been near the porthole of our own cabin.

As I entered the cabin, the stuffiness of the room struck me and did nothing for my already delicate stomach. I opened the porthole and lay on my bunk beneath it, hoping the breeze from the window would alleviate my symptoms.

A few moments later I heard voices as two people took shelter under the overhang of the upper deck near my porthole. It was beginning to rain and I recognized the voices immediately. It was Holmes and Sarah. Curiosity made me sit up and lean closer to the window; they obviously had no idea I was there.

"Sherlock," she was saying, "the other day was the first, and I hope the last time that I have ever lied to my husband."

"Pardon?"

"When I told him that I loved you like a brother. That wasn't true. I'm sorry if my words hurt you."

"You did not hurt me. There was nothing else you *could* say," replied Holmes evenly.

"I do love you, you know, and most definitely *not* like a brother," said Sarah, her voice intimate. I could imagine her reaching for Holmes' hand. Holmes did not reply to her statement, so she continued, "I wish I had met you before Cathcart."

For a moment I thought Holmes would remain silent, but his reply came clearly, despite the words being whispered and choked with emotion. "So do I," he said.

"Oh, Sherlock!" She sighed. I dared to raise myself for a quick peek out the window. She stepped closer to Holmes and wrapped her arms around him. He hesitated a moment before reciprocating. His eyes were closed as he held her and he took in a deep drawn breath. Perhaps he was savouring the memory of the moment.

"When I was in the water getting colder and more exhausted by the minute and heard your voice calling me, I thought I'd died and gone to heaven."

Holmes chuckled briefly. "I, too, was relieved to see you," he said. "I would never have forgiven myself had you drowned."

"You know, I could come up to London and visit occasionally," she suggested looking adoringly up at him.

Holmes released her suddenly and stepped away from her. "No!" His tone was vehement. "No," he repeated. "Please promise me you will *never* do that!"

"Not even if Cathcart dies and I'm a free woman?" she asked, almost pleadingly.

"Don't go poisoning him on my account," Holmes replied, humour returning to his voice.

"Oh, Sherlock, what a wicked thing to suggest. I would never do *that*! I meant if he died of natural causes."

"Don't count on it. His father is in his nineties and still going strong. I will be long dead in *my* grave before Plymouth sees his."

"Will I never see you again?"

"Never. It is for the best, Sarah. We have no future together you know that as well as I."

She sighed mightily. "I know. I just wish things were different."

"Perhaps it is just as well they are not," Holmes replied. "I am not exactly the marrying type. You are much better off with Plymouth."

I felt a sudden pang. Poor Holmes, he was just saying that to make it easier for Sarah. I was quite sure of that; after all, that is what I would do in his situation.

"Don't you want a wife and family?" asked Sarah and I listened eagerly for Holmes' answer. This was one question I too had often wondered about, but never dared to ask.

"What I want is irrelevant. My work would never permit it. A family would make me vulnerable to my enemies. My work is everything to me, I cannot

[343]

readily give it up, yet I would have to if I chose home and hearth over occupation. And, even then I would live in fear that old enemies would seek me out. No, it is not for me. I could never marry you, even if you were free, Sarah; it would make no difference. You *are* better off with Plymouth, believe me and you will realize that in time."

"I guess. But really, that's quite sad," she said and I silently agreed with her. Perhaps I was wrong then; he was not trying to let her off easy; he was merely being practical, like always.

"Each to their own, young Sarah."

"Don't 'young Sarah' me," she said, but there was no anger in her voice, more a wistfulness. "I will think about you, you know, often. Will you think of me?"

"I shall try not to," he replied.

"Not even once a year?" Now she was teasing him.

"I promise I will think of you if ever I see a woman drowning in the Thames." His voice had also taken on a lighter timbre.

"Well, as long as she's dressed."

"If she was, she would not remind me of you," laughed Holmes, the seriousness of the moment gone.

"Sir, you are no gentleman!" returned Sarah, also laughing.

"The weather is worsening, Sarah, we had better go inside."

"I guess," she said reluctantly, before the pair of them left their sheltered spot and went to join Plymouth inside.

I lay back on my bunk, my seasickness forgotten as I thought about the conversation I had just overheard. Holmes' self-control was truly phenomenal, almost inhuman. I say almost, for there was that one burst of anger at Plymouth's stupidity in risking his wife's life. That at least betrayed the fact to me that, despite all his nonchalance, Holmes did have feelings, intense, powerful emotions that he kept buried deep within his soul. I knew now that the indifference he often displayed towards his clients when they became emotional or the sneers and jibes he made whenever the softer passions were mentioned were nothing more than an act. It was his way of coping with such situations without betraying his own feelings.

The only time he gave vent to those hidden emotions was when he played his violin. The instrument expressed his every mood. I smiled to myself. I would have to pay attention when we got home to see what sort of music he played. For an instant I wondered if Holmes would dream about Sarah and what might have been, but quickly put that thought from my mind. He was too pragmatic for that. No doubt he would do exactly what he told her. Put her from his mind completely. Holmes, after all, was Holmes, and if anyone could disassociate themselves from their emotions, it was he.

The reader no doubt will think rather meanly of me for having eavesdropped on such a personal and private moment, but Holmes was a mystery man, an enigma. He seldom revealed his inner thoughts or desires. This brief glimpse into his heart, taught me more about the man in five minutes than I had learned about him in the past five years. He has always impressed me as being superhuman, so often machinelike, that this incident served to remind me that Holmes, despite his desire to avoid all emotions that would foul up his finely balanced mind, was nevertheless, as human as I. Perhaps this was part of the essence of the man, part of the qualities that endeared others to him. For a man as bohemian and unsociable as he, he had a great many admirers. I was merely one of them.

THIRTY–THREE

The next morning the ship steamed into the port at Southampton. It took a while to organize our luggage as Sarah had quite a lot. While I set about hiring a wagon to take us to the train station, Holmes went to the nearest post office to telegraph Sir Eustace and inform him of our arrival and that we were on our way to Sheffield. It felt strange to be back in England again.

I could not help smiling at the curious looks we were attracting. In America we had stood out for wearing our English clothing. In England, we were being stared at for wearing American clothes.

We caught the train from Southampton to Paddington Station and hired several cabs at Paddington to take us and the Plymouth's baggage on to St. Pancras Station, from where we would journey to Sheffield. As we drove through the streets bustling with traffic and more people than Sarah had ever seen in her life, she stared wide eyed about her. Plymouth pointed out the sights to her as we drove. At St. Pancras Station, we transferred to our train and were soon on our way to Plymouth's birthplace. Sarah was like an excited child, staring out the window at the passing terrain with enthusiasm.

A wagon and monogrammed carriage awaited our arrival, as did a telegram for Holmes. He read it and slipped it into his pocket without comment. There were two liveried footmen with the wagon and coach and they quickly set about loading the baggage. Sarah oohed and ahhed at the scenery.

"It's *so green!*" she enthused. "Ooh, ooh, look at those funny looking sheep! Oh aren't they cute, with their little black faces. Can we get one, Cathcart?"

"Sarah, my dear, we have hundreds," replied Plymouth, smiling indulgently. Now that he was home again, he was in his element. He had fallen easily into the role of nobleman and ordered the footmen about as he had all his life. Not so Sarah. She had said please and thank you to the men, causing them to look at her with surprise. She would learn, I thought. More's the pity. I admit I liked her in her natural state, unfettered by society's rules and customs. I was sure that a year from now, should we chance to meet, we would not recognize her.

She became silent as we drove into view of Plymouth Castle. She stared at the impressive structure in awe.

"My gosh!" she gasped. "You weren't joking. It really is a castle."

"Complete with dungeons, turrets, battlements and ghosts," offered Plymouth with a grin.

"And ... are those cannons?"

"Yes. There are sixteen cannons in all, four to each wall. Father fires them once a year on his birthday."

"I can't wait to see inside!" She looked excited at the prospect. This was her first visit to a real castle for there were none in America which was, by comparison, a rather young country. England had centuries of history behind it.

We drove up to the house and were let in by

the butler. He smiled when he saw Plymouth. "It is good to see you again, Sir," he said. "Welcome home."

"It is good to be home, Samuels," replied Plymouth, handing him his hat and gloves, as did we. "How is father?"

"Much better, Sir. His condition began to improve the moment he received Mr Holmes' telegram from Phoenix that you were on your way home."

"We will go up now," decided Plymouth. He led the way, holding his wife's hand. Holmes and I followed at a slower pace. This after all, was a private moment for the Plymouths, both young and old. A reunion after a long separation.

In the huge old bedroom, Plymouth went over to the bed. His father was sitting up, smoking. His eyes lit up when he saw his son. "Cathcart, my boy!" He grinned and held out his hand. They shook. "Well you look none the worse for your experience in that barbaric land. So, what is this surprise you have for me?" he asked, referring to the letter Plymouth had written him.

Young Plymouth grinned and stepped back to collect Sarah, who had stopped near the doorway with us. He took her hand and led her forward.

"This. Father, I would like you to meet my wife, Sarah. Sarah, this is my father, Sir Eustace Plymouth."

Sarah smiled shyly at him. "How do you do, Sir," she said.

"Come closer, girl," said the old man and she did. He studied her with his shrewd eyes, missing nothing as she stood nervously before him. Then, suddenly he smiled. "Well, I used to say Cathcart could do nothing right. Seems he's improved some to have married you."

Sarah smiled with relief and glanced at her anxious husband. "Oh, Cathcart. You said your father was an ogre, but he's perfectly sweet."

Sir Eustace chuckled. "If I were ten years younger, I'd marry you myself," he said.

"And, if I were sixty years older, I would be just as happy to marry you," she returned, cementing their friendship for life.

He chuckled again, before calling out, "Sherlock Holmes, are you lurking in the shadows?"

Holmes moved forward. "Yes, Sir," he said.

"Not bad going for an impudent young pup," said Sir Eustace, still smiling. "I trust you had no difficulty finding my son."

"None whatsoever, Sir Eustace," replied Holmes blandly.

"Mmm, didn't think so. Still, a promise is a promise. You can start expecting to receive a better class of clients in the near future," he said. "I have passed the word around."

Holmes inclined his head slightly in a gesture of acknowledgement.

"Where's that doctor fellow?"

"Here, Sir Eustace," I said, also stepping forward.

"If you want a practice in Harley Street ..." he began.

"Perish the thought," I replied. "I am happy as I am."

"Well I have to do something for you," he

insisted.

"I would not say no to a box of fine cigars," I replied, smiling faintly.

"Good, good! You will be my guests tonight," he said.

"Surely you would rather be alone with your son and daughter-in-law?" I protested.

"Actually, it is getting late," interrupted Holmes, much to my surprise, for I thought he was keen to leave. "We appreciate the offer, Sir Eustace."

We left the Plymouths alone then and went out.

"I am surprised you want to stay, Holmes," I said to him as we walked down the long wide corridor to the staircase.

"You forget, Watson that the killer is still about. I am hoping he will make a move tonight."

"What if he doesn't?"

"Then I will have to tell Sir Eustace my suspicions and advise him to hire guards for his son and daughter–in–law."

We went downstairs and met the butler, who then showed us to our rooms. I did not see how Cousin Wilbur would be able to strike here; the place was like a fortress. It just didn't seem possible.

✠ ✠ ✠

That evening, dinner passed uneventfully. Sir Eustace left his sick bed and joined us in the dining room. He was quite a jovial host and not at all like the intimidating old tyrant he was on our first meeting. It was a merry meal.

Towards the end of the meal, he looked at Holmes, "You lied to me, young man," he accused sternly.

"Sir?" Holmes looked at him politely.

"You told me you had no trouble finding Cathcart."

"We didn't. His trail was quite easy to follow."

"But it wasn't exactly a safe one, or so Sarah tells me."

Holmes shrugged. "Nothing we couldn't handle."

"Your father must be proud to have a son like you," said the old man.

I smiled behind my napkin. He was obviously favourably impressed with Holmes. It was rather funny how everyone seemed to compare Holmes with Cathcart. Holmes came out ahead every time!

"My father is deceased, Sir," replied Holmes.

"Too bad."

After dinner we joined Sir Eustace in the library. He wanted a full account of our adventures. Sarah went upstairs and Cathcart Plymouth stayed with us for a short while before he, too, excused himself to join his wife.

As we were relaxing with our cognac and cigars, Sarah entered the room. She peered at us and glanced about the room as if searching for something.

"Lose something?" asked Holmes.

"Yes, Cathcart. The butler told me that Cathcart asked me to join him in the library."

Holmes leapt to his feet, spilling his drink and dropping his cigar, in an ashtray fortunately. Without a word he raced from the room. I followed as quickly as I could move and Sarah trailed behind. Holmes ran up the stairs two steps at a time, to the young couple's bedroom. He threw open the door. The room was empty. He hurried back out into the hallway and saw a footman coming along the corridor. The man saw him and made to turn, but Holmes was upon him in an instant and grabbed him by his shirt front, demanding, "Where is he?"

"Wha–who?" gasped the startled servant.

"The butler?"

"Samuels?" The other looked vacantly at Holmes.

Holmes shook him roughly. "Tell me, or by God you will hang as an accessory!" he threatened.

"H–he went out towards the battlements."

"Which way?" It was a necessary question for all the walls that surrounded the main building were equipped with battlements and there were several ways of reaching them.

"Th–the north wing turret exit," said the footman, thoroughly intimidated by Holmes.

Holmes shoved him aside and ran down the corridor towards the door which opened onto a narrow passageway that led to the north wing turret, which in turn was connected to the northern most wall and battlement.

At that moment, poor Sir Eustace finally caught up to us, puffing and panting and demanding to be told what was going on, all said between his gasps and wheezes. Sarah and I ignored him and chased after Holmes, who was well ahead of us.

As we hurried through the turret and onto the wide stone battlement, we had an uninterrupted view of the drama that was unfolding before us. It was nightfall, but a full moon bathed the scene with an almost surreal light setting the scene like a stage.

Plymouth was struggling helplessly with the butler, Samuels, who was doing his best to toss him over the parapet. He had managed to get Plymouth up onto the two-foot wide edge and it was onto this that Holmes bounded.

He struck out with his fist at the butler, who staggered but continued to clutch at Plymouth. With a remarkable feat of strength, Holmes wrenched the butler's grip from Plymouth and shoved. The killer screamed as he fell and plummeted to his death.

Plymouth's situation was still perilous as the butler's tugging had destroyed his equilibrium and he teetered on the edge. In a deft, almost graceful move, Holmes pivoted and grabbed Plymouth's arm, swinging him around bodily and tossing him off the parapet and down onto the relative safety of the battlement. Plymouth literally flew off and landed heavily on the hard stones.

Meantime, the force Holmes used to thrust Plymouth to safety worked against him, causing his self to lose balance on the precarious ledge. With a desperate grasp at the smooth stonework, Holmes disappeared over the edge.

"Holmes!" I cried my voice hoarse with shock.

"Sherlock!" screamed Sarah, leaping over her prone husband, and running to the edge of the battlement.

I joined her my heart heavy. It was a good hundred feet down with a rough cobblestone surface at the base. No one could survive such a fall.

I reached Sarah just as she climbed up onto the parapet. Quickly I stretched out my hand and caught the back of her dress, fearful lest she should fall also. Can you imagine my utter surprise when I heard Holmes' voice floating up from the depths calmly saying, "It is always a pleasure to see you, Sarah my dear, but is Watson there?"

"Holmes?" I too climbed up onto the wall and peered over. Holmes was some eight feet below us, sitting astride the barrel of a cannon which jutted out from the wall.

"Holmes! Thank God!" I gasped. And thank God Sir Eustace was a traditionalist in that he maintained the castle in all its glory, including the keeping of cannons. I could not reach Holmes by leaning down, so I looked around for something I could use. Flying proudly from a flagpole on the nearest turret was Sir Eustace's monogrammed flag. I hurried over and pulled it down, ripping it in half with my penknife. I tied the two ends together to increase its length and checked that the knot would hold before going back to Holmes.

By this time, he had managed to stand up on the cannon. I lowered my makeshift rope and within minutes he joined us on top of the wall.

Sarah hugged him tightly, not hiding her relief or her feelings.

Holmes gave her a pat on the back before helping her down off the parapet and onto the battlement where Cathcart Plymouth had only just now regained his feet. I climbed down also, still holding the destroyed flag. It occurred to me that Sir Eustace would probably be livid at such wanton vandalism on my part.

Plymouth was holding his right arm. "Holmes!" he cried. "You broke my wrist!"

Holmes glanced at him one eyebrow raised in surprise at Plymouth's complaint. "So?"

"My father will have your head when he hears of this, you broke my wrist!"

"Shut up, Plymouth," replied Holmes tersely, disgust plain in his eyes. Plymouth really was too contemptible for words.

My emotions were already on a tight rein, what with having thought that Holmes had just plummeted to his death saving this spineless weasel, so his whining now over a trivial injury raised my ire.

"Damn it all, Plymouth!" I snapped, forgetting for a moment that Sarah was present. "Stop your whining, you pathetic ingrate. Holmes just saved your worthless life, again, and at considerable risk to his own, I might add. If he hadn't thrown you off the wall onto the battlement, you would have fallen to the cobblestones below and you would have broken your neck. You owe him your life. Why don't you bloody well act like it!" I was furious. The selfishness of the man was almost too much to tolerate.

"Sarah," whined Plymouth to his wife, "are you going to let them talk to me like this?"

Sarah's own eyes gleamed with anger. She strode forward and to Plymouth's astonishment and embarrassment, gripped him by the ear and twisted, pulling him along towards the parapet. He howled like a banshee as she dragged him along. If the huge grin on Holmes' face was any indication, he thoroughly approved her actions.

[356]

Unmindful of her husband's injured wrist, she pushed him onto the parapet and for a moment I feared she was going to push him over. Instead, she only pushed him far enough to be able to see over the side.

"Look down there!" she ordered, forcing his head down. On the ground below lay the butler; a dark stain spreading out from his shattered skull and visible in the moonlight. Plymouth gagged as nausea from the sight beset him. He tried to straighten up, but Sarah held him down. She was quite strong for a girl.

"If Sherlock hadn't caught you and pushed you to safety, that would be you," she said. "After he saved you, *he* fell. What if that had been Sherlock lying down there? Just because you're rich doesn't make you better than anyone else. Would it even bother you if a brave man died in your place? How can you be so selfish, so ungrateful Cathcart? He nearly died saving your life, and not for the first time, and all you can think about is your lousy arm. I don't know who you are anymore Cathcart; you're not behaving like the man I married. You have changed since we got here. In fact, you're not behaving like a man at all. You're acting like a spoiled brat." She let him up. His face was pale and clammy with perspiration.

"Now, thank Mr Holmes for saving your life. Start acting like a man and stop whining. Dr. Watson will fix your arm soon enough."

Plymouth stared at his wife, aghast.

"Do it!" she demanded, her voice and expression hard.

"Th–thank you, Mr Holmes," he muttered. "I–I'm sorry, I didn't realize ..."

[357]

"You never do," said Holmes bitterly, interrupting his apology.

Unbeknownst to us, Sir Eustace had made his way to the battlement. I don't know how long he stood there listening to us berate his son, but his face was expressionless when he came forward.

When Plymouth saw him, he looked hopeful. Perhaps he expected support. If so, he was disappointed.

"Father!" he cried hurrying forward, but before he could start whining about his wrist, Sir Eustace said, "Sarah, take your husband to your quarters. Dr. Watson will be along shortly to tend to him."

Sarah nodded and took Plymouth's good arm, leading him away.

Sir Eustace looked at us. "You don't like my son very much, do you?"

Holmes met his eyes. "He is a weak, pampered jackass," he replied.

I glanced at Sir Eustace, expecting him to explode in a fit of temper that he was so notorious for, but instead he merely nodded sadly.

"That's his mother's fault. Spoilt and cosseted him. I should have had more of a hand in his rearing, been firmer, perhaps then he would have turned out more like you, Mr Holmes."

Holmes snorted. "I doubt that!"

"What Holmes means," I said hurriedly, "is that he is one of a kind and..."

"Indeed he is," agreed Plymouth senior. "Now, perhaps you can tell me why my butler wanted to kill my son?"

"Before I do that, answer me one question.

How long has he been in your employ?"

"Five years."

"Five years!" Holmes repeated, frowning. The answer obviously did not fit into whatever theory he had hatched. He lapsed into silence; head sunk upon his chest and began to pace back and forth.

"You haven't answered my question, Holmes," said Sir Eustace a little impatiently.

"Shush!" I hissed at him. "Can't you see he's thinking?"

Sir Eustace turned and glared at me. Perhaps he wondered how an upstart such as I dared to shush someone like him. Deciding that I had aggravated him enough, I dropped the concealed flag to the ground and casually pushed it off over the edge of the battlement with my foot, so that he would not notice it.

Seeing that Holmes was lost in thought, Sir Eustace gave up and sat himself down on the inner edge of the parapet to wait him out. Having disposed of the flag, I joined him.

Ten minutes or so passed before Holmes deigned to acknowledge us. "Sir Eustace, do you have a man who can get to London and back here again in four hours at the most?"

"Not in four hours. However, I do have a man in London. Name of Scott Henrick, an ex–soldier and very reliable. He could make it here."

"Good. Watson, do you have your notebook with you?"

"Yes."

He held out his hand for it as I passed it to him along with a pencil. He scribbled a list of some sort and a brief note. Then he ripped the page out, folded it and handed it to Sir Eustace.

"Have that telegraphed to Mrs Hudson at 221B Baker Street at once and also contact your man to go there and collect what she hands him. He has to bring the bag back here as quickly as possible. Watson will now tend to your son, while I take a look at the body and organize its removal. We will meet again in the library when our respective tasks are completed." With his instructions issued, he turned to leave.

"Wait a minute!" Sir Eustace called out, rather put out by Holmes' imperious manner. "What is all this about? I demand to be told."

"All in good time, Sir Eustace. Just get that note sent as quickly as you can, it is imperative. Surely you want the threat to your son to end once and for all? Do exactly as I say and it will." Holmes' masterful air worked to subdue even Sir Eustace's protests, who, I am sure, had never been spoken to in such a manner.

As Holmes and I returned to the main building, I noticed that his gait was somewhat peculiar. "Are you all right, Holmes?" I asked. "You are walking oddly."

Holmes's expression was rueful. "You would walk oddly too, if you fell eight feet and landed astride a cannon," he replied.

My face contorted in a grimace of male empathy. "Ooh," I half groaned. "That would hurt!"

"It did, Watson. It did."

We parted company at the top of the stairs. Holmes going down to examine the body, while I went to tend Plymouth's wrist. Contrary to his complaint, his wrist was not broken, just badly sprained. I bandaged it, gave him a shot of morphine to shut him up and helped Sarah put him to bed.

As she escorted me out, she said softly, "You know Dr. Watson; I have never been as disgusted with anyone as I was with the way Cathcart behaved tonight. It's like having these servants and other folk running around after him has changed him, and not for the better. At least he had showed some gumption when he had to fend for himself. But I didn't know him tonight. He was like some pampered Eastern dude and for a while I was tempted to toss him over the wall myself."

"And, I was tempted to help you," I replied. We laughed companionably at my comment, until she became serious again.

"Well, I guess I married him for better or worse. Tonight was definitely the worse, I hope it will get better. The problem is, I keep comparing him to Sherlock and I know I shouldn't do that because they are so different. I shall just have to pull him into line."

"You are certainly the girl to do that," I agreed, smiling at her with admiration. I had not forgotten how she dealt with her husband on the battlement.

"I do like his father, though. Sir Eustace kind of reminds me of my dad in a way. He would have liked him I think. They're both strong, forceful men. Sherlock is too."

"True enough, but strong men do not need strong women to guide them. Young Plymouth does."

"That's the hell of it," she agreed sadly. "You know, up on the battlement there, when Cathcart was acting so abominably, all Sherlock would have had to do was crook his finger at me and I would have left

Cathcart for him in a flash.

"You know he would never do that."

"I know," she sighed mightily. "Oh, Doc, why is life so hard?"

I shook my head, having no answer for her question.

"If only you fellers had shown up a month earlier…"

"Don't waste your life on if onlies, Sarah. Life in England is all new to you. You are unaccustomed to servants and British customs and classes, but you will get used to it in time. You will be Lady Plymouth and, no doubt, successor to Sir Eustace, for he is unlikely to leave his business dealings in his son's hands. Over time, your strong influence should improve Cathcart's behaviour and if I were you, I would encourage him to paint. That will keep him out of mischief and will improve his confidence.

"His mother doted on him as a child and protected him excessively. When we first met you that was what you were doing also. You were merely a surrogate mother to him. You need to be more. What you did tonight might be considered cruel by some, but it was necessary. Plymouth needed to have his eyes opened. He is living in a dream land that revolves around him.

"If you continue to bring him down to earth, make him face reality, you might yet make a worthwhile man out of him. Just don't mollycoddle him; you won't be doing him any favours."

Sarah took my hand and gave it a squeeze. "Thanks, Doc. You're talking horse-sense and I'll heed it. Only you will forgive me if I occasionally dream of Sherlock, won't you? He's just so different from Cathcart."

I gave her hand a pat in return. "I wouldn't be surprised if he occasionally dreamt of you, my dear," I replied, wondering if I was correct or not, for I had no idea what Holmes dreamt off and it was highly unlikely he would ever tell me.

✠ ✠ ✠

We gathered in the library, Sir Eustace, Holmes and I.

"Now, Mr Holmes," began Sir Eustace.

Holmes held up his hand. "All in good time, Sir Eustace. First, I need you to do one more thing before the servants retire for the night."

"What?"

"Ring for a pot of tea to be brought in here, then when the servant enters act like he has arrived in the middle of a discussion. I want you to declare angrily that first thing tomorrow you intend to change your will to ensure that there are no beneficiaries other than your son and his wife. That if they should die your property will then go to charity."

"But, why?"

"Can you do that?" asked Holmes, ignoring the old man's perplexity.

"Yes, of course, but ..."

"After you have carried out that little charade, I shall explain all. Watson, be so kind as to ring the bell."

The servant who answered our call was not a maid but none other than the footman, whom Holmes had almost choked in his earnestness on the upstairs landing when we were looking for Plymouth. Sir Eustace carried out his part to the letter and declared his intention of sending for his lawyer first thing in the morning.

The footman returned with the tea and left. Holmes, a finger to his lips hurried to the door, stood still and listened for a long moment before opening the door and peering out into the deserted hall. "Good. It is safe to talk now," he said.

"About time! Now, young man, perhaps you will explain yourself?"

"Certainly, Sir Eustace." Holmes helped himself to a cigar, lit it and began to speak. "There is only one person who stands to benefit from your son's death and that of course is your nephew Wilbur Carstairs."

"Wilbur!"

Holmes ignored him and continued. "There have been several attempts on your son's life. The first was in America where murderers were hired. They failed miserably in their endeavour. There were two further attempts on his life on the ship, one which nearly succeeded but for Sarah's intervention at considerable risk to her own life."

"And Holmes'," I interjected, not wanting him to miss out on the credit.

"I succeeded in killing him, but he also turned out to be merely an employee of Carstairs. My first thought was that your butler was actually Carstairs, but his having been in your employ for five years put paid to that notion." Holmes reached into his pocket and pulled out the telegram he had received earlier in the day.

"You told us that Carstairs was with the Third Northumberland Regiment in India. On our return to England, I sent them a wire. Carstairs was dishonourably discharged six months ago. He is a gambler, a cheat, and has a violent and drunken temperament. A man like that would need money but be disinclined to work for it.

"Samuels, your butler was contacted and perhaps bribed. Through him, Carstairs learnt about your will making him your beneficiary, so when you became ill he must have thought his luck had changed. However, you also became remorseful and changed your will making your son your major beneficiary, but, unfortunately you left Car-stairs in as the default heir. While ever your son remained in America he was no threat, for on his own it was unlikely he would survive very long, and if it were necessary, he could be disposed of at leisure. The situation only became urgent when you hired us to find Cathcart and bring him home." Holmes took a long puff on his cigar, before continuing.

"He hired someone to go to America and dispose of Cathcart once we found him. When we arrived safely here, he talked the butler into having a go. In fact, and of this I have no doubt, if Samuels were successful in murdering your son, he himself would also have been killed, as this man doesn't like to leave witnesses or anyone that can tie him into this business. Our prompt arrival thwarted Carstairs. He was on his way up to the battlement, firstly to help in tossing Cathcart over and secondly to push Samuels over and make it appear that the two struggled and plunged to their deaths accidentally."

"But there was no one upstairs except the footman," I protested.

"Exactly. How long has that man been in your service, Sir Eustace?"

"I think his name is Peachman, about two and a half months."

Holmes nodded. "It fits. Tonight an attempt is going to be made on *your* life, Sir Eustace. That was the purpose of declaring your intention to write Carstairs out of your will. He will have to act now or it will be too late. Your son is no longer the primary target."

"I say, Holmes, was that wise? I mean you have just put Sir Eustace's life at risk."

"He can take it, and anyway, his life will not be at risk. I will masquerade as him. Sir Eustace you will retire to our room and we shall wait in yours. Carstairs will make his move and we, in turn, will catch him red-handed. That shall put an end to the danger once and for all."

"How can you pretend to be me. You look nothing like me," objected Sir Eustace.

"I will, as soon as your man arrives from London with the things I requested. In the meantime, Sir Eustace, I am afraid you must stay up until my disguise arrives. Watson and I will keep you company. It would be fatal for you to go to bed until we are ready to spring our trap."

"Would it not be easier to just get hold of that footman and check his right shoulder?" I asked. "If he has Carstairs' birthmark, we will know we have the right man."

"We may know it, but what would that achieve?" countered Holmes. "We cannot prove he hired assassins. He was clever to get others to do his dirty work. We cannot prove anything against him. It is not a crime to work as a footman in one's uncle's house. My way is the only way to stop him once and for all."

THIRTY–FOUR

Sir Eustace's man, Henrick, arrived at midnight with a valise packed by Mrs Hudson. I could imagine her surprise at being disturbed by a request from Holmes. She did not even know we were back in the country. Still, she was long used to the unexpected where Holmes was concerned and complied to the letter.

I woke Sir Eustace up—he was dozing in his armchair by the fire and we escorted him to his room. He sat on his bed while Holmes quickly changed his appearance to resemble the old man. Grey hair, whiskers, age lines. It was always fascinating to watch him transform himself into someone else. He then undressed and put on one of old Plymouth's nightshirts, which was far too short for him.

"Never mind," he said in reply to my glance. "I will be in the bed. Carstairs will not notice. He only needs to see my head and upper arms."

I was going to escort Sir Eustace to our room in the conventional manner, but he stopped me and led the way to a secret door.

"This passageway leads to the landing where the other bedrooms are located," explained Sir Eustace.

"Excellent!" Holmes enthused, as he climbed into the big four-poster bed. "Less risk of you being seen."

I escorted Sir Eustace to our room just to ensure his safety and wished him good night.

"I hope young Holmes knows what he's doing," growled the old man.

"He always does, Sir Eustace. He always does." I returned via the secret passage and closed the panel. Holmes had snuggled down in the big bed already and looked exactly like Sir Eustace Plymouth.

"Hurry up, you impudent young pup!" growled Holmes and I grinned, for he sounded exactly like the old man.

"Where are you going to hide, Watson?" he asked in his normal voice. I glanced around. "How about behind the bed head?" I suggested. It was tall enough and wide enough to shelter half a dozen men. Holmes nodded.

"Don't go to sleep will you?"

"Not on your life, Holmes," I replied, taking up my position behind the bed head and reflecting that my comment was literal. Holmes, masquerading as Sir Eustace was literally putting his life on the line. I had to remain alert to be ready to help him, for we knew that Wilbur Carstairs was more than willing to hire help when he needed it. There was no guarantee that he would come alone.

Holmes turned the bedside lamp off leaving the room lit only by the moon which peeped through the open drapes. All was silent except for the ticking of the clock on the mantelpiece. We waited. I was starting to feel rather cramped and was just thinking of standing up and stretching for a moment when I heard the unmistakable creak of the large, heavy door opening. At the same time, I also became aware that the pattern of Holmes' breathing had changed. Now, instead of his quiet, regular breathing, he had a sighing

[370]

wheeze, similar to that of Sir Eustace. Trust Holmes to think of that, he never left anything to chance so thorough was he.

I did not hear the intruder approach the bed his footsteps muffled by the thick carpet. In fact, I heard nothing but Holmes' breathing until there came a muffled grunt.

I leapt to my feet, ignoring the pins and needles which shot up through my numbed legs and dashed around the bed. I threw myself bodily at the attacker who was forcing a pillow down over Holmes' face, which Holmes was struggling to push off. As the attacker and I thudded to the floor, Holmes leapt out of bed and joined me in attempting to subdue the ruffian who fought like the devil. I received a clout to the jaw which sent me staggering. The man was fierce and extremely strong. He did his best to throttle Holmes and until Holmes poked him in the eyes, he nearly succeeded.

I quickly struck a match and lit the lamp in time to see Holmes strike the final blow, which knocked the man, the footman, Peachman, unconscious. Holmes was panting by this time and my jaw throbbed.

"Give me a hand, Watson. We'll check his shoulder," said Holmes.

I helped him half strip the fellow and sure enough, there was a great red birthmark glaring at us.

"You will find a pair of manacles in my valise, Watson. We should secure him before he rouses."

I fetched the manacles and Holmes secured Wilbur Carstairs alias Peachman's hands behind his back. Then, together we hoisted him up into a chair.

While he was still unconscious, Holmes removed his disguise and dressed

It was a good twenty minutes before Carstairs roused to glare at us malevolently. He swore obscenely in a vehement tirade of anger and defeat.

"When you are quite finished, Carstairs, we will have a   discussion in a more civilized manner," said Holmes calmly.

"You can't prove anything against me!" he snarled.

"On the contrary, I can prove everything. I even know you hired Craggill to kill Cathcart Plymouth. He talked before he died."

"That damn fool!" Carstairs went off on another blasphemous diatribe so foul that I was glad young Sarah was not present. Interspersed with his profanity were comments that proved he knew Craggill well.

"Actually," said Holmes when Carstairs stopped for a breath. "He died without talking. I am afraid you have just incriminated yourself in front of two unimpeachable witnesses. Now are you going to be reasonable?"

Carstairs clamped his lips tight and sat silent, glaring murder at us.

"Craggill tried, but he failed miserably. I do not know what you promised the butler to enlist his aid, but I do know you had no intention of paying him off. When we encountered you on the upstairs landing, you were on your way to the battlement to finish Samuels off. Our arrival gave you no choice but to pretend to be intimidated. In the surprise of our sudden appearance, you accidentally told the truth, not having time enough to think up a convincing lie or send us on a goose chase. You must have been grati-fied that Samuels did not survive to talk."

Carstairs continued to glower, so Holmes car-ried on with his story. "When you learned Sir Eustace was writing you out of his Will, you became desper-ate. You needed the Will to remain as it was. I knew you would make your move tonight and so took Sir Eustace's place."

"Think you're smart do you, Mr Sherlock Bloody Holmes? Well, if I were you I wouldn't sleep easy in my bed at night. While ever I breathe, I will be thinking of ways to destroy you. No one messes with me and lives to brag about it."

"So others have said to me, but I am still here," replied Holmes unconcernedly. "And they are not."

"You will be lucky if you do not get the rope for these murder attempts," I said, glaring at him.

"You'll get yours," he muttered, his eyes full of hate.

"Watson, can you go down and see if Mr Hen-rick is still on standby. Ask him to fetch the local po-lice to take this miscreant into custody. If they move fast we may still get a few hours' sleep before day-light."

I nodded and went downstairs. When Henrick had delivered Holmes' bag, Holmes had asked him to be prepared for a late call. The ex-soldier was dozing on the library couch, fully clothed. I woke him and quickly explained the situation to him. He was more than happy to ride to town and fetch the police.

They arrived within the hour and took Carstairs away. Holmes advised them against waking Sir Eustace and suggested they return at a more fitting hour. It was four in the morning before we finally retired, still fully clad in our day clothes, too weary to bother changing.

✠   ✠   ✠

At breakfast that morning, Holmes and I were a tad bleary eyed, but triumphant. Sir Eustace was expressive in his gratitude and even Plymouth condescended to thank Holmes for catching Wilbur Carstairs. He was looking a little shamefaced this morning. I had a feeling that Sarah probably had a few more words with him regarding his petulant behaviour of the night before. She, herself was as bright-eyed as always, although, now that I think about it, her eyes were perhaps a little brighter than normal, her cheerful manner, a little more forced. Without a doubt she dreaded saying goodbye to Holmes and was overacting to compensate. I knew that she would not make a scene though. She was a remarkable young lady, with a good deal of self-control. If she were going to cry over the parting, she would do it in solitude.

After breakfast we packed our bags and returned to the reception committee downstairs. Sir Eustace handed me a package. "Cigars," he said and I smiled my thanks, before we shook hands. "I thought you still deserved them, young fellow, despite what you did to my flag."

I grinned sheepishly.

He then shook hands with Holmes. "I could use a man like you. How would you like to work for me full-time?"

"Thank you, Sir Eustace, but I am a free agent.

prefer to choose my work and for whom I work."

The older man nodded, understanding completely. Holmes gave Cathcart a curt nod and would have bypassed him if the latter had not held out his uninjured hand.

"I am sorry for all the trouble I caused you, Mr Holmes. I know that I do not measure up to your standards, but I hope that one day you will be able to respect me for the things I *can* do."

Holmes looked him over for a moment. When Plymouth wasn't behaving like a spoiled child, he was actually quite likable. Holmes accepted the olive branch offered and shook his hand, saying: "Perhaps one day."

Sarah was next in line and she did not worry about the propriety of her actions. She threw herself at me and hugged me firmly. "Thank you, Dr Watson, for all your help and good advice," she said.

I patted her on the back. "You will be fine, young Sarah. You're a natural lady," I said, smiling at her. She reached up and kissed my cheek before turning to Holmes. He frowned slightly, but that did not stop her. She was not interested in maintaining decorum. She hugged him tightly. "And thank *you*, Sherlock," she said, looking up at him, her eyes beginning to brim with tears.

"Good luck, Sarah. It has been an education knowing you," replied Holmes, his eyes kindly as he looked down at her.

She kissed his cheek and with tremendous effort, blinked her tears away and smiled back at him tremulously, not game to say another word, lest she break down and start howling. Hardly acceptable behaviour in the presence of her husband and father-in-law.

Holmes gave her a rather weak smile in return as she released him and stepped back. To my surprise, I noticed that he swallowed hard several times as he turned away. This farewell was just as hard on him as it was on her. They had formed a bond, that had the circumstances been different, may have led to a very different ending.

"Well, we must be off if we want to make our train," he said with forced heartiness. With a final nod to the Plymouths, he turned on his heels and walked rapidly outside. The coachman was waiting for us. Our bags had already been loaded and all that was missing was our presence. We journeyed to the train station in silence. I did not want to interrupt Holmes' deliberations.

The silence was maintained until we reached the outskirts of London. Holmes butted out his cigar and asked,   "Well, Watson, are you ready to return to a life of normality?"

"Life is never normal living with you, Holmes," I replied truthfully.

He chuckled.

"Still," I continued. "It certainly beats the tedium of my life prior to meeting you."

"Kind of you to say so, Watson. I would certainly be lost without my trusty sidekick."

I chuckled at his Americanism. "You can count on me, pardner," I returned in a not so accurate American accent.

EPILOGUE

The snow-covered peaks glistened in the distance and the firs and pines were covered by a blanket of white as the pristine wilderness spread out from the mesa. Tepees stood in a circle, smoke emanating from their centre point openings. For the most part the Indians went about their business, their summer breech clouts exchanged for buckskins and bear-hides. Near the biggest tepee, with the five red hands on its side paced an old man anxiously, awaiting word from the medicine man.

At that instant a baby's wail echoed from the birthing tepee. Chief Red Feather looked up at the sound and glanced apprehensively towards the tepee. A moment later, a squaw emerged and marked a symbol on its side. He sighed and grinned, for the sign meant another brave heart had been born this day.

Several hours passed before his daughter, Plump Beaver appeared carrying a tiny squirming bundle. She was smiling with motherly pride. As she approached her father, the tribe gathered around for the naming ceremony. The Chief looked at his new grandson. His little pink face looked back at him. He studied his light brown hair and dark brown eyes and ran a finger along his cheek, intrigued by the sprinkling of freckles across his chubby round cheeks and nose.

He took the child and held him up for all to see. In his native tongue he announced to all that a new Indian warrior had that day been born.

"I name him Spotted Deer," he declared.

"Spotted Deer!" chorused the tribe.

Plump Beaver smiled proudly. Her marriage had been brief; her husband deserting her on her wedding night, but she had what she desired most, a son on whom she could dote. She would teach him and he would become a great warrior. She had been angry when the white man left her and demanded she be avenged for the humiliation, but when she found she was with child, she forgave him as he had given her the most precious of gifts. She knew that Spotted Deer was destined for great things.

Read about the continuing adventures of Holmes on Watson in:

Return to the Wild Frontier

OTHER BOOKS BY THIS AUTHOR

ANDROMEDA FOX SERIES
1. Deathbringer
 2. Art for Art's Sake
3. A Friend in need
4. Kidnapped

NURSING THRILLERS
Night Moves
God's Disciple

SHERLOCK HOLMES BOOKS
Sherlock Holmes on the Wild Frontier
Return to the Wild Frontier
The Private Diaries of Dr. Watson
Sherlock Holmes and the Femme Fatales
Sherlock Holmes in the 21st Century

MISCELLANEOUS TITLES
Natural Progression

NEPTUNE KING SERIES
1   Introducing Neptune King.
2.   The Casebook of Neptune King.
3.   The Adventures of Neptune King.
4.   The Revenge of Neptune king.
5.   The Exploits of Neptune King.
6.   The Marriage of Neptune King.
7.   Neptune King Investigates.
8.   Neptune King Down Under.
9.   A Surprise for Neptune King.
10.   The Friends of Neptune King.
11.   Neptune King and the Newly Weds.
12.   Neptune King and the Psychic Witness
13.   The Bizarre Cases of Neptune King.
14.   The Singular Cases of Neptune King.
15.   The Challenges of Neptune King.
16.   Neptune King and the Counterfeiters.
17.   Neptune King of Baker Street.
18.   Dosvidonia, Neptune King.
19.   The Enemies of Neptune King.
20.   The Charity Cases of Neptune King.
21.   The Deductions of Neptune King.
22.   Neptune King and the Lunatic Asylum.
23.   Neptune King and the Gallant Thief
24.   Neptune King and the Missing People
25.   The Miscellaneous Cases of Neptune King

Manufactured by Amazon.ca
Acheson, AB

13131768R00210